THE ROSE AND THE
GUARDIAN

Ethereal Ties
Ties
World Map

Sea of Stone

Sea of Fire

The Barrier

Gráyárk

Ávera

Tárnov

Thrä'kkor

Znavarā

Vathéria

Sea of Stars

háven

Vodāny

Yáarim

Róstan

Sea of Moon

N
W E
S

THE ROSE AND THE GUARDIAN

ETHEREAL TIES
BOOK 1

NICOLE A. STERLING

You've faced challenges and storms with grace. This is for your strength, your courage, and your spirit. You've fought your battles, and you've risen.
You did well.
You deserve that thick monster cock.

CONTENT WARNINGS

This novel contains dark and intense themes that may be disturbing or triggering to some readers. It explores the brutal realities of power, control, and survival through a fantasy lens, but it's also a story of resistance, rage, and reclaiming autonomy.

Some scenes are inspired by real histories of systemic violence and oppression. Please proceed with care and prioritize your well-being. You're in for a wild ride, but your peace comes first.

Themes and content include:

Graphic violence and gore

Torture and physical abuse

Sexual violence and nonconsensual bodily invasion *(brief, not MC)*

Captivity and forced marriage *(not MC)*

Emotional manipulation and blackmail

Psychological and emotional abuse

Systemic oppression of women

Grief, PTSD-like symptoms, and bereavement

Starvation, poverty, and imprisonment

War, conquest, and large-scale slaughter
Humiliation, domination, and disturbing imagery
Obsessive behavior toward corpses (sexual context, *not MC*)
Abuse of power and betrayal
Sexual content
Alcohol and substance use
Death of a parent
Coercion involving a minor (off-page, *not MC*)
Suicide (off-page, *not MC*)

Your mental health matters. Please take care of yourself and skip or pause if needed.

The world of this book is dark and unjust.

Remember: I might leave your heart bruised, but your soul will sing.

It will be worth it.

CONTENTS

"She didn't listen to the serpent. She ran with the wolves."
— Nina

PROLOGUE

This is a story of a girl who was never meant to leave. They locked the gates and sealed the walls, bound her in tradition and called it peace. Her name was Noël Ársa, born beneath cold skies and colder laws, raised by a woman who taught her that silence was a cage and pain was a teacher. They will tell you she followed these laws, that she bowed her head. But that is not the truth.

Noël was a rose, and the truth is: *Roses grow thorns when ignored for too long.*

"One, two, one, two."

Noël's mother's sharp commands cut through the quiet of their secret garden. Noël moved her body in time with the words she'd heard over and over, her bruised hands gripping the wooden sword as she struck the dummy before her. This garden, hidden from the eyes of Tárnov's rigid rules, was a place of defiance. High walls circled the village like a fortress, ivy creeping along the old cracks in the stone as if nature itself sought to break free. The streets were lined with cobblestones, perfectly even and slick from the melted snow. Each stone sat in its place, just like the homes they led to, identical gray blocks of cold stone and pointed roofs, lined up in regimented rows. Even the wind moved in straight lines here, whistling past shuttered windows and locked doors.

Every building and every street served one purpose: to maintain control. Women walked in silence, skirts brushing the polished stone. Children were sorted before their voices had deepened. Boys sent to drills, girls to domestic halls where they learned how to listen without being told.

No woman left Tárnov.

No girl was raised to believe she could. That wasn't how the world worked.

A woman who is born in Tárnov dies in Tárnov. The phrase had been etched into Noël's mind since birth. A truth known among the village women but never spoken above a whisper.

In Tárnov, the trees didn't reach the walls. But here, in this garden, the blue roses flourished, glowing in the early morning gloom. No one knew they truly existed outside tales of old, and that was the way it had to remain. This place, where Noël could be more than just a daughter bound by the laws of men, was her mother's gift, her rebellion against an empire that saw women as nothing more than vessels for bearing children and slaves for men's greed.

"Come on, Noël, you can't rest now."

Noël's chest burned from the effort, her muscles trembling as she lifted the sword again. Sweat beaded on her brow, blended with the dirt and dust of the garden. But she wouldn't stop. Not here. Not with her mother's eyes on her.

The dummy swayed, spinning on its base as the wooden sword smacked into its body over and over again.

"Push harder!" her mother urged, and Noël listened. She always did.

From a young age, Noël trained under her mother's guidance. She woke early, always beginning with chores. The floor had to be swept before breakfast, and the table set with clean plates for the staple porridge. Buckwheat, millet, or oats, depending on the season. Tárnov was a village favored by the tsar, and there was always enough if you had a coin.

Noël had a sweet tooth and often added berries or honey when she could, something her mother, Eyleen, loved too.

Every day was filled with training. The body and mind had to be honed in equal measure, and Eyleen made sure her daughter understood that.

Discipline, she would always say, was the key to keeping the soul at ease.

"One, two, one, two."

Noël gritted her teeth, focusing on the movement of her arms, the flow of her strikes, and the sting in her muscles. She swung with all her strength, her mind blocking out the pain as the dummy spun faster. She could hear her mother's footsteps circling behind her, the soft crunch of leaves under her boots, her gaze never leaving Noël's back.

Noël's final strike came with a crack. The wooden dummy broke apart, its pieces falling to the ground as she stumbled back, gasping for air. Her arms trembled from the effort, her chest rose and fell with every ragged breath. Wiping the sweat from her forehead, she dared to glance at her mother.

For a moment, she thought she might see pride in her mother's eyes. But her mother simply looked down at the broken pieces of the puppet.

"Better," she said. "But not enough. Tomorrow, we start earlier."

Noël swallowed, panting heavily as she wiped her hands on the hem of her damp tunic. "Yes, Mother,"

Noël always wondered when the day would come, the day her mother would finally see her. When her effort would be enough. But it never was. Not the perfect strikes that could put seasoned soldiers to shame. Not the disciplined routine she followed without fail. Not even the lessons she memorized word for word.

Nothing was ever enough for Eyleen Ársa.

As the morning sun rose above Tárnov's stone walls, the blue roses surrounding them danced gently in the breeze. Her mother turned and disappeared through the archway of blue roses, her back straight and graceful as she walked. Noël stared at the empty space she left behind with a narrow gaze.

She wondered, as she often did, when the day would come.

It seemed though, once again, today was not the day.

Years Later

"One, two, one, two."

The sharp command rang out across the training grounds, echoing off the stone walls of the base. Noël stood at the front, her voice firm and demanding as she paced between the rows of her soldiers. The men swung their swords in time with her commands, their movements precise, uniforms damp with sweat.

Tárnov's base was an extension of the village, as cold as the stone from which both were built. It was said to be the strongest in the world, or so the Tárnovers all believed.

The walls were tall and bare, save for the banners of crossed swords and the symbols of blue roses.

Inside, the halls were narrow and exact. Barracks were lined up in strict rows, with beds of stone, thin sheets, and floors scrubbed daily. The training yard never emptied. The armory was organized down to the last blade.

"Faster!" Noël barked. "You think the enemy will wait for you to catch your breath?"

The metallic sound of swords clashing against shields filled the air alongside the harsh breathing of tired men. Noël's leather boots dug into the dirt as she moved among them, her eyes scanning the lines of warriors before her for any sign of weakness.

Who would dare to rest under her command? Who would dare to speak up? To ask why she was so harsh with them?

No one would.

She spotted one soldier. His arms shook, the grip on his sword loose. Noël was on him in an instant to grab the front of his uniform and yank him toward her.

"Are you tired, *rookie*?" she asked. Her voice was cold, but the heat in her chest was too familiar. She'd been where he stood, trembling under the weight of expectations that felt impossible to meet. And yet, she couldn't go easy on him.

Weakness had no place in this world. Just as her mother taught her. The very thought of it made her chest tighten, but she pushed the burning feeling aside.

She had no room for softness.

"N-no, Sergeant ..."

"Then why are you slowing down?" she demanded, shoving him back into place.

The man stumbled before fixing his stance.

"The moment you hesitate is the moment you die. Is that what you want?"

"No, Sergeant Ársa!" Fear flashed in his eyes as he snapped to attention and tightened his grip on his sword.

"Then fight like your life depends on it." She leaned closer, narrowing her gaze as she slowly pronounced the last words, "*Because it does.*"

With a step back, she watched as he straightened and swung his sword with energy, intention, and the desire to please her shining in his eyes. The soldiers at his sides stood tall, expressions wary. They, too, were afraid to displease their sergeant. The cold sergeant who had joined them years ago. The one who beat them in every drill and rose through the ranks like a fire spreading in a dying forest.

Satisfied, she continued pacing the line as her soldiers pushed themselves harder and harder under her watchful gaze.

The clanging of steel against steel, the grunts of effort from tired men, and the shouts of her commands echoed through the training grounds of Tárnov's base. The heat of the early sun bore down on Noël, but she didn't let it affect her focus. This was where she thrived—leading, commanding, shaping these men into something stronger than they thought possible.

"One, two, one, two," she repeated.

The men responded, their swords cutting through the air in perfect unison. Noël watched them, her eyes hard but proud. She would make sure they were strong. She would make sure her mother was proud.

After several rounds, she finally called out, "Enough!"

The soldiers' chests heaved as they lowered their weapons, turning their gazes to their sergeant.

"Take a break," she said. "Then we'll begin again."

As the men collapsed onto the dirt, wiping the sweat from their faces, Noël stepped away from the training grounds and made her way through the dark corridors of the stone base toward her office. Her boots echoed against the floor as she passed the cafeteria, already empty after morning drills, the classrooms lined with chalkboards and stacked gear, the communal washrooms, the officers' quarters. At the end of the hall, she stopped in front of a familiar door and unlocked it with the key only she carried.

As she stepped into her office, her gaze drifted to the back of a framed picture on her desk. Her mother's portrait, one she had painted as a child.

"I'm coming home soon, Mother. I have so much to tell you," she whispered, a small smile tugging at her lips. It had been months since her last visit.

She sat down, and her eyes caught on the painting once more. The smile faded. As a girl, she had glued a few blue rose petals to it, plucked from their secret garden. The petals had never withered. Not in all these years.

Loud steps echoed outside her office. Every thud of heavy boots against the floor became louder as the seconds passed. When the door swung open, her lieutenant colonel stepped inside. His face was still, as always, his expression cold.

Even as he walked across the room to place a white gown on the worn sofa.

"Sergeant Ársa, put this on."

Noël looked at the white gown, clenching her fists. She knew what it meant. There were only two options: new beginnings or the end.

That day, the petals on the painting turned black.

1

THE VOID LEFT BEHIND

"A leader does not rise from triumph, but from loss. It is grief that carves the shape of a ruler, and only those who survive the carving will stand."
—Láda Veléša, Goddess of Leadership and War

Noël

"Don't touch her! I'll burn this place to the ground!"

I thrash, but I can't move. The two soldiers holding me by my arms refuse to let go. My boots scrape against the cold ground of Tárnov's village square, the rough stone biting into my soles. The men don't speak. Don't say a word.

They are statues, void of feeling, dragging me back like I am nothing.

It's daytime, but the world is dark. The sky above is bleak, a muted gray that swallows the sun. Cold seeps into my bones. It wraps around me like a second skin.

This isn't real. It's nothing but a nightmare.

"Let go of me! That's an order!" I scream. I am an officer! I can throw them into the pit and forget their existence! My word holds weight.

But they don't listen. They pull me back, farther away from her. "Mother!" My cry tears from my throat, but it does not stop them.

The dark wooden carriage lunges forward, wheels grinding against the hard soil as its black horses carry my mother's lifeless body toward the main gates of the village. She is inside. Wrapped in white. Motionless. Her knees bounce beneath the thin shroud, and I can see their shape through the fabric.

What's going on? They never take corpses out of the village.

"Keep your tongue behind your teeth, Ársa." My lieutenant colonel's silhouette grows bigger as he approaches.

"Where are you taking her?" My voice breaks. My heart slams against my ribs. I can't breathe. There is nothing left now. Nothing but the blurred spin of the wheels, the cruel trudge of the horses, the tightening of the soldiers' grips as they keep me in place.

"Who do you think you are?" he says, stopping a few steps before me. "Got a rank and now you speak?"

My eyes narrow, and my teeth grind as my pulse pounds in my ears.

"We arrived here at the same time, Ársa. You've seen what I've seen."

I shake my head. No. "You don't *take the dead* out," I rasp. "You bury them. You burn them. But you don't—" I gag on bile. "You don't cross the gates."

This is it. Sobs tear through me, leaving only emptiness, as if each one is hollowing me out from the inside. "You don't take her. No one takes her!"

The soldiers say nothing. Remain cold fingers and locked jaws. Like they don't hear me. Like I'm no one. I twist, trying to headbutt one. He dodges, but only barely.

It hurts too much to scream again.

"Heart failure," he finally says.

Nonsense. My mother was always so healthy, so full of life. Everywhere in our house, there was salt and rosemary, herbs to ward off illness like magic amulets. She couldn't just . . . die. It doesn't make any sense.

The colonel steps forward, hands clasped behind his back. He looks at me as if I've lost my mind. That detached gaze, the coldness in his lifeless eyes—I want to burn them.

"Release me!" I scream again, thrashing against the soldiers' grips. The colonel slaps me across the face. It stings.

"Take her home," he orders. "She's unwell."

They drag me down the narrow path toward my mother's home, past the rows of stone houses that watch with shuttered windows and silent doors. I twist hard, once, twice, and manage to rip my arm free from the soldier on my right. My elbow shoots up to slam into his chest. He grunts and staggers back.

I almost break loose.

But the moment I think I've got a chance, the other lunges, and both their hands clamp around my throat.

My back slams against the wall of a nearby house. The stone is cold. Their grip is colder. I choke on air, eyes wide as they squeeze just enough to make the edges of my vision blur.

"Shut up," one of them hisses. "You want to make a scene?"

I snarl, trying to fight, but my strength is slipping. My tears haven't yet dried.

The second soldier leans in close. "Show the others what order looks like."

Through the fog in my head, my chest heaving, throat burning, I glare at him. But there's no point in fighting now. The carriage is long gone. *Mother* is long gone.

"Where is this house?" the first growls as they drag me against the wall.

"The colonel said it should be somewhere around here," the other replies.

Are they blind? My home is right in front of us.

I twist, grab the front of their uniforms, and slam them both into the stone wall. Their pained grunts as they fall to the ground almost bring me a dark satisfaction. Almost.

Grabbing the sides of their heads with both hands, I shove them back again, hard. These two are nothing compared to me. I've sent countless men just like them to the healer over my years in the army.

"I can walk on my own."

Without waiting for a response, I leave them there, crumpled outside my mother's home, and walk toward the door.

I exhale deeply.

But today is not about them. It's about her.

After all, she was the reason I joined the army in the first place. She never yielded to those restrictive rules set by men who think themselves gods to rule over everything else in existence. She taught me to think critically, to wield my strength, to never take anything at face value. Defying their conventions, surpassing their expectations, I climbed the ranks. Where women were silenced, my voice was heard.

My mother was the light of my soul. She was a strong-willed woman who always urged me to question everything around me. "Never let anyone say you can't do something, Noël." Her eyes used to flare with the same spark that lived in me until today.

Our home was a stronghold, where intellect and influence were nurtured. She taught me how to read, how to be strong, and how to fight for what I believe in. Many nights were spent out in our garden, training with wooden swords, secretly, as she commanded every step I took. "Strength comes in many forms," she would remind me often. "Physical, mental, spiritual—you must master them all."

I am a few steps away from the door when something dark

catches my attention, and I move to crouch beside a stain on the soil to the left of the entrance. What is it?

I run my finger through the earth and lift it to my nose.

My heart sinks.

It smells of blood. What? Mothe— No. This can't be it. There were no blood stains on the shroud that covered her body. This just cannot be true.

I rise to my full height and smear the dried blood on my skirt, wrinkling my nose, and turn to the door.

The handle is cold in my grip, and as the door creaks open, the sound is a twisting knife in my gut. I will walk in, and she won't be there. Because she is gone.

Bracing for something that will never come, I step inside. No scolding. No *tsk* as she eyes the dirt on my gown. She's supposed to be here, supposed to tell me not to walk around like this.

But the silence is too loud.

Every step I take feels like a violation, like I don't belong in this space anymore. The familiar scent of herbs lingers in the air with the cold seeping in from outside. It's comforting and painful all at once. It reminds me too much of her. It feels like she's still here, just out of reach, tending to her herbs.

But she is *not*.

The kitchen. It's filled with herbs and flowers, exactly like it was a few months ago when I last visited. Tears blur my vision.

I would complain about the pain in my neck, or the smack these soldiers gave me just a few minutes ago. But who will hear my pain if not her?

My hands on the counter, my arms holding my full weight, I lean forward, and my tears fall into the sink to darken the wood with every drop. Could it be the colonel? Maybe any of the soldiers?

Impossible. They were all with me at the base. Then what happened?

But the blood outside...

Shaking my head, I walk into the living room. Her sanctuary, the place where she'd sit by the fire, read to me, teach me everything I know.

I can almost see her there, curled up in her chair by the hearth, her fingers tracing the pages of the book she read so often. The same book that sits there now, left open, as if she had just been reading it again.

My hands tremble as I pick it up and flip through the pages. One of them is marked with a folded piece of paper. Carefully, I pull it free and read the passage she bookmarked.

It describes an ancient ritual, one designed to undo the most binding of enchantments. The text speaks of breaking the "chains of blood" that hold entire forces at bay, forces so strong they can only be contained by spells woven from ancient bloodlines. The final passage hints at a great cost, a sacrifice required to unravel such powerful magic, followed by crossing a path of blood.

I swallow hard.

Why did my mother mark this?

She always spoke in riddles, said things I struggled to understand, did things I never dared to ask about. My every question was left unanswered.

After I close the book and set it back in its place, I move deeper into the house, and with every step, the air gets colder.

When I reach her bedroom, the door creaks as I push it open. My breath catches at the sight of her bed, unmade, the furs still piled where she last lay. I freeze.

Mother never left her bed like this. It was one of her rules: everything in order, *always*. Seeing it now, messy and abandoned, sends a shiver down my body. It's wrong.

Swallowing hard again, I rush to make the bed. I pull the white blanket neatly into place, smoothing the plush furs on top.

My eyes move to her bedside drawer, one I never touched. My fingers brush over the wood, rough and worn from years of use. Maybe there's something inside. A clue? A sign? Because I refuse to believe she died of heart failure.

Hesitating, I pull the drawer open to find empty envelopes and a bit of white fabric. My gaze softens. It's her embroidered handkerchief, the one she sewed herself, with blue rose petals stitched into it. Her favorite flowers.

My throat tightens as I take it out and hold it close, pressing the fabric against my chest. It feels like the last piece of her I can cling to. The last part of her in a world that suddenly feels so empty. I stare at it longer than I should before shoving it into my pocket. I don't know why . . . it just feels right. Like keeping her with me, even in the smallest way, is something I need to do. My vision blurs again.

It's too much. The scent of herbs in the air, the unbearable silence of the house, the way everything still feels like it's waiting for her to return—it's too much.

I can't stay here.

My legs shake as I make my way out of the house, wiping my tears as I go. The air outside is biting and cold, but it's nothing compared to the void she left behind.

The soldiers are gone, and the village of Tárnov is bathed in the dull light of a pale moon struggling to pierce the clouds above. Even the stone buildings, which have stood for generations, seem lifeless, like cold statues in the night.

When I first joined the army, they told us Tárnov was one of the largest villages in the world. A place shaped by the great tsar himself, who, as the stories go, poured his soul into its very foundation, making it second only to the capital, Velháven, in size and resources.

His influence is etched into every stone, every road paved with care, not for beauty, but for control. Every path, every towering wall designed to ensure that no woman escapes. Our lives dictated by rules we did not create.

The vast granaries, always full, are said to be proof of his foresight to ensure Tárnov never knows famine. The aqueducts, a marvel of engineering, carry fresh water from the mountains, a luxury envied by other villages. Tárnov's workshops produce the finest weapons and armor, forged with techniques passed down by the royal smiths themselves.

The marketplace, the heart of the village, still bustles despite the late hour. Military men patrol the streets or stand stationed at every corner, scanning their surroundings. Women, clutching their children's hands, make their way home. In the shadows of dark alleys, cloaked women blend into the dim light. The night workers, watching for the soldier who might become their next customer.

The hard stone that shapes every wall and path was meant to symbolize the empire's strength and power. But tonight, it feels like a prison.

It always has.

Ahead of me, the inn stands, the interior glowing warmly against the cold night.

For now, it's my only way out.

A figure stands just outside the shadows, her familiar face lit by the inn's windows. An older woman, her gray hair wrapped in a scarf. Her knowing eyes lock onto mine.

"Noël?" Her voice is soft, and I stop in my tracks. "Is that you?"

Swallowing against the knot in my throat, I nod. "It's me, Nina."

I remember her from childhood. One of the few women who sometimes came by our house for herbs. She always kept to herself, quiet but kind.

"I heard what happened to your mother," she says. "I'm so sorry."

"Thank you." The words feel heavy as I say them. I try to move past her, but something in her expression stops me.

There's a look, one I can't quite place, but it makes my heart quicken.

She steps closer, lowering her voice to a near whisper. "Not long ago, your mother came to the market," she says, her eyes narrowing. "She never spoke much, never stayed long, but that day . . . that day, she bought bundles of rosemary and salt."

I blink. "She used them to keep us safe from illness," I say, my voice coming out more defensive than I intend.

Nina shakes her head. "No, child. This was different. I thought it was odd too. Those herbs, they weren't just for sickness. They're used in old rites, ancient ones, for protection against things far worse."

A chill runs through me. "Protection?"

She hesitates, then continues, "I asked her why—why she needed so much. She looked at me, Noël, and . . . she was afraid."

Afraid? The word feels foreign. My mother was never afraid. She was strength itself. "No, you must have been mistaken."

"I wasn't." Nina's gaze searches mine. "Your mother was never scared, but that day, she was."

Her words hang between us, and my skin prickles.

"You . . . you think something else happened to her?" My voice barely comes out.

Nina glances at the patrolling soldiers before settling back on me. "I don't know what to think. But you should be curious, Noël. Ask questions. Look deeper. Things in this village, in this empire, are not always as they seem."

I've always known Tárnov has secrets, always felt them pressing beneath the old stones. There are things we were never allowed to talk about, rules we had to follow that seemed to go against everything natural. I always believed that nature should not be restricted, but here I am, standing in a village that has never allowed me to touch a living tree. But standing here, with Nina's warning in my ears, it suddenly feels too real.

I steel myself. "I will. I'll find out the truth."

She nods, a sad smile pulling at her lips. "Be careful, child. They're watching. *Always* watching."

I murmur my thanks, and she slips back into the shadows, vanishing as if she were never there. But her words stay with me as I turn toward the inn.

The warm light ahead no longer feels like a refuge. It feels distant. The world is far darker than I ever realized. I have no strength left, but I know one thing.

I will not stop until I know what really happened to her. I owe her more than grief. I owe her truth. And I won't rest until I find it.

2

TEARS, ALE, AND BLOOD

"The moment you raise your fist, you have already declared
war. The moment you stand in defiance, you have already
chosen your enemy. But war is never fought on the battlefield
alone, it begins in the silence, in the spaces between words,
where no one dares to stand beside you."
—Láda Veléša, Goddess of Leadership and War

Noël

I was here not long ago, buying ale for Winter's Farewell.
My mother taught me from a young age the importance
of that day, a time to celebrate surviving the brutal cold
and to honor those we lost along the way. In our village, the
homes of the fortunate were adorned with early spring flowers,
a mark of gratitude after making it through another winter. For
mourning families, it was a day of reflection, their homes left
bare, the silence louder than any decoration.

Some families hosted feasts, sharing what they had as a
symbol of endurance and resilience. My mother believed in the
act of giving, and she always made it a point to gift a meal or

warm fabric to those grieving their loved ones, a gesture that spoke to her view that community is a bond stronger than any season. She was always so different from the others in Tárnov, or even the soldiers from other villages who came to train with us at the base.

Our own house would be filled with the smell of freshly baked bread and the ale set out for any weary traveler who might pass by, because my mother believed that even in hardship we must show kindness. She would say that we are all bound by the same cycle of life, death, and renewal. It has been a tradition in our family for many generations.

The familiar musty air of the inn, and the scent of vodka, settles around me. The heavy door closes behind me with a thud, and for a moment, the world outside feels far away. But as I make my way to the bar, Nina's words haunt the edges of my thoughts.

My mother, *afraid*. The idea feels wrong. Nina saw something in her, something I didn't. What did I miss? Why didn't I press Nina for more?

But what else would she say? Mother barely spoke with anyone.

I slide onto a worn wooden stool, and the bar creaks under my weight as I press my elbows into it. The innkeeper's wiping down the counter, his back to me and his shoulders hunched as if the air in here weighs him down too.

I catch my reflection in the dusty mirror behind the bar. Hollow eyes, pale skin, my dark hair one big mess. The grief has etched itself into my face so deeply I barely recognize myself.

"An ale, please," I murmur, my voice rasping from the dryness in my throat.

The innkeeper grunts in acknowledgment, his movements mechanical as he pulls a bottle from the shelf and pours the drink. I stare at the liquid as it sloshes into the cup, golden and bitter. I've never been fond of ale. My mother used to say it dulled the mind. But tonight, that's what I need.

I pay with one silver coin. It's too much for one cup, but I don't have less. The innkeeper tosses the change, a few copper coins, onto the bar, and I let them rest where they are. As I sip the drink, the burn spreads down my throat, but it doesn't take away the pain in my chest. Ale can't answer the questions running through my mind. It can't bring my mother back. It can't erase the fear that something far worse than I know is hiding beneath the surface of Tárnov.

The barmaid moves like a ghost, her eyes flicking to mine as she passes. They're tired, but in them there's something like . . . understanding. She doesn't ask how I'm doing. She knows. Women in Tárnov always know when to stay silent.

I take another sip as I scan the room. A few men sit in the far corner, their faces dark in shadow. One of them catches my gaze. Commander Barric from the tsar's court. I remember him from the day I met the tsar. He was standing at a distance, and he even smiled at me then. But now, he holds my eye for a moment too long to be casual, then turns away. A prickle of unease crawls down my spine.

When I set my cup down, the dull thud against the wood barely registers over the pounding in my chest. Everything feels different tonight. Or maybe it's just me that's different.

The door creaks behind me.

"Noël, darling, you look sweeter than ever."

The voice grates on my nerves before I even turn to look at him. Arnold, the commander of the newbies' troop. If you could even call him a commander. After a few loud steps and a smack to the barmaid's behind, he leans on the bar, his grin as oily as the smears on the counter. He brushes his hair back in a way he must think looks charming. It doesn't.

"Did you miss me?" he asks, his voice cloying and irritating. "Even when you're grieving, you're a beauty."

My skin prickles with annoyance, but I don't let it show. I know what Arnold's doing—needling me, waiting for me to crack. He's always been like this, even back when he was my superior. Back when I was just another soldier under his command, working twice as hard for half the respect. He's the kind of man who thinks power comes from the uniform, not from the person wearing it.

I told my mother everything about him. Every smug remark, every ugly smile, every time he tried to undermine me. I can't count the nights I'd gone home, ranting about the way he treated me. How he always found a way to turn every little thing into a battle for dominance. She always told me to be careful, to not let his bitterness drag me down. She knew the kind of man he is, maybe better than I do.

He leans closer, his breath hot with the stench of vodka and tobacco. "You've been working too hard, Noël." His eyes rake over me like I'm some prize he's entitled to. "You should smile more. It wouldn't hurt to show a little softness now and then. Might even win you a few points with the higher-ups."

I can't help the tiny bit of rage that rises in my chest. Smile? Softness? What would he know about surviving in this world with nothing but grit and strength? He's never had to prove himself like I have, never had to claw his way up from the bottom while everyone told him he didn't belong.

Because I'm a woman, and women don't belong in the army.

I turn to face him fully, locking eyes with him and projecting a calm I don't feel. "I smile when there's a reason to, Arnold. Your face isn't one."

He chuckles. "Oh, I don't doubt it. You've always had that fire. But you know . . . you'd do a lot better if you stopped pretending to be one of the men. Femininity suits a woman like you. A pretty face and eyes like a rotten tree."

I grip the edge of the bar to keep myself grounded. If he weren't so predictable, I'd laugh at how wrong he is.

"Come on, Noël," he murmurs. "You know you've always wanted a man like me on your side. We could make a great team. You and me"—he traces a finger over the counter—"in one bed . . ."

"I don't need a man like you." I narrow my gaze, and my voice is hard as steel. "I've done just fine without." I brush his finger off, and he stumbles. His elbow slips from the wooden surface, and I fight to keep my smirk from stretching too wide as I say, "I think it's time for you to close your legs, isn't it?"

His grin disappears, and I savor that tiny victory. But I know better than to think he'll back off. Men like Arnold never do. He clamps down on my arm with a grip like iron, yanking me from the stool before I have a chance to react.

I grit my teeth and plant my feet as the burn of rage surges through me.

"Oh, you think you've earned the right to talk back now?" His grip tightens, the pressure around my arm bruising.

Is that the only phrase men know?

But I'm not one of the fresh recruits he pushes around. I'm not weak.

My body reacts before I even realize it. A sharp twist of my torso, years of training taking over, and I wrench free from his hold with a snap that surprises even him. "You're drunk," I spit, stepping back to put space between us. "Stop this nonsense."

But Arnold isn't deterred. His eyes gleam with something dark, something far more dangerous than the usual drunken state. He moves forward, trying to catch my arm again. "You don't walk away from me," he snarls, his voice more menacing by the moment.

I move on instinct to knock his hand away. Caught off guard, he stumbles, and I see the realization in his eyes. I'm not someone he can push around.

The lanterns cast shadows on his face, deepening the ugly twist of his mouth as he lunges again. But I'm ready this time.

In one motion, I sidestep and drive my elbow into his ribs. The satisfying sound of his grunt fills the room, but I don't stop there. I follow through with a quick fist aimed at his stomach that has him doubling over.

You're pathetic, Arnold.

The inn feels smaller, the shadows longer, as if the walls are closing in. I can feel every gaze on me, the other patrons watching but none of them moving. No one's stepping in. Typical. If I were a man, everyone would be involved by now.

Arnold straightens, gasping for air, his face twisted in rage. "You think you're better than me?" he spits, voice rough, as if each word scrapes his throat. He swings, his mead-soaked brain slowing his reflexes.

I duck easily, and my fist connects with his gut once more, even harder than before. The force sends him staggering back, knocking over a chair.

For a second, I think it's over. He's down, clutching his stomach, struggling to catch his breath. But I know he won't stay down for long. He's not just angry, he's humiliated. And a humiliated man is far more dangerous.

As expected, he lunges at me again, his hand shooting out to grab a fistful of my hair.

Wrong move. I dodge him as my hand snaps to catch his wrist and twist it behind his back. He lets out a yelp, and his knees bend as I force him down.

"You are too weak, Arnold," I whisper into his ear, tightening my grip on his arm. The room is quiet, I can nearly hear his pulse. But no one moves.

And then, as I'm about to release him, he breaks free with a burst of energy fueled by rage and humiliation. His hand comes fast—too fast for me to block—and the next thing I feel is the sting of his palm as it strikes my face. The force of it sends me reeling, my vision swimming. The sharp sting spreads across my cheek, but I push the pain aside and will myself to stay upright.

I lock eyes with him. I will *not* show weakness. But something's different now. The room feels colder, and as my gaze moves around the inn, I realize it's not just about Arnold anymore.

The men sitting in the far corners rise slowly from their seats, looking at one another, then back at me. They're not here to help.

Arnold smirks as if he's already won. "Oh, not so tough now, are you?"

The innkeeper pretends to wipe down the counter, avoiding eye contact, while the barmaid stands frozen, still clutching the tankard she was pouring. The tension in the room tightens around me. I can hear the crack of knuckles, the creak of leather as more men circle closer. Commander Barric gets up, then sits back down. Looks around the room.

What was that about?

Arnold's grin widens. "Come on, Noël," he taunts. "You should know better than to challenge me."

I don't think. I lunge. My fist slams into his face with enough power to send him flying backward into a table. The wood groans under his weight, hitting the wall as mugs and shards of glass tumble to the floor.

Before I can steady my breath, something hard slams into the back of my head. The pain is blinding, like fire spreading through my skull. The world tilts as black spots swarm at the edges of my vision. My legs give way, and I collapse toward the cold, unforgiving stone floor. Sounds become distant, and Arnold's leering face is the last thing I see before everything turns black.

3

THE EDGE OF NIGHT

"Fear is a blade sharper than any sword. It does not strike, it festers and weakens before the first wound is ever made. A warrior must decide: Will she wield it, or will it wield her?"
—Láda Veléša, Goddess of Leadership and War

Noël

"**A**re you sure this is a good idea?"

"Of course it is. The wench needs to know her place. I don't give a flying boar shit that she's the only female in the military. Even better, this will be a lesson to others that there's no place for a woman in the army."

Arnold's voice would wake me from the dead. Even half-conscious, I'd recognize that sound anywhere.

My pulse quickens, and my head throbs in time with each word I hear. My skull feels like it's being split open from the inside, and for some reason I feel weak. It's hard to move—physically. A deep, burning anger bubbles up, cutting through the sting of pain. How did I end up at his mercy?

I don't know if it's the fear of what he's planning or the pure rage of being in this situation that stirs me more, but I know one thing: He'll regret this. I'll make sure of it.

My eyes are heavy, and it takes every drop of effort to open them. It's even harder as the carriage jolts side to side over uneven ground. What happened?

"Oh come on, don't be so harsh. Everyone knows you have your eyes on her."

That voice, it's not Arnold. Someone else is with him. I try to focus. My memories are vague, flashing through my mind in broken fragments. And then it hits me.

Right. I punched Arnold in the face, and then someone knocked me out from behind.

"I'm not being harsh!" Arnold laughs. "Well, maybe I am. Who else would've thought to drug her like that? Had to slip the innkeeper a few pretty silvers. Though I'm surprised she's still breathing. I heard this herb is deadly, but somehow she's managed to survive."

I think I might throw up. What a sick—

"That's why she hasn't woken up yet? It's been days and nights, Arnold, and she's still asleep."

Days? How long have I been unconscious?

I try to shake my head out of habit, but it hurts, so I stop moving and focus on my surroundings.

The carriage is old, dark, and musty. The air hangs so thick with the smell of worn leather that it clings to my throat. My fingers graze the rough wooden walls, tracing the scratches and grooves gouged into its surface. Thin light seeps through torn curtains, barely enough to cut through the gloom and leaving most of the carriage swallowed by shadows. It's disturbingly quiet, save for the murmurs of my captors outside. And the horses. My heartbeat fills the silence, pounding in my ears. I feel a sick unease, like I'm being buried alive.

"I still think throwing her to the vólkins is way too harsh, Arnold. The poor girl just didn't want to talk to you. Besides, you know it's illegal to get close to their territory, not to mention to let a woman outside the gates. If the knyaz finds out, we could be jailed for the rest of our lives."

"That's why you'll keep your mouth shut. Once we toss her to the vólkins, they'll tear her apart, and no one will ever know she was here. Let them do the dirty work."

Arnold, you sick, sick man.

The military painted a clear picture: Vólkins are savage, bloodthirsty beasts created from cursed wolves of old. I still remember the day during our early lessons, back when I had just joined the ranks, when one of the commanders drilled it into us. We stood in formation, the cold biting through our uniforms as he paced.

"You think you can survive out there? You think your swords or strength will protect you from a vólkin?" he said and his voice boomed, silencing the yard. "These monsters don't care about rank or skill. They'll tear you apart before you can even lift your blade."

We were always told that no human could match one of those creatures, that we must stay away from them. Once, while I was checking to make sure all the candles were extinguished in the rookies' barracks, I overheard a soldier say the tsar couldn't be that powerful if he was so afraid of the vólkins. He was hushed immediately by his roommates. Speaking negatively about the tsar is a serious crime in Vathéria. When I stomped my foot, they all fell silent.

These monsters . . . The colonel described them in detail that day. Their bodies are hulking, fur matted with blood, glowing eyes that pierced the night, always lurking just beyond the edge of Ávera, their home. "They're territorial," he'd warned, looking into every soldier's eyes. "They'll kill anyone who crosses into their land without hesitation. And no one ever returns."

It was a lesson meant to scare us into submission, a warning to stay far from their territory. Even though, as a woman, I'd never left the village, the stories of soldiers who strayed too close and vanished without a trace lingered in my mind. They were supposed to keep us in line, to keep us afraid.

But my mother told a different story. To her, the vólkins were not monsters, but guardians—ancient beings who watched over the land, protected the balance between nature and humanity. She always said they aren't beasts, they are part of the earth, the forest's soul. They keep the wilds in check, ensuring that the land thrives.

"You don't fear them, you honor them."

But now, as I sit here, bound, hearing Arnold talk of throwing me to them, doubt claws at my chest. What if my mother was wrong?

Mother was never wrong.

Lately, I've been experiencing strange dreams, visions of a time long past, of women standing alongside wolves, sharing in the guardianship of nature. In these dreams, I felt a deep connection to something, a yearning I couldn't understand. My mother always said I was special, but I never knew what she meant. Every woman has her own talent. Some are good at arts, some knit, and I am good at what my mother taught me my whole life. After twenty-five years of learning, I dare say that anyone would be good at anything.

But these dreams, these visions stirred something burning within me. I remember her always saying, "Under the crescent's glow, the Leader shall unite and guide, her vision piercing through the shadows of doubt." It was one of her many riddles. But for some reason, it feels connected to my dreams.

But what if the military's tales were more than simple fear-mongering? My mother, same as any woman in Tárnov, never went outside the village. She was smart and knew more than most, but the military knows what goes on beyond the walls. She didn't. What if the stories of bloodthirsty beasts are true?

I don't know which version to believe, and not knowing feels worse than the fear itself. It's like standing at the edge of a cliff with nothing but shadows below.

I try to get up, but my wrists are bound in many knots in front of me. The coarse twine bites into my skin, the fibers digging deeper every time I move. My wrists throb with every beat of my heart, and the pain makes it hard to focus on anything else. I grit my teeth. I must ignore the pain. I can. But it's the helplessness that bothers me most.

A hot, panicked breath escapes my lips, and my pulse quickens. I am trapped. Completely trapped. The air in the carriage feels thicker, like it's squeezing my chest. My hands tremble, my breath comes faster, and the tight grip of fear starts to coil around my ribs, pressing tighter and tighter.

I won't let this be my end. I won't let Arnold be the reason for my death. I will calm myself. Breathe in, and out.

Focus, Noël, push the dread down.

I've survived worse. I've trained for this. I close my eyes, letting my mother's voice echo in my mind. "You are strong, Noël," she used to say.

As I shift to a more comfortable position, a sudden jolt of pain stings my hip. Something pointed is digging into my skin, and I wince as I reach for it. My fingers brush against something hard—my mother's handkerchief. Not that. There's something else. A small blue crystal wrapped up in the handkerchief, its edges sharp enough to catch on the fabric and tear at my gown. *Where did this come from?*

Perhaps the crystal was hidden in the handkerchief all along, and I was too blinded by grief to notice. But this is good. This is my way out.

With shaking hands, I maneuver the crystal against the fibers binding my wrists. It's hard to do it right as the carriage continues to jostle and jerk. The edges dig in, sharper than I expected, and with each glide, the threads begin to fray. Good.

Sweat beads on my brow as I work, every slice urgent and uneven. The fibers weaken, and then, with a snap, the rope falls loose.

Heart racing, I fumble to free myself from the rest of the knots. My hair falls into my face, and without thinking, I shake it away, making the pain in my head throb harder. Shit. My fingers tremble. It's a challenge to stay steady, but I can't afford mistakes. I don't have time.

"Just imagine it," Arnold says, snapping me back to the present. "No one will ever find her. Not even 'scary Noël' will stand a chance."

We'll see about that, Arnold. The rope slips through my fingers, and I nearly cut myself. This crystal is like a razor.

"You think they'll just . . . take care of her like that?" His friend sounds unsure.

Arnold lets out a laugh. "They're beasts. We're doing them a favor."

The last knot gives way, and I nearly drop the crystal in my haste. My hands shake as I push at the carriage door. It's tied. No, no, no.

"We're not too far out," Arnold says, his voice louder now. "Get ready."

Goddesses, Mother, please. I must survive. I pull the torn curtains from the small windows. Bars. A quiet exhale escapes my lips. Getting on my knees, I reach between the bars and begin cutting the rope that ties the doors.

The crystal digs into the thick fibers, each stroke more frantic than the one before. Every second stretches into an eternity. I hold my breath. Goddesses, please let them not hear me.

Finally, the last rope falls away. I ease the door open, and the cool night air rushes in. My eyes widen. For the first time in my life, I'm beyond Tárnov's stone walls. The forest stands before me, its shadows dark yet strangely exhilarating. The thought of freedom dances on the wind, but there's no time to enjoy it.

The carriage rattles on, wheels clattering over rough ground. Every jolt of the carriage sends a fresh spike of fear through me, but I brace myself.

It's now or never.

I swing my legs out of the carriage. The damp earth meets my boots with a quiet thud, and I crouch low, listening. Nothing. Arnold's voice is so close, but he's too distracted to notice.

I have to move.

So I bolt.

Let the forest take me. I will not die in silence.

4

A PATH WRITTEN IN PROPHECY

"In the silence of the night, he will hear the call of the one who was made for him."
—Ánya Volkóva

Theron

The cool night greets me as I leave the council room of Ávera. The forest's flourishing fauna surrounds me, the sounds of night creatures filling the air, yet there's a strange quiet underneath it all. It makes me uneasy, as if something is just out of sight, waiting.

Lately, my dreams have gripped me like a paw around my throat that refuses to let go. Each night, I wake in a cold sweat under my fur, my chest heaving. The human female in my dreams . . . I can almost scent her. Her presence is like a ripple in the wind.

I'm built for battle, all muscle and fur. But these dreams . . . they're battles I can't fight. They shake me, leaving me disoriented in a way that's foreign to me. When I wake, my claws flex into the furs beneath me, muscles ready to grab at something that isn't there.

I've never seen her face, but I know she's important. There's a heat in her gaze, I know even though I can't see it. She's waiting for me, and I can't escape the feeling that I need to find her. *Now.*

For centuries, we've been trapped in this invisible cage, behind a barrier that keeps us tied to Ávera and its surrounding forest. It's more than a boundary we cannot cross, it's a prison. We've trained, studied, and prepared, hoping to understand why it appeared and how to break free. Despite our efforts, nothing has changed.

I've lost count of the years I've spent staring at the invisible wall, feeling its silent presence. It's not something you can see, but every vólkin and spirit can feel it. The way the air grows dense when you get too close, the way the land beyond blurs, the promise of freedom unreachable.

Some have grown restless, their once-bright eyes dulled by centuries of waiting. Éldir, who tore at the barrier with his claws until they bled, or Ásen, who sits in silence, rarely speaking anymore. They've given up hope, accepted this prison as their fate. Others have become angry, lashing out at the world inside the barrier, knowing there's no escape. The longer we stay caged, the more we lose our strength and our *minds.*

The goddesses themselves are bound by the barrier's magic, powerless to help us escape. Their voices, once clear, have faded with each passing century until they became nothing but whispers.

Yet I refuse to give in to that silence. I have to believe that one day, the barrier will fall. One day, we will break free from this cage. And when we do, the one responsible won't be ready for us, the starving beasts we are.

I roll my shoulders back, muscles tense beneath my thick pelt, and my claws flex against the ground as if digging into the earth will give me some sense of control. But it doesn't. It's too quiet.

"Theron." Kaël's voice pulls me back. His white crystals glow against his golden-brown fur. My trusted warrior and dear friend, standing with his hip cocked to the side. "You look troubled."

"They've changed . . . They're more than just visions now."

Kaël frowns, and Zephyr, overhearing our conversation, steps in to ask, "You think it's connected to the prophecy?" His yellow crystals gleam in the night, his deep brown fur moves with the bristle of wind that moves between us.

I shrug. The prophecy. It speaks of a leader, not from our own kind, but a human—a female whose vision will guide us, whose spirit will unite the six to restore harmony to our world. She is meant to lead us. But who is she? Where is she? The prophecy offers us no name, no face, only a promise. "It could be. But we've studied it for so long, and we still don't know exactly what it means."

Zephyr crosses his arms, his brown fur seems darker from this angle, and he too cocks his hip to the side. After spending so much time with Kaël, he's begun to mimic his stance. "We've never seen blue roses, yet you see them in your dreams. Maybe . . . maybe the time has come."

"Maybe," I repeat, looking down at my paws.

When I first saw the blue roses, I was as excited as a young pup. But the more I saw them without anything happening, the more my excitement faded. Maybe Zephyr is right.

Kaël shakes his head. "You've always believed, Theron. Now we have to believe the most. Who knows, maybe our mates are near."

I nod. "Thank you. You're right. We need to stay sharp."

We head toward the edge of the village and into the forest. *Mate.* The mate I haven't found yet. Völkins are supposed to know their mate by scent, even from a distance. I've heard the stories from Elder Aïna, how everything changes the moment a vólkin catches that scent. It's not only emotional. It's physical, instinctual, like they cannot control their body.

That longing has been with me for as long as I can remember. Every day I wonder if today will be the day the barrier falls, the day I finally find her. What will she smell like? What will it feel like when I recognize her? I've heard it's overwhelming, that nothing else matters anymore. But I can't let myself get lost in that thought. Not *yet*.

I have to stay strong. For her, for my people. They rely on me to lead, to be the one who stands between them and whatever's out there, waiting beyond the barrier.

We are near the ancient trees around Ávera. The patrol begins soon.

This forest is home to us. Every trail, every root is ingrained in our memory. The procedure for these patrols is mine—small groups moving in rotations, never following the same path twice. It keeps us alert and ensures no corner is left unchecked. Even though we've never fought an enemy, I treat these patrols as if we could face danger at any moment. It's a discipline my people need, something that reminds them we must be ready for the day that everything will change.

"It's been a while since I was assigned to this route," Kaël says as he moves a big stone back to its place, covering the mouth of a cave, then sighs. "And still, nothing."

"You were at the barrier yesterday." I scan my surroundings.

Every warrior has their role. I've divided the borderlands into sections marked by ancient trees and hidden stones only we vólkins would notice. Each team reports back after their circuit, giving me a complete report of our land's status by dawn. It's painstaking but necessary. This land is too important to leave unguarded, even if no one has crossed into our territory for four centuries. Because one day we will have to fight for our land, because the prophecy was born for a reason.

As the night deepens, we return to Ávera, where homes are grown from the earth itself. My own stands in the middle of the village, shaped from the ancient trees, their roots and branches twisted together to form walls and archways. The living bark hums with a pulse as it breathes with the forest. I walk in, and it's too quiet.

I made this place with her in mind. Every curve of wood, every vine hanging from the ceiling was grown for the day my mate will arrive. The nest in the center of the room, lined with furs from beasts I've hunted, lies empty, too large for just me. For centuries, I've waited, each night spent alone, knowing the space beside me is meant for her.

But century after century, she hasn't come. The thought of finding my mate keeps me going, but one thought bothers me as the years stretch on. *Humans must have changed over the centuries.* Their connection to the spiritual has faded, and they've lost the bond we vólkins honor. I wonder if my mate will even understand what it means, what *we* mean.

The thought of her not recognizing me, of her not feeling the bond as I will . . . is torturous.

Humans no longer live as long as we do. We were taught that over thousands of years, humans have died earlier and earlier, a sign of their lost connection to the world.

What if my mate has already died? What if she hasn't even been born yet? I cannot think of it. The goddesses know what they're doing.

I look through the open door. The fires outside burn low, lighting the paths. The village is silent, younglings long asleep in their nests. But even this peace can't calm the unease in my soul. Sleep won't come, it never does on nights like this. My home, though grown for two, feels emptier every night.

There's no purpose in staying in, so I make my way toward the sacred glade, where the goddesses have spoken before. The path is familiar. My paws know every root and herb.

I kneel before the ancient stone at the heart of the glade and bow my head. "Great goddesses," I whisper, "I seek your guidance. The dreams you've sent are powerful, but I need to understand. Please, show me the way."

A faint sound pulls my attention upward. Through the gaps in the trees, I see a white dove flying through the night sky. Its wings spread wide, catching the moonlight as it circles above me, glowing against the darkness.

My chest tightens as I watch the bird dip lower. Something falls from its talons. A single blue petal floats through the air.

When the petal lands on my shoulder, so light, it feels too delicate for someone like me. I stare at it, my clawed fingers hovering just above, as if touching it might make it disappear. Could it be...?

Since the barrier appeared, signs from the goddesses are not common. But this is unmistakable. The petal's deep blue hue stands out against the dark fur covering my shoulder, and a shiver runs through me.

I glance up, catching the glint of the white dove soaring above.

My gaze jerks as Kaël and Zephyr approach, their eyes wide as they take in the scene.

"Theron," Kaël breathes, "is that...?"

I nod, feeling the soft petal beneath the pads of my fingers. This is it.

"Gather the others," I say, my voice firm. "We leave now."

The day the prophecy was spoken, blue rose petals fell from the sky above.

5

ROOTS OF GRIEF,
SEEDS OF STRENGTH

"A warrior's grief is not a burden. It is the forge that tempers her steel. Let sorrow carve you, but never break you."
—Láda Veléša, Goddess of Leadership and War

Noël

Holding my skirts with both hands, I run through the forest. The wind howls through the trees, like whistles that taunt me with every step. My heart pounds in my chest, the rhythm matching the rapid snaps of twigs beneath my boots as if the forest is chasing me. Every sharp inhale feels like a sword scraping against my throat, which burns with each desperate gasp for air.

The darkness is thick and murky, and though moonlight slips through the branches, it does little to ease my fear. My fingers graze the rough bark of a tree as I stumble forward. The brush of the coarse surface over my skin reminds me that I'm not safe yet.

I have no idea where I am, only that I have to keep moving, put as much distance as possible between myself and the carriage that had become my prison. I don't know if Arnold stopped to check on me or not. Maybe he's already running in my direction. I still can't believe he drugged me. But it's not only Arnold I'm running from.

Vólkins. Every shadow in the forest seems to move, every rustle of leaves makes my heart race faster.

I'm out here now, near their territory. Alone. And so far away from home. The thought of them finding me—of claws ripping through my skin, of fangs sinking into my flesh—sends a chill down my spine and a burst of speed to my legs, even as they ache with exhaustion and my head spins.

It seems like I've been running throughout the whole night. The moon is no longer high above, it's setting. My legs are growing numb, and I know I can't keep this pace forever. I need to stop and rest, just for a moment. So I do.

I look around, and it's only now that I truly take in the forest surrounding me. The trees stretch in all directions like a big colony of birds flying over my village, their trunks impossibly tall, rising like pillars holding up the skies. The leaves, dark and glinting in the moonlight, sway in the cool night breeze. It's more than I ever imagined, more beautiful and alive. The air smells different here, crisper, richer, with the vague scent of pine and damp earth. For the first time in my life, I'm seeing the world as it truly is, not through the cold distance of a window or the lifeless pages of a book. The trees aren't just illustrations in an old tome. They're real and massive, each one unique in shape and texture.

It's not polished wood like Tárnov's furniture.

I run my fingers along the rough surface of a tree. It's uneven and knotted, with deep grooves where rainwater has carved its path over centuries. It feels ancient, as though it has witnessed the world change and grow around it but stood firm. I never knew bark could feel so alive.

Even in our garden we didn't have trees. Only roses, lots of them.

A tiny movement catches my eye, and I lean close. It's a caterpillar. Its body is green, little dots at the end of the hairs glowing in the silver light of the moon. It moves slowly, its tiny legs gripping the stem of a plant as it crawls upward. I watch, fascinated, as the caterpillar arches its back and then inches forward. Its world is so small.

I've only ever seen creatures like this in my mother's books, in the sketches she made as she told me stories of the wild. But this . . . It's right in front of me.

I follow the caterpillar's path with my eyes as it crawls over a leaf, the surface glistening with dew that sparkles like stars in the darkness. I reach out, touch the cool, waxy surface of the leaf, feel the moisture cling to my fingertips. How many times have I studied pictures of leaves like this?

Above me, the trees sway, their branches dancing in the moonlight. The sound they make isn't like the hollow creaking of wood back in Tárnov—it's a soft rustling, like a thousand whispers all at once. I tilt my head back and stare up at the canopy where the moonlight slips through like threads of silver woven between the leaves. The sky is wider here, unbroken by the walls that trapped me for so long. It's endless, and for the first time, I feel like I'm standing in a world without limits. I take a deep breath, savoring the freshest air, and exhale slowly.

The ground beneath me is uneven, the forest floor thick with layers of fallen leaves, moss, and small plants I can't even name. I crouch down and run my fingers through the soft, spongy moss that carpets the earth. It's cool and damp under my touch, a strange comfort in the middle of all this wildness. Little shoots of plants I've only ever read about poke through the soil. My mother used to tell me the names of plants like these, pointing to their pictures in old books. But seeing them here, growing in the wild, it feels like discovering them for the first time.

I glance up again at the trees, towering above me like guardians. I used to imagine what it would be like to touch one, to feel the rough bark under my hands, to breathe in the scent of real, living wood. Now, standing here, surrounded by them, I feel small, but not in the way I did in Tárnov. Here, in the wild, I feel connected. Like I'm finally part of something I longed for.

I've never felt this kind of freedom.

Even when I commanded my soldiers, they were the ones out here in the wild—tracking, scouting, and pushing the boundaries of their skills—while I was kept inside, chained by the unbreakable rules of Tárnov. It didn't matter that I had trained harder or fought better. I was still a woman, and women are not allowed outside the village walls. Not for safety, not for protection. No, because in their eyes, we didn't belong in the world beyond.

I remember one mission all too well. My unit was assigned to scout the northern border near the forests where bandits were rumored to gather. It was a critical task, one that I spent weeks preparing for. I poured over maps, strategized routes, thought of every risk. This was my chance to show them that I wasn't just a "female officer" but a true leader.

But the morning we were to leave, my lieutenant colonel called me into his office.

"You're not going," he said simply, his eyes hard as stone. There wasn't even room for discussion.

I remember the tension in my chest, my fists clenching at my sides as I demanded an explanation. I knew why, of course, but I needed to hear him say it. I needed to hear the words from his mouth.

"You know the rules, Ársa," he said, his lips curling into a smirk that made my skin crawl. "Women don't belong outside the walls. You're useful here, with the reports and the paper-work. Leave the real work to us."

Leave the real work to them.

No matter how much I proved myself, no matter how much I outpaced them in every training, they would always see me as less than. A woman's place is behind walls, behind men, behind limitations they created to keep us small and obedient.

That day, I watched from the tower as my men rode out without me, the sound of their horses fading into the distance while I was left to pace the cold stone halls like a caged animal. They returned days later with stories of battles fought, victories won. They wore their bruises and cuts like badges of honor, while I had nothing.

I find shelter under a large tree, its roots stretched wide enough to offer me some safety while my head aches. I sink down onto the damp forest floor, half lying on the trunk behind me.

Despite my limbs heavy with exhaustion and my stomach aching with hunger, I know I can't risk lighting a fire. The crackling flames would surely betray my presence and draw unwanted attention from lurking animals. Or Arnold. I wonder what that arsehole's face will look like when he sees the empty carriage.

I sigh with my whole body.

Mother always encouraged me to join the military because she believed it would make me capable and independent. "You have a strong spirit, Noël," she would say. "In the army, you will learn to channel that strength." Her voice echoes in my mind. She stood tall the day I left for training, pride shining in her eyes as she bid me farewell. While other parents were sending their sons, I stood tall with her, full of determination as the first woman to join the military in history. Warmth swells in my heart at the memory.

In my early days in the army, my squadron was subjected to a brutal training in the dead of winter. The relentless cold seeped into our bones, but we had to keep moving. And though we all struggled, I was singled out.

"Push through the pain, Ársa," the sergeant barked at me. "I knew a woman couldn't handle it, what were they thinking allowing this madness?"

I clenched my teeth, focused on my mother's words, and let her belief in me drive each step forward. By the end of the exercise, I was exhausted but proud. I had proven to myself and my comrades that I could. That I'm no less than a man.

I smile at the memory, but it quickly fades as the weight of grief settles on my shattered heart. My mother's absence hurts more than any wound. Her presence now nothing more than a precious memory I can hold on to.

How I long for her comforting embrace, her words of wisdom to guide me through this darkest of nights. But she's gone, taken from me too soon, leaving me to navigate this cruel world alone. *Mother, how will I survive without you?*

No matter how independent I am, I always listened to her. Always asked for her advice and always relied on her. I can't even imagine a life without her.

What now? What am I supposed to do now?

My chest tightens. Each breath is a struggle, as if the air around me is filled with sorrow. Hot tears stream down my cold skin, and I bury my head in my hands, my body shaking with the effort to keep my cries muted. Each sob is like a scream into the void, a scream into a world that has turned its back on me. The grief feels unbearable, and I find myself gasping for air, the sound of my uneven breaths the only noise in the heavy silence.

I pull the handkerchief from my pocket. My mother's scent still clings to it. It's faint, but enough to make my chest hurt even more. My hands tremble as I press the fabric to my face, inhaling deeply. I want to bring her back, even if only for a moment. More tears spill down my cheeks, and I rub the handkerchief against my skin.

"Mother . . ." The word is barely a whisper.

After sobbing for what seems like forever, I wipe away my last tears. I must focus on what I need to do next. Hunger overwhelms me.

As I walk through the forest, I find edible berries and apples. My military training has honed my survival skills, so I know how to find nonpoisonous foods in the wild. However, there are many I've never seen before. So, for now, I'll enjoy the juicy fruits and berries I know. Luckily, I stumble upon a patch of peppermint leaves. Their aroma lifts my spirits as I chew, freshening my breath and calming my nerves.

With a full stomach, I turn my attention to protecting myself. I find a sturdy branch. Without a sword, I won't stand the smallest chance against a vólkin, even against an animal, but I need to at least know that I tried.

I pull the crystal from my pocket in hopes that it might help me carve the wood. But when I glide it over the end of the branch, my hand slips. The crystal is too small to be effective, and instead of carving the wood, it slices into my finger, leaving a shallow cut. I hiss, the pain sharp and stinging. More tears begin to fall. They blend with the blood from my finger, and the cut burns. Shit.

The frustration, the fear, the overwhelming grief, it all pours out in my tears, and I feel miserable. How did it come to this? How did I end up here, alone in the dark, without my mother?

I find a rock with a bladelike edge and use it to finish the tiny spear. My knuckles turn white around the branch as the image of my mother fills my mind. Her smile, her long hair, our breakfasts before I left home. I tighten my grip until my fingers ache and more blood drips from my cut. But I don't stop. I don't care. The pain drives me forward.

"Mother, I swear to the goddesses," I growl through clenched teeth, "whoever did this to you, I will rip their spine out with my bare hands."

They will pay.

When the spear is finally complete, I feel accomplished despite it all. It reminds me of my mother's strength and the spirit that burns in me.

I pace under the trees, my grip tightening on the spear. She was distant with everyone, always kept us at a safe distance from the rest of the village. I used to think it was because of me, or maybe because she just didn't like anyone.

She said it was to protect us, but from what? From whom?

She never answered my questions.

A sense of betrayal lingers in the back of my mind, though I shove it down. I know she was hiding something, something that was probably too much for me to handle, but what? Did she know this was coming? Is that why she kept me at arm's length all these years?

Her voice, soft and calm, but always with steel beneath, as if she was speaking through a veil of secrets. She never let anyone get close, never involved herself in the gossip and petty dramas that consumed the village. She stayed aloof, above it all. But that only makes it worse. There was no one who hated her. No one who had a reason to kill her.

So why?

I wipe my tears. Enough.

My questions will not be answered now either.

I need to cleanse my body. I hope to find a stream that will ease my soul. Mother always believed in the purifying power of water, a belief she passed on to me.

With my spear in hand and my mind strengthened, I

venture through the trees, ready to face whatever comes my way. The night is dark and full of dangers, but I am not the same woman who was taken from her village. I am stronger now.

I have no choice but to be stronger.

6

THROUGH THE FOREST, INTO FATE

"The wild does not beg to be tamed. It calls, and only those strong enough to answer will find their fate within it."
— Vládan of Ávera, Warlord and Mate to Ánya

Theron

"**D**id you feel it too?"

Halfway through braiding his fur, Zephyr pauses, his gaze locked on me, eyes wide. Around us, the other warriors stand silent and ready, muscles tense, waiting for my command. *The barrier has fallen.*

But excitement cannot cloud judgment. "Listen all," I growl.

As much as my heart races at the thought of what lies beyond, I know we must be cautious. We know nothing of the lands outside the border we've patrolled, nothing of the dangers they might hold. Ávera must remain guarded.

We've prepared for this exact moment since we were cubs. I have trained each of my warriors well, and each one knows their role and responsibility. When I give the word, they will sprint to their designated positions at the edges of the forest.

These locations were chosen with purpose, every one providing a clear vantage point to scan the surroundings and protect our land. Each warrior must reach their post, assess the area, and return to Ávera to report before anyone is tempted to explore farther. Exploration will come later. First, we secure our home.

"You know what to do."

Without hesitation, they spring into action, their powerful bodies blurring as they vanish into the forest's shadows. This is what we've lived for, what we've sworn by the goddesses to protect. I, too, bolt into the night.

There's a flood of new scents. They're unfamiliar, impossible to sort through. My snout twitches, searching for something recognizable, something that makes sense, but it's too much and too fast. The air is thick with a thousand different aromas swirling together from the world beyond the barrier, a world we've been shut off from for so long.

I stumble to a halt, my breath catching in my throat. My body tenses, and the fur along my spine bristles as I try to ground myself. For the first time in my life, my senses feel out of control. I shake my head. I've trained for centuries to stay sharp, to never let anything slip past me, even when I'm overwhelmed.

But then, there, hidden beneath the flood of new scents, something catches my attention. A hint of sweetness rises above the rest like a single thread of silk in a web of thorns.

I close my eyes, focusing on that one scent, letting it guide me. It's floral, but not like any flower I've ever smelled. It's soft and alluring . . . luscious, like a blue rose.

Everything else fades away. The overwhelming blend of new scents, the chaos of the barrier lifting, the uncertainty of what lies beyond. All I can focus on is that precious note in the air.

My muscles flex, and before I realize it, I'm sprinting through the forest, my paws barely touching the ground as I chase that unseen thread. Branches snap beneath me, leaves rustle in my wake, and I keep pushing.

It's pulling me, guiding me like it's tied to my chest, tugging me deeper into the trees. The scent grows stronger with every breath. I need to find the source. *Now.*

Then it hits me—a scent so powerful, so intoxicating, it knocks the air from my lungs. My knees buckle, and my entire body shudders. Heat rushes to my groin. Every inhale fills with a sweetness so pure, it's like nothing I've ever known. My blood roars in my ears. I'm paralyzed for a heartbeat, my claws sinking into the earth as I try to steady myself.

It's her.

My mate.

My body is trying to push me forward, to follow, to claim what's mine. *Mine. Mine.*

I surge through the forest. The scent is all that matters. It fills my senses, making everything else disappear. *My human is here.*

My blood burns hotter, my cock hardens with a need so fierce it borders on painful. My body responds before my mind can even process it. I can't stop it, don't want to stop it.

I burst through the thicket, panting, my chest heaving like the beast I am. Then I see a small scrap of tattered white cloth caught on a bush and fluttering in the breeze. My paws shake as I lift the cloth to my snout, and the scent floods me.

It's her. This . . . this is what I've been waiting for.

I inhale deeply. My eyes roll back, and my body shakes with pleasure as her scent fills me completely. My cock hardens even more, pulses with every breath I take.

She's close. So close I can almost taste her. I will have her.

I have to feel her.

My paws tremble, claws dig into the earth with each stride, the dirt sinks under my weight. Every step is a war between control and instinct. The want turns every breath into a struggle to keep from losing myself entirely.

Goddesses, it's too much. My jaw clenches hard, fangs grinding together as I try to focus. I must control myself.

I lunge and sink my fangs into a thick branch. The bark splinters beneath my teeth. The taste of raw wood fills my mouth, earthy and bitter, *but it's not enough.* I tear at the branch again, biting into it with more force, feeling it give way under the pressure. The sound of it breaking echoes in the forest, a sharp crack like the bone of a prey animal snapping.

I have to calm down. I can't show myself to my mate like this.

Slamming my claws into the nearest tree, I rake the bark with a growl, pulling chunks of it away in strips. The rough wood tears under my claws, splinters fly, but the frenzy inside me keeps building. Nothing—nothing—can soothe the madness. I snarl, snapping at the air.

Nothing helps.

My paws shake with every step as I keep walking, and I know no matter how much I fight it, I won't be able to hold back much longer.

She's close. Too close. And I'm barely holding on.

And then I see her.

A human female rises from near the water, bathed in the early morning sun. The sight of her stops me dead in my tracks. My breath freezes in my throat. The world around me fades into nothing. She's not just beautiful, she's ethereal, like something the goddesses crafted in secret, hidden from the world until this moment. Her long, dark hair falls down her back, the silky strands reaching her waist.

She's . . . perfect. So small, yet there's a quiet strength about her, something that radiates from her very soul. I've never seen a human before, and I never expected anything like this. Not the way she makes my body roar with need, nor this burning hunger. My muscles tense, every part of me on edge. My claws dig into the tree beside me.

She lifts her face, slowly rising to her covered feet. Those are shoes. She looks around, and I take in her whole form. Small face. My paw could cover her whole head, front to back. Her eyes are swollen—why? What happened?

She moves back a step, and her clothing sways with the motion. Truly, there is no fur anywhere on her except for her dark brown hair and . . . eyebrows? Patches of hair above her eyes. We have them too. I don't know why that part surprised me, but Elder Aïna wasn't joking. Humans are so different.

My little mate looks around, *she's wary*. She moves slowly, trying not to make a noise. Smart female.

I grab my cock. It's leaking, and I hiss as I squeeze it. If I just take a few steps, she will see her mate. She will see my cock.

But she is so tiny . . . Goddesses, how can I claim this small female?

It's a fight to keep my body from lunging forward. My knees tremble from the effort. The tree groans under the pressure of my grip as I try to calm my need. I clench my jaw, but the sound of wood cracking fills the air before the tree crashes to the ground. Shit.

The little female takes a few more steps back.

With a shuddering breath, I try to calm myself, but I only inhale even more of her delicious scent. Wrong move.

I can't scare her, but I'm so close.

She takes something out of her pocket. A weapon.

Right.

She doesn't know me. She probably doesn't even know what I am. I grit my teeth.

She's human, so delicate, and I'm . . . I'm a beast compared to her. I have to approach her, but goddesses, I can't. Not like this. Not when every part of me is screaming to claim her, to take her. My cock is hard as stone and dripping on the ground.

"Shit," she whispers. Oh, that sweet voice.

We both said *shit*.

Slowly, I take a step forward, trying to keep my movements controlled, though every hair and every fiber begs to pounce. She moves her head to look to the side, exposing a new angle to me, and I nearly groan aloud from the pleasure of it.

I can't lose myself. Not now. I can hear her soft breathing, the way she exhales, how fast her heart beats. She points the weapon in my direction.

Please, little human. Don't run.

Because if you run, I'll chase.

7

A KNEEL, A GROWL, AND A CHOICE

"Some would call them monsters, but those who've truly
looked a vólkin in the eyes know, there is no creature more
bound to protect what he calls his."
—Eyleen Ársa

Noël

Did I just hear a tree fall?

I hold my spear with both hands. They shake, but it's the most I can manage for now. My heart stutters in my chest, and I instinctively hold my breath. Every part of me is screaming to run, to move, but my legs feel like they're anchored to the ground.

Could it be a bear? I've never seen one, not in real life, only in my mother's books. *But something doesn't feel right.* Mother said they're more afraid of humans than we are of them. If I don't bother them, they won't bother me. They live far from the villages, in the depths of the forests, and rarely venture out. *But a bear wouldn't make trees fall.* Arnold said there wasn't much farther to go, that we were almost there.

I'm close to vólkin territory.

I swallow the lump in my throat. The vólkins should be avoided at all costs. But I'm not in Ávera, I'm still in the forest, right? The forest that surrounds it. It can't possibly be a vólkin ... right?

Run, Noël. Run.

But I can't. My heart is pounding so loudly in my ears that I can't even think straight.

Another crack makes my head jerk to the side. Something heavy is moving through the trees, snapping branches like they're nothing. I force myself to scan the spaces between the trunks, but all I see is shadows. The forest feels darker. The sunlight that offered soft comfort now barely reaches through the dense canopy above.

I need to move. But my body isn't listening. The fear is paralyzing, and I curse myself for standing here like a helpless child. *Mother ... please. I need you.*

I hear a growl, it's unmistakable. Low, deep, and so close it vibrates through my bones. It's here. *Goddesses, please.*

If you hear a growl, it's already too late.

A massive figure emerges from the mist, and with every step it takes, the ground quakes under its weight.

This ... this is a vólkin.

Nothing could have prepared me for the sight.

The vólkin is massive, easily twice my height. A living wall of violence that dominates the space around it. The sunlight glints off the thick, grayish-blue fur that clings to its body, and as it steps closer, the fur ripples, revealing muscles so enormous they look unnatural. Its entire body is carved out of raw power, built not just for strength but for war. I can't even imagine a whole army of beasts like this one. Humans have zero chance.

I'm rooted in place, staring at it, feeling like a mouse caught in the shadow of a predator. I force myself to look away from the broad expanse of its chest, and my eyes move down its arms to catch on the—large, terrifying things that hover somewhere between paws and human hands. Claws glint in the light, long and vicious, capable of rending flesh like it's paper. The thought sends a cold shiver down my spine. I swallow, my throat tight, as I imagine those claws slicing through me.

But when I lift my gaze up to its face, I stop. Its features are fierce, chiseled like stone, yet the eyes . . . The eyes are what make me pause. They're a deep hazel, but there's something in them, something that doesn't match the rest of its terrifying appearance. A gentleness, a softness that almost feels . . . human. How?

I blink fast. There is no way I'm humanizing it.

Blue crystals embedded in its forehead in a V shape, they glow like stars. With such strong features, that's definitely a male. A he.

He's godlike, like he stepped out of some ancient legend meant to frighten and awe all at once. How . . . How is this possible? Is this what all vólkins look like? We were shown paintings of them in the army, but they looked nothing like the beast before me. He's not matted with blood, doesn't even look like a normal wolf.

I tear my eyes away from his face to take in the sheer mass of his torso. With every breath, his muscles ripple. Each one sharply defined and solid. I've seen men, soldiers, bare-chested after training, their bodies honed for battle. But this . . . is something entirely different. His body . . . No.

No. No. No.

Look down, Noël. Stop staring at his abs. There is no way I feel my most private parts heating. What is wrong with me?

I swallow hard, my eyes widening. I try to dart my gaze away, but it's too late. The sight of him, fully erect, is right before me. His cock is massive, thick and pulsing. It's pulsing! And a ruddy pink color with a pointed tip, like a wolf. Literally.

Blood rushes to my cheeks, my skin burning at the sight of it. Why does he breathe so heavily? His knees tremble.

I snap my gaze upward. No. I can't focus on that.

His nose twitches, moving ever so slightly left to right. What is he scenting? Is there another vólkin around? This is not good.

He lowers his gaze to my thighs, and his pupils expand. Shit. Could it be . . . ? Can he scent *me*?

I have to charge him. I have to end this madness. *Come on Noël, take a step forward, and—*

Is he . . . kneeling?

The massive creature lowers himself before me, a gesture so out of place I can only stare in disbelief. He bows his head, averting those piercing eyes and showing a vulnerability I would never have expected from such a monstrous being.

"I have been waiting eons for you, my mate."

Did Arnold's friend hit me so hard I'm imagining a vólkin kneeling and speaking? He is speaking to me . . . speaking! What is going on here?

And what is this mate nonsense? Is it his mating season?

No matter. He can say whatever his heart desires. I simply do not care.

When he rises, he looks even more massive straightened to his full height, but his gaze doesn't leave mine. "My name is Theron," he says, his voice low and rumbling but surprisingly gentle. "I speak because my kind are not the monsters of your nightmares. We have voices, thoughts, and emotions just as you do. We live, we feel, and we desire balance."

My expression says it all. He didn't even need to hear the question.

He takes a slow step, his massive paw-hand reaching out as if to reassure me. My gaze turns to his lowered paw, and I catch sight of his cock again, fully erect. Shit.

My cheeks burn, heat rushing down to my chest, and I force my eyes up quickly. I hope he didn't notice.

He follows my gaze, looking down at himself before his mouth curls into a grin, the amusement lighting up his face in a way that makes my cheeks burn even hotter.

Not quick enough. He noticed.

"Ah," he rumbles, his voice teasing. "I see I've . . . distracted you."

I swallow hard. He doesn't seem embarrassed, far from it. There's confidence in the way he stands, completely unashamed, as if this moment were as natural to him as breathing.

"I . . ." My voice cracks, and I have to tear my eyes away, focusing on anything else—anything but the intense heat rolling off him, the way his grin makes something inside me stir. What is going on with my body today?

Theron chuckles. "Don't worry, I won't bite. Not unless you ask."

Did he really just say that?

How did I find myself in such a horrific situation? Mother, look what's happening right after your death. Everything you taught me about being strong, about surviving, and now here I am . . . standing before this . . . this creature. This beast. And I'm letting him unnerve me like I'm some frightened girl?

My knees are weak, so much they almost give way under the emotions burning inside me—fear, confusion, shame—but I clench my fists around the spear and force myself to stand tall. No, I can't afford to show weakness. Not in front of him. Not in front of anyone.

"Do not," I spit out through gritted teeth, "come any closer!"

My legs may be shaking, my body betraying the fear pumping through my veins, but I won't back down.

His eyes soften, the teasing grin slipping away as he watches me stand my ground. "You've got fire, I can see that." He straightens, giving me space, his gaze never leaving mine. "I won't come closer."

Why isn't he attacking? Why am I not attacking? Why do I feel warmth in my heart?

"I don't care what you are or what you want, but don't you dare move!" My voice quivers, but I force the words out with as much strength as I can muster.

The vólkin's eyes move to the weapon in my hand, but instead of advancing, he lifts his paw to his chest. "I understand your fear"—his voice sends goose bumps prickling across my skin—"but I mean you no harm. If holding that weapon makes you feel safe, you are welcome to do so."

"How can you speak?" I need more than *I'm not a beast.* "And why would you call me your mate?"

"We have voices and minds, same as you do. The barrier has kept us separated for centuries, but that doesn't mean we are without understanding or speech. As for why I call you my mate . . ." He pauses, and his voice drops lower. "It's not something I chose, human. It's a bond, deeper than blood, woven by the goddesses themselves. I felt it the moment I caught your scent."

I narrow my gaze. Mother never said anything about mates. Only that vólkins are guardians of nature. She might have been tricked before. Although thinking that Mother would believe nonsense feels foolish.

"You may not believe me now," he continues, "but I would never harm you. The bond between us . . . it is sacred. It's more than words, more than what you've been told to fear. You are not just a human to me. You are my mate—the one I've been waiting for."

How could Mother be wrong? But how could the military be wrong? They've always prepared me to survive, to fight, to shield myself from the vólkin. Yet here I am, torn between everything I've been taught and what my mother believed.

As I stare into the eyes of this creature—this *Theron*—I see no malice, no aggression. His gaze, piercing as it is, holds something gentle. Nothing like the feral, bloodthirsty beasts I was warned about.

I want to believe my mother, to trust in the wisdom she imparted. But what if she was wrong? What if this creature is simply biding its time, waiting for the perfect moment to strike?

I trust my mother.

But not this vólkin.

8

A PROMISE IN THE PETALS

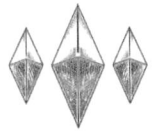

"The bond between a vólkin and his mate isn't only about claiming. It's about knowing, without question, that even your soul is no longer your own, it belongs to her."
— Ánya Volkóva of Ávera, Mate to Vládan

Theron

My mate is afraid of me.

I can barely contain my body. My knees still tremble, but only slightly now. I must breathe. If I tear apart more trees, she'll run away. But now she stares at me with wide eyes, and a soaked cunt. Our bond is real. Her soul responds to me. But she is still afraid.

The sight of her tiny body, shivering before me, only fuels the storm inside. Her fear, it excites me. She *sees* me. She sees my strength, my size, and there's no denying it—I'm the male who can protect her. When her gaze lingered on my shaft . . .

A surge of pride floods my chest, and I suppress the grin threatening to surface again. She saw it. Saw *me*. I can feel the pulse of desire in my blood making my cock throb. She knows now what I can offer her. She knows I am capable, not just as a protector but as a male. *She sees me as strong*, I hope as my muscles flex involuntarily. The thought makes my fur stand on end.

To be the first vólkin in centuries to meet his mate . . . It's a great honor. I am the luckiest being in the world to have found her, yet with this fortune comes heavy responsibility not to overwhelm her, to approach with the care she deserves.

I can hear her rapid breathing, the faint sound of her heart pounding in her chest. My senses are so attuned to her that it's almost painful. *Almost.*

I lower myself slightly, trying to appear less intimidating, even though I know it won't change much. Maybe the gesture will ease her. I'm not only taller than any human, I'm also one of the biggest vólkins.

"Why wouldn't you want to harm me?"

The very thought sends a pang of pain through me. I could never harm a female. Even if she wasn't my mate, I'd never dare. "Because you are my mate," I say, willing my voice to be as gentle as possible, even though my instincts want to roar the truth for the entire forest to hear.

Her eyes narrow, her posture straightens, and the confusion on her face is beyond charming. She's trying to understand, trying to process words that sound foreign to her. "Your mate?" she repeats. "I'm not interested in participating in your mating season."

I can't help the chuckle that escapes me. The sound of it surprises her, and truthfully, it surprises me too. But her response, her fire . . . Oh, I love it so much.

"It's not like that," I begin. *Goddesses, she's fierce.* "A mate isn't a companion for a season. A mate is . . . far more. A soul bonded to mine, chosen by the goddesses. It's a connection that can't be broken. You are mine, just as I am yours. Two halves, one fate."

Her brow furrows as she studies me, her weapon still held defensively between us. She's so small yet so brave, standing her ground. "What makes you think *I'm* your mate?" Her eyes search mine for answers she clearly doesn't want to accept.

My heart swells with pride. How sweet. "It's in your scent," I say, choosing my words carefully. I don't want to frighten her, but I need her to understand. "Your scent is unlike anything I've ever encountered. It's . . . intoxicating. It draws me to you in ways I can't explain, and my body, my soul, react. There's no mistaking it."

Will she get more defensive if I tell her that her body reacts as well? I don't want to lose the fragile thread we're spinning between us.

She raises an eyebrow. "So, what? It could happen with any other female. You just follow a scent?"

I shake my head, moving a fraction of a step closer. *Careful, Theron.* "No." I keep my voice as steady and firm as I can manage. "It only happens with the one chosen by the goddesses. The connection is unique, only with you. It's not just a scent. It's deeper than that, a pull . . . a bond."

The air between us feels charged, heavy with both tension and unspoken truths. I can see her struggling, torn between disbelief and the pull she must feel too. At least I hope so.

"Prove it. Show me you speak the truth," she demands. There's something in her eyes—curiosity, maybe even hope.

I nod. *Very well, my mate.*

I focus, drawing on the natural energy that hums beneath the earth, the connection that binds me to this forest and to her. The air around us shimmers, but soon, the ground at her feet stirs with small vibrations that ripple through the soil.

A delicate gasp escapes her as tiny shoots burst from the earth, unfurling into beautiful blue roses. The petals are a vibrant, rich blue, glowing in the misty air. They mirror her—this beautiful, fierce human standing before me—because they're tied to her essence, what I've sensed from the moment her scent reached my snout.

"These roses," I say, my eyes never leaving her face, "are not native to this land. They bloom here because of you. Your scent, the sweet scent of blue rose petals, led me to you. They're a reflection of your soul."

Her eyes widen, and she turns in place, taking in the growth around her. The way her dark hair flows as she moves, how it frames her pale skin that seems to glow in the dim forest light, captivates me. She's breathtaking, like the goddesses carved her from stardust.

I take a slow step closer, but not too close, I don't want to frighten her. Not now. Not when she's seeing the truth of our bond. "As you see," I continue, "these roses are not a random choice. They are connected to you, to your soul. Only a mate can sense and create something so personal. This bond, though new and unfamiliar to you, is ancient. It's deeper than either of us can understand, but it's real."

Her fingers brush the petals. Her touch is gentle, hesitant, as if she's testing whether this moment is real. The roses sway under her fingertips, responding to her presence.

"You . . ." she starts, breathless and full of wonder. "You made them appear because you sensed them in me?"

"Yes, little human," I confirm as gently as I can. "It's part of the bond between mates. We connect with what is most precious to each other. These roses . . ." I gesture to the blooming flowers surrounding her. "They are my heart reaching out to yours. They are proof that we are bound together." Soon, it will be my responsibility and my honor to create a blue rose crown for her. Very, very soon.

For centuries, I've trained and led my people, each day pushing forward, every step driven by purpose. But no amount of respect earned could ever fill the hollow ache inside me. We are taught from birth that each of us has a mate, a soul connected with our own. To find one's mate is to find the missing piece of your very being, to become whole in a way nothing else can ever achieve.

And now . . . she's here.

Right in front of me. Real. Flesh and blood. I can scent her, feel her presence with every breath I take.

But joy and fear, they're two sides of the same leaf, aren't they? The bond is a force of nature to me, absolute. Yet what if she doesn't feel it the same way? What if it's only *me* who is consumed by it, by this instinct, this pull that cuts me to my core?

She's human, and I'm vólkin. We come from two different worlds. How can I make her see that she's the missing piece of my being? And I'm the missing piece of hers?

I must help her understand.

The beauty of the moment turns bitter as her expression changes, curiosity fading into something darker. "How dare you," she snaps. Her chest rises and falls with each heavy breath, her hands gripping the fabric of her white sarafan. Her eyes blaze with fury. "You reach into my soul without permission and presume to call me your mate? Who do you think you are?"

Her words are sharper than any fang, but I don't move. I can feel the heat of her anger, the fire burning inside her, and I understand. Of course she's afraid. She's human. She didn't grow up with tales of bonds and mates woven into her every thought like I did. She knows nothing of the goddesses' ways, or the destiny I've been waiting for my entire life. To her, this must all feel like an invasion. Her world suddenly exposed to someone she's never met. Even if I am her *mate.*

She takes a step back, then another. The distance between us grows, and my heart clenches at the sight of her retreating. I should have been more cautious, more patient. Her reaction is a reminder of the boundaries I must respect. I was too eager, too consumed by the bond I feel with her.

Her eyes meet mine one last time before she turns on her heel and bolts. The sight of her disappearing into the forest, her long, dark hair flowing behind her like a shadow, leaves an ache in my chest. But I don't move to follow.

Not yet.

I let her run. Let her feel that she can escape. My cock throbs with every breath I take, as if her scent alone has chained me.

Because little does she know . . . I love the chase.

9

A VOW IN THE MIST

"Where love is torn by grief, and grief is sharpened by fear, hatred is born. And hatred, left to bloom, will always lead to war."
—Láda Veléša, Goddess of Leadership and War

Noël

I dart away, weaving between the trees as branches claw at my face and arms, drawing thin lines of pain across my skin. It's like the forest is resisting me.

The cold bites at my cheeks, my limbs burn, but none of it matters. I can't stop. I have to keep moving. If I stop, I'll fall apart, completely and utterly shatter into pieces that no one will ever bother to pick up.

The mist clings to the forest, smothering everything in its path. Damp leaves brush against my arms and droplets collect on my skin, but I hardly notice them. My thoughts are too tangled, my mind too heavy with everything that's happened, everything I've lost, and now this—this vólkin, this creature claiming me as his *mate* like I'm some object the goddesses handed over to him.

Anger roars through my veins, but it's not enough to overcome the fear curling inside me. How dare he? How dare he look into my soul without permission, dredging up the deepest wound left by Mother's death? The sight of those blue roses, her favorite flowers, was like a slap in the face. They were *hers!*

Mother . . . Why aren't you here? Why did you leave me to face this by myself?

I stumble over a root and barely catch myself as I run. My head is still spinning from the smack Arnold's friend gave me, and my vision swims for a second. I push it back, focusing on the pain in my legs, the stinging cuts on my arms, anything to keep myself grounded.

My lungs burn. My heart pounds so hard it drowns out the sound of my footsteps. But it doesn't drown out *his*. The snap of branches behind me grows louder. Closer. I know it's him. It has to be the vólkin.

A shiver crawls up my neck as I glance over my shoulder and catch a glimpse of dark movement through the fog. He's there, somewhere. There's no way I can outrun him. *Look at him! He's huge!*

He could break me in half if he wanted to.

I search the area, desperate for somewhere to hide, but there's nothing. No shelter, no crevice, no hollow tree. How foolish am I? How did I think I could outrun a vólkin? They've surely trained their entire lives for the hunt, and here I am, tripping over roots like a scared animal. He's been gentle so far, but that could change. His thighs quivered when he was pretending to be calm.

I stop beside an ancient tree. My chest heaves as I lean against it, but the bark digging into my back grounds me. Still, my breath comes in short, shallow bursts, and my body trembles from exhaustion and fear. The mist curls around me, choking in its embrace, and when I try to draw in air, every breath feels like pulling water into my lungs.

I can't run anymore. There's no point. He'll catch me. He'll *always* catch me.

My knees buckle, and I slide down the tree, resting against its trunk as the damp earth soaks my gown. Tears sting my eyes, but I refuse to let them fall. Not now. Not in front of him. I clench my fists, nails digging into my palms as my anger simmers. I don't want to be this weak. I don't want to feel this helpless. How did it all go so wrong?

Enough.

Something inside me snaps. The fear, the confusion, the overwhelming grief, I push it all aside, letting the anger flood through me. *Yes. Anger is good.*

How dare he call me his mate, acting as if he has any claim over me? I've been tossed around like a pawn in everyone else's game—my mother's death, Arnold's kidnapping, and now this vólkin, this *beast* who thinks he can dictate my fate. *No more.*

My entire body shakes with fury. If this monster thinks I'm going to cower and run, he's wrong. Dead wrong.

I hear him before I see him. His growls echoing through the mist, the heavy pounding of his paws against the earth like the drums of war. My heart still races, but it's no longer from fear. It's from the heat that pulses through my veins. The sound of snapping branches and the thunder of his approach send a surge of vigor through me. Bracing myself, I plant my feet firmly on the ground.

Come here, wolf.

I whirl around, jaw clenched, just in time to see him burst through the trees. His massive body crashes through the under-brush, but I don't flinch. I stand my ground, glaring at him with all the strength I have left.

As he rears onto his hind paws, rising to his full height, I meet his gaze. "BACK. OFF!"

Theron's hazel eyes lock onto mine.

The ground beneath my feet vibrates as he comes closer, closing the distance between us.

I take a step toward him, my right hand holding the spear tighter. "What do you want from me? You think you can just . . . take me? Is it that simple for you?" My voice cracks, but I press on. "You think you have a right to decide my future? To say I'm your mate? Who do you think you are?"

He needs to understand that I'm not some weak, fragile creature he can do whatever he wants with.

Without wasting time, I step forward again, and so does he, the ground shaking beneath his enormous paws. The heat of his body draws me to him. I feel my right leg aching to move closer still. It's like he stares into my soul, calling me, forcing me to listen. I'm angry, it pisses me off. Why, why can't I control myself?

Stupid, foolish, delusional vólkin!

With my left hand, I grab a fistful of his fur and pull, making him lower himself toward me. His massive body bends easily to my demand.

I shove the sharpened tip of the spear into his chest, press it into the thick fur over his pounding heart. "I've lost everything!" I shout. "Everything! And now you . . . you dare stand in front of me and act like this is what the goddesses want?" I can barely breathe. "I don't care about your bond, or your destiny, or whatever it is you're talking about. I won't be claimed by anyone!"

My hands shake, my grip tight on both the spear and his fur, but Theron doesn't move. He doesn't flinch. The spear digs into his chest, but it's as if he doesn't even notice it.

Gritting my teeth, I push the spear harder against him, desperate for some reaction, some proof that I can still do something, that I have some power in this situation. But still, nothing. His body doesn't even tense. He just watches me. My anger burns hotter, frustration swelling inside me like a dam about to burst. I want him to hurt like I hurt. I want him to be afraid of me like I'm afraid of the whole world. My hands might shake, but I don't let go of the fire burning inside me. I won't let him take that from me too.

"We both carry burdens that the world will never understand," he says, the rumble of his voice soothing me. I hate it.

What does he mean? He doesn't know me. He doesn't know what I've been through, how much I've lost. He can't.

"Do what you need to," he continues. "But I will never harm you. And I will not leave you to carry your pain alone."

With eyes wide open, I feel the fire in my chest flicker, then die. He doesn't care about the spear drawing blood from his flesh. He doesn't care that I'm shaking with rage. And worst of all, he's not afraid of me.

The spear slips from my fingers and falls uselessly to the ground between us. The anger I've held on to, the fury that's been burning inside me since my mother's death, since Arnold's attack, since this entire nightmare began—it crumbles. All of it crumbles.

Tears blur my vision. I try to hold them back, but it's too much. I can't keep it together anymore. A sob tears itself from my throat, and I collapse against him, tears falling down my face as my heart bursts open.

Theron doesn't move. He stays perfectly still, letting me cling to him and bury my face in his chest. With my fingers still twisted in his fur, I sob—loud, ugly, broken sobs that I can't control.

I don't know how long I've been crying. Time feels meaningless in this moment, swallowed by the grief, the anger, the exhaustion that weighs down every part of me.

He still doesn't move.

The warmth of his body seeps into mine, so unlike the cold dampness of the forest, and somehow, that makes me cry harder. It's too much, everything is too much. I've lost everything, and now I'm here, clinging to a beast I injured, soaking his fur with my tears as if that's somehow going to make any of this better.

I hate this. I hate how weak I feel. I hate how broken I am right now, standing here, vulnerable in front of him. I should be able to handle this, but I can't. I can't!

I'm so sorry, Mother. I'm not strong. I'm sorry I'm not the daughter you wanted me to be.

I push my face deeper into his chest, trying to hide the ugly sound of my sobs, trying to muffle the humiliating way I'm breaking apart. Only Mother ever saw my tears. It's not fair.

I feel so small next to him. His body towers over mine, his presence so . . . overwhelming.

It's infuriating. It's confusing. And it makes me want to scream.

"Why?" The word rips from my throat, barely audible through my sobs. "Why are you just standing there?" My voice cracks, and I hate it. I hate how desperate I sound.

My legs threaten to give out beneath me, but before I can collapse, I feel him move. His massive, clawed hands sliding beneath me as if I weigh nothing.

And then, before I can protest, he lifts me.

I freeze, my breath catching in my throat as he cradles me against his broad chest. My feet dangle above the ground, and suddenly, I'm staring directly into his glowing hazel eyes, close enough to make my heart race in ways that have nothing to do with fear.

I blink. Up close, he looks even more inhuman, and yet . . . not monstrous. The blue crystals on his forehead shine, casting reflections that dance across his fur. It's mesmerizing, and my mind can't make sense of any of it. Why did he pick me up?

All I can manage is to stare back at him, completely baffled.

"Put me down," I whisper, though the words lack conviction. My voice sounds pathetic even to my own ears.

He doesn't. He just holds me. His heart beats as fast as mine, but he stands still. Gaze calm. How can he be so composed while I'm falling apart in his arms?

"It's so hard not to chase when the sweetest thing runs," Theron whispers, his deep voice vibrating through his chest, so close to me now that I can feel every breath he takes.

I don't know him. I can't trust him.

"We are creatures of the chase, but it's not fear I want you to run from. It's the bond that pulls me to you, a force I've never felt in my life."

I swallow hard, narrowing my eyes. "What are you talking about?" My voice trembles, but I force the words out. "You don't know me."

Theron's eyes seem . . . sad.

Why does that sadden me? This is foolish.

"You're right," he says. "I don't know you, but I *want* to. I want to understand everything about you."

My hand tightens in his fur. "How can you talk about bonds and connections when I've lost everything? My mother is dead."

I know he had nothing to do with it. I know he couldn't know, but still.

Theron flinches at my words, his ears pulling back, but doesn't let go. His grip is firm but not painful. He holds me as if afraid I'll shatter in his arms. "I cannot take away your pain," he says, and the tenderness in his voice makes my heart ache, "but I can offer you a future where you are cherished and respected. I want to protect you, not because I think you need it, but because I want to."

I shake my head, biting back the sob that rises in my throat. "I don't need anyone. I don't need you."

The tears come despite my effort to stop them, and my

chest feels like it's about to cave in under it all. How much more can I take? How much more until I shatter?

Why am I fighting so much?

"We both carry burdens"—he says those painful words again—"burdens that the world will never understand. But I'm not asking you to trust me right now. Let me prove myself, one step at a time. Let me show you that I am a worthy male, worthy of being by your side."

Why does he smell of blue roses?

10

GUARDIAN OF HER GRIEF

"To touch a heart without force is the true measure of strength.
A male who cannot calm his storm will drown the very thing
he was meant to protect."
—Vládan of Ávera, Warlord and Mate to Ánya

Theron

Goddesses above, you blessed me, and I will forever be grateful for your decision.

I've spent centuries imagining this moment, but nothing could have prepared me for her. So fierce, so small, and so full of blue fire. It's overwhelming, this need to know her, to understand the storm inside her . . . But I have to wait.

Her body trembled against mine just moments ago, her anger and grief pouring out in a way I hadn't expected. And yet, beneath all of that, she had the strength to pull a weapon on me. Did she truly mean to hurt me, or was she just driven by emotion?

Either way, it didn't matter.

NICOLE A. STERLING

She could have stabbed me a hundred times, and I wouldn't have moved. A wound like that wouldn't kill a vólkin. Not even close. If anything, I would've let her do it. If it helped her find control in this chaos, I'd gladly bear the pain. A sharp edge is nothing compared to the torment I see behind her dark eyes.

I can still feel her touch, the way her small human hands gripped my fur, pulling me down to her. I'm glad she broke down, glad she let go of the burden she's been carrying. I won't ask questions now. I won't pry into her wounds. She needs time to breathe, to let her spirit calm before she can even begin to share her story. I'll wait for her, no matter how long it takes.

But even as I want to focus on giving her what she needs, my body betrays me. The way she leaned against me, her lush figure pressed into my chest, her tears soaking into my fur . . .

My shaft throbs, heavy and hard, and I curse my body for its timing. It's inappropriate to feel this now, when she's crying in my arms and tears stream down her face. She doesn't need me like that—at least not now. She needs comfort. And as much as the beast inside me craves the moment he can fill her, I won't let it happen like this.

That's why I pulled her into my arms, holding her higher so the tip of my cock wouldn't press into her belly.

I cradle her carefully and look at her. Small face with red cheeks and nose. How could anyone hurt her? How could anyone see someone so precious and try to take her freedom? Whoever has wronged her, whoever has put her in this state, goddesses, I swear, they will die.

But that's not what she needs right now. Revenge can wait. For now, she simply needs to know she's safe.

Her face is still tear streaked, her eyes shining and swollen, but she no longer looks at me with the same fiery defiance. Instead, she seems . . . tired. Her breathing is steadying, the harsh sobs beginning to quiet. She has me now. There's no need to be on guard like that anymore.

The silence between us is finally gentle, no longer tense. I can almost hear the way her mind is working, spinning, still trying to figure out what's going on.

"What is your name?" I ask, keeping my voice low.

She hesitates, as if weighing whether or not to answer me. Then, finally, in a hushed voice, she says, "Noël."

It's a beautiful name. Strong and soft all at once, just like the female resting in my arms. "Noël," I repeat. It fits her perfectly.

She doesn't pull away any farther. She even looks up at me, her dark brown eyes searching mine as if trying to understand what she sees in them. We're getting there. Slowly.

Noël. My Noël.

My eyes move over her face. Her hairline is refined, a delicate curve framing her forehead. Unlike me, she has no fur, just the thinnest layer of small hairs across her skin. How do humans stay warm without a pelt? How does her body survive the cold? I understand now why she needs clothes, even though her sarafan is dirty and torn from her journey. And stained with blood from my chest.

I force myself not to grin in satisfaction. *Not the time, Theron.*

Her eyelashes are wet, clumped together with the tears that have yet to dry. Her pupils are wide, a bottomless black framed by the most mesmerizing dark brown irises. I study her lips, swollen and tender from crying. The exquisite pink of her mouth draws my attention. It looks so delicious.

Humans kiss with their lips, I know that much. It's considered an intimate act, something shared between lovers. My mouth, though . . . it's different from a human's. Would kissing her be awkward, strange? I can't imagine pressing my lips to hers in the same way humans do. It would be too clumsy. But I would kiss her in my own way, taste her, worship every part of her skin. Still, I wonder if she'll be disappointed that I can't kiss her like a human male would. Has she kissed anyone before? The thought sends a growl rumbling through my chest.

If any male dared to touch her, I'd r ip his jaw off.

Now that she's calm in my arms, her breathing even and her eyes fixed on me, I can finally let my attention shift to something I've been aware of for some time but had to set aside—the faint, delicious scent of her blood. It's been teasing my senses ever since I found her, stirring my cock even as I tried to calm it. Vólkins are drawn to the scent of blood in a way that's difficult to describe. It calls to our instincts, but I was never hard because of it.

"You're hurt," I say, more of a statement than a question. Carefully, I lift her hand, examining the small cuts and bruises littering her skin.

"It's nothing." She attempts to pull her hand away, but I hold firm.

"Let me help," I insist. "Our saliva has antiseptic properties. It will help heal your wounds."

Noël watches me, her eyes fixated on my mouth as if she's both curious and uncertain about what I'll do next. Her cheeks turn the subtlest shade of pink. I've seen that color before . . . when she first caught sight of my cock. So that is *definitely* blushing.

"Really?" she asks, her voice betraying that tiny spark of wonder.

I nod, holding her gaze. "It does. We vólkins heal quickly, and we can help others heal too."

Her eyes study me, and I can see the intrigue in them. This is good. She isn't planning my death, for now.

"We have many abilities," I continue, "beyond what you might expect. Our senses are heightened—we can see in the dark, hear even the faintest of sounds, and track scents over great distances. We can also speed up healing through a form of energy transfer."

Her brow furrows as she processes what I've said. "Energy transfer?"

"By focusing our energy, we can help others heal more quickly. It's a skill that takes time to master."

She glances down at her hand where it still rests in mine before looking back up at me. "What else can you do?"

"Many things," I say, "but let's start with healing you first."

I bring her hand to my mouth, eyes locked on hers, letting her know exactly what I'm about to do. I trace my tongue over her cuts, slowly, and her fingers twitch. Her skin is silken, warm, so real on my tongue. The slightest taste of blood hits me, awakening the beast deep inside, but I push him down. This isn't about hunger. It's about her. About the way her body responds to me, the way I can feel her pulse under my touch. Each stroke of my tongue feels like claiming a piece of her, and I can't help myself. The connection pulls tighter with every breath. That hint of sweetness from her cunt is teasing me again. *Yield, Theron.*

Noël's curious eyes follow my tongue, and they widen as the cuts heal before her.

After I've tended her hand, I trace my tongue over the tears that still cling to her cheeks, tasting the salt and sorrow they carry. She looks at me, startled. Will she pull away?

"Can you heal my soul too?"

"I wish I could, Noël."

She shifts in my arms. Her plush lips part as she searches for the right words. "I wanted to wash myself in that stream," she finally says, her voice quieter than before.

I nod. "Then we'll go back."

Keeping her secure in my arms, I turn around. It feels so natural to carry her like this, her small body fitting against me as if she belongs here. Because she does. I could get used to this, holding her, keeping her close. Even though I know she'll protest eventually.

Right on cue, she shifts again, crossing her arms. "I can walk,"

A grin tugs at my lips. "I know."

She rolls her eyes, and I chuckle, but I don't stop walking.

As we move through the forest, I can feel every creature around us—bears lumbering farther into the brush, boars moving quietly, and smaller animals darting away. None of them dare come close. They know better than to cross paths with their Lidéřen. I wonder if Noël has noticed, if she's aware of the power radiating from her, even in this state.

I glance down at her. "Have you seen any animals since you've been here?"

A hint of pride creeps into her voice as she says, "No. I was careful not to attract any predators."

I suppress the urge to smile. She's pleased with herself, and I'll let her have this. She doesn't need to know that no predator would have dared approach the leader from the prophecy, so I hold my tongue and keep walking.

But then she hesitates, a slight smirk crossing her lips. "Except for one."

I raise an eyebrow. "Me?"

She nods, her gaze dropping to my chest. "I hurt you, and you didn't even feel it."

"I did," I say. "I'd keep the mark as a gift, if I could, but I can't help that my body heals itself." My jokes aren't nearly as good as Kaël's, but—

"Watch yourself, vólkin," Noël warns, grabbing my mane. She narrows her eyes, leaning close to my snout. "If you think I'd fall to my knees and thank you for healing a few cuts, you're delusional."

"There's no need to thank me, *human*," I say, the glow of my crystals shining in her eyes. "This is my duty as your mate."

"Again with this nonsense." With those words, she pushes

me away, drops to the ground, and walks toward the stream. She doesn't even pause to say, "Go home."

"I am home," I reply, following behind her. She doesn't realize *she* is my home.

We walk in silence, and it's clear I've crossed the line again. My mate doesn't like being called a mate, that much I understand. But she is . . . Is it because of me? Am I unpleasant to her? She knows I won't harm her. She's no longer afraid when I'm near. So then, what is it?

"Your home is Ávera. Go there."

"Come with me."

She turns to face me, wrinkling her nose. "I don't need whatever fantasy you've got in your head. I'm not your mate, and you're not mine. I have too much on my mind, and I must—"

"How did your mother die?" I ask. The grief feels fresh. Maybe that's why she keeps denying me.

Her shoulders sag, and she looks away. "I don't know."

"Was she ill?"

"No."

Such anger doesn't come from the grief of losing someone after a long life. Perhaps my mate is mourning a mother who was taken from her by force.

I should help my mate heal. She needs me as a supportive male before she needs my cock. "Did your mother like any herbs?" I ask as I follow her.

She falls silent again.

I know little of human customs now, but history rarely changes. Even centuries ago, humans spilled each other's blood for the sake of pride. For worshipping different gods. For daring to speak. For being born on the wrong side of a wall. They called it justice, or righteousness, but it was always blood.

Vólkins fight for dominance, but that's how nature works.

Wolves, lions—we are no different. But even wolves do not take a mother from her child. They never place pride above life.

We reach the waters, and I watch Noël approach the blue roses I grew for her. She kneels beside them, her fingers brushing against the petals. "These beautiful roses were my mother's favorite," she murmurs. "And now they're mine as well."

And mine.

"This flower is the rarest," I say, watching her expression as I speak. "They never bloom without purpose."

Her eyes lift to meet mine. "How do you know that about them?"

"These roses are very ancient," I explain, crouching beside her. "They belong to only one bloodline in the human race, and we are taught about them from the time we are pups. Their history is rich and sacred."

Noël's lips part, her disbelief written across her face.

"In our culture," I continue, "we bid farewell to the dead in a way that honors their spirit and their connection to the world. Let me show you."

I move to gather materials, picking up pieces of wood and leaves. "We create a circle, a small arrangement of things connected to the soul we honor. Flowers, herbs, and other elements that had meaning to them. It symbolizes the continuation of life, the cycle that never truly ends. It's called svytyn prócha."

Noël watches me, then takes the branches in her hands. "I want to do it myself."

"I'd like to honor your mother too."

"Why do you care? You didn't even know her. And don't start with any 'she's my mate's mother' business."

That is part of it, but also, "No mother would want to leave this world before her child."

My mate lowers her gaze and lets me arrange the svytyn

prócha. I weave thin branches together to create the foundation for the boat. Then, I gather moss and leaves, arranging them in a circle, leaving space in the middle. Noël watches my every move, then gathers more leaves to fill the empty spots. I notice that she avoids touching me, moving her wrists at unusual angles so she won't brush against mine.

The svytyn prócha is usually the size of a large leaf, so we don't take much from nature to honor the departing souls.

I watch my mate as she leans toward the roses.

There's a tenderness in the way she handles the roses, carefully placing them at the center of the small farewell boat we're crafting.

"When we say farewell to the dead," I add, "we light a flame to guide them. In Ávera, we often use wax with leaves, but here we'll improvise."

"Like a candle?"

"Humans call it that?" I smile as she nods. Her curiosity is adorable.

Together, we finish the small boat, weaving branches and leaves together, and placing the blue roses in a wreath around the edges. It's simple, but beautiful, and as I kneel by the stream, I focus inward.

I form two small orbs of energy in my hands, rubbing them together until a small flame ignites in my palms. My Noël watches carefully as I guide the fire down to the tiny boat, and it catches quickly.

Noël leans forward, takes another rose in her hands, and lifts it to her lips. I lower my head, and I hear her move to place the rose on the boat. From the corner of my eye, I see her hands tremble as she releases the svytyn prócha into the water. The boat drifts, carried by the current, the blue roses glowing against the dark surface.

"How beautiful," I whisper, looking at her.

Tears glisten in her eyes, but there's peace there too, a calm that wasn't there before.

"It is," she says. "Thank you, Theron."

"It is my hono—"

She jerks her head toward me before I finish the sentence, drawing her brows in. "I did this for *her*."

11

BETWEEN THE STREAM
AND THE SPEAR

"There are men who will touch your hand and claim your life.
You were never meant to belong to an earthly soul."
—Eyleen Ársa, to her daughter

Noël

Maybe it's not a bad idea to have a vólkin guard me while I bathe. It doesn't mean I won't stab him again if he dares to look, but for now, it's a good solution.

I place my spear and the handkerchief on the ground, my fingers brushing over the worn fabric as if it holds the last pieces of my sanity along with the crystal wrapped up in it. The stream's gentle waves lap against the shore, a soothing sound that should calm my racing thoughts, but it doesn't. So many emotions come and go, one after the other, as I crouch to unlace my boots.

Theron, a creature so big and fierce, calmly held me while I cried uncontrollably in his arms. He tended to my wounds with a care I hadn't expected from anyone, let alone him. I can still feel his touch. His tongue tracing over the cuts on my hands, his eyes locked on mine the entire time. His gaze was so intense I could barely breathe.

I kick my boots off and mutter to myself, "This is madness."

A part of me wanted to pull away, but I didn't. Instead, I stayed there, letting him heal me. I don't know what came over me. Maybe it's because I've never had a man tend to me like that before. Maybe that's why my chest felt tight, why I couldn't look away from him.

He didn't retreat when I stabbed him. He didn't run away when I fell apart. He stayed. He stayed and held me as if I were something precious. That confuses me so much.

I've spent my whole life believing that vólkins are monsters, creatures to be feared, and yet, here is this beast, cradling me like I'm fragile. His demeanor doesn't match what I've been taught to fear, and it's throwing me off balance.

I shake my head. *Foolish woman, what are you thinking?*

He grew blue roses for me. With nothing but his will, he made them bloom right before my eyes. They glowed like the roses in my mother's garden. He made fire from nothing, just by concentrating his energy. It doesn't make sense. How can any of this be real?

I glance over at him, watching as he stands confidently with his back to me. Why wouldn't he go? I said I'm not his mate. I don't understand.

His presence is too much—too large, too powerful—and yet, he's shown me nothing but kindness.

I bite my lip. Mother, maybe you were right. Maybe the world outside Tárnov is not what I thought. *Maybe I'm not who I thought I was.*

I sigh deeply, my heart heavy with everything I've lost and everything I don't understand. It's confusing. Everything is confusing.

As I'm about to slip out of my dirty gown, tinkling, ethereal laughter echoes through the trees. Tiny dots of light fly around me, and I pause, my initial intention to bathe forgotten momentarily as I observe these glowing, leaflike figures.

Leaves with faces? How is that possible?

"What are you?" I whisper, reaching out to touch one.

The tiny leaf creature hugs my finger and nuzzles against it.

"They're leaf spirits," Theron says, walking closer. "Guardians of the forest's growth, very playful and quite curious about visitors, especially those they have been waiting for for ages."

The spirits' touch tickles, their feet brushing against my skin like tiny balls of cotton. It feels surreal, as though I've stepped into a dream come to life. One of them lands on my shoulder and looks up at me with big button eyes. They're black, contrasting against their light green bodies. Some of them even have little rounded bellies. What do they eat?

"Can they hear us?" I ask.

"They feel more than they hear," he responds. "They're mischievous but gentle. I think they came to welcome you."

I step toward the stream, and the spirits grow more excited, their movements quickening as they rush around me in different directions. I turn to Theron, who watches with an amused grin.

"How am I supposed to bathe with all this attention?" I ask with a big smile on my face. They're just so adorable!

His grin widens, and he leans in, his voice low like he's sharing a secret. "Just tell them you need a moment of privacy. They will listen to you."

"They will?"

Theron nods.

Skeptical yet very intrigued, I turn to the leaf spirits. "I appreciate your welcome, but I need some privacy to bathe. Please, could you give me a little space?"

To my surprise, the spirits pause, their tiny faces tilting as if they're considering my request. Then, they back away, flying over to the nearest rock. From there, they continue to watch, but from a more polite distance.

I glance back at the smiling Theron, raising an eyebrow. "You too."

He dips his chin and steps back to his previous position. "Call if you need anything."

Did his tail just wag?

I take off my dirty gown and put it near my boots. The leaf spirits fly over to inspect it, and I smile. They're so cute. I'm left in only the bandage over my breasts and my linen undergarments. My heart pounds as I slowly remove the bandage, my gaze never leaving Theron's back—just in case. He really won't look, right?

I place my soldier identification card, which I always keep with me, even when I'm not in uniform, on the handkerchief. And every few seconds, I glance at my spear, and the tip covered in his blood. It's dark red, like mine. He sure felt at least a sting. A grin stretches my face.

A cool breeze travels along my skin, and I'm grateful that all of this is happening after winter so at least the water isn't freezing. Theron wanted to heat it, whatever that means, but I said I was fine. Mother made me practice enduring cold water since I was a child, so it doesn't bother me at all.

The water brushing against my skin and washing away the dirt and grime is refreshing, so I take my time. Letting the water cleanse not only my body but also my spirit.

Mother . . . You always believed water cleanses the soul. But what happened to you?

The uncertainty is torturing me. I need answers.

So far, this vólkin has not shown me anything to suggest he wants to go our separate ways. From what he's said, he believes I'm his mate and we're fated to be together forever. Obviously I can't stay with him. I have my whole life in Tárnov. My mother's home, our secret garden, my military career . . . I wonder how my soldiers are doing.

I dip my face into the water and then rise, my heavy, wet hair clinging to my back. I gather some fallen leaves from the bank near me and look for the ones that have the strongest veins, or leaf skeleton, Mother never told me what it's called. Picking a few, I begin scrubbing my arm.

I remember the one moment that defined my time as my soldiers' commander. It was early, the sun's first rays peeking over the high stone walls of our base and the morning mist lingering on the training grounds. As usual, I greeted my soldiers with a firm, "Good morning," but Joren, a recruit with a mouth bigger than his balls or his brain, couldn't resist the chance to take his shot.

"Sergeant Ársa, I'm having some trouble with my morning wood. Would you have a look? That would definitely make it a good morning." His grin was wide enough to split his face, like he'd forgotten who he was talking to. The group burst into loud laughter, exchanging glances that only fueled each other's egos.

Joren's idiotic grin didn't waver as I marched right up to him, but when I grabbed him by the collar and yanked him so close our noses almost touched, the shock in his eyes was beautiful.

I hissed, "I'll cut it off if that's what it takes to shut you up."

The laughter died instantly, replaced by a tense silence. I didn't let go of him right away. Instead, I held him there, eyes on his, making sure the lesson sank in. My grip tightened, and I could feel his heart beating fast.

When I finally let go, he stumbled back, eyes wide. From that moment on, none of them dared to talk back to me again. I had made my point. I was their commander, and they would follow my lead, no matter how hard it was for them to follow a woman.

In the end, it wasn't only about earning their respect, it was about showing them that I belonged just as much as any of them. I made sure they understood that, while I might be different, I was someone they could rely on. And eventually, they did. We became a unit, a team, and the memory of that morning became a story they shared with new recruits, a reminder of the line they'd never dare to cross again.

With a smile, I wash myself as the leaf spirits jump on a rock near me.

I pause with my hands resting on my inner thighs, feeling the cold water travel over my shoulders. My skin is flushed, and a strange heat creeps up my neck. I've never really taken the time to look at myself like this, never had a reason to. My life in Tárnov was one of duty and discipline. I never let men court me, never felt the need to entertain their advances.

Mother always said there were more important things than men.

She wasn't harsh about it, no, she was always matter-of-fact, as if her words were a simple truth I'd eventually come to accept. And I did, until now.

"You don't need the distractions of men, Noël," she would say whenever the topic of courtship came up. "Your life is meant for more than that."

At the time, it made sense. My life was different from the other girls in the village. While they spent their days fussing over gowns and braiding their hair to attract a wealthier man, I was training, learning to lead, pushing myself to be stronger. To some degree, it felt right to stay focused rather than waste time on love like everyone else. "Romance will only weaken you," she'd say. "You have no need for it."

I believed her. But now, looking back, I wonder if there was more to it. Why was she always so intent on keeping me isolated? Why did she tear up every letter or gift I received from men in the village? Why did she burn them without ever showing me, as if she wanted to erase any sign of them from my life?

I walked into the kitchen once to find her crouched by the fireplace, tossing another letter into the flames. When I asked her about it, she brushed it off with a smile. "It was nothing, Noël," she said. "Nothing you need to worry about."

But why did she do that? Why was she so intent on keeping me from any sort of connection? I never understood, and I still don't.

And now, here I am, standing in the forest, washing away the dirt of a life I don't recognize anymore. I need to stop thinking about it, at least for now.

I scrub my abs and grab a few more leaves because the ones I had have gone soggy. As I take a step out of the water, I feel a wetness between my thighs that I can't blame on the stream. *What is wrong with you, Noël? Just stop!*

Grunting, I scoop some water into my palm and wash between my folds. I'm so sensitive, and I don't understand what's happening to me.

That stupid vólkin! There's no such thing as a mate bond, and I don't care that he grew blue roses out of nowhere. It means nothing! Tomorrow, he'll grow peonies and confess to another woman.

I turn around to look at him. Still standing tall, with all those muscles.

It scares me. I've never let anyone get this close before, never let anyone tend to me, never let anyone make me feel . . . like this.

I bite my lip. It's only because I've never experienced this before. That's why I'm so affected. That's all it is.

Isn't it?

But his cock . . . He's saying I'm his mate. Does he plan to . . .

Oh goddesses above, what am I thinking?

My cheeks flamed when I saw Theron's massive shaft. It's so ...
big. The thought of it makes my cheeks burn again. There's a
strange tightening sensation in my chest as I run my hands over my
skin, tracing the muscles of my body, and for the first time, I feel
aware—aware of the way my body reacts, the way my heart races.

I huff out an exhale.

It's just curiosity, stupid girl. Just because I've never had
anyone look at me the way he does, never felt a man's presence
so acutely, it doesn't mean anything.

My heart pounds in my chest, and I shake my head. This
isn't me. I've never wanted this before. I've never even thought
about it.

But now, I can't stop thinking about it.

I need to go back to Tárnov.

12

THE SOUL'S FIRST LAW

"A vólkin without his mate is strong. But a vólkin who chooses his mate above all else is unstoppable. The mate is the soul's first law."
—Elder Aïna, Lesson of the Sacred Bond

Theron

While my mate bathes, I stand guard, every muscle in my body tense. The forest is alive with its usual sounds—the rustling of leaves, the whisper of wind—but my attention is tuned to the splashes of water behind me. Each one sharpens my awareness of her. I listen to every movement she makes, how the water slips over her skin, the way her fingers caress her body as she washes. My cock leaks. Just at the thought of her behind me, so close and yet entirely out of reach. *Calm yourself, Theron.*

She deserves this moment of peace after the chaos she's endured. I want to offer her a life where she's never forced to suffer again. My every instinct demands I provide for her, care for her in ways she doesn't yet understand, but I know I must give her time.

Clenching my fists, I try to focus on the task at paw. *Stay alert.*

I scan the forest for any threat, but the only sound I hear is my mate's soft murmur to the leaf spirits near her, guarding her as I am. There's something about hearing her speak to them. She's interacting with my world. It's finally become hers too.

Human females, according to what we've learned from Elder Aïna, require frequent nourishment compared to vólkins. That knowledge was once nothing but a piece of information, something to remember from lessons. Now, it feels vital. She'll need food soon. She's *my* responsibility, and I must feed her. But I can't leave her to go hunting. Not when she might bolt at any moment.

Even though she's starting to let her guard down, I know fear and distrust are present in her heart. I must ensure she stays by my side long enough to realize she's already home.

In human-lore lessons, Elder Aïna taught us everything she knew about them, about their bodies, their needs, their way of life. I was always fascinated by how much she knew. She spoke of humans with deep respect, as if they were vulnerable yet strong at the same time. I'd never seen a human before, but her descriptions painted vivid pictures in my mind. Their bodies, so different from ours, require care in ways I hadn't imagined before.

How will my mate adapt to our ways? Will she accept the life I can offer her, or will she always long for the world she left behind? She had a life before she met me, in a place I know nothing about, and I wonder if she'll ever truly feel at home here.

What foods does she prefer? What does she enjoy in her quiet moments? Does she like mornings, or is she more content in the embrace of night? What simple joys bring her happiness? And what does she look like beneath her—

My ears twitch, catching a distant noise. A voice. A human voice. Two of them.

Humans. Here, in the forest. It shouldn't be possible, wasn't before the barrier fell. I strain my hearing, tracking the direction of the voices. They're distant but still too close. Who would dare wander this far into the woods?

A threat. It has to be. This part of the forest, the lands surrounding Ávera, was untouched by humans until last night, when everything changed. It can't be a coincidence.

A low growl rumbles in my throat. Her safety is my priority. No one can touch her. No one can disrupt this fragile peace we're beginning to build.

I inhale deeply. If they are here searching for Noël, they will not find her. Not unless I allow it. My paw tightens into a fist, claws flexing against my palm as I prepare myself for whatever may come. But I can't leave her alone. I can't abandon her, not even to investigate the source of the sound.

"Is something the matter?" Noël's voice pulls me from my thoughts, and when I turn to face her, she's standing with her hands resting on her hips. Dampness makes the fabric of her dress cling to her curves, outlining her body in a way that tests every drop of my self-control.

Goddesses help me. She's torturing me without even realizing it.

"Nothing to worry about," I manage, keeping my voice steady. I force my gaze to stay on hers, even though my instincts are screaming at me to do anything but. I don't want to make her uncomfortable.

She tilts her head, her dark eyes searching mine, but she doesn't seem satisfied with my response.

"You must be hungry," I say. "Let's find some food."

As we walk through the forest, the underbrush parts for her. The trees are watching my mate. Branches sway above us, leaves rustling in response to our passage. Every now and then a twig snaps, and I find myself tensing, hyperaware of everything around us—both the unseen humans I can still hear and the rhythm of her steps beside me.

She moves with intention and focus, her eyes scanning the environment. Her movements are graceful, her steps almost soundless, and I can tell that even though she's new to these woods, she knows how to survive. She might be small—so small that the brush barely touches the hem of her gown—but she's not weak.

"Noël," I say, unable to curb my curiosity any longer, "do you know how to identify which plants are safe to eat?"

"Actually, yes." She stops and turns toward me, a spark of excitement lighting her eyes. "My military training covered basic survival skills, including foraging." She points toward a bush nearby, its branches heavy with bright berries. "See those? They're safe to eat. The uniform color, bright sheen, and how plump they are are good indicators. Also, I recognize them from our training simulations."

I nod, my chest swelling with pride. My mate is smart. "You continue to surprise me,"

She turns away and keeps walking.

"What's a military?" I ask, the word foreign on my tongue.

Noël blinks, clearly not expecting the question. She turns to face me fully. "It's . . . an organized group of people trained to defend their land, their people. We follow orders from commanders, go on missions, and protect our villages from threats."

A part of me relates to the structure she describes. It sounds so similar to the way vólkins train and protect our own. "So humans have their own warriors," I muse aloud. "Like us."

"Yes, I suppose so. We train to fight and survive, to protect what matters. It's probably not so different from your kind."

Interesting. The concept of a human defense system fascinates me. I've always known humans have their own methods of survival, since they don't have sharp claws or thick pelts, but hearing it firstpaw from my mate makes it feel more real.

"So, you were a warrior," I say. Both of us, then. A deadly pair.

"I had to be," she answers, crouching beside the berry bush. "It was expected of me. But that doesn't mean I wasn't questioned or doubted at every step. Especially since I'm a woman."

"What does that mean?" Was her life more difficult because she's a female? In Ávera, females are precious.

"In my world," my mate begins as she picks a berry, "women—females—are looked down on. We can't even leave our villages . . . A woman born in Tárnov, dies in Tárnov. We all know that."

Her words make me realize how different human societies must be. The more I learn about her, the more I want to understand the world she comes from.

But when a world forgets the worth of its females, it writes its own end. And I won't let that happen.

As Noël munches on the berries we've gathered, we approach an apple tree, its branches laden with ripe fruit. I've always preferred the taste of meat, but Elder Aïna said humans love sweet tastes and that fruits are healthy for them. I wonder if Noël enjoys all fruits or if some aren't to her liking.

Leaf spirits move around us, their tiny lights dancing playfully in the leaves.

Noël's gaze locks onto an apple hanging just out of her reach. How did she choose that exact one? They all look the same, but she's been looking at them as if they're not.

Her eyes shine with want as she prepares to jump for it, her body tensing. But before she can make the leap, she pauses, noticing the leaf spirits fluttering toward the branch. A few grip the stem, while others gather around the fruit, trying to pluck it free for her.

I lower the branch so my mate can have the apple she wants. There's a snake wrapped around that branch, so I snap it away. My mate wanted that specific apple. The spirits pluck it for her, and she takes her first bite.

A low growl escapes my throat before I can stop myself.

Noël's body stiffens in response, her head snapping up to look at me, concern lacing her expression.

The voices are near.

"What is it?" she asks. "You were tense by the stream too."

I step back, my ears straining to catch more of the conversation. "There are two men not far from here," I murmur. "They've been moving in our direction for some time now."

Noël's eyes widen. But fear isn't what flashes across her face —it's anger. She knows something I don't.

"Two men?" she echoes through gritted teeth. "It's Arnold . . . it has to be him, and his friend."

At the mention of this male—Arnold—something cold and dark unfurls inside me. "Who is *Arnold*?" I ask, my voice low.

"Arnold is the man who kidnapped me," she spits out, her free hand curling into a fist. "He tied me up, gagged me, and threw me into a carriage, planning to take me far away from Tárnov, my village. He wanted to . . . to take me to my death."

She pauses, cracking her knuckles. "He's always been like this. Always trying to break me. But this . . . This time he went too far. He knocked me unconscious, and I woke up bound, completely powerless. I had to escape before he could finish what he started."

My claws dig deep into my palms as I try to keep control of the boiling rage inside me. The idea that someone, some *male*, dared to harm her—*my mate*—sends red-hot fury through me.

"He did *what*?" I growl, the words barely escaping through clenched teeth.

I will personally erase them from existence.

Noël nods, her expression hardened by the anger she clearly still holds. "He's a coward. Always was. But this time, I swear . . ."

"He is dead," I roar.

13

THE HAUNTING SILENCE

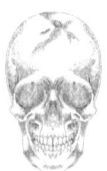

"They burn the earth for power, silence their women for pride, and call it order. But even the soil chokes on their footsteps."
—Ánya Volkóva of Ávera, Mate to Vládan

Arnold

How the fucking son of a whore did that wench manage to escape the carriage? It was empty, and she had nothing on her. I kick at the dirt. It was supposed to be a simple thing. Grab the bitch, throw her at the vólkins' territory, and be done with it. But no, she had to be a cunning little slut.

I searched every part of her, every curve. Her gown, her undergarments, even the strands of her hair, nothing was left unchecked. She had nothing on her, nothing but the fabric that clung to her body and a stupid handkerchief in her pocket.

"Arnold, calm down," Gregor says, walking beside me as we follow alongside a stream, so we can make our way back to the carriage when I finally have my hands on this wench. "We'll find her. She couldn't have gone far."

I glare at him, my temper barely in check. *Snap.* I freeze. My heart pounds in my chest. Just a twig, probably, but the echo through the forest feels too loud.

"Calm down? That bitch made a fool out of me! Do you have any idea what will happen if the knyaz finds out we took her past the village walls?"

Gregor shrugs. His ugly face grates on my nerves. "We still have time. Let's focus on tracking her down."

I take a deep breath. I need to rein in my anger, and we have to hurry. Women aren't allowed to leave the village. If she's found, I'll claim she ran away after a night with me, and the shame alone will be enough to condemn her. In Tárnov, a woman defiled before marriage is as good as dead. No one would question it. And Noël can't accuse me if she's dead.

But still, what if she escapes? What if she speaks to someone before I can finish her off? *Snap.* Another twig, a rustle in the bushes. I jerk my head toward the sound, breath stuttering. But there's nothing. Only shadows.

"Let's move," I mutter, trying to shake off the creeping sensation crawling up my spine.

My childhood in the rougher parts of Tárnov was hard. Growing up, I had to fight for everything—respect, power, survival. The military was supposed to be my escape, my chance to rise above the filth of common life. And I did. I'm a commander now, feared and respected, and a man who doesn't take kindly to being outsmarted by anyone.

I will never understand why they let Noël join. After that day, everything changed. Now a woman in the army, and then what? Talking back? Choosing her own path in life? Who to marry? It's madness enough that we have to send gifts to those whores before using them for the only thing they're worth. Ridiculous.

She couldn't have gone far. Despite her skills, she's still just a woman, a thought that both angers and reassures me.

Gregor follows, and we move through the trees. Noël has always been a thorn in my side. Defiant, strong willed, and way too competent for her own good. I underestimated her, and now she's out here, somewhere, making me look like a fool. Unless I make sure she's dead. There is no way I'm letting her go so easily. How did I get here? How did I let myself get dragged into this?

It all started with a letter.

It arrived like a whisper, a folded piece of paper in an envelope slipped into my quarters, unsigned and unmarked. I might have ignored it, dismissed it as a joke, but the words . . . They hooked me like barbed wire.

Noël doesn't belong in the military. You've seen it yourself, haven't you? She's out of place, out of her depth. But soon enough, she'll rise higher. And when she does, you'll be left behind.

I crumpled up the letter the moment I finished reading it, but the words stuck. Whoever wrote it knew what I was thinking. They understood my frustration, the way Noël constantly overshadowed me. How could a woman be better than me at everything? She's just a girl.

Recently, our troops were competing against each other, and of course, hers won.

Noël's soldiers were stronger, better, and they fought well. Too well. For some reason, whatever she does, she does perfectly. She arrived at our base a few years ago, and since then, my life has been a nightmare. Whenever I get the chance to show off, she steals my spotlight. She always does everything better. No matter how hard I try, she wins. She's nothing but a woman, how can she be so strong? It pains me. The thought of a woman being so good drives me insane.

Weeks passed before the second note arrived. This time, it felt more direct, like the writer had been watching me.

Imagine what it would be like without her. No more competition.

No more endless defeats. The village would see you as the leader they need. Think about what could happen if she were gone.

That word, "gone," echoed in my head for days. *Gone.* No more Noël. No more battles where I came second to her. No more sneering soldiers laughing behind my back because a woman outshined me. The idea festered like a poison, seeping into my every thought.

Soon, Noël. Soon, you'll regret ever thinking you could escape me.

The third letter was the final push. By then, I was already obsessed with the idea of getting rid of her. I couldn't stop thinking about it. And the writer knew exactly how to make me act.

I know how to help you. Take her to the vólkins' territory. She'll never return. You'll be free, and the village will never know. After all, you know what happens to women who defy the laws of Tárnov.

It was almost too easy. The letter suggested the idea, but it felt like my own. I could kidnap her. And so I did. But now she's out here, playing with my mind.

Once I get my hands on her, I won't even bother with the vólkins. I'll take my time, savor every moment of her suffering. She'll cry, she'll beg, and I'll relish her every tear. I want to break her, to see the fire in her eyes extinguished, and when she's nothing but a shattered, whimpering mess, I'll make her endure it all over again.

I grin at that mouthwatering thought.

We walk deeper into the forest. The trees seem to close in around us, denser than I remember. A strange hush hangs over the woods, the usual sounds of birds and animals oddly absent. I glance at Gregor and catch a flicker of uncertainty in his eyes.

"Don't tell me you're spooked by the stories," I say, my own voice almost trembling.

Gregor smirks, but there's no humor in it. "The vólkins aren't roaming here, Arnold. You've said it yourself."

But something is off. I can't shake the feeling that we're

being watched. My fingers tighten around the hilt of my sword as we continue forward, the silence scraping at the edges of my sanity. *Snap.*

I whirl around, eyes scanning the area. For a split second, I see her. Noël. A flash of her dark hair disappearing between the tree trunks.

"There!" My voice cracks, and I break into a run, heart hammering as I crash through the bushes. She's there, just ahead, slipping through the trees like a ghost.

"Arnold!" Gregor shouts behind me, but I don't stop. I can't. I have to catch her. My boots pound against the ground, my breath coming in sharp inhales as I chase after her.

But then— She's gone.

I skid to a halt, chest heaving. I look around frantically. No footprints, no broken branches, no sign of her at all. The trees are silent. My pulse thunders in my ears.

"Arnold, you're losing it," Gregor says when he catches up to me. He's panting, sweat beading on his forehead. "There's no one here."

I open my mouth to retort, but something stops me, a low, distant whisper, like someone calling my name. *Arnold.* The hairs on the back of my neck stand on end. I grip my sword tighter.

"You hear that?" I ask, voice low.

Gregor shakes his head. "Hear what?"

I turn back to the trees, eyes narrowing. The sound is gone, swallowed by the terrifying silence of the forest. But I swear I heard it, my name. It was my fucking name!

"Let's go," I mumble. We push forward again, farther into the heart of the forest.

It's my first time so deep in the wild. We mostly trained at the base or in the woods around Tárnov. We never went this far, not even during the most intense trainings. The trees here seem new to me. Taller, darker, with twisted roots that rise from the earth like skeletal hands. The atmosphere grows heavier with every step. Dusk slowly falls, silencing the familiar sounds, the breeze, rustling leaves, birds perched on branches. All of it is replaced by a weird quiet, making me sweat.

It feels as if something lurking within the thicket is watching me. Every shadow seems to move as we do, every branch snaps under something unseen. The farther we go, the more unsettling it becomes. The ground grows rough, tangled with roots and moss, as if the forest is resisting us, urging us to turn back.

I need to see her dead.

I should be more confident. I've led countless expeditions, navigated dangerous terrain, and fought battles that most men wouldn't survive. Yet this place ... It's different. The forest here feels alive with malice, like it's watching us, watching me, waiting.

Sweat drips down my forehead to my mouth, slipping between my gritted teeth.

A few steps later, something catches my eye—massive claw marks slashed viciously into the trees. I stop to inspect them. They're not just big, they're brutal, like something tore through the trunk with great force. I trace my fingers along the jagged grooves, feeling the depth. Shit. Whatever did this wasn't just marking territory, it was showing off its strength. I've never seen anything like it.

"What in the ...?" I murmur.

Gregor steps close, his eyes widening as he takes in the markings. "I don't like this, Arnold."

Fear flickers in his voice, and I feel it too. The stories of the vólkins, beasts lurking in the shadows, waiting to rip any man who dares to enter their territory to pieces, start to feel a little too real.

This cannot be right, we're still far from Ávera.

"We don't have time for this," I snap, trying to shake off the creeping dread. But as we move on, the markings become more frequent, etched into almost every tree we pass.

Snap. Within seconds, the air around us changes. It grows thicker, choking. I catch sight of a figure ahead, Noël, standing by a stream, her back turned to us.

There you are.

My lips curl into a grin as I signal Gregor to move quietly. The idiot stays close behind me, panting like a dog. Noël looks down into the water, unaware. I can practically feel her silky skin in my grip already.

But . . . something's wrong.

Her hair sways, but there's no wind. It moves unnaturally, almost like smoke curling in the air. I stop.

"What the . . . ?" I whisper, then shake my head. *Noël. It's Noël. It has to be her.*

But as I step closer, the hair shifts again, and I notice . . . it isn't hair. It's moving too fluidly, too unnaturally. My heart pounds harder.

"Noël?" I call out, my voice faltering. She doesn't turn. Doesn't move.

Something in me screams to stop, but I take another step. And another. I curl and uncurl my hands, my fingers trembling despite myself.

She turns.

And everything inside me sinks.

It's not Noël. It's not even human. Her face . . . too smooth, too perfect. Eyes glowing with an ethereal light. I can't breathe. I can't—

From the shadows, more figures emerge, slipping through the trees too lightly, as if floating. Women, their eyes gleaming, their bodies shimmering like water under the moonlight. We're surrounded. Trapped.

"You are not welcome here," one of them says, her voice echoing in my head, vibrating through my bones.

My legs refuse to move. I try to reach for my sword, but it's like my arms are made of stone, frozen in place by their gaze. Beside me, Gregor stumbles, his face pale with fear.

"What . . . what do we do?" Gregor's voice shakes, his knuckles white as he grips his blade.

I grit my teeth, struggling to breathe. "We need to go . . . get out of here. Now."

But the women close in, their beauty hiding the danger beneath. My skin crawls. And for the first time in years, I feel true fear.

14

THE WRATH OF THE VÓLKIN

"She will not come like a storm, but like a wound. She will not
restore the world with mercy but with memory. The one who
carries the ache of every mother, the fire of every daughter—
she is balance."
—Mother of All

Noël

Theron's entire presence changes before my eyes. His
fur bristles, fangs bare, and his breathing slows. I take
an involuntary step back.

I thought I'd seen his strength earlier, but this . . . this is
something completely different. It's raw, wild, and terrifying. He
didn't look like that before.

I take another step back, but he moves forward in perfect
sync, closing the distance between us with a single stride.

"Theron . . ." I start, but he doesn't give me the chance to
finish.

His massive paw tightens around me, and before I can
process what's happening, he lifts me into his arms. It's not the

careful, tender gesture it was earlier. Now it's like he's acting on pure instinct. The world blurs as he moves through the trees, and I cling to him, my fingers gripping the full fur of his mane, trying to steady myself. Strands of his fur catch on the bushes and low branches he runs past, a part of him scattered through the forest. Is he shedding after winter?

"Where are you taking me?" I demand. "Theron, tell me what's going on! Did you hear Arnold again? Are we going to him?" My voice is uneven. I fight to keep myself steady, but my stomach twists with the thought of facing Arnold again.

Theron doesn't answer right away. His jaw is clenched, his focus locked in, and every muscle in his body tenses as we speed through the forest. Fury radiates off him, a force so powerful it feels like it's pressing against my skin. But I'm not scared of him. Even in his rage, there's no danger to me. I feel it.

"Yes, I heard him," he growls finally. "He's close." His grip flexes, pulling me even tighter against him. "Too close."

My heart pounds at the thought of Arnold, at the memory of what he tried to do. Anger bubbles up along with the fear I've been trying so hard to suppress.

Theron's pace quickens. I can feel the strength in his every step, the way his muscles coil and release as he carries me through the woods.

"What will you do when you find him?" I ask. He said he would kill him, but will he really?

"I will do what is necessary to keep you safe," he says, his voice dark and final. There's no hesitation in his tone.

The forest opens into a small clearing, the trees giving way to an exposed patch of land, and there, in the distance, I see Arnold and . . . Gregor?

The shy, quiet newbie who barely said two words during our few mutual trainings? He wasn't in the inn when everything fell apart. Why is he here with Arnold?

Gregor always seemed so different from Arnold—awkward,

hesitant, the kind of person who kept to himself. He wasn't the type to be involved in something like this. Or at least, that's what I thought. But now, seeing him here, my stomach twists. Could I have been so wrong about him?

He looks like a caged animal. He's visibly shaking.

As we get closer, I see breathtakingly beautiful women. No, not women. Spirits, perhaps, like the leaf spirits, but far more haunting and powerful. Their ethereal bodies shine like they're lit from within and bathe the forest floor in silver.

Their skin is unnaturally pale, almost translucent, as though carved from moonlight. Long strands of hair fall down their slender bodies. For some it's as dark as the midnight sky, others the color of fiery autumn foliage, all flowing as though caught in an invisible breeze.

They, like Theron, have crystals embedded in their fore-heads, glowing brightly with a white glow. They have large shimmering eyes. Eyes that are fixed on Arnold and Gregor, as if ready to strike them down.

Their movements are graceful and fluid, and though their bodies appear fragile, there's a strength in the way they glide across the forest floor. How can something so magnificent be so fearsome?

Where the leaf spirits are playful, these women—no, these creatures—are deadly.

How beautiful.

Arnold and Gregor are frozen in place, their faces drained of all color. Neither of them has seen us yet.

Theron slows, his growl deepening into something far more feral. His entire body seems to swell with raw power, and I feel the ground beneath us tremble every time he takes a step.

"Stay here," he commands, setting me down with surprising gentleness despite the fury radiating off him. "Do not move." He pauses, turning those intense hazel eyes to mine. "Please."

I can't speak, only nod, my heart racing in my chest, thundering in my ears. I watch as he strides forward. The spirits—if that's what they are—part for him. Is he some type of tsar? Leader? Why do the spirits obey him?

The women's radiant eyes follow him, their postures straight. They know him. They respect him. A leader among creatures I've never even imagined, let alone heard of. Just how much more is there in this world that I haven't seen yet?

Theron's form is a menacing silhouette against the misty background of the forest. Arnold finally notices him, finally sees the massive vólkin bearing down on him like some nightmare come to life. His eyes widen in sheer terror, his face contorting into something that would almost be pitiful if it weren't Arnold.

"What . . . what is that?" Arnold stammers, stumbling backward, all his arrogance and cruelty stripped away.

Theron doesn't give him the chance to run, doesn't even give him the chance to finish his sentence. In a blur of motion, he lunges, his claws extended, the sharp tips catching the last glimmers of light coming through the trees. The crystals on his forehead flare a brilliant blue.

But I don't see the strike. I don't see what happens next.

One of the women rushes to me, covering my eyes with her slim fingers, her pale hand cold against my skin. Her touch is gentle, but it firmly insists that I should not witness what is about to happen. "Not for you." Her voice, a whisper like the wind, brushes against my ear.

Two more of the women move closer, surrounding me like guardians. They embrace me from every angle. Their presence is oddly comforting, a shield from whatever is happening in front of me.

And then I hear it.

Arnold's scream cuts through the air like an animal's cry, but it's cut short by the sickening sound of claws ripping into flesh. My whole body tenses as the sounds of violence fill the space around me.

I don't need to see it. I can hear everything. The quick, panicked gasps from Arnold, the sloppy sound of tearing flesh followed by sharp cracks, the unmistakable sound of bone snapping in Theron's paws. Blood splattering onto the forest floor, meeting the dampness of the earth.

Arnold's cries fade, replaced by choked, wet gurgling as I imagine Theron tightens his grip on Arnold's throat. It's as though the forest has been stunned into silence, waiting for the carnage to be over. The only sound that remains is the heavy thud of what's left of Arnold hitting the ground, piece by piece, and Theron's deep, even breaths.

Goose bumps prick my skin. I've seen bloodshed before, during my military trainings. I've watched men be beaten down, watched them break, but this . . . this is different. This isn't brutality for brutality's sake. It's something that feels more like nature taking its course than a man's vengeance.

The smell of iron, blood, reaches my nose. My stomach churns, but I force myself to breathe. Just breathe.

Slowly, I remove the hand that shields my vision, blinking against the harsh reality before me. Gregor, his face pale. He's panicking. Trying to flee, floundering, but he's not fast enough. He won't get far.

Before he even makes it two steps, the women surround him. Their graceful movements are now predatory, the light in their eyes changing from ethereal beauty to something much more dangerous.

"You are not welcome here," one of them says, her voice echoing in layers as if a thousand voices are speaking inside my head. The air around her hums with power, the ground beneath her pulses in response.

Gregor staggers back, his eyes wide with terror, shaking his head as if he could somehow will himself to wake from this nightmare.

"You and your kind have brought poison to these lands," she continues. "There will be no mercy."

Theron stands over Arnold's lifeless remains, his burning eyes on Gregor, who is shivering uncontrollably.

"Please . . ." Gregor stammers. "I didn't mean to . . . I-I was just following orders! Arnold— He made me come along! I didn't know!"

Theron's eyes narrow, the glow of his crystals deepening as he takes a step closer. "You are both guilty of harming Noël. There is no excuse." His voice is low. Blood drips to the ground as his claws extend, preparing to finish what he started.

"No, wait!" I scream, rushing forward before I can think. "Please, Theron! Stop!"

Theron freezes mid-step, his head snapping in my direction. The rage in his eyes vanishes.

I turn to Gregor as I step between him and Theron. My body quivers but I force myself to stand firm.

"Gregor," I say, looking straight into his eyes, "why were you with Arnold? Why were you in that carriage?" I need to understand.

I need to know if he's guilty or just got caught up in Arnold's madness.

Theron ripped through Arnold with such ferocity, the smell of his blood still hangs in the air. Even now, I can almost feel it clinging to my skin, as if it's seeped into me somehow.

I don't feel sorry for Arnold. Not after everything he did, not after what he had planned for me, but that doesn't mean his death hasn't left a mark.

If Gregor is not guilty, I cannot let him face the same fate as Arnold. *Answer me, Gregor.*

Gregor's eyes dart between Theron and me, sweat dripping down his forehead.

"I didn't know!" he pleads. "I swear, I didn't know you were in the carriage. Arnold told me to meet him, that it was a job, just a job. He didn't say . . . he didn't say it was you. I only found out after we'd already left, and by then, it was too late." His voice cracks, and he sinks to his knees. "I swear . . . I'm so, so sorry. Please . . . please, you have to believe me."

I see the fear in his eyes, the regret, and I feel pity for him. He's scared and confused, just like I was. Is it so unlikely that he was dragged into this by Arnold's manipulation? My mind is torn. He doesn't deserve to die like this, not when Arnold was the true monster.

I open my mouth to speak, but before I can make a move, the ethereal, ghostly women who were surrounding the clearing appear beside me. Their luminous hands grip my arms, holding me back, their touch like a caress.

"Please, Your Majesty," one of them whispers, her voice like the rustling of leaves in the wind. She stands beside me, her long fingers wrapped around my waist, her glowing eyes pleading. "Do not harm yourself for the sake of this man."

Your Majesty? I blink, confused, but before I can question it, another woman speaks from beside Theron.

"Leave him to us," she says, her voice low and full of authority. Her pale, translucent body moves toward Gregor, her dazzling eyes fixed on his face. "We will take care of him. There will be no harm done."

She turns and offers me a gentle bow.

Theron's gaze doesn't leave mine, his muscles still tense, but I see the conflict in his eyes. He wants to protect me. But he also hears my word. Why would he listen to me? Why would my opinion matter so much to him?

Slowly, he steps back, his claws retracting to their normal length.

I glance back at Gregor, whose face is wet with tears, his breath shuddering with relief. The women move closer to him, their hands resting on his shoulders as I watch them guide him away. For now, I'm grateful that no more blood will be spilled.

Theron tears his gaze from Gregor, his expression softening as he approaches me. "Are you alright?" he asks, his voice now gentle, the fury gone as if it never existed. The way he says it, his eyes so tender and concerned, like he didn't just rip Arnold apart, sends a strange warmth through me. *Am I losing my mind?*

I nod, but as he steps closer, I focus on his fur. Arnold's blood stains his claws, streaks are smeared across his chest. The sight of it freezes me in place. My breath hitches, and for a second, my feet feel like they're rooted to the ground. I have never seen so much blood in my life.

Theron's eyes follow mine, and he stops. Without a word, he takes a step back and turns toward the stream where he crouches low. When he dips his claws into the flowing current, the red seeps off him, swirling in the water before disappearing entirely. He scrubs at the fur on his chest, washing away every trace of the violence he unleashed only moments before.

When he finally stands again, his fur is clean, and he walks back toward me more cautiously, as if testing the space between us.

My pulse quickens.

The spirits clinging to me slowly move away, giving us room.

"You're safe now," he says. His paw hovers near my hand, as if waiting for permission to close the distance between us fully. "I won't let anyone harm you ever again."

My eyes search his. A part of me feels drawn to the safety he offers, but another part of me—a much more wary part— remembers what he's capable of.

"I . . . thank you," I finally manage. His presence is overwhelming, but instead of pulling away, I find myself standing still. I'm not sure if thanking him for killing a person was appropriate.

I glance back at the stream where the last traces of blood have already faded away, and silently, I remind myself: Be careful what you say to him. He ended Arnold's life because of me, because Arnold hurt me. And that power . . . it's comforting and terrifying. A dangerous combination.

As I step back to look at him, the spirits begin to gather, their movements synchronized as if driven by something unseen. They form a perfect circle, their brilliant eyes fixed on the shimmering water.

Theron, now at my side, watches with the same intensity. His body is still, but I can feel that he, too, is waiting for something.

The air shifts. A hum fills the space around us, vibrating through the ground beneath my boots and into my bones. The surface of the water ripples and glows, brighter and brighter, until it's almost blinding.

"Stay close to me," Theron says quietly. His paw brushes against my hand.

I nod, barely able to speak, too captivated by the unfolding scene before us. The light from the water pulses as if in sync with my own heartbeat.

Then, from within the shining depths, something moves.

A figure of a woman, but all made of light. I can barely make out the silhouette.

This is no spirit. This is something far greater. I can feel it in my very soul. My entire body prickles with goose bumps, a chill racing down my spine. I try to breathe, but the air feels heavy with her gaze as if every part of me is exposed before her.

She turns her head ever so slightly in my direction. The connection is immediate, intense, and I freeze, unable to look away. There is something ancient about her, a deep well of understanding. She can see through every layer of my being. It's both frightening and welcoming at the same time.

I clutch at Theron's fur for support, my fingers trembling as

I cling to his warmth, needing to remind myself that I'm still here, still in this world.

She tilts her head, and her lips part, though no words escape. Instead, I feel it. A voice, not spoken but sensed, like a whisper that stirs in the back of my mind.

Noël.

She slowly raises a hand and points toward the center of the water. The spirits around us bow their heads.

I don't know what she wants. What does this all mean?

Beside me, Theron finally speaks. "You're in the presence of a goddess."

15

THE WEIGHT OF THE OATH

"Six of you shall rise, each marked by fate, each bound by soul. When your mates awaken, the world will begin to heal. Guard them with your life, for through them, the balance shall be restored."
—Elder Aïna, during the Oath of Guardianship

Theron

The air feels sacred. Even with my strength, I feel small under the goddess's gaze. The forest, the air, the world bows to her presence—and so do I. My crystals pulse with the energy surrounding her, but they feel insignificant in the face of her divine light.

Yesterday, I was running through these trees, following the barest hint of sweetness in the wind. Now, here I stand, having found my mate and torn apart the man who dared to harm her.

It's been a lifetime of waiting for some word from the goddesses, any word. Each century that passed, their voices grew fainter. We'd begun to wonder if they had left us entirely.

And now, here she is. A goddess, standing before my mate

in all her glory. It's more than I ever thought I'd witness in my life, more than any vólkin has experienced in generations.

Noël stands beside me, eyes wide, mesmerized by her presence. Her wonder mirrors my own, though for entirely different reasons. This is all new to her—this world, the spirits, the goddesses—but for me, it's a return to something ancient that was lost to time.

"My beloved children." The goddess's voice vibrates deep within my very soul. "Hear my words."

Six goddesses rule the lands: Láda Veléša, Vodínaya, Zárya, Dušava, Beregína, and Dalyéora. However, I don't know which one is speaking. I know what they're supposed to look like. Elder Aïna describe them to us as pups, but now, with all the blinding light, it's hard to tell. Every goddess has her own unique powers and characteristics, and each one represents a different aspect of nature and our lives.

"Noël, chosen Lidéřen," the goddess says, her voice tender and powerful, "your journey has just begun. The strength within you is greater than you think, and your heart, though wounded, holds the power to heal this world."

Lidéřen, an ancient word from a language long forgotten. It means *leader*.

"In the depths of Ávera lies the sacred glade," the goddess continues, "where the roots of our world's balance intertwine. You must seek this place, for there you will find the key to restoring harmony."

When I glance at Noël, I catch the slight tremble of her lips as she processes the words. She's strong, but I can see her heart is heavy, full of questions and doubts. I find myself reaching out without thinking, brushing a lock of her silky hair behind her ear. She doesn't flinch, doesn't pull away. Her trust in me is growing, little by little.

"Theron, noble guardian." The goddess turns her gaze to me. "Your bond with the Lidéřen is the light that will guide you both through the darkness. Trust in each other, for your spirits are intertwined by destiny's thread."

Destiny. Her words are a command, a vow I'm bound to fulfill. *My mate. My Lidéřen.*

I nod. The oath I took during the Coming of Age Ritual weighs heavy in my heart, woven into every level of my being. This is who I am and the purpose I serve. That night, under the glow of the full moon, each of us who had reached a hundred years stood in the sacred glade. We were so young then, on the cusp of becoming warriors, each offering our lives to the goddesses.

The Oath of Guardianship was etched into our souls, becoming a living part of us. With every challenge I've faced, that promise has thrummed in the back of my mind, guiding my every decision. From the moment we are born, we are taught that our role isn't only to fight but to be the guardians of our mates, their protectors, their strength in the darkness. But never in all my life did I think my duty would become so clear.

Now, that oath has a name. Noël.

The promise that once seemed distant has now become the center of my existence.

"Know this: The path ahead is perilous, but you are never alone. The spirits of the forest, the whispers of the wind, and the goddesses' essences are with you. Together, *you shall mend what has been broken.*"

The goddess's eyes are now fixed on my mate.

"Remember, the power of the blue rose lies within you, Noël. Let it guide you as you embrace your destiny."

Then, with a final gesture, she lifts her hands and says, "We will meet again at the bonding ritual, Ethereal Leader."

As the goddess fades into the air, the light disappears fully, but I can still feel her presence, a hum of warmth beneath my fur. The glowing nýmphí, who stood so silently, lower their heads in deep devotion before slowly dispersing back into the forest. The clearing falls back into stillness, but nothing feels the same.

Everything is about to change—for Noël, me, and all of Ávera.

Noël is too quiet, and though her expression remains neutral, I can sense something isn't right.

"I know it's a lot," I tell her. I want to reach out, to hold her, but something about her posture keeps me rooted in place.

Her eyes shift toward me, her brow furrowing. "A lot? That doesn't even begin to cover it." Her tone is sharp but not aggressive. I can hear the exhaustion in her voice. She's holding it together, but only just.

I give her a nod of understanding. "Ask me anything. I will answer your every question." I want to ease her burden, but I know this isn't something that will go away with a few answers. She's carrying the prophecy now, a role she never even knew about.

She takes a deep breath, looking around as if searching for the right words. "Why me?"

"You are the leader—the Lidéřen—from an ancient prophecy, Noël." I can feel the tension rising, but I remain calm. "The blue rose has always been the sign. And when I first saw you, I knew. It wasn't just the prophecy that told me, Noël. It was you—the strength you carry within."

She crosses her arms, her gaze hardening. "Strength? You've known me for what, a day? You don't know anything about me."

I nod again. "I may not know the details of your past, but I see the strength in you. The goddess herself spoke it. You are more than you think."

She falls silent, her lips pressing into a thin line. She doesn't reject my words, but she doesn't accept them either. "You called me your mate. What does that actually mean? Why me? Is it because of this prophecy?"

"The bond between us is fated," I explain, trying to keep my tone gentle. "It's more than just prophecy. It's the connection the goddesses have woven between us, something neither of us can fully understand yet. But it's real."

She's quiet again, and conflict sparks in her eyes. She wants to say more, but she's holding back. I can feel it.

A few moments pass in silence, and then, she speaks again. "The goddess said, 'you shall mend what has been broken.'" Her voice is quieter this time. "What does that even mean?"

"The earth . . . it's suffering from an imbalance," I explain. "This imbalance has disrupted the natural flow of energy between the ethereal and physical realms. The land itself is in pain, and that pain affects everything—plants, animals, even the seasons. The role of the leader, of you—us—is to restore that balance. To heal what's been fractured for so long."

She frowns, her eyes narrowing. "Restore the balance," she repeats slowly. "And I'm supposed to . . . what? Fix the entire world?"

"I'll be with you the whole time," I say quickly, trying to reassure her. "You won't be alone in this. I'll help you, guide you—"

"Stop. You keep saying that, Theron. That you'll be with me. That I'm supposed to do this. But you don't understand."

I freeze, my heart beats faster. But I stay quiet, giving her space to say what she needs to say, even though the intensity of her gaze makes every muscle in my body want to reach out and comfort her.

I don't know what to do.

She runs a hand through her damp hair, nose wrinkling. "You don't understand what it's like to have all this thrown at you, to be told that you're supposed to save the world when you barely understand any of it." Her voice rises with every word.

I open my mouth to respond, but I stop myself. Something tells me this isn't the time for me to reassure her or tell her she's strong enough. She doesn't need that. She needs something I can't quite grasp yet.

Noël's breathing is heavier now, her chest rising and falling rapidly as she tries to keep her emotions in check. But I can see the frustration, the confusion, the anger, all swirling inside her, ready to explode.

I clench my fists at my sides. Then, as I'm about to speak, she looks up at me again.

"What makes you think I'll go to Ávera with you?"

16

THE CALL OF FATE,
THE WEIGHT OF LOSS

"One day, the world will kneel to the woman with blue roses in her blood."
—Eyleen Ársa

Noël

These past few days have been nothing but chaos. Everything I thought I knew about the world has been shattered, and I haven't had a second to breathe, never mind process anything. Now, a goddess—*an actual goddess*—has appeared and told me I'm some kind of leader and that I'm supposed to restore balance? Restore what? How?

Frustration claws at the inside of my chest. I'm angry. Furious. How could everything fall apart so fast? I had my whole life planned: become a commander, change the stupid laws of Tárnov, take control of my life.

I already made so many changes in the foolish military system. I even proposed jobs "suitable for women," at least according to men's egos. But that's alright, we can start small by letting women have jobs. It might begin with office roles, but then it could expand to every position. I believed I could make a change.

But now, I'm . . . lost.

"Why me?" The words spill out, my voice rising without my permission. "Why do *I* have to be the one to fix everything?"

Mate? Leader? Restore balance?

"Noël . . ." He moves closer. Theron. His presence, so calm, doesn't soothe me at all. It just reminds me of the expectations everyone has heaped on top of me.

I snap.

"You have no idea! I've been kidnapped, thrown into a prophecy I never asked for, and now a goddess tells me I'm supposed to restore balance? I don't even know what that means!" My voice cracks. "And all of this after my mother . . . after she—" I swallow hard, tears blur my vision. "After she died. I didn't even get a moment to grieve, not a single moment!"

Theron's expression softens, his hazel eyes filled with sympathy. It only makes me angrier.

"Don't look at me like that!" I shout. "Don't act like you understand! You weren't there. You didn't see her die. You don't know what it's like to lose everything in a matter of days."

Theron's massive body is shading me, but I don't care how big he is. I glare up at him. I refuse to back down.

As soon as I felt I could finally take control of my life . . . it all crumbled.

"Remember when I told you I felt the blue rose within you?" he says, his voice so calm, so *infuriatingly* calm.

I grit my teeth. "Yes, and what does that even mean?"

He drops to his knees beside me, reaching out to take my hand. Even when he kneels, I'm not as tall as him. "The blue rose is a symbol of power. It's been with you all along, guiding you, giving you strength."

I yank my hand out of his grip. "Strength? What strength?"

My breath comes in short bursts. "The only thing that happened was that I had my mother's handkerchief. It had a crystal in it—"

Theron dips his chin. "The blue rose has been with you all your life. It's more than a symbol. It's part of you. The goddess spoke of it because she knows how important it is."

I can't take it anymore. His calmness, his explanations, his talk of destiny and blue roses, it's all too much. I feel like I'm drowning, and no matter how much I fight to stay above water, I'm still sinking.

My body shakes with frustration. "I don't *care* about the blue rose! I don't *want* it! I don't want *any* of this!" I turn away from him, trying to breathe, trying to calm myself down, but it's useless.

"Thousands of years ago, humans, vólkins, and spirits lived in harmony. Nature provided for us, and we nurtured and respected it. There were no wars or hunger, and no suffering," Theron says, pointing at the flora and fauna around us. "Then something happened, and the balance in nature was disturbed." He sighs. "For a reason we do not know, we have been trapped behind a strong barrier that didn't let anyone escape. For four centuries."

Why is he telling me all this?

"A barrier? What do you mean?" I didn't see any barrier.

Theron looks into my eyes, his expression serious. "It was an invisible wall that surrounded Ávera and its forests. No one could pass through it, not vólkins, not spirits, not even the goddesses."

"I walked into the forest just fine," I say, but the words feel wrong even as they leave my lips. When I ran into the woods, I crossed whatever invisible threshold Theron's talking about. I didn't feel anything. No force. No barrier. And yet . . . When I was running through the forest, I did notice changes in my surroundings. I thought it was normal, given the fact that I've never been in a forest before, but now that I think about it, the berries Theron and I gathered were sweeter than the berries I ate in Tárnov. Even the apples were rounder, and their color was deeper.

A four-hundred-year-old curse, undone in an instant. Because of me?

I don't know whether to laugh or be sick.

"That was when you started restoring the balance," he says, giving me a flower that he just picked from the ground near me. "I believe the moment you crossed it, the barrier lifted."

It can't be so simple. But also . . . Why would he lie? And . . . a goddess appeared. I don't know what to think, truly. "Why would that happen?"

"I think because you are the blue rose, my Noël. Blue roses are sacred, and the ones who carry them in their blood are very powerful."

For generations, women couldn't leave the villages . . .

A woman who is born in Tárnov, dies in Tárnov.

That's what we were taught since we were little girls. Whenever I looked at the main gates, I always saw the sad gazes of the village women. No one dared to question it. But now I know why. *Of course.*

If we couldn't leave the village, and I was the one who lifted this barrier . . . It can only mean one thing—the barrier is known, and the tsar and the army didn't want it to be destroyed. And yet . . .

I was a soldier, a commander. But never a leader of prophecy. Never the kind of woman Theron's talking about.

I glance up at him. "How do you know all this?"

"Every spirit, every vólkin, and all the goddesses know it. A woman is born, radiant like the dawn, a beacon of light. She grows with the essence of the earth and sky. Her spirit is tied to the soil, and her soul dances with the winds." He looks into my eyes with a kind of awe that both confuses and terrifies me. "You are a child of nature, Noël."

Something stirs within me, something buried so far down I didn't even know it was there. The warmth of his words, his gaze—it's all too familiar.

Mother.

We were in our secret garden. I was young then, and she taught me about the blue rose. The light of the setting sun bathed everything in gold. Her fingers ran through my hair as she spoke. "The blue rose is special, Noël. It represents the power and potential inside us, something that connects us to the world in ways we can't always understand. You have this power within you, my dear. You are a child of nature, don't ever forget that."

I remember the pride in her eyes, the same kind I see now in Theron's.

Tears well up inside me. "She always told me I was meant for great things," I whisper, my voice cracking, "but she never told me it was for this."

Theron moves closer, his large paw cupping my cheek. His warmth spreads through me, and the tears spill over.

"I miss her so much," I choke out. "She taught me how to care for the blue rose, how to keep it alive. She trained me to lead. She pushed me into the military, prepared me for . . ."

I have to fight to breathe now. "But she never told me this. She never said it was for *this*. Restoring balance, being some . . . leader!" My voice rises in desperation. "Why didn't she tell me? Why did she leave me to figure all this out on my own?"

I clutch Theron's fur, gripping it tightly, my tears soaking his chest. I feel like I'm drowning. "Why didn't she prepare me for *this*?"

Theron stays silent, his stone-like arms pulling me tight as I cry into him. The comfort of his fur surrounds me, but it's not enough to dull the pain twisting in my chest. Nothing can take away the ache of being left in the dark by the one person I trusted the most.

"She knew, didn't she?" I sob, looking up at him through my tears. "She knew the whole time, and she didn't tell me."

Theron's eyes glisten, his own sorrow reflecting mine. "Noël," he whispers, "I'm so sorry." He brushes his paw over my head, but there are no words that can fix this. He can't give me back my mother. He can't make sense of this mess.

So I cling to him, holding on like he's the only thing anchoring me to this world. My heart feels like it's being ripped in two—one half lost in grief for my mother, the other half breaking under the weight of this prophecy I never asked for.

Theron holds me, nuzzles into my hair, and I feel his breath against my scalp. His embrace cages me, wraps around me like a shield against the chaos in my mind.

"I am so sorry," he repeats, his voice rough but tender, as if my pain is his own.

I melt into the hug, my cheek presses against him, and I murmur, "Thank you."

But . . . this doesn't change what I have to do.

"But," I begin, my voice muffled by his damp chest. "I need to find out what happened to my mother." I pull back just enough to meet his gaze. "I can't go with you to Ávera and leave everything behind."

I don't break eye contact. He needs to understand. No matter how this prophecy will unfold, I can't abandon the truth. My mother's death— There's still so much I don't know, too much left unresolved.

Theron's paw moves to my face, brushing my hair back as he searches my eyes.

"I went to the holiest place in Ávera, The sacred glade, to ask the goddesses for guidance before I found you," he says. His eyes shift, reflecting the thin silver light of the moon. I hadn't even noticed how the day went by, and I spent it with Theron.

His silhouette shines with the moon's glow. The contrast between his dangerous appearance and the gentleness in his voice makes my heart beat faster.

"The goddesses had been giving me signs," he continues, "showing me that you were near, that my destiny was close." He looks up, his gaze distant. "As an answer to my prayer, a beautiful white dove appeared in the night sky, blessing me with a single blue rose petal."

I follow his gaze to the sky, my eyes tracing the outlines of clouds passing over the moon. The cool breeze tugs at my hair, and my skin prickles as his attention moves back to me. "Blue rose petal?"

"The goddesses have been guiding me to you," he says, caressing my cheek, his thumb brushing over my skin. "And you, to me."

Theron straightens his posture. "We will find out what happened to your mother." His expression sharpens. "You can trust me."

I realize then that I've been holding my breath. The tension I've been carrying for days finally finds a release. Goose bumps rise along my neck where his paw rests, and I can't help but lean into his touch, even though my mind still reels with questions.

"Little dove," he whispers.

I blink up at him. What?

I don't know how to respond. My mother used to call me "my little rose," but no one has ever called me a dove. And yet, when I look up at him, I don't pull away.

I should. But I don't.

17

GUARDING THE DOVE

"To each, a mate will be given—not to possess, but to protect. In the arms of their chosen, the earth shall begin to breathe again."

—Elder Aïna, Oath of Guardianship, spoken beneath the moonlit trees

Theron

"It's getting cold, and you should rest," I tell my brave Noël. "Let me prepare a nest for you."

She furrows her brow, tilting her head. "A nest?" she asks. "Like what birds make?"

I grin. "In a way, yes. A place of comfort, safety. For us, it's where we rest and where we find peace after a long day."

She blinks. "You mean . . . a bed?"

"A bed?" I repeat. "Yes, I suppose that's what you'd call it."

She raises an eyebrow. "It's called a bed," she insists, though her voice is gentle, not harsh.

I smile and nod. "A bed, then. Let me prepare your bed."

"I can make my own bed," she says as she sits on a log, one

leg crossed over the other. I have never seen such a sitting position. I don't think I could even sit like that, not with a sac. I haven't seen our females sit like that either. Humans are so different.

"I know you can, but let me do this thing for you." As she opens her mouth to protest, I say, "After you stabbed me, I should get to."

She closes her mouth and looks to the side. Pride? I hum in amusement.

I begin gathering leaves and moss and arranging them beneath a large tree. Each piece I place is meant to cushion her, to make her feel at ease. The moonlight filters through the branches, glowing over the clearing and my beautiful mate.

The plush plants beneath my paws remind me of the nights I spent alone, waking from dreams that left me with an aching emptiness. Instinctively, I would reach out beside me, searching for someone, only to grasp at nothing but the cold air.

That emptiness, it's all I've known for so long. And now, with her here, I feel the pull even stronger, the need to fill that void, to have her beside me. And to make her mine.

The way her body would fit perfectly in that space, the warmth she would bring to the cold, lonely nights. I want to be the one who comforts her, who protects her, who wakes beside her.

But I understand her. I see the anger and frustration in her eyes. I want to tell her that I feel it, too, that the weight of it all crushes me as well. But I can't force her to understand, to feel the bond between us like I do. I can't make her accept this fate because it's what I want. And that's the hardest part of all—holding back when every part of me, down to each individual hair, itches to claim what is mine.

I've never been patient. Never been this kind. Before her, my life was simpler. Train, lead, protect. It was all so clear. But now, I feel like I'm walking through the fog, lost in my own wants and needs. I don't know how to make her see it, how to explain the depth of this bond, how much I need her.

While I make the nest—no, the bed—I steal glances at Noël. She sits quietly, lost in her thoughts, her face bathed in the glow of the moonlight. Even through the fatigue I see in her eyes, there's still that spark of will burning in her. She's been through so much, yet she remains strong.

"It's ready," I say, stepping back to admire the bed-nest. "I hope you find it comfortable."

Noël smiles, a tired but genuine smile. "Thank you, Theron. It looks perfect."

As she settles into the nest, I sit beside her.

"I need to go back to Tárnov," she whispers, almost as if she's confessing something forbidden. "I need to understand what happened to my mother."

"You told me her death was . . . sudden," I say as I brush a leaf from her arm, "but what makes you think going back to Tárnov will give you answers?"

Noël's gaze hardens as she turns her head, fire flaring in her eyes. "If I go back, maybe I'll find something she left behind. I can't just leave all that unresolved. I didn't even go through the whole house yet."

Though I understand her drive to uncover the truth, my instincts scream caution. "Do you think it's safe to return to Tárnov now? You've said yourself that women aren't allowed to leave. It's dangerous."

Her lips press together. "I know it's not safe," she admits. "But I can't ignore what happened. People saw me with Arnold. The inn was crowded, there were witnesses. By now, the whole village is probably looking for me."

She lets out a bitter laugh. "They'll want to drag me back, or worse. There was this woman, years ago, who tried to leave. They caught her and hanged her in the village square. That was before I was even born, and since then, no woman has dared to try again."

My stomach tightens at the thought of anyone harming her, and I struggle to keep my voice level. "So, they're on high alert now. And you'd be putting yourself at risk by returning."

Her expression falters. "But what choice do I have? If I don't go back, I'll never know the truth."

I lean in. "There will be a time to find the answers you need, but rushing into Tárnov right now without a plan is not worth the risk. That makes you a target."

She falls silent again. After a long, tense moment, she sighs, her shoulders slumping. "You're right," she murmurs. "I can't just walk into Tárnov like nothing happened."

I reach out, taking her hand in my paw. "When we get to Ávera, we'll seek guidance from the goddesses. They might be able to show us the path forward, to help us find the answers we need—safely."

Noël looks at me, her eyes softening as she takes in my words. The tension in her body eases just a little. "Alright, we'll go to Ávera."

"We'll find out what happened to your mother, Noël. I promise."

Her voice is barely audible over the rustling of the woods around us when she whispers, "Thank you."

"Of course," I say, adding more leaves under her head for comfort.

In the sacred glade, we will be able to speak to the goddesses. One of them appeared, and I received a sign. That is good. Perhaps the world is truly opening its arms to its Lidéřen. And that Lidéřen is *my* mate.

"You're not going to sleep?" my little mate asks, her eyelids fluttering as she fights to stay awake. She's adorable.

"Vólkins don't sleep as much as humans," I reply. "You need

it more than I do, so rest well. We have a whole day tomorrow before we get to Ávera."

"If you get tired, wake me up, alright?" She can hardly manage to finish the sentence before she yawns. "I wake up to stand watch all the time. We do it in rotations in the military, so it isn't new to me."

As she settles in to sleep, I pull out some of my fur and add it into the bed-nest. She should be surrounded by my fur, should smell like *me*. The shedding season has begun, and I already left so much of myself on the forest floor.

"The goddess said something about a bonding ritual," my mate murmurs.

"She did."

"What is that? Sounds like a wedding."

"I do not know what a wedding is, but a bonding ritual is a ceremony that binds two souls together: an earthly soul and an ethereal being," I say, brushing out more of my fur.

"I'm not marrying yo—"

And just like that, she's asleep, faster than any cub I've ever seen. I shall ask Elder Aïna what's *mar-ry-ing* when we arrive tomorrow.

My little dove's breaths are soft and even, her body relaxing into the nest I made for her. She looks peaceful.

The way her gown drags over her as she moves, revealing a bit of her legs, the moonlight casting a lustrous glow over her skin—I feel it again. My shaft hardening despite my attempts to push the feeling away. *Fuck.*

This is not the time, not when she's finally found some peace.

But it's as if every instinct in me is drawn to her, begging for that connection. I take a deep breath. I must focus on anything else, but the sight of her, so serene, only makes it worse. I want her in every way, more than I've ever wanted anything in my four hundred years of living.

The day we're close enough to sleep together, in every sense of the word, will be the day I howl my lungs away. I'll be the happiest vólkin alive. But right now my cock throbs painfully even thinking about it. It stings. The torn part of her gown reveals smooth skin beneath, and I can't hold back anymore. I never thought a furless creature could be so irresistible.

I grasp my shaft, and I fight to suppress the growl rising in my throat. If I make too much noise, I'll wake her.

My grip tightens as I begin to stroke slowly, inhaling her scent. Goddesses, forgive me. Each stroke is torturous. I speed up, unable to tear my eyes from her. Her cheek is smushed against her hand, her lips parted slightly. I want those lips on me, tasting me, wrapped around my beast. I can't control it. I . . .

My hips start moving, meeting my paw. I've never been this desperate. If she saw me like this, she'd run, and I wouldn't blame her. I'd run too. Calling myself a worthy male but stroking myself like this while I watch her sleep, it's wrong.

Precum leaks over my paw as I stroke faster, rougher, holding back the growls and grunts of pleasure that want to rip from my chest. *I want her to hear what she does to me.*

Then she stirs, turning over in her sleep. Her gown rides higher, exposing more of her legs. I need those legs spread for me, need them wrapped around my waist as she takes my knot. As it stretches her hole that was made for me. For my seed.

My cock burns. I squeeze it, desperate to will the need away, but her scent . . . My mate. My Noël. This isn't right. Not yet. But goddesses, it hurts.

It has never been painful before, not like this.

My head drops back, and I bite down on my tongue to stifle the sound, holding in the roar that threatens to escape.

My hips keep moving as I spill, every thrust filled with a single thought—I'll breed her, fill her so full she'll have no choice but to take it all, to carry my scent. Even as my release hits hard, the need doesn't fade. I can see her, swollen and full with what I've given, hers and mine. The vision drives me, pushing me over the edge again, unstoppable, until there's nothing left but the thought of her beneath me.

I pant heavily. I will never forgive myself for this.

As the night deepens, my ears twitch at every subtle sound in the forest. We will restore the balance, one step at a time. After a final glance at Noël, I call upon the leaf spirits. The leaves rustle in response, their inner light intensifying as they gather around me.

"Did you listen to our conversation?" I whisper.

They nod and circle me, then drift toward my mate.

"Of course you did." I wave my paw, and they rush back to me. "You have smaller hands, spirits," I whisper, getting down on all fours. "I want more of my scent on her. Having just a few of my hairs in her bed-nest is not enough." I shake my body, and many hairs fall to the ground. The spirits rush to gather them, while others pluck clumps of fur from all over me.

It feels amazing, and I stretch. Kaël usually scratches himself on a tree or annoys Zephyr until he does it for him.

Will Noël brush my fur? I roll onto my back, arms and legs extended into the air, so the spirits can pluck fur from my chest and abs.

Once we're finished, I sit up, and the spirits begin weaving the hairs together. I have a feeling I'm missing a step, but they seem to know exactly what to do.

The sun will rise in a few hours, and the fur blanket is ready. "How should I thank you for your kindness?" I ask the spirits, and they giggle in response. They fly over to my mate, circling around her as she sleeps.

"Will it be enough?" I tilt my head. I lift the blanket and it falls nearly to my knees. The leaves fly away from Noël and, in a perfect line, measure the blanket.

"It will." I nod. "Let's get her some food before she wakes."

They move quickly, gathering fresh berries and water from the nearby stream. They arrange everything on a broad leaf, and I cover it with larger leaves to keep it fresh.

As dawn breaks, Noël stirs, and though her eyes gently flutter open, her movements are sharp. She's alert. Her body tenses, ready for action. Her gaze sweeps her surroundings before settling on the food I've prepared. Her eyes widen, but she is still tense. Perhaps it's a habit she built up through years of training in the "military." It's a side of her I haven't seen until now.

"Theron," she says, "did you do all this?"

"With help from the leaf spirits. I wanted to make sure you had everything you needed."

She looks at me with those alert, curious eyes, her expression softening in a way that makes my chest tighten. "Thank you," she says. "This is really thoughtful."

I reach out and gently squeeze her hand. "You're welcome, little dove. We have a long journey ahead, so eat well."

She nods, and then when she takes a bite of a strawberry, her eyes light up. *Hm.*

After she sips from the water, I take the empty leaf from her, and she goes back for another satisfied bite of the strawberry.

"Did you eat already?" she asks, stopping mid-bite.

"I'm fine. My focus is on you. We'll have plenty of time to eat together when we reach Ávera."

Watching her smile, unguarded relief crossing her expression, makes the long night of starving worth it.

Once she's done with the berries, the leaf spirits take the empty leaf bowl and fly away. As my mate gets up and stretches, I turn to get the blanket from a branch. The leaf spirits hung it so it'd stretch and even. I think.

"What's that?" Noël asks, walking over to me as I turn around with the blanket in my paws.

"You will be cold on the way, so the leaf spirits and I made you this blanket from my fur."

She blinks at me. Is she confused?

"I . . . I don't even know what to say, Theron. Thank you. That's . . . also very thoughtful."

She takes the blanket from my arms and puts it over her shoulders. Then, she takes a handkerchief from her pocket and ties it at the front so it stays on her. Resourceful, so resourceful.

"Let's get moving," I say, standing and offering her a paw. "Ávera awaits."

She nods.

"It will be faster if you ride on my back,"

Noël furrows her brows. "Ride on your back?"

"Yes," I reply, getting on all fours. "I can run much faster this way. It will save us time."

She hesitates. "But what if I fall?"

"I won't let you fall. Hold on tightly, and I'll make sure you're secure."

Her light touch sends a shiver down my back as she climbs onto me. Her fingers weave into my mane, and I wrap my tail around her waist, pulling her closer. Once she is secure, I rise.

She brushes her hand over my tail. A thrill zips through my veins.

"Noël," I warn.

She chuckles. "Don't tell me you're ticklish here!" I can hear the smirk in her voice. She leans down to my ear and whispers, "Now I've got a weapon, just in case."

My little dove is so innocent. "Yes, very ticklish," I say, trying to calm myself.

Not now, Theron, not now.

I have never before wished for the ability to hide my cock. Thank the goddesses I'm on all fours, and Noël is on my back and cannot see it.

With a powerful stride, I set off, the wind rushing past us as we head toward Ávera. Noël holds on to my mane and the support of my tail, and she yelps in delight as I run. She reminds me of the pups frolicking about.

It's been more than a day since I left my warriors, since I took that leap into the unknown to find her. Ávera is open. For the first time in centuries, my warriors can leave. The world beyond the border is no longer a myth, no longer a dream we prayed to see. They will be tempted. And I can't let that happen.

The forest blurs around us, the distance to Ávera shrinking with each stride.

Running with a hard cock will be a challenge.

18

A DEAL IN THE DARKNESS

"Don't worry about me, brother. I'll be just fine. As long as I
wear this necklace, the gods will keep me safe."
—Linnéa Fenrówe, the night before Gregor left for Tárnov

Gregor

The morning light is my only hope that I'll get out of
here. Out of this chaos I got myself into. I walk along
the dusty road, my legs aching. For some reason, I
couldn't find the carriage Arnold and I left by the edge of the
forest. And no sign of the horses either. I've been walking for
hours, driven by fear and a desperate need to find my way back
to Tárnov. I've never been anywhere near here. Where do I
even go?

The events of yesterday play over and over in my mind:
Arnold's violent end, those inhuman beings, and the terrifying
power of the vólkin. I shiver despite walking so much and
sweating like a tired dog.

I knew that dealing with Noël would end up a mess. She
always comes out on top, is always a few steps ahead of anyone

I know. The moment Arnold told me there was a job, I jumped at the opportunity. It was good pay for something so easy. Little did I know we were going to smuggle Noël out of the village and leave her to the vólkins. All Arnold told me was that we were delivering something outside of Tárnov, and he needed someone with him in case we had to spend the night in the forest. Arnold was one of my friends. Well . . . I don't know what friends are, really. Would someone who bullies you for months but is nice sometimes be considered a friend? I don't know. Arnold always berated me, always looked down on me . . .

He also helped me many times. But still.

Funny how life works. Arnold was the one to die at a vólkin's hand instead of Noël.

I sigh deeply. Why am I always involved in these sorts of things? One day, I'll end up dead for my stupidity, just like Arnold.

The road is quiet, the usual sounds of the forest behind me replaced by the occasional rustling of leaves and the distant sounds of crows. I try to stay alert, but exhaustion clouds my thoughts. I need to find help, but who can I ask? Everyone I know is either dead or too far away to reach.

I don't even know how to survive out here. I joined the military a mere few months ago. I'm so tired. My feet hurt like shit. My stomach growls, reminding me I haven't eaten well for so long. On the way to find Noël, we had only dry bread, and Arnold found some berries and apples in the forest.

Joining the army was supposed to be my way out of poverty, a chance to escape my starving village for Tárnov, a place full of opportunities and dreams. Instead, it's been one hardship after another. The endless problems, the constant fear of doing something wrong and getting punished. I'm not cut out for this life, but there's no turning back now.

In Tárnov, rank is everything. The officers, born into privilege, look down on recruits like me, their eyes full of disdain as they bark orders. We were all the same in the barracks—desperate and replaceable. The cold stone walls and thin blankets did little to chase away the chill that settled deep in my marrow each night.

They said Tárnov was built on the bones of giants, that its foundations were laid in blood. We were nothing but the latest in a long line of sacrifices to keep the village strong.

It wasn't much different from Róstan, really, except that in Róstan, the chains were invisible but just as heavy. The poverty there was crushing, fields barren, bellies empty, hope in short supply. My parents had worked themselves to their deaths trying to scratch out a living from the unforgiving earth, but it was never enough. I'd gone to sleep more nights than I could count with nothing in my stomach but a constant hunger that kept me awake till dawn.

Róstan's winters were the worst. The cold bit into our skin, leaving us numb. The coughs that echoed through the thin walls of our home, the endless rationing of what little food we had. I joined the military because it was the only way to survive. But here, in the unforgiving world of Tárnov, I wonder if all I did was trade one nightmare for another.

I've been walking all day, and my throat is as dry as the bread in our cafeteria. As the sky darkens, I catch a flicker of light down the road. A spark of hope pushes my legs forward, and I quicken my pace toward the glow. As I get closer, I see a wagon, its lanterns shining in the fading light. Someone sits at the front, holding the reins of two horses, and they look up as I approach.

The smile that spreads across his face is a little too slow to reach his eyes, but his voice is smooth and inviting when he says, "Well, well, what do we have here? You look like you've had a rough day, my friend."

I hesitate, every instinct screaming at me to be cautious. Something in the way he's looking at me, too intent, like he's inspecting each crease on my face, makes my skin prickle. But I am too tired to care. "Please," I say, my voice trembling. "I need help. I . . . I don't know where I am."

The person gestures to the back of the wagon. "Hop in. You look like you could use a ride and a good meal."

My mouth waters at his words. A hot meal would be amazing.

I climb into the wagon, my legs barely holding me up. The warmth of the blankets inside is a welcome relief, and the smell of food makes my stomach growl even louder. I settle onto the seat. This wagon isn't the rickety, worn-out kind I'm used to seeing back in Tárnov. The wood looks polished, the seats lined with clean fabric.

The stranger follows and carefully ladles stew from a small pot into a bowl. I'm *so* hungry.

My hands shake as I take the bowl from him, and its heat seeps into my fingers. When I look up, his eyes are fixed on me, unblinking, as I lift the bowl to my lips. He probably made it himself, since he's so eager to see my reaction.

The first sip is rich and savory, and I can't stop myself from drinking more. The soft potatoes melt on my tongue, and I think I'm tasting beans. They're different from the ones we have in the cafeteria. This stranger must be wealthy.

His gaze remains on me. I should express my gratitude.

"Thank you, it's delicious," I say, feeling a bit more at ease with each gulp of the stew. "I . . . I was with my friend, but we got separated. There was a vólkin and . . . and something terrible happened."

The person's left eye twitches. "A vólkin, you say? Fascinating creatures." He watches me intently. "Tell me more. What happened?"

He's talkative too. That's a relief. I can finally talk about everything with someone. I tell the stranger about Arnold,

Noël, and everything that happened. He nods as I speak, makes me feel comfortable. I should ask for his name.

When I finish, he leans back, his eyes narrowing as if he's considering what I've said. If I heard so much nonsense, I wouldn't believe it either.

His voice is almost sympathetic when he finally says, "It sounds like you've been through quite an ordeal. You must be careful, my friend." But his tone changes from one second to the next. "There are dangerous people out there. People who wouldn't hesitate to use someone like you."

Fear twists in my gut. "Who . . . who are you?"

The stranger's smile turns sharp and rigid, as though carved from stone. "Let's just say, I'm someone who keeps an eye on interesting events. And you, dear Gregor, are now part of something much larger than you could ever imagine."

I stiffen. I never told him my name.

"What do you want from me?" Each word tastes bitter in my mouth.

"I want you to continue on your journey," he says, his smile frozen. "Keep doing as you're told, and everything will be fine. But if you think of running or betraying us, well . . ." He leans in. "We have ways of making sure you stay on the right path."

What in the . . . ? He changed so suddenly. How does he know my name!

"No! You know nothing about me!" I shout, louder than intended.

He watches me, expression unchanged, calm, as though amused. "Linnéa . . . still wears that yellow ribbon in her hair, doesn't she?"

At the mention of my sister, my heart clenches painfully. Her face flashes before my eyes. The one person I couldn't bear to lose. I nod quickly, sweat dripping down my forehead, my mouth dry. "I understand."

"Good," the stranger says, leaning on the wall. "Now, rest. You'll need your strength for what's to come."

With shaky hands, I stare at him.

"GO!" he shouts through the window, and the wagon jolts forward.

My heart drops. There are more outside?

The stranger's words echo in my mind, each one sealing my fate. There is no turning back now. I am trapped. With a heavy heart, I lie down among the blankets. My choices are no longer my own.

19

A NEW ROAD, A HEAVY CROSS

"One day, our Noël will begin her path where the veil is
thinnest . . . and in that sacred place, her soul will bind not only
to him, but to something far older than this world."
—Eyleen Ársa

Noël

Moonlight and shadows blur around us, and
Theron's coat rubs between my thighs with his
every stride toward Ávera. I grip his fur tight,
trying to steady myself by focusing on the rhythm of his paws
pounding the earth.

Sometimes it seems like he slows and steals glances at me,
as if he senses it too. I squeeze my eyes shut, my face burning.
Despite my attempts to push the thought aside, it stays, quickening my pulse even more. Theron said he could pick up even
the faintest scents, which means . . . he can likely sense me now.
Goddesses.

I need to put a piece of cloth in at some point. I can't enter vólkin land with so much wetness between my legs. I don't understand any of this.

Every few hours, Theron would pause, letting me stretch and shake the ache from my muscles. Without a word, he'd hand me small bundles of fruits he'd gathered along the way. Even when I insisted I wasn't hungry, he'd hold them out, worry clear in his eyes as he muttered about needing strength for the long day ahead. It was strange, this attention, and unexpected from someone like him, a vólkin warrior. Each time he did it, I couldn't help but think how thoughtful he was. He was trying, really trying to make this journey easier, even with everything stacked against me. Who would've thought a vólkin could be so . . . human?

When I first told him I needed . . . relief, I could barely get the words out, mumbling and stumbling, unsure how to say it. Theron only tilted his head, asking if my stomach hurt, and I wanted to sink into the ground from embarrassment. I tried to explain without saying *the word*, and eventually, his eyes lit up.

"You need to urinate?" he asked, as straightforward as a child.

Goddesses, I just nodded, feeling my face heat even more as he took a few steps back, gestured for me to go ahead, and promised he'd keep me safe. I had to tell him to turn away, and he only looked at me in confusion, his head tilting like a puzzled pup. I told him it was like when I didn't want him to watch me bathe, and he let out a soft "Oh!" and nodded.

It strikes me how primal he is, how even with all his tenderness, he is still a beast. Somehow, though, I almost find it . . . adorable.

Except for the part where he pissed right on my own puddle after I was done. He said that since we aren't fully bonded yet, he needs to have his scent on me at all times. To be honest, I'm too exhausted to argue. It is probably a vólkin thing, and I just . . . I can't.

So, what have I learned so far?

He wags his tail when happy, tilts his head when confused, and pisses on my piss so it smells of him. And all of that with so much confidence, as if everything is normal, like that is simply how things work for him.

For me? I don't know what I think about it. Interesting? Weird? I still can't believe he made me some sort of coat from his fur.

"Theron," I finally say. "Could you let me down?"

He slows, lowering himself with that natural grace of his, his muscles moving beneath his fur like a river in motion.

The moment my boots meet the earth, my legs wobble, unsteady from hours of holding on to him.

I used to ride horses back in Tárnov, but never for so long. A full day of riding, even with breaks, has left me aching. And this was no ordinary ride. Theron is much wider than a horse.

"You alright?" His voice rumbles beside me.

I look up, and he holds my gaze as he rises to his full stature. He is definitely at least twice my height.

I nod, rolling out the tightness in my legs. "Yes, just . . . not used to traveling like this." Or traveling at all, really. The sight of the world sprawling out before me still leaves me in awe—the endless trees, the sky, the shadows over everything.

I expect him to make fun of my inexperience. What warrior would say they're not used to traveling? But he doesn't. He just watches me. Studies me in a way that doesn't make me feel small or weak. If anything, he makes me feel seen, like I'm a person, not a duty or a burden. For all his strength and wildness, there's a gentleness in him that surprises me every time we have the smallest interaction.

He walks beside me, positioning himself just slightly ahead. With every step, he surveys the path, his ears twitching in response to even the quietest sounds around us. I catch myself glancing at him more often than I mean to.

When I breathe in, I taste the crisp night air as my gaze drifts to the horizon, a line of shadowed mystery stretching endlessly before us. "How much farther?" I murmur, half to myself.

"Not long now." Theron's reply is low. "We'll be there soon."

As we walk, my eyes move over the powerful lines of his back and shoulders before lingering on his thick tail swaying with each step. It's funny how he jerked away when I traced my fingers over it. He's surprisingly ticklish for someone so scary, and there's something charming about that tail of his. I stifle a chuckle. How can someone as fierce as Theron have such a fluffy tail?

The forest around us changes as we walk. The trees stretch taller, their trunks twisted and gnarled. They look ancient, as if they've stood here for centuries. Their bark is dark and rough, with tendrils of mist clinging to their roots. The leaves above us glow with the moonlight, and their shadows shift and sway.

Along the path, colorful flowers bloom. Their petals glisten, yet the colors are robust, reds like blood, purples like bruises, and blacks as dark as the night. They're beautiful and haunting all at once, as though they were grown in both light and shadow.

Small, luminous orbs flit around. They leave trails of light that fade into the darkness behind them.

This place is unreal.

I feel like an outsider. How could someone like me be destined for something so grand?

Theron's presence beside me keeps my nerves in check. For now.

"We're almost there," he says. "Just beyond these trees."

As we make our way through the dense forest, the trees gradually part, revealing the entrance to Ávera, and my breath catches in my throat.

Towering, timeless trees, their trunks as wide as houses,

stand like guardians around the village. Their branches weave together high above, creating arches adorned with shining flowers and creeping vines that pulse with light. Streams of crystal-clear water wind through the earth, reflecting the moon's silvery sheen.

The homes, nestled high within the colossal trees, appear to have grown from the wood itself, as if the trees and structures are one and the same. Water flows down from every dwelling, and vines coil around the trunks, creating stairways that spiral upward, leading to platforms and terraces that seem to float among the branches. Clusters of glowing flowers illuminate the pathways with a pale radiance that lights up the faces of those passing by. Of *vólkins* passing by.

The place is a perfect harmony of nature and architecture, where the boundaries between the living forest and the crafted homes blur into one. I try to hold in my countless gasps.

Bridges woven from leaves and vines as wide as carriages stretch between the trees, their surfaces strong, allowing the giant vólkins to move easily between the different levels.

"Theron," I call.

"Yes, little dove."

"I have never seen such beauty," I whisper. The wind flows through my hair, and I turn to him. "This is unbelievable."

"Welcome to Ávera."

A hush falls over the village as we approach, and curious faces turn our way. Vólkins of all ages pause in their activities, their gazes fixed on me. Small vólkin children peek from behind their parents, their wide eyes following my every move as if I were something mythical stepping into their world.

A group of vólkins approaches, their expressions kind and welcoming. A relief, really. If I hadn't met Theron first, I'd probably be running for my life at the sight of them. They're all so large and imposing, covered in thick fur, and their presence makes me want to retreat.

The one leading them comes forward, bowing with the others. "Your Majesty, welcome home," he says, his tone respectful, though, is he holding back a grin?

Golden-brown fur covers him completely, and he has white crystals on his forehead, shaped in a V just like Theron's. He's tall and lean, his build more athletic than Theron's bulk, with a line of fur along the top of his head that stands up slightly. Do all vólkins style their . . . fur? Hair? Theron's looks styled too.

He studies me with icy-blue eyes, a color I've never seen in any human.

"I am Kaël, one of the warriors of Ávera. We've been expecting you, Your Majesty."

Will I ever get used to being called *Your Majesty*? The goddess called me *Ethereal Leader*, and Theron agreed without hesitation. And now, hearing it from Kaël, it's clear they all know. They don't look the least bit surprised by the title. But what unsettles me is the way they're looking at me. Back in Tárnov, my soldiers look at me because they're afraid to look away. But these vólkins . . . they're curious. Of course they wouldn't be afraid of me. Between us, I'd be the first to run. But still, it makes me uneasy. Their eyes studying every part of my existence.

I clear my throat and turn my gaze back to this Kaël vólkin. "It's an honor meeting you, Kaël, and everyone else. My name is Noël."

Kaël grins, stealing glances between Theron and me. "It is my pleasure."

"They all came to welcome you, little dove," Theron says.

"I'm glad you two are already lovey-dovey," Kaël says, baring his fangs in a . . . smile?

My face heats up instantly, and I'm caught between embarrassment and the need to flee, not entirely sure how to respond.

Kaël turns to Theron, his grin widening. "Welcome back, Theron."

Kaël leads us farther into this unbelievable place, with Theron close beside me. I'm glad he stays near. He's the only one here I know, the only one I can somewhat trust in this strange and beautiful lair of beasts.

"This is the communal gathering area," Kaël says, gesturing to a large open space with stone benches arranged in a circle. "Here, we share stories, hold meetings, and celebrate our traditions."

Why would vólkins need benches?

I imagine this place filled with giant vólkins sharing their tales under the open sky. There's an air of timelessness here, as if countless generations have gathered in this spot.

It makes me feel like this place has been standing strong since creation.

As we continue walking, I notice more details. Hidden within the massive trees are archways carved directly into the trunks, blending so perfectly with the wood's natural patterns that they almost vanish if you don't know where to look. Small shrines, adorned with offerings of flowers and stones that seem lit from within, rest in corners as though they are part of the forest's very soul. Each shrine is the shape of a small, wooden figure. Intrigued, I lean in to examine one of them. The figure's face and decorative patterns are beautifully carved into the wood.

"These are crafted to honor the goddesses," Kaël explains, watching me. "Each shrine is shaped in their likeness."

"For example, Vodínaya, goddess of healing and endurance, loves the water. So our ancestors carved waves into the wood," Theron says.

I study the carved face. Its expression looks like it's

watching over the forest. Tiny patterns spiral across every figure. Spirals and lines. And small faces.

Following Kaël to one of the bridges, I'm aware of the other vólkins moving around us. Each one is so heavy, their steps make the wood tremble with their weight. They're all so large, but even among them, Theron stands out as the most commanding looking. The vólkins bowed to us, but was it because of me, the so-called ethereal leader, or was it for him as well? Perhaps Theron holds a place among them that I have yet to understand.

Theron brushes his fingers over my back and draws my attention to a small group of vólkin children playing nearby. They chase after small, luminous orbs floating through the air. Their laughter is the most precious thing I've ever heard. It's been so long since I've heard laughter like this, a sound so pure and alive. I feel a warmth I haven't felt in years.

"The cubs are taught to respect and care for the spirits of the forest from a young age," Theron explains. "It's a crucial part of our culture."

"They're very sweet," I murmur as they jump and run, giggling in delight.

"They are," he whispers near my ear, close enough to send a thrill down my neck.

He did *not* have to whisper it like that.

One of the tiny glowing spirits darts in my direction, and the cubs follow, their eyes wide and excited as they chase the orb. Suddenly, more spirits fly over, circling me, each one a small ball of light that glides around me like a dream. I can hardly believe this is real.

"Children! Do not disturb Her Majesty," calls a gentle voice. "She has only just arrived. Show some respect."

I turn toward the sound to see a beautiful vólkin female approaching. She's smaller than the male vólkins, with dreamy gray fur and the most stunning green eyes I've ever seen—an earthy, vibrant shade that seems to hold the warmth of the forest. Wildflowers are woven through her fur, and a small crystal necklace rests at her mane.

Although she doesn't have crystals on her forehead like the others. I wonder why.

"I am so sorry!" she says, bowing low. "They've never seen a human before, let alone our leader."

The little ones pause, staring up at me with wide-eyed awe.

"Don't worry." I smile, glancing back at her. "I already adore them."

Theron rests a paw on one cub's head and introduces the female vólkin. "This is Mina," he says. "She's a healer and the one who educates the pups."

"We're honored to have you here, Your Majesty." Her voice is so warm, like a gentle melody.

I return her smile. "It is my pleasure, Mina."

"This is our sacred glade," Kaël explains as we move past a serene area. "A place for reflection and communion with the goddesses. It's where we come to seek guidance and strength. We perform most of our rituals right here."

Goose bumps prick my skin. This is where I'll be able to speak to the goddesses. My eyes sweep across the glade, taking in the sight before me. Ancient trees encircle the space, their branches growing together to form a natural dome, the moonlight seeping through in silver rays. The ground is covered in a plush carpet of moss, its vibrant green color shining.

At the center of the glade stands a stone altar. It's adorned with strange carvings—spirals, runes, and symbols that throb with an ageless feel as if the goddesses themselves carved them. The sight makes my heart race. *This is where I will find my answers.*

As the night deepens, Kaël brings us to a large, tree-covered area with several platforms woven into the branches.

"These will be your quarters. Theron worked hard on this place." He winks.

"Thank you, Kaël." I turn my gaze to Theron. Did he build this house? "This place is truly incredible."

Kaël smiles. "Rest well, Your Majesty. Tomorrow, you will meet the elder and begin to understand your role in the prophecy."

As I walk in, I admire the beautiful home. The path ahead feels overwhelming, but soon, I will be able to talk to the goddesses and ask about my mother. Ask for directions. For anything, really.

20

A HOUSE FOR TWO, A STORM WITHIN

"To scent her is a right, not a reward. But to have her, you must first be the male who would burn for her and never touch."
—Elder Aïna

Theron

"I brought you some broth with meat. You've only been eating fruits and berries for a little while," I say as I step into our home. The word *home* feels right now, especially with her in it. The space is grand, befitting her status. Although I didn't know I'd be the mate of the leader, I knew my mate would have the fanciest home. The walls are constructed from broad branches and leaves, sturdy and alive, as all things in the world should be. Cozy mats cover the floors, woven for my mate's comfort, and the room is lit with clusters of glowing flowers and large crystals embedded in the walls, their facets reflecting colors that dance across the room and their soft brilliance creating warmth I hope makes her feel welcomed.

I worked hard to grow this place, with her in mind even before I met her face-to-face. Seeing her here, sitting within these walls, was once just a dream. But now, she's here, real and within reach. She fits like she belongs. I wonder what she thinks of it all—of Ávera, of her new home.

"Thank you," she says, her eyes lighting up at the sight of the bowl. One of the many bowls I carved, a skill I honed for her. The first few were uneven, far from perfect. I imagine she's used to finer things made by human hands.

"I didn't know you cook," she says, her eyes following me. "Considering you're . . . well, some type of wolf, don't you eat the meat raw?"

"We do," I say, placing the bowl in front of her, the aroma of herbs and meat wafting between us. "But we've learned human ways, preparing for your arrival, knowing one day you'd come to Ávera."

Her eyes widen.

"All the homes you saw earlier," I continue, "they're built for your comfort. Our males have been growing them for ages."

She pauses, glancing around the room, then leaning forward. "Growing them? How do you grow houses?"

"Energy transfer," I say with pride. "The better a vólkin masters this skill, the more he can connect with nature—bend it, shape it, and make it grow. Those who have mastered it," I add, a grin spreading on my mouth, "can grow anything. Flowers, vines, even homes like this from the very bark of trees."

Her eyes travel across the walls and over the curves where branches and leaves blend into the structure.

"But not every vólkin can do this," I say, watching her closely as my chest puffs.

"This is incredible," she whispers.

Vines, heavy with blossoms, drape from the ceiling like a canopy, filling the air with their sweet scent. The furniture, made from the strongest, healthiest wood I could find, is adorned with luxurious cushions and silky furs from my hunts. It invites her to relax.

With me.

A stream flows along one side of the room, its clear water shimmering with tiny luminescent stones like scattered stars at the bottom, and small orbs float above, pulsing like fireflies.

Every piece, every detail, has been chosen and shaped for her, to be a place worthy of her. My mate will *always* have the best of everything.

"I'm glad you like it," I say, keeping my voice steady. I should try to stay composed. "If there's anything else you need, anything I might've missed, let me know. I've done what I could, but our knowledge of human ways is limited, given that we've been isolated behind the barrier for over four centuries."

She glances at me. "You've adapted so much . . . All this, just in preparation?"

I nod, feeling those long years, the waiting, the learning. "We always knew the day would come that our lives would be shared with our mates." I sit beside her, close enough to catch the warmth from her body. "So, we've studied your customs, your needs, and prepared ourselves."

Noël takes a spoonful of the broth, and her face softens as the warmth spreads through her. "This is delicious," she murmurs. "You've all gone to so much trouble for me."

"You are worth every effort."

While she eats, I step outside to check on my warriors. Two of them stand guard, one on either side of the porch, while a few others patrol the surrounding area. With the barrier gone, we must be ready for anything.

"How lucky can one be?" Zephyr says, nodding toward the house.

Kaël leans in. "Human females are so tiny. Are they supposed to be like that?" His eyes are wide, genuinely perplexed.

I chuckle, shaking my head. "Yes, they're small, but don't let their size fool you. Their strength lies in their spirit."

Kaël's expression shifts, and he lowers his voice. "Do you think the other humans will accept us too? I can't wait to meet my mate. I'm both happy and jealous!" He sways his hips from side to side, wrapping his arms around himself as if already embracing his mate.

Zephyr sighs and places a paw on his forehead. "Kaël, control yourself."

I smirk. "You were so serious when you explained Ávera to my mate earlier, I almost didn't recognize you."

Kaël rolls his eyes. "Just because I can be serious when it counts doesn't mean I'm not allowed a little excitement."

Every vólkin longs for the day they'll meet their mate, and I understand their impatience well. We've spent centuries preparing, trying to understand human customs, hoping we'd be ready to welcome our mates and honor them.

I gesture to Kaël and Zephyr to follow me, and together, we walk into the heart of Ávera. The night is still, yet the air feels charged, alive with the energy of our people. Vólkins are gathered across the land, unable to sleep, drawn by the promise of change. As we pass, they bow, and I feel the awe in their gazes.

They feel it as I do—the shift in our world, the beginning of something new.

I acknowledge each vólkin, exchanging greetings. Some aren't warriors, only residents of Ávera who now share in this anticipation.

One elder walks up to me. "Balance is close, Theron. May the goddesses bless us with strong cubs and harmony." His words echo others I've heard throughout the night, a longing for unity and restoration.

Another, a younger vólkin with bright eyes, murmurs as we pass, "You've brought our leader home, Theron. May her presence heal the land."

I nod in response. Their hopes are on my shoulders, and I will bear them all.

We approach the council room where two guards stand at attention by the entrance. They bow low as I come close, paws pressed to their hearts, and then step aside to allow us through. I meet their eyes before crossing the threshold with Kaël and Zephyr at my sides.

Inside, my warriors stand tall, their postures straight, attention fixed on me. These are the warriors who stood with me on our last patrol, each of them prepared and loyal, ready to face the unknown at my command. These are the finest of Ávera.

"Brothers," I begin as I move toward the council table, "today marks the start of a new era for Ávera. The arrival of our leader—of Her Majesty—and the fall of the barrier have set events in motion. Everything will change."

I see a spark in their eyes, pride, eagerness, hunger. These warriors have prepared for years, just as I have, for this exact moment.

"The outside world is open to us now, and with it come new challenges. We must be cautious. The humans may not yet know the barrier is gone, but it won't stay that way. We stand as Ávera's shield, its protectors, and we will ensure our territory remains secure," I say, narrowing my gaze. "I hope I'm being clear."

The warriors straighten further, each one pressing a paw firmly to their heart.

"Reports from the borders," I command.

Zephyr speaks first. "We found remnants of a campfire near the edge of the barrier. The embers were still warm when we arrived, suggesting it was abandoned not long before. Around it, blackened stones were arranged in strange patterns . . . ritualistic, maybe."

Rituals, so close to our borders—not a good sign.

Another warrior speaks, his brow furrowed. "We found footprints, Theron, clearly human, leading in and out from the area. But there were no signs of a struggle. Whoever they were, they were careful."

I meet his gaze, clenching my jaw. "Yet not careful enough to cover their tracks."

Kaël steps forward, his earlier lightheartedness gone. "There's more, Theron. We picked up the scent of dried blood nearby. Strong enough to linger, but no sign of a body. No trails to follow either."

A low growl rumbles from the assembled warriors. They share in my unease. The scent of blood with no clear source could only mean one thing: magic. And dark intentions.

Orïon crosses his arms. "I think it was human blood."

Zephyr nods. "The air felt strange. Even the forest around the campsite felt . . . different, like it had resisted whatever ritual was practiced there."

"For so long, we've known only the stories from our elders about the lands beyond the barrier. But now, with these strange scents, these ritualistic markings . . . It's clear that whoever came here had a purpose."

The warriors exchange uneasy glances, some shuffle on their paws, some lean on the table.

"We'll have to investigate further," I continue. "I want to understand what we're dealing with before it encroaches on Ávera. Elder Aïna has a greater understanding of the world outside our lands. I'll go with her to the site and uncover what I can."

I pause. The new moon marks new beginnings, the time to honor our leader's arrival with the welcome ceremony. It's vital, especially with my mate's doubts, that everything goes perfectly. Any delay could threaten the order until the bonding ritual.

I take a breath. "No, I've changed my mind. Three will accompany Elder Aïna to the border. Ívar, Yoren . . ." I pause, assessing the warriors before me. "And Nér, you'll lead the patrol. Report every detail back to me by dawn."

The three nod in unison.

"Until then," I add, "we maintain our watch. All of you, keep your senses sharp and track every movement, every sound. If you catch the scent of blood or magic again, report it to me immediately. Ávera is our sacred home, and we will not allow this new world to darken it."

The warriors press their paws over their hearts, and so do I.

"We are protectors first," I say, meeting each of their eyes in turn. "For Ávera, for our leader, and for the future of our people."

Without a moment's pause, the warriors tilt their heads back, ready to release a howl. But I lift a paw, a small smile tugging at the corner of my mouth.

"Hold it," I say. "I'd rather not startle our new leader—at least not tonight." I lower my paw, and a few of them grin. "There will be time for howling soon enough," I add, my smile widening. "For now, let's keep it calm. My mate is adjusting. Let's not make her wonder what kind of beasts she's come to live with."

I roll my shoulders, the tension easing with each slow circle.

"Get ready for tomorrow," I say to bring them back to focus. "It's a big day for all of us. Make sure Mina meets with my mate in the morning."

My mind pulls back to Noël as soon as I dismiss them. I haven't left her side for long, and already, I feel her absence like a hollow space. Tomorrow will be difficult, I can hardly bear to be away from her now. I spent a mere two days with her.

Time to go home. To our home.

I stride back toward our quarters, very excited to see her again. As I walk in, I'm met with a sight that roots me to the spot.

There she is, sitting in the stream, facing me, *completely bare.* The glow from the stones dances over her skin, every part of her bathed in the soft light. Instantly, my cock twitches, the need to be inside her threatening to be the death of me.

"Theron!" she gasps. Her gaze falls to my unsheathing shaft, and a flush rises on her cheeks as she averts her eyes. "What are you doing here?" Her voice is small and flustered as she sinks down into the water.

"Can't a vólkin enter his own home?" I tease, unable to hold back a smirk.

She presses her lips together, looking everywhere but at me. "I thought you went to . . . to your own house," she mumbles, moving closer to the edge of the stream to hide herself.

Stepping farther in, I chuckle and shake my head. "This is my house, little mate. Our house."

Her blush deepens. How can a furless species be so arousing?

"Wait here," I say, walking away. My cock only grows from her scent filling the room. It's the best feeling a vólkin could have—a mate's scent that consumes everything.

I want her to sit on every plush and every fur. To walk in every corner so that, wherever I go, her scent will meet my snout.

Moments later, I return with a small wooden container in my paws, which I open to reveal a dark paste. The fragrant scent of herbs fills the air.

She looks at me, eyes round and curious. "What is that?"

"It's a blend we use to clean ourselves," I explain, kneeling beside the stream. "Herbal ash with oils from the forest. Let me help you wash your hair."

My mate looks hesitant, moving back in the stream, only to return to where she was as she realizes that moving away gives me an even better view. "You don't have to, Theron . . ."

I hold her gaze. "I want to."

She furrows her brows, then slowly turns her back to me as

she sinks farther into the water. I watch as she settles, her muscles easing under the warm stream. Every part of her is so unlike my own kind—her skin, smooth and flushed, her defined muscles that speak of her strength. My fingers itch with the need to reach, to feel her, to explore each and every part before my eyes.

I dip into the herbal paste and rub it between my paws to create foam. Leaning forward, I let my breath graze her exposed skin, and goose bumps rise along her shoulders and arms, her reaction as immediate as my own. Slowly, I bring my paws to her scalp, the sensation unfamiliar and electrifying as her silky strands slip between my claws. It's so different from the thick texture of my own fur.

As I begin massaging, I watch every change in her expression, the way her brows unfurl and her eyes close in relief. Noël lets out a quiet moan as she leans back into my touch. *What a sweet sound.*

"This feels wonderful," she says. Her soft, airy voice, her little moan . . . they do nothing to ease the strain of my arousal. My balls swell between my thighs, a deep ache building, pressing me to claim what's mine.

"Theron?" Her voice melts me, soft and so tentative.

"Yes, my mate?" My claws glide slowly across her scalp, each movement is like a battle to maintain control even as my heart pounds like thunder.

She tilts her head, exposing her neck, the bare, vulnerable curve inviting me to sink my fangs deep while I pump into her. "You said only mates can scent each other." She's testing me, knowing the effect she has on me. She has to know. She has seen my leaking cock a thousand times already.

"I did." Sliding my fingers from behind her ear, down along her neck, I feel every curve, every line, before moving back up. Her skin is impossibly smooth.

"Did you know I can sense your scent too?" She tilts her

head back farther, her eyes meeting mine, bright and unguarded. This is dangerous.

"Oh really?" I grin, though my voice comes out rough.

Calm down.

"You smell like blue roses ... mm-hmm ... just like from my mother's garden."

Her words are followed by another soft moan, her breaths deepening. Each sound, each movement, tightens the tension in me until it's unbearable.

"And what do you think of my scent?" I ask, my voice barely a whisper as I lean down, my breath warm against her ear.

"It makes me feel safe," she breathes. "And ..."

"What else?" I press, leaning closer, the tip of my nose grazing her temple as I move to the other side of her neck.

Her breath catches, and when she manages to respond, her voice is featherlight. "And ..."

I catch the faintest hint of her arousal, and it hits me like a punch to my aching sac. Her scent is everywhere, seeping into every breath, making it impossible to think of anything but her. My cock throbs, pulsing so fiercely it's torture.

"Noël." My voice is rough. "I need to step out."

Her eyes lift to mine. "Why?"

"Because," I say, standing, forcing the words out as my gaze moves anywhere but her, "if I stay any longer, I won't be able to control myself."

She has no time to react before I move, crossing the room in a few strides. I throw open the door and step out before shutting it hard behind me, my claws piercing the wood as I grip it for stability. My body trembles. Her scent is maddening, filling my mind with sights of her—waiting, wanting. She is aroused. She feels it *too*.

The cool night air brushes my face, but it does nothing to ease the tightness in my shaft, the beast roaring inside me, the urge to claim what's mine. I grit my teeth, press back against the door, feel the pain. I have to wait. I need to. She's there, but I can't. Not yet.

"Theron?" One of the guards approaches. "Is everything . . . alright?"

I force myself to answer, though my breaths come out ragged. "Everything's fine."

He squints as he steps even closer. "You don't look—"

"Do NOT get near the house," I snarl.

They stare at me, taken aback by the sharpness in my tone. Without another word, I shove away from the door and run. The night air whips against my fur as I push myself, the burn in my chest is a relief to the ache everywhere else. I need distance. Control. The forest blurs as I force myself faster, every step a fight against the raw instinct driving me back to my mate.

She is in the stream, bare and aroused. *My mate* is aroused.

I won't lose myself, not tonight. But her scent is on my fur, between my claws, and it only drives me to run harder, to find the calm I need. For her sake and for my own.

21

A BRAID OF THREE

"The body may hunger, the mind may wander, but only the soul can choose the path of becoming. She who braids all three shall awaken the world."
—Láda Veléša, Goddess of Leadership and War

Noël

Oh goddesses, what is wrong with me?

Every time he's close, my body betrays me. His touch was so gentle, so . . . caring, as though his paws could calm and ignite me all at once. I've never felt this way before, this pull toward someone, especially someone like him. So powerful and intense, so much more than human. It's confusing, and yet, I find myself craving it. Craving *him*.

You can't, Noël. What is going on with you? Since when do you even use such words? Craving?

When he touched me—running those claws through my hair, moving closer, breathing in my scent—it felt as if he were peeling back all my walls, seeing me in a way no one else ever has. His eyes were full of something so warm, something so protective. They held none of the harshness, none of the empty lust I've seen in the men back in Tárnov.

But he's not human. That truth clouds everything else. He's vólkin. He's unlike anyone or anything I've been taught to want, and yet . . . that difference only draws me in more.

Back in Tárnov, I thought I knew what men were: harsh, self-serving, built more on ego than on character. I've seen so many of them, lined up in the barracks, in the army—muscles and raised voices, but no tenderness. No care. They were all so unappealing, so predictable, and whatever curiosity I might have had died under their gazes. I could never imagine myself with any of them.

But Theron? He's the opposite of everything I've known. His strength is real, his power silent, and he's twice the size of any man in Tárnov. His fur, so thick and warm, is unexpectedly soft, something I want to curl into—

I'm losing it.

Also, there's . . . *that.* His reaction every time we're close, the way his body responds to me. I can see his arousal, see it in the way he moves, the way he fights to control himself. It's thrilling. The effect I have on him is exciting, and it makes me feel powerful in a way I've never felt before. I may have felt powerful every time I stood in front of my soldiers, but this is a different kind of powerful.

I am *not* supposed to enjoy this.

Part of me is terrified by it, by the strength of his desire and my own, but another part—deep down, hidden far away—wants to be the cause of it. Wants to explore it. Wants him to lose control, just for a moment. But one moment leads to another. I can't have that.

Can I?

I don't understand why this feels so *right*, but maybe what he said is true. Maybe it's the bond he speaks of, this connection that ties us together, binding us in ways I can't understand.

But if this bond is what draws me to him, why does it feel like I'm choosing it?

The goddesses are playing with my mind. But he also smells of blue roses . . . No one else does.

My fingers trace where his nose brushed against my neck, and I close my eyes. I can still feel his warm breath. His tail hit the floor with rhythmic thumps. Why is that so . . . precious?

My hand slides down to cup my breast. I imagine how his giant paw might feel on me. It'd probably cover my whole torso. A shiver runs through me as I sink into the water, letting my head fall back. My other hand moves lower, slipping between my legs, where the tension burns hottest. The sensation is good, but it's never enough. The release I crave always feels just out of reach, teasing and retreating, leaving me more frustrated every time.

I tried exploring deeper once before, slipping a finger in, but the pain stopped me.

My mother never prepared me for this. We never spoke of it, only filled my days with other lessons, leaving me to figure this part out on my own. And here I am, at an age where other women in Tárnov are long married, all with children, while I'm left fumbling through this mystery, still uncertain.

What would Theron do to me?

The thought sends heat through me yet again, raises a flush of shame. His touch alone was incredible. In Tárnov, I never once felt this way. The men there . . . they're all the same, so much like Arnold—cruel eyes, harsh hands, eager to dominate, eager to remind a woman she's nothing more than property. I'd never seen a happy wife or a happy daughter, only women whose spirits were trapped and fading, told to obey, to accept their place.

Marriage was something to escape from, not a dream. My only path out was the military, where I could at least hold a weapon and stand on my own two feet. Love, intimacy, all of it felt like a trap, something that could destroy everything I'd worked to become.

But Theron . . .

A part of me wants to trust him and let down my guard. But the battle inside me won't allow it, fear and longing clashing until I'm torn apart, like two halves of me can't decide which will win.

The warmth of the water slips from my skin as I climb out of the stream and wrap myself in a heavy fur I find nearby. It smells of Theron, earthy, like blue roses from Mother's garden after rain.

I can finally look around without Theron distracting me. This house is *alive*. The walls, a weaving of branches and leaves, seem to stretch if I look too long. It's as though the trees are watching me as I watch them. I had a similar feeling in the forest.

The glow of flowers and stones dapples the room, and the light softens the edges of everything. I look back at the stream, noticing how it weaves in and out of the breathing walls. Like from one branch to another. How is it warm?

My gaze settles on a small puddle near the stream, right where Theron washed my hair.

Oh dear goddesses.

Shaking my head, I force myself to move, taking slow steps toward the sitting area. Theron created this place for me, and I can feel his effort in everything.

My eyes trace over the carvings on the furniture, vines and leaves etched in beautiful patterns, each detail too perfect to be casual. Theron didn't just build this house, he poured himself into it. And that thought, of him working, carving, shaping it to be so beautiful for me, makes my chest warm. I trace my fingers over the grooves. I wonder if he thought of me with each stroke, if he imagined what it might mean for me to sit here, to call this place home.

Home.

The word tastes foreign. This home isn't mine. It doesn't matter how beautiful it is or how carefully it was made. It only highlights what I've lost—the kitchen shelves packed with my mother's herbs and charms, the warmth of her presence in every corner. Here, the shelves are bare, waiting for me to fill them, but I can't bring myself to make this space my own. It feels like accepting something I'm not ready for. Like admitting that what I had is truly gone.

I wander to the cabinet, open it. Inside, there's nothing but earthy soap—his soap. I lift one of the containers, raising it to my nose. Did he think I'd like this? Did he wonder if it would remind me of him when he wasn't here?

Finally, I turn toward the bed, a nest of furs and blankets so inviting, it might swallow me whole. I sigh.

It's too much. Every detail in this house is too much. Too much effort, too much care, too much expectation. And yet, standing here, wrapped in a fur that smells like him, surrounded by his work, his hard work, I've never felt so alone.

It's so quiet here.

It was quiet *there* too.

Back in Tárnov, I knew how to endure loneliness. I knew how to build walls around myself, to survive without the warmth of connection. But this place that breathes with life makes the absence of my mother, of everything I've lost, unbearable.

My pulse quickens with the urge to leave and find him when I look at the door. I want to ask why he did all this, why he would go to such lengths for someone he doesn't even know.

I'm his mate.

I shake my head again. I don't need to think about him. Yes, he's great. So far, he's shown me nothing but kindness. But I'm here for a different reason.

I glance back at the door, taking a few steps closer.

Furrowing my brows, I look down at my body. The fur is wrapped tight, I know it won't slip. Besides, all the vólkins I've seen were bare. But then again, Theron's eyes widened when he saw *me* bare.

I tighten the fur into a firm knot and open the door.

As I step out of the house, the cool night air brushes against my skin. The forest hums in the distance, and I feel freedom. For a couple seconds.

Two vólkins stand near the entrance, their giant forms silhouetted against the glow of the flowers and the barely noticeable moon. As they see me, both bow low, their paws pressed to their chests in that gesture of respect I've yet to grow accustomed to. I'm still wet down there . . . Can they tell? Oh goddesses.

"Your Majesty," one of them says. "Are you going on a walk?"

A walk? The thought hadn't crossed my mind, but now that he mentions it, it feels like exactly what I should say. So I nod.

I had no idea there were guards. They're so quiet.

The two vólkins exchange a glance, subtle, but I catch it. Then the other speaks. "My apologies, but Theron has instructed us to keep you safe. Please, allow us to accompany you."

My brows knit together. "No," I say, shaking my head. "I'll be fine on my own."

I don't need nursemaids.

The first vólkin hesitates, his ears twitching as he glances at his companion. "I truly apologize, but w—"

"Am I not your leader?" I interrupt, taking a step toward them.

Both vólkins straighten, their eyes wide. "Of course . . . of course you are," the second stammers.

"Then why am *I* hearing orders?" I cross my arms, meeting their startled gazes. "Isn't my word enough? Or is Theron's word stronger than mine?" My challenge hangs heavy in the air, and I watch as panic draws across their faces.

Their silence already feels like a victory, but I go on. "Then stay here and guard the house."

They both stiffen, straightening even more, as though I just issued a royal decree.

"As you wish," one of them murmurs, bowing once more.

Without another word, I turn and stride into the village, my heart pounding in my chest.

Well, that was easy.

The soft thuds of my bare feet on the earth fill the silence as I walk away, leaving the two vólkins behind.

I can't help the small satisfaction curling in my chest. But it's fleeting. Their wide-eyed stares and the unspoken tension between us stay. I got what I wanted, but was it too much?

Ávera is quiet as I slip through the shadows of the impossibly large trees. Their massive trunks stretch high into the night, their grand branches giving me cover, though I know it's hardly enough. The fur wrap clings close to my body, shielding me from the cool air as I walk.

They'll sense me anyway, the vólkins, if not by scent then by sound. I can't escape that, but I won't make it easy. Not when I'm this close.

Why do I feel as if I'm doing something wrong?

Theron wanted the guards to be with me all the time. What for? Would other vólkins want to hurt me? That's unlikely. The two guards listened to me even though they've known me for a whole five minutes.

The faint bubbling of water trickles through the air. Vines draped in dew shimmer under the light of the glowing orbs that hover between the trees. It's a breathtaking sight, one that should be calming, but instead, it tightens something inside me. The village seems to sleep, it's peaceful. It's the perfect moment. If anyone is awake, they're hidden away.

I glance upward, catching glimpses of the homes nestled high above, their outlines blending into the branches and leaves. Water spills from their edges in thin streams and flows down to the earth like veins feeding life into this place.

So each home has its own water stream.

Alright. Focus. Where was th—

The sacred glade. I feel its pull before I see it—a hum in the air, a whisper threading through the trees. Kaël's words echo in my mind. "This is where we speak to the goddesses."

I quicken my steps, running between the ancient trunks, my breath shallow but controlled. *Quiet, Noël, stay quiet.*

If Theron placed guards near the glade, they'll sense me soon enough. For now, the silence is on my side.

If I don't do this now, I don't know when I'll be able to.

Waiting for permission, for the perfect moment, it's not an option. There's too much I need to know, too many unanswered questions. The prophecy. My mother. Why she left me with nothing but riddles and a hollow strength that barely holds me together.

The glow ahead grows brighter, the trees thinning as they give way to a clearing bathed in silvery light. The sacred glade.

I swallow hard, my grip tightening on the fur wrapped around me.

This is why I came. To demand answers. To face whatever power dwells here. To stand before the goddesses, if they'll listen.

I force my feet forward, stepping into the light.

A massive, ancient stone, its surface etched with carvings. The spirals and symbols feel alive, pulsing with radiance, and yet, there's no one here. Just me.

My shoulders slump, and I force myself to move closer, then stop in front of the stone. It is so massive I have to lift my chin to see the top. I take a shaky breath, clutching the fur tighter around me. I should say something. I should . . . try.

For my mother.

"I'm here," I start, my voice breaking the silence. "I . . . I'm here to seek your guidance." The words feel strange in my mouth, like I'm speaking into a void. "I need help. Please."

The glade stays silent. The weight in the air doesn't change. Alright, that wasn't enough.

I take another step, my voice rising. "I don't know what I'm supposed to do. I don't understand any of this. I don't—" I stop, my throat tightening as I try to gather myself.

I swallow hard, my gaze falling to the ground before I force it back up to the carvings. The lines in the stone look sharper now, and the weight in my chest grows heavier. "I don't know what's happening. I don't know why—why any of this is happening to me. Someone took her from me. Someone *took* her." My fists clench around the fur as I take a shuddering breath.

"My mother—she was all I had. She was everything to me." The words pour out before I can stop them. "She . . . she prepared me for everything, but not for this. Not for what it would feel like to lose her. Not for the emptiness she left me with."

I blink back the tears that sting my eyes. "You let her die. You let her die without telling me why, without telling me what I'm supposed to do. And now, I'm here. Alone. And I don't even know if I'm strong enough for this." Anger and desperation take over as my tears finally break free to streak down my cheeks.

"Please," I whisper. "Please, I'm begging you. Just let me know what happened to her. Tell me who did this to her. Tell me why. Tell me something. Anything."

I squeeze my eyes shut, my voice breaking as I speak again. "I'll do it. I'll fulfill your prophecy. I'll do whatever it takes. Just . . . just let me do this one thing for her. Please."

I stand, my chest tight, my tears falling freely, staring at the ancient stone and its silence. I wait. But nothing comes. *It's not fair.*

"Most souls do not know who they are."

My eyes snap open. I turn around, my heart pounding. An elder vólkin female stands at the edge of the glade, her figure slender and quiet against the luminous orbs floating in the air.

My stomach drops. I've been caught.

The silver of her fur gleams, streaked with white, a clear sign of her age. Her eyes, white and without pupils, are unnerving yet strangely wise. Crystals adorn her forehead, white as well. She is unlike anything I've seen. She's not like Mina, nothing like the vólkins I've met so far. There's something about her, something . . . timeless. *The other vólkin females didn't have crystals.* Though her crystals seem larger than Theron's.

"I am Noël Ársa," I manage to say, trying to steady my voice, though I feel small under her scrutiny.

"No," she replies, her tone firm and calm, as though correcting a child. "These are just names. Two words. That is not who you are. That is what you are called."

Her words confuse me, and I frown. "What do you mean?"

"When someone says their name, their status, their role, it means they do not know who they are," she says, her presence growing more commanding. "My name is Aïna, but that is not who I am. Your name is Noël because your parents called you that. But it is not you."

I blink, caught off guard by the statement. My mind scrambles to process what she's saying. She lifts a paw and gestures to herself. "You could say I am a vólkin, that I have fur, fangs, claws. But that isn't me. It is my body."

She moves closer. I find myself frozen, unable to look away. "You do not say, 'my fur is hungry,' do you?" she continues. "You say, 'I am hungry. I am sleepy.' So, tell me, who is 'I'?"

I can't find an answer. My lips part, but nothing comes out.

She watches me, and then, slowly, she lifts her arms. The floating orbs that light the glade gather near her paws, drawn to her like moths to a flame. They hover, pulsing as though listening to her.

"We are spiritual creatures," she says. "And we must seek the answer to this question: Who are we really? We have physical bodies, but because we lack awareness of who we truly are, our minds remain trapped in the physical world. We let what is outside of us—circumstances, fears, others—control us."

The orbs float from her paws to circle around my body. The glow feels warm, like sunlight kissing my skin, and something inside me burns. It's not just warmth, it's . . . A hum. A vibration.

"Most earthly souls are simply reacting to life, not living it at all," Aïna says.

What is she saying? What does she mean?

Before I can find the words to respond, she takes another step forward, her gaze locked on mine. Her tone softer now, gentler, when she asks, "Do humans still wear braids?"

The question takes me by surprise, but I nod. "Yes. Most girls start wearing them at seven. It's a tradition in Tárnov, the village I come from."

Aïna's white, pupilless eyes hold mine. "And do you know why?"

"Not really."

She hums, motioning for me to turn.

I hesitate but comply, feeling her claws brush through my damp hair.

"May I?" she asks.

"Yes."

Her paws move slowly, delicately gathering the strands. Her claws don't snag or scrape my scalp but glide through my hair as she begins to braid it. It's so soothing. It is strange, this feeling. Mother used to braid my hair when I was a child. Once, she even wove blue roses from our garden into the braid, complimenting how thick my hair is.

It hurts so much to remember that.

"In a braid, there are three parts," Aïna begins, her voice low and gentle, like the hum of the glade itself, "woven tightly together. It is a symbol of balance—body, mind, and soul."

I glance down at the ground, moving my toes.

"Each strand alone is weak," she says. "Fragile. But together, they become something strong. Whole. Complete."

"No one ever told me that," I admit.

She hums again, this time even quieter, almost amused. "Most do not know. They follow tradition without understanding its purpose. But you are not like most, Noël. You carry the weight of knowing. And that weight can break you, or it can guide you."

As Aïna finishes the braid, she drapes it over my shoulder. Her paw stays there for a few moments before she steps around to face me. She looks at the braid, sleek and smooth under my fingers, then into my eyes.

"This is who we are. And when we begin to understand that," she says, taking my hand in her paw, "we begin to understand that the world knows only one word. Yes."

I glance down at our hands . . . and paws, then back at her face. I stare at her, then at the orbs still circling me, their glow reflecting in her pale eyes. "My mother used to say that I must master my body, mind, and soul."

Aïna tilts her head, her expression remaining calm, though her white eyes seem to sharpen. "She knew that?"

"Yes," I say, nodding as I look away, my fingers still brushing the braid. "She used to say it when she worked in our garden. She always seemed to know so much, more than I ever realized. And now . . ." My throat tightens. "Now I'm only beginning to understand how much she knew, and she's not here anymore."

"It is rare for humans to hold on to such wisdom. Most of your kind lost their connection to spirit long ago."

"She did. She knew so much," I murmur. "But she never told me everything. She always spoke in riddles or gave me pieces of things I didn't understand. And now it's too late to ask her why."

Aïna studies me, her gaze searching. "Perhaps she knew you would need to find the answers yourself."

I swallow hard, shaking my head. "It doesn't feel that way. It feels like she left me with more questions than I can handle."

"Tell me, what did she teach you, aside from this wisdom?"

"She taught me how to fight," I say. "She taught me to be strong, to defend myself. But she never explained why. She only said I'd need it one day."

Aïna nods, her eyes narrowing as if she's considering my words. "And what of the spirit? Did she teach you how to nurture the soul?"

The question catches me off guard again. It seems like I can never expect her next turn.

"She . . . taught me to trust the goddesses," I say. "But it was always in riddles, never direct answers. She focused more on my body and mind than anything else."

"That is because she knew the soul is something you must awaken on your own," she says with a hum, combing her claws through her mane. "But it is clear to me, Noël, that your connection to spirit is . . . faint. Like a thread barely holding. Do you feel it?"

I look down, shame prickling at my chest. I don't like not being good at something.

"I tried to speak to the goddesses," I admit. "Here, in this glade. Just before you came, I begged them to give me answers, but nothing happened. They didn't respond."

"Do you know why?"

I shake my head again, swallowing the lump in my throat and whispering, "No, why?"

"Because the goddesses do not answer to the mind alone, nor to the body. They speak to the soul. And until you learn to quiet the noise within you—your fears, your anger, your grief —they cannot reach you. The connection is there, Noël, but you are the one who must strengthen it."

My chest tightens with frustration. "How am I supposed to do that?" I ask, looking up at her, desperation creeping into my voice. "I don't know how. I don't even know where to start."

"You start by understanding that spirituality is not something you do, but something you are. It is in the way you breathe, the way you listen, the way you open yourself to what you cannot see or control. It is not about forcing answers but allowing them to come to you."

"But . . . it worked for Theron," I say after a moment. "When he called to the goddesses, they answered him. A white dove appeared and gave him a blue rose petal."

Aïna tilts her head. "Theron is different from you. Völkins are inherently spiritual beings, tied to the land, the sky, and the energy of life. We see what humans often cannot, feel what they are unable to."

Her paw touches my braid again, as if to ground me. "Theron is unique. His spirit is deeply attuned, more so than even most völkins. He does not seek the goddesses with doubt or fear. He simply listens. That is why he was chosen to be mated with the leader. With you."

"So . . . what does that mean for me?"

"It means that you must walk a different path," Aïna says. "Theron's connection is natural, instinctual. Yours will be harder won, but no less powerful. You are human, Noël, and humans have lost their connection to spirit over thousands of years. You must rebuild what was broken—piece by piece, step by step."

With every passing day, I get more confused. More things come my way and nothing resolves. I . . .

"That is why you are here, to reclaim what has always been yours. The strength of your soul, the wisdom of your bloodline, and the balance your kind has long forgotten."

"Your Majesty, Elder Aïna."

I turn toward the voice and see three vólkins standing between the trees, their immense forms bowed low, paws pressed to their hearts.

They call her Elder Aïna.

"What is it, Ívar?" Elder Aïna asks, half turning to face them, her tone firm and calm. She exudes authority effortlessly. If I didn't know they meant me when they said *Your Majesty*, I'd think they were speaking to her.

Ívar steps forward, his gray fur swaying with the breeze. "We've been sent by Theron, Elder Aïna. He requests that you accompany us to the border. There are matters requiring your expertise."

Elder Aïna arches an eyebrow, and I'm not quite sure if it is a good thing or a bad one. "Theron couldn't solve it himself?" she remarks, though there's a hint of humor in her tone. "What has him so rattled this time?"

The corners of Ívar's mouth twitch, though he quickly stifles any sign of mirth. "It is . . . unusual," he answers, choosing his words carefully. Is it because of me that he's so uncomfortable? "He believes your insight is needed."

I look between them. The border? What could be so important that they'd summon Elder Aïna so late at night?

As if sensing my thoughts, she says to me with a soft smile. "We'll speak of this tomorrow, Ethereal Leader. For now, you need rest. We'll begin working on your spirit in the morning."

I nod, though unease moves through me at the mention of "working on my spirit." Her tone leaves no room for argument, though, so I swallow my questions for now.

With a grin, she walks toward the vólkins, and I notice her crystals pulse with white light. "Let's not keep him waiting then, shall we? Knowing Theron, he's probably rearranging rocks in a straight line."

The smallest vólkin lowers his eyes, a quiet chuckle slipping out. The others remain stoic, though their ears flick, betraying their amusement.

As they prepare to leave, Ívar glances at me. He exchanges a quick look with his companions before stepping in my direction. "Your Majesty," he begins, his rumbling voice hushed. "Would you permit us the honor of escorting you to your chambers before we depart?"

For all their size and strength, there's a gentleness in the way they address me.

Approval glints in Elder Aïna's eyes as if she, too, is curious to see my response.

I hesitate before offering a small nod. "Thank you. That would be . . . kind of you."

The vólkins bow deeply again. As they lead the way, I notice how their gazes flick to me from time to time, not with suspicion or distrust, but with curiosity. It's as though they've never seen someone like me before. And perhaps they haven't.

Four centuries trapped behind a barrier. It's impossible to imagine what that must feel like.

I know what it's like to feel caged, to long for something more. My years in Tárnov were nothing compared to their centuries, yet I understand the ache of it, the way it wears on you.

These warriors, strong though they are, are just as vulnerable as I am. I decide, then and there, that I won't make things more difficult for them. For any of them. They've endured enough.

22

A RESTLESS MIND

"The world coils in pain, and no one listens. We come to you barefoot, not crowned. If you choose to rise, your howl will echo beyond the skies. Not as beast. Not as woman. But as memory made flesh. You will not be born. You will be remembered. Say yes, and we will shape you from the storm itself. Say yes, and you will become what the balance forgot. Say yes, and become vólkin."
—The Circle of the Unmated

Noël

I sit on the massive fur bed, large enough to fit at least two vólkins like Theron, weaving small blue ribbons together. It's been a while since I crafted something like this. The last time was the spear I made for protection, but before that . . .

Maybe it was when I made trinkets with my mother.

I nod to myself, taking another ribbon from the wooden container I set beside me. Earlier, as I explored, I came across a room with a small stream flowing through it. The air in there was cooler than the rest of the house, and the scent of herbs and earth filled my nose the moment I stepped inside. Smooth stones lined the edges of the stream, and large leaves formed natural basins.

There was a hollowed-out log that looked like a sink with a smaller stream of water constantly replenishing it. Beside it, I found a box filled with blue ribbons.

These ribbons seem like they're made for humans, unless Theron secretly ties his fur into tiny ponytails. I smile to myself as I finish weaving the blue strands together.

Standing up, I secure the furs around me once more—just in case—and head to the door.

Taking a deep breath, I open it to find the same two vólkins standing guard by the porch.

The moment they see me, they snap to attention, bowing in unison. Once they straighten again, they look at me quietly, but I can feel their unease.

"I wanted to apologize for my tone earlier," I say, switching my gaze from one guard to the other, my fists clasped behind my back.

One of the vólkins furrows his brows, and their shoulders stiffen.

"Your Majesty," the first begins. He swallows hard, and I can see his jaw clenching.

"We're the ones who should apologize," the other says, his voice quiet. His tone makes me feel even guiltier than before.

"Your word is beyond anyone's, beyond Theron's or Elder Aïna's. We shouldn't have hesitated."

"No. How can you follow me blindly?" My voice is calm but firm. "If I were in your place, I'd want the so-called ethereal leader to prove themselves first." I lift my chin higher. "I took your kindness for granted, and my bad mood wasn't your fault."

I pull my fists from behind my back and extend them toward the two vólkins. "Here," I say with a small smile. "A token of my apology, a braid for each of you."

Their eyes widen simultaneously, and after a short pause, they reach out. Slowly, each takes a ribbon braid from my hands, careful not to damage the tiny strands with their claws.

"You were kind to me, and I wanted to repay that kindness," I say, my smile lingering on my lips.

They look at the braids in their claws, and their gazes soften as their postures become less rigid, their guardedness easing.

"Thank you, Your Majesty," one of them says.

"We do not deserve such kindness," the other adds.

I offer them another smile and turn to head back inside, wishing them both a good night.

Closing the door behind me, I look at the ribbon container. Should I make one for Theron as well?

A braid from his own ribbons compared to the house he grew for me . . . I'll just embarrass myself.

Settling into the bed, I let out a long breath, the weight of the day sinking into my body. The softness the furs beneath me feels inviting, almost too much, but I don't resist. Instead, I pull another fur blanket over me, tucking it close as though it could shield me from everything that runs through my mind.

Curling into myself, I let my body relax, my knees drawing toward my chest as I rest my cheek against the plush bed. It's strange, this comfort feels foreign. And yet, here, surrounded by Theron's care and Elder Aïna's wisdom, I feel a sliver of it breaking through.

Body, mind, soul.

The braid she wove into my hair feels heavier, as though carrying the weight of her lesson. She saw something in me I'm not sure I can see in myself, but her faith in me was so real. I hold on to that.

As I shift under the layers of furs, I glance at the empty space beside me. The house feels so large, so quiet without him here. My fingers curl into the edge of the blanket. He said this was his home . . . and mine. But if it's his, why hasn't he come back yet?

I try to push the thought away, to convince myself it doesn't matter. He's out there somewhere, probably fussing like Elder Aïna said. Or maybe tending to something important. I shouldn't expect him to return.

I'm tired—too tired to wrestle with these feelings—so I focus on my breathing, letting it lull me into sleep.

I did the right thing tonight. I think. I hope. Elder Aïna's approval felt like the first step forward. And maybe . . . maybe I can learn to take the next step too.

My breaths slow, and I let myself sink into the warmth of the furs, the softness wrapping around me like a cocoon. It feels like the house is sheltering me, as though it knows I need this.

The darkness is choking me. I gasp for air.

No. No. No.

It comes in flashes: Theron's claws slashing into Arnold, the snarl ripping from his throat, the sound of flesh tearing. Blood pooling, dripping into the earth. Arnold's scream echoes, loud and raw, fading into nothingness as Theron delivers the final blow.

I can't move. My legs are frozen, my voice locked in my throat. All I can do is watch as the life drains from Arnold's wide, terrified eyes.

"Theron!" I scream, but no sound escapes my lips. He doesn't stop. He's unstoppable, his massive body coated in crimson, his eyes cold and detached. He's not the Theron I know—he's something else entirely.

A monster.

Then his head snaps toward me, his gaze locking onto mine, fur matted with blood, teeth bared in a snarl.

I take a step back, tripping over the roots of the forest I don't see, and he lunges toward me. His massive claws reach out—

My body jolts upright, and I wake with a desperate need for air. Each erratic beat of my heart slams against my ribs. It hurts.

My chest heaves as I clutch the fur blanket to me, feeling its dampness from the sweat clinging to my skin. Goddesses. It was a nightmare.

Willing myself to breathe, I press a shaking hand to my chest and fight to remember where I am. I'm in Ávera. In the house Theron grew for me. Not in the forest. Not with Arnold.

The handkerchief!

I immediately reach under the bed-nest. It is there. Oh, thank the goddesses.

The room is dim, the glow of the stones on the walls soft, as if they too are waking with me. My fingers tremble as I run them through my hair, damp with sweat. My skin feels clammy, the air around me too cold despite the furs I'm wrapped in. I look to the side, noticing the cloak-like blanket Theron made me from his fur lying nearby. I shiver.

Eyes closed, I suck in deep breaths to calm the storm inside me. It's over. Arnold is gone. I'm safe. But the safety feels fragile, like it could shatter at any time.

Knock, knock.

The sound startles me, and my eyes snap open. It takes me a moment to register that it's the door.

"Your Majesty?" A female voice.

Knock, knock.

"Is everything alright? I'm coming in."

I exhale, running my fingers from my face to my scalp. "Yes, come in," I say, my voice barely carrying. "Come i—"

The door opens, and Mina steps inside.

Right. They can hear everything. I straighten my back instinctively, and the furs tumble from my shoulders onto the bed. The cool air brushes over my bare chest, and heat rushes to my cheeks. Panic sets in as I pull the furs back over myself. "My apologies, Mina," I blurt out, my voice quicker than my thoughts.

She rises from her mid-bow, her expression calm, as though unbothered by my naked body. "You seem distressed," she says.

I clutch the furs tighter around me. "Oh, don't worry about it. Everything is just . . . a lot."

Mina's gaze shifts to the table across the room. She strides over and picks up a large wooden bowl resting there. "Theron left you breakfast," she says, her face lighting up as she turns back and offers it to me.

Breakfast? Was he here?

My brows knit together as I take the bowl from her, the warmth of it seeping into my palms. If it's still warm, that means he left it not long ago.

"Thank you," I say as I set the bowl on my thighs. There's cooked meat and strawberries. I haven't seen strawberry bushes here. Do they have gardens?

"How do you like to start your mornings, Your Majesty?" Mina asks as she picks up my gown from one of the cushions near the bed.

"Oh, that gown is dirty. Let me—"

"It is clean, though."

What? I didn't clean it. I set the bowl on the furs and stand up. Looking at my gown in Mina's paws . . . It is clean.

Mina looks at me, tilting her head.

"Tell me, Mina," I begin, picking the bowl up again. "Are there strawberry bushes in Ávera?"

"There are not."

I hum. "Did you clean my gown before I woke up?"

"I did not."

Another hum escapes me. Holding the furs tightly against my skin, I walk through the house, scanning for anything else he might have done.

I pause near the door. "Do you know if any of the guards entered this house?"

Mina shakes her head. "Unless it is an emergency, they're not allowed to disturb your rest."

A sigh escapes me as I walk back to her. "Theron did it, didn't he?"

Mina's gaze softens, and she nods. "It is a great honor for a vólkin to care for his mate."

I sit on the nearest wooden chair, the bowl warm in my hands. The strawberries don't touch the chunks of cooked meat, each piece resting perfectly in place as though he arranged them on purpose. Well . . . he did.

I take a bite, the meat's smoky, savory flavor hits my tongue, and I nearly moan in pleasure. I've never had meat for breakfast before, but I could definitely get used to this. After savoring the last bite, I move on to the strawberries, their sweet juice a perfect distraction from the nightmare I had.

As I eat, Mina busies herself around the house. She fluffs the cushions, rearranges the furs, and even checks on the flora growing from the ceiling.

It's better than her standing here, watching me eat. I'm grateful for her thoughtfulness, even if the house already looks perfectly in order.

As soon as I'm done eating, she takes the bowl from me with a smile.

"Thank you," I say, standing.

"No need to thank me for such a small thing, Your Majesty. Tonight is your welcome ceremony, so before that, we have a lot of things to do!"

"A welcome ceremony? There's no need for such grandiosity, Mina."

"How come! Our prophesied leader had finally arrived and freed us from the barrier. It is a grand celebration."

I look over at my gown in Mina's hands—paws, and my eyes widen. The crystal!

My heart pounds as I begin to frantically search the house.

"Your Majesty? What happened?"

"My crystal! Mina! It's from my mother!" Black dots fill my vision. Where is it? Where did I put it? What is wrong with me?

"A vólkin crystal?" Mina asks.

What.

She takes the crystal out of my gown's pocket and shows me. Goddesses, it was there. I sigh in relief, but I'm breathless when I thank her.

What is going on with me? Since when am I so unorganized? I have never *not* known where my belongings are, never lost a thing in my life. Except for my mother.

Mina puts the crystal in my hand, and I ask, "Why did you call it a vólkin crystal?"

She sounds perplexed when she says, "That's what it is, Your Majesty. Only vólkins carry such crystals. They're born from energy, from the bond vólkins share with the soul and their mates."

I blink, looking down at the crystal in my hand. "But this crystal was my mother's."

Mina's ears twitch. "Your mother had this? That's . . . unusual. Only a vólkin would carry such a thing. Perhaps she—"

"She wasn't vólkin," I interrupt, shaking my head. "She was human. She was . . . my mother." My voice lowers, and I tighten my grip on the crystal, feeling its cool surface.

"Of course she wasn't vólkin," Mina says, her calm tone so matter-of-fact that I almost missed what she just said.

"Mina."

"There are no vólkin females. Well, no natural vólkin females. Except Elder Aïna." She says it so casually, her tail swishing lazily behind her, as though she hasn't just upended everything I thought I knew. To her, it's a simple truth. To me, it's as if she's pulled the ground out from under my feet.

And yet . . . why am I so surprised? Since my mother's

death, nothing in my life has made sense. I'm in a vólkin's house—a vólkin who calls me his mate—when a few months ago I was throwing knives at vólkin training dummies in the barracks. I'm speaking to Mina, a vólkin female, who is telling me there are no vólkin females. I witnessed Arnold being shredded, and instead of falling apart, I'm standing here clutching a crystal I thought belonged to my mother, eating strawberries fetched by a creature I was raised to fear, who insists I'm the leader of a prophecy.

No, nothing makes sense anymore.

"I think y—"

Knock. Knock.

Oh, for the love of the goddesses! I snap my head toward the door, my irritation bubbling over as I call out, "Yes?"

The door opens, revealing one of the guards—and behind him . . .

A dozen nýmphí. At least.

Before I can process the sight, they stream into the room, their movements fluid and graceful, like they're gliding rather than walking. They bow deeply in unison, their bodies glowing in the soft light of the crystals.

"We wish you a good morning, Ethereal Leader," they say in melodic voices that send a shiver down my spine. The harmony of their greeting feels otherworldly, both beautiful and haunting, like a song.

Nothing. Nothing makes any sense.

And that is how I find myself in the stream, the warm water flowing around me as Mina gently rubs fragrant oils into my arm. The nýmphí have taken over the house entirely. Two of them crouch near the edge of the stream, inspecting my mother's crystal with curious eyes.

The others move, flitting in and out of the house, returning each time with something new—bundles of herbs, strands of woven flowers, or glowing stones that pulse in their hands. Every time they enter, they bow briefly before me, their fluid movements so synchronized it feels like I'm witnessing a dance.

Mina hums as she works. "They're quite eager, aren't they?" she says, her voice amused. Her tail flicks as she glances at the nýmphí holding the crystal. "The nýmphí rarely visit this part of the village, they're usually in the forest around Ávera, but now that you've arrived . . ."

I glance at the nýmphí. "They came just to see me?"

Mina chuckles, dipping her paws into the container the nýmphí brought to gather more oil. "Of course. You are the ethereal leader, after all. To them, you are practically a goddess."

"A goddess," I repeat, the words tasting strange on my tongue. "I'm just . . . me."

Naked me in front of Mina and all the nýmphí.

"That doesn't matter to them," Mina says. "They see what you've done, what no one else could. The barrier is gone because of you."

I look down at the water, watching the gentle ripples distort my reflection. A goddess. I want to tell Mina that I don't deserve such awe, but the nýmphí's presence makes the words stick in my throat.

One of the nýmphí tilts her head, her eyes locking onto mine. She rises gracefully and walks over, holding the crystal in both hands. "This," she begins, her voice like a tranquil melody, "is no ordinary stone."

My breath catches. "What do you mean?"

She kneels at the edge of the stream, holding the crystal just in front of me. "It carries an energy. Strong, but dormant. It's waiting for something . . . or someone."

"Waiting for what?" I ask, leaning forward so Mina's paw glides down my arm.

She looks up at me. "That is for you to discover, Ethereal Leader. But if you wish, we can shape it into something you can carry. A pendant, perhaps. It may guide you when the time is right."

My fingers brush over the surface of the water. The idea of altering something that belonged to my mother feels wrong. But if it helps me, if it keeps her close . . .

"Yes," I say. "Please."

The nýmphá dips her head in acknowledgment, and her golden hair flows as she rises. She hands the crystal to another nýmphá, who immediately disappears into the house, her movements almost too quick to follow. The others continue their work, their low chatter blending with the quiet murmur of the stream.

Mina's paws move to my other arm, her touch gentle as she works the oils into my skin. "It is a beautiful crystal," she says. "And now it will be something even more. Something tied to you."

"Tell me, Mina," I begin, looking above her eyes. "Why don't you have crystals? And does it relate to what you said earlier that the only vólkin female who has them is Elder Aïna?"

Mina pauses and turns to me. "Yes."

I swallow, narrowing my gaze, waiting for her to continue.

"When the barrier appeared four hundred years ago, the goddesses' powers began to weaken. As if something was sucking out their spirit. After approximately two hundred years, the goddesses saw that nothing could break the barrier from the inside, and the vólkins and spirits were becoming desperate. Being trapped for so long did no good to anyone. And so, the goddesses' connection to our world was fading, and they were afraid." Mina breathes deep, taking my hand. "The vólkins would go extinct, and the balance in the world would completely disappear."

My eyes widen at her words. It doesn't take long to see the profound connection vólkins have with nature. I might have arrived here only yesterday, but the thought of vólkins leaving the earth makes my heart . . . ache. I trace over her paw gently.

"When the goddesses felt that they might lose connection to this land completely, they decided to go against nature for the first time."

Mina's words hang in the air.

"Against nature? What do you mean?"

She hesitates, her ears flicking, as though weighing how much to say. "They decided to create vólkin females out of female wolves in the forest, using dark magic, to continue the vólkin race."

A breath I didn't realize I was holding escapes me in a rush. "Dark magic . . . the goddesses? I thought they were pure," I say, half to myself.

"They are." Mina's grip on my hand tightens. "But even purity can be forced to act in ways it shouldn't when the balance is at stake. The goddesses sacrificed their own spiritual energy to save us."

I can't help but picture these wolves—wild, free—being turned into something they weren't meant to be. "And . . . the females? How did you . . . ?"

"We accepted the change and adapted to our new forms," Mina says.

A shiver runs through me. "And Elder Aïna?"

"She is the only natural-born female vólkin. Her connection to the goddesses kept her spirit intact when others began to fade," Mina explains.

The goddesses broke the natural order to save their creations, but at what cost? The thought of such sacrifices—

both theirs and the wolves'—sends a pang of sorrow through me.

"Mina . . ." I rise from the stream, water trailing down my body, and wrap her in a tight embrace. Her fur is warm against my wet skin, and for a second, words fail me. "I didn't know," I whisper.

"This is why the vólkin females don't have crystals or powers like Elder Aïna or the males." She whispers the words into my neck, her arms holding me as tightly as I am holding her.

I pull back slightly, searching her eyes. "But are you—are you truly happy with this life?"

A small, warm curve of her mouth. "I love my life, Your Majesty," she says. "No female was ever forced. Those who became vólkin did so willingly, and there are some who chose never to have cubs. We are free to live as we wish. Also, I like being able to speak and walk on two legs." She chuckles.

Her words bring both comfort and guilt. As if sensing my thoughts, Mina tilts her head, her gaze soft.

"We are not broken," she says. "We are whole. And we stand strong because of our choices."

I nod. "Thank you," I murmur, brushing a strand of wet hair from my face. "For telling me."

Mina steps back, her tail flicking side to side. "Now, Your Majesty," she says with a playful smile, "let's not let the nýmphí finish all the preparations without us. You still need to get ready for tonight."

Her tone pulls a smile from me. "Right. Tonight."

23

TAMING THE WILD HEART

"Let the soul-bound wither where they kneel. Let the ash of
love silence the land. What once howled beneath the moon
shall sleep beneath our seal."
—Council of Crown

Theron

I lead my hunting party deeper into the forest, but my
mind is not here. It's with Noël. Every memory of her
wakes the beast inside me, a need to protect, to provide,
to claim.

To take what's mine.

The moment in the stream replays endlessly in my mind.
Her voice, the softness of her moans, the way she leaned into
my touch, it's maddening. I ache for her in ways that words
cannot describe. I am becoming obsessive.

Last night, I ran until the stars faded. My body demanded it,
the need was too much to contain. I pushed myself hard,
leaping through the trees, the burn of muscle and the
pounding of my heart barely dulling the fire inside me. When

morning came, I started the hunt alone. Providing for her—it's all I could think about. She deserves the best that this forest can offer.

But even as I hunted, I couldn't escape her. So I gave in to my need more than once, unable to silence her moans in my mind. I sought release over and over, for hours.

Now, my warriors follow close behind, their movements quiet, but the tension is hard to miss. They've sensed my mood.

They've said nothing. Yet. They understand that today's hunt is different. It's not just for survival or for Ávera. It's for her. To show her that I am the best male, her best choice.

"Stay alert," I command. Zephyr and Kaël nod, their ears pricked and their gazes scanning the shadows. Every step we take is calculated, every sound in the forest noted.

"Will you tell us what happened?" Kaël finally speaks up.

Well that didn't take too long.

"Theron, you don't have to if you don't want to," Zephyr adds. His respect is clear, but I can see the question in his eyes too.

"There's nothing to worry about," I answer, keeping my focus on the trail.

"Nothing to worry about?" Kaël snorts, his voice rising. "You snapped, Theron. You—"

"Enough," Zephyr cuts him off with a stern look. "It's between him and his mate."

I glance at Zephyr, grateful for his understanding. What happens between Noël and me is ours. It's not something to be dissected or discussed. Her victories, I'll share with pride. But our struggles? They're private.

Even so, this struggle is mine. All mine. I can't stop wondering what might have happened if I'd stayed with her. Would she have accepted me? Would she have leaned into the bond? Let it pull her the way I feel it pulling at me? Or would I have scared her away?

I force the thoughts aside. It's too soon. She's learning me, testing the waters of what we are.

We move in silence after that, the forest alive with its usual sounds. The rustle of leaves, the faint tread of paws, the calls of distant creatures—it all grounds me, reminds me of who I am and what I'm here to do.

"We should split up," I say. "We'll cover more ground that way."

Kaël and Zephyr nod without question, fanning out as we go farther into the forest. I catch sight of fresh tracks, a deer, judging by the size and pattern. It's a good sign. My movements are silent as I follow the trail.

Soon, I spot it. A large buck grazing in the clearing. It's the perfect catch for the feast. My muscles coil, my claws readying to strike.

"Theron."

I freeze, lowering my arms. I turn toward the shadows, and there she is, her silver fur glinting in the light filtering through the leaves above.

"Elder Aïna," I greet her, my tone respectful as I step back from the hunt.

"I didn't want to wait until you returned,"

My muscles tense instantly, and I move closer to her. "Tell me."

"Theron, the barrier's fall is not only a gift. It's a warning."

This new world—this life beyond the barrier—is a test for me. Leading the vólkins behind the shield of the barrier was one thing. It was safe. Now with it gone, every decision, every instinct carries the weight of survival. One wrong move and I risk not only my people but Noël too.

A low growl rumbles in my throat. "What did you find?"

"The magic tied to it, it's dangerous. Old. And it lingers still."

I narrow my gaze, the tension crawling under my fur.

She exhales, her ears flicking back. "The campfire's embers seem fresh, but they are not. Those who were there left in a hurry, but not before completing a ritual. The stones they used were arranged in patterns I've only seen in the darkest of practices. A summoning, perhaps. Or a *binding*."

Fresh but not . . . That can only mean one thing.

"There's more," she says. "The air around the site was heavy with pain. The forest remembers what was done there. And the blood the warriors scented . . ." She pauses, her pale eyes sharpening. "It was sacrificial."

A growl rises in my throat. My claws flex, itching for something to strike. "A sacrifice?"

She nods. "The ritual wasn't a harmless spell, it was fueled by suffering. Death. Whatever they did, it wasn't ordinary magic."

I bare my teeth. "The barrier."

"Perhaps," she replies. "Or something tied to it. Whatever their intent, they failed. The barrier is gone, but their purpose remains. They'll come back, Theron."

A cold rage simmers beneath my fur. The idea of those responsible returning, bringing darkness into Ávera, is enough to make my blood burn. "If they come back," I say, "we'll make sure they won't return."

"If they come back, they'll bring with them the same magic that created the barrier. And they'll be more desperate, more dangerous. We must prepare. For ourselves. For Ávera. And most of all, for *her*."

Noël. She's not just my mate, she's everything. Our future, our balance. The thought of her in danger twists my anger.

"Nothing will touch her," I snarl. "Or Ávera. Not while I breathe."

Aïna's gaze softens, but her voice remains firm. "Theron, this is a new beginning. Beginnings are fragile. One misstep, and everything we've fought to protect will crumble."

"We'll be ready," I say, my voice low and final.

She studies me before nodding. "Then let us see it done." I dip my chin, and she places a paw on my shoulder. "The goddesses are with you."

With that, she disappears into the forest, leaving me with my thoughts.

Noël has suffered more than anyone should—losing her mother, facing the cruelty of men who sought to crush her. Yet she stood against it all, unbroken and fierce. But strength shouldn't come from such pain. It shouldn't come at the cost of her peace.

And she's never known true safety. Anyone who dares to harm her, who even dreams of bringing her pain, will answer to *me*. They will face my claws and my fangs. They will face their end. The same as that weird-looking human male did.

We must find the six, restore the balance, and reshape this land into something worthy of my mate. I will not fail her.

Zephyr and Kaël join me, carrying their game.

"Let's finish this hunt," I say, turning to face them. "We have a feast to prepare and a leader to feed."

After a while, we take a brief rest. I lean against an ancient tree while Zephyr holds Kaël's legs so he can try to clean the blood from his torso without dipping fully into the water.

Sometimes he does things I don't understand, but I've stopped asking. If he wants to clean only half his body, so be it.

After Kaël falls into the stream and splashes water everywhere, including all over Zephyr, they both walk away shaking their soaked fur.

And I watch them.

"Why do I go along with your ideas, Kaël?" Zephyr sighs,

squeezing his braid and twisting his paws in different directions. "Always making the same mistake."

"His mate will have to deal with a lot," I say with a laugh.

"I can't stop thinking about her," Kaël says, shaking off the water once more. "What will she be like? Will she accept me?"

Zephyr chuckles. "You worry too much, Kaël. But I wonder about mine too. What if she doesn't like the way we live? What if she can't adjust?"

"Humans are more adaptable than you think. Look at Noël. She knew how to make a nest and almost didn't let me make one for her."

Kaël sighs. "In the human-lore lessons, there were so many things I couldn't believe. But now, after seeing a real human, I feel like I need to go through everything again. I'm not sure I know everything about them."

"You should've listened to Elder Aïna's lessons," I say.

Kaël scratches his mane, humming in thought. "When do the cubs have their lessons with her again? Maybe I should sit in with them."

"You'd better catch up quickly before your mate arrives and finds you studying with the young ones," Zephyr adds, smirking. "I can't imagine anything more embarrassing than that."

Kaël stretches, then leans back on his elbows. He hasn't even dried yet. "There's just so much to learn," he groans, shooting us a pleading look as Zephyr licks the remaining blood from his wrist. "How am I supposed to sit still and study?"

"It's about understanding them, respecting their differences," I say. "Noël is strong, but she still needs reassurance. She needs to feel safe. It's a *balance*. You show strength, but you temper it with gentleness. That's what they need."

Zephyr nods. "I suppose it's not so different from how we care for our own, just . . . more delicate?"

"Exactly," I reply, leaning back against the tree trunk, the bark rough against my fur. "Humans aren't like us. They express things differently. They need words, gestures, and small acts of care. They're not built like we are—they're smaller, more fragile. They don't have fur to shield them, and their skin tears at the slightest scrape of a branch. You have to pay attention to their needs. When you do, you'll find a way to connect."

Kaël rolls over to Zephyr and me. "I just hope I can make my mate happy."

"You will," I say with confidence. "But it takes time. Noël was terrified of me at first. She thought I was some kind of monster. It wasn't until she saw the truth—that I would never harm her—that she began to trust me." I grin. "The first time we met, she pointed a weapon at me. Fierce little thing."

Kaël lets out a laugh, his fangs flashing. "That's adorable."

My chest swells with pride. "It is. Everything about her is."

Pushing off the tree, I stretch and motion for them to follow. "Let's head back. I'm curious to see how she's doing with Mina."

24

BENEATH THE HEAVY CROWN

"Tsars rot faster than corpses when they crown themselves
gods. Let him wear the crown. Let him rot beneath it."
—Unknown

Tsar Varyán II

T he candlelight glows in the cold study. Old tomes line
the shelves, their spines worn from centuries of use
by my ancestors. Maps and documents, detailed
lands and plans known only to me, are lain across the large
wooden desk. The crown is heavy on my head, and my
migraines trouble me constantly.

I trace a finger over the map, stopping at Ávera. My gaze
narrows as I contemplate the mistake I made when I allowed
her to join the military. The moment comes back to me like a
nightmare every time I close my eyes.

It was a visit to Tárnov to greet the people, a routine display
of my power. There, I saw her, a young woman fighting with the
boys her age, making them eat dirt. I had never seen a woman

behave in such a manner. Amused, I told my guards to stay back and approached her.

"How can you fight like that?" I asked.

"I've been training," she said simply. She didn't bow or tremble. No, she looked directly into my soul.

The poor boys, shaking with fear, looked at my feet and struggled with words as if their mouths were full.

I dismissed them with a wave, and they darted away on unsteady legs.

"Why would you need to do that? A woman should be in the kitchen or, at your age, nursing her child."

"I train to keep my mother and myself safe from men and boys like those who attacked me."

I laughed, a sound that echoed through Tárnov's stones. "Where is your father?"

"I don't have one," she replied, apparently unbothered by the presence of the tsar.

I hummed, looking at her toned figure, studying her face. "What happened to him?"

"I don't know."

"What do you want to do in life, young maiden?"

"I want to join the military," she said as if she had been waiting for this question to come. I had never been astonished so many times in one day.

I laughed again, harder than before. But she didn't smile. And so I asked, "Do you think you can do it? Those men would eat you alive."

She smirked. "I'd love to see them try."

At that moment, I decided to do something no one would ever think of. I allowed her to join the army.

From that day, I received detailed reports of her progress. She was different, stronger. I was fascinated by her achievements, her ability to talk back to me without fear, and her strength against the men around her. But then her extraordinary abilities began to frighten me. She won every competition, broke the men into pieces, and memorized every lesson. She was unstoppable.

I had plans for her, to make her strong and bring her under my command, but everything changed when I discovered who Noël's mother was.

The day is so clear in my memory. Suspicion made my nights sleepless, so I sent one of my shadows to infiltrate her home and search for clues.

The ache behind my eyes returns. Pinching the bridge of my nose, I breathe slowly, then rise from the desk and make my way to the tall window that overlooks the southern garden in the hope fresh air might offer some relief. And there she is. Elara, my lovely daughter.

A streak of light against the dark green of the grass, her pale gown spilling around her like she was placed there by an artist's hand. Her back is straight, and yet, her shoulders are relaxed. She sits beneath the old maple, head tilted, light catching the gleam of her golden hair as she turns a page. One leg is tucked beneath her, the other stretched out, her shoe kicked off without thought.

I've told her nursemaids time and time again not to let her sit directly on the soil. Not only is it improper, it's dangerous. But of course, she never listens. And worse, now they join her. Three grown women in pressed gowns, skirts soaking in dew, sitting in a circle like they are her sisters. Not her keepers. Not her servants.

I hear their giggles even through the glass.

She's reading again. Of course she is. The book lies open in her lap, resting on the same embroidered shawl her mother once favored. I narrow my eyes. Green cover, gold trim, I recognize the book immediately. Some fairy-tale nonsense about a knight who saves his fragile wife from a vólkin. The knight slays him, is praised by the people, and the couple live happily ever after.

Elara looks up as one of the nursemaids leans in and says something, likely some foolish comment about finding a handsome knight of her own. Tipping her head back, Elara laughs, a sound that rings like bells in the garden. Her hand flies to her mouth, as if trying to hold in her amusement.

"One of them has a chin too large," another nursemaid says, and the others erupt with laughter. Elara slaps the book closed and presses it to her chest, leaning forward as she whispers something, and now all four of them are nearly in tears from the joke.

They are children. All of them.

Yet I watch in silence.

Elara is everything they once said a daughter of mine could never be. She's soft, untouched by the shadows this stronghold was built upon. She walks through these halls as if they were made for her. Servants bow, courtiers perk up at the sound of her voice. She's beloved by all who meet her. She is the light of this place.

And they call it innocence.

But I know better.

Elara is not weak. Not truly. Her softness is not fragility. She listens, she smiles, she obeys just enough to be praised. But I have seen it. The moments when her eyes sharpen, when she asks too many questions. When she lingers in the temple corridors longer than she should. When she copies the old symbols from the archives into her personal journal.

She is more like me than anyone realizes.

She does not yet understand what I've protected her from, what I've planned. She plays in the garden now, giggling about cleft-chinned knights and beast-slaying husbands, but soon, she'll grow into the crown I carved for her.

"One day, little rose," I promise quietly, "you'll learn the stories aren't real. You'll see the beasts wear crowns. And still, you will choose me."

The ache behind my eyes begins to fade.

A slight noise pulls me back to the present. From the corner of my eye, I see my trusted shadow, Bard he is called, slip through the other window to land silently on the cold floor. The shadow's hooded cloak blends into the shadows of my study, and only the gleam of his eyes is visible.

"Your Imperial Majesty," Bard begins, bowing low. "It is done. Eyleen is dead."

Good. This is very good. "Where is she, then?"

"Ice chambers, Your Imperial Majesty."

I nod, brushing my fingers through my beard. "Noël . . ." I mutter under my breath. "Is she dead yet?"

Bard stays silent for a few moments before closing his eyes. "We lost sight of her."

Black dots begin to swim in my vision. I turn my gaze from Elara to him.

The barrier has stood for four hundred years, proof of the control and order my ancestors and I maintained for so long. I know all too well what would happen if women were free— chaos, rebellion, the end of my rule, perhaps the end of everything. I should have punished her that day in Tárnov, should have sent her to the work camps to break her spirit like I did with so many others. Allowing her into the military was a grave mistake, one that might cost me everything. "Where is *Noël*?"

The shadow bows his head. "We do not know, Your Imperial Majesty. She escaped into vólkin territory, and we've lost track of her." He pauses, then adds, "But we do know how she was taken out of the village."

I narrow my gaze. "Speak."

"Two soldiers took her. One of them, a fool named Arnold, thought he could dispose of her. We know he hated her since she enlisted, and he severely underestimated her. He was killed by a vólkin, probably the son of Vládan, who had blue crystals, likely indicating the blue rose. The other man, Gregor, managed to escape."

My brows furrow. "This Gregor is alive?"

"Yes, Your Imperial Majesty," the shadow replies. "He was captured while wandering, attempting to return to Tárnov. He's being interrogated as we speak."

Why would everything happen so suddenly? Is this also Eyleen's doing?

"What has he revealed?" I demand.

The shadow pulls a sealed scroll out of his cloak. "This contains everything he's confessed so far, though we believe there is more he has yet to reveal. We are . . . persuading him to speak further."

I tear open the scroll, quickly reading its contents. Gregor's account aligns with Bard's report. Noël is out there, beyond the barrier, and the vólkins have already caught her scent. If she ventures too deep into their territory, she may slip beyond our grasp. Perhaps she already has. If what I'm reading is true . . . she was last seen with a vólkin.

"We have the perfect plan for dealing with Gregor," Bard says.

Sitting in my chair, I put the scroll on the desk and lean forward. "I'm listening."

The shadow outlines the plan, detailing each step. The candles flicker, and the shadows dance across the room as my mind races with possibilities, each more dangerous than the last.

As the shadow finishes, I nod. "Very well. Proceed with the plan. And keep me informed of every development."

Suddenly, the room grows dark and quiet, and my heart almost stops beating. *If Noël met a vólkin . . . This could mean only one thing.*

"Your Imperial Majesty?"

I slowly turn to Bard.

"There's something else." After taking a deep breath, he says, "She slit her own throat, Your Majesty. Eyleen . . . chose her death."

25

A GARDEN OF BLUE ROSES

"When the air stills, and white weeps upon the wind—not snow, not ash, but something softer still—you will know. The earth will hush, the stream will silence its song, and she will walk where balance once broke. You will not chase her. You will wait. And when the braid is whole, you will kneel, not only in body but in soul."
—Elder Aïna, to Theron

Noël

I try to focus on the preparations for the welcome ceremony. Mina has been by my side all morning, guiding me through each step.

"We want to honor your customs as well," she says, presenting me with a gown unlike anything I've ever seen. "Elder Aïna made this for you herself."

Elder Aïna. She had lived for thousands of years, though she'd long since stopped keeping count. I'm still struggling to wrap my mind around it. How does someone even live that long?

"We know humans prefer to be covered," Mina adds, her tone kind. As though she hadn't bathed me with at least two dozen nýmphí running around mere hours ago.

The gown is stunning. The fabric is airy and light, a pristine white that feels ceremonial. Mina explains that white symbolizes new beginnings for the vólkins, which feels oddly familiar. It does in Tárnov too.

Blue patterns are embroidered along the edges and seams. They depict the flora of Ávera—vines, flowers, and leaves—all woven together like a story. The threads shimmer when the light catches them, giving the gown an ethereal look, as though it belongs to this land more than I do.

The fitting takes place in a spacious room within one of the ancient trees. I finally walked along one of the branch bridges that connect the trees.

The walls are made of intertwined branches and leaves, allowing the sun to gleam through and create patterns on the wooden floor. The air is filled with the rich scent of fresh flowers and pine. In the center of the room, a large, shallow basin filled with clear water acts as a mirror, making the room look even more spacious.

Mina and two vólkin females with the same soft gray fur as her, Naïa and Essin, circle me. I stand in the center, unsure whether to be grateful or embarrassed.

"Raise your arms, Your Majesty," Mina says, her voice soft but firm, leaving no room for debate.

The last time someone dressed me was my mother. The last time anyone bathed me, brushed my hair, or did anything this intimate . . . it was her. It makes my chest tighten.

I hesitate, but Mina clicks her tongue and shakes her head at my resistance. "It's our honor to assist you," she says, holding the gown out of my reach. "Please, trust us."

Reluctantly, I lift my arms to let Mina slide the gown over my head. The fabric feels cool against my skin as it falls into place. The bodice is fitted but not restrictive, hugging my figure enough to feel secure while also not limiting my movement. Small silk blue roses are sewn into the fabric, their vibrant color standing out against the white. The neckline is modest, dipping just enough to be flattering without making me self-conscious, with a button to secure the cleavage.

The sleeves are wide and bell shaped, flowing past my hands with beautiful embroidery along the cuffs, and the skirt flares out from the waist to fall to just above my ankles. As I move, the fabric sways, making me want to run around with bare feet and watch the gown flow behind me.

Mina adds a final touch, a sash of deep green, made to resemble a leafy vine. She wraps it around my waist, tying it in a loose bow at the back. The ends drape over the skirt, mingling with the blue embroidery.

Running my fingers over the patterns, I trace the shapes of leaves and flowers. It's beautiful. Here it is, waiting for me to step into a role I still don't understand.

Naïa steps in without a word. Her paws smooth the material down over my shoulders and back with a touch so light, it's as though she's afraid I might shatter.

Essin crouches to adjust the hem. "Hold still," she says with a smile. Her tone is playful, almost teasing, and it helps ease some of the tension knotting my stomach.

Mina fusses over the neckline, tilting her head to examine every detail. Her paws move quickly as she makes tiny adjustments I can't even see. "Perfect," she declares at last before stepping back with a satisfied smile.

Naïa and Essin follow her lead and stand back to admire their work. "You look beautiful," Naïa says.

Essin's smile widens. "Better than we imagined."

Naïa stands calm, composed, her posture steady and confident. I've noticed she doesn't say much, preferring to observe. Her green eyes are as beautiful as nature, like Mina's. Around her wrist is a band with small, bright green crystals that match her eyes. Essin, on the other hand, is her opposite—lively and full of energy—with eyes like amber, even leaning toward yellow. She's about the same height as Mina, her mane woven with dark purple flowers. Her laugh is light and bright, and it fills the room like a spark of life wherever she goes.

They're both so sweet to me.

"This fabric is so smooth." I run my fingers over the delicate material. It's lighter than anything I've ever worn, softer than even the silks the nobles in Tárnov used to boast about.

"It's made from the finest silks we could find," Naïa explains. "We wanted you to feel comfortable. And beautiful."

Before I can respond, Mina steps behind me and begins combing through my hair, her claws working carefully to untangle the strands. "You have such lovely hair, Your Majesty," she says. "It's like the deepest pines after rain."

I don't know what to say to that. "Thank you," I manage, feeling a blush rise to my cheeks. "You're all so . . . kind."

Essin smiles as she weaves small flowers into my hair. "We're just excited to have you here. You're already fitting in so well."

I glance at her reflection in the water mirror, raising an eyebrow. "Why do you say that?" I ask, curious but unsure how to take the compliment.

"Because," Mina says as she meets my gaze in the reflection, "you broke the barrier."

"Not to mention," Essin adds, holding my hand as she works, "you're not screaming, fighting us, or even complaining about life here."

I blink, taken aback at her honesty.

Naïa steps closer, her voice calm as she adds, "Elder Aïna told us humans might react that way—afraid or overwhelmed —since everything here is so different from what you're used to."

I hadn't considered how they might have expected me to behave. How have I behaved so far? Confused, yes. Scared, definitely. And overwhelmed by these strange connections I can't seem to shake. But I haven't complained, at least not out loud. Not about the ridiculous distances I've had to walk from one tree to the next, to each building seemingly grown straight out of the forest itself. And those trees? They're colossal, far beyond anything I ever saw from within Tárnov's walls.

I didn't say a word about it, though. Probably because I can handle it. I'm fit, always have been. Years of training have made sure of that. I remember back in the barracks, when the soldiers would compare their six-packs, joking and flexing like fools. I wanted so badly to join in, to roll up my tunic and show them what real definition looked like. But I didn't. Authority and all. A grin tugs at the corner of my mouth at the memory.

"Is that smile because you're thinking of Theron?" Essin teases, her paws planted on her hips.

Oh goddesses, no!

Heat rushes to my cheeks, my face betraying me in the worst possible way. With a sharp breath, I try to look anywhere but at them, eventually landing on the entrance like it might offer some escape. A white dove is sitting on the windowsill looking at me, and then it cocks its head to the side. This bird is really staring. How strange.

"Essin! Would you stop that!" Mina scolds as she rushes to my side. I turn toward her, absolutely lost for words, feeling more cornered than ever. Naïa, however, takes matters into her own hands . . . paws by pinching Essin's snout with an exaggerated huff of disapproval.

"Um," I blurt out, entirely by accident. Of course, that draws all their attention. Their gazes lock onto me, and I freeze, blinking like an absolute fool.

Then, without warning, the tension snaps. One moment of silence turns into a burst of laughter.

The air is warm and sweet, wrapping around me like a gentle embrace. These girls have been nothing but kind to me, their lighthearted teasing and careful paws a balm I didn't know I needed. I'm deeply grateful for them. It's been so long since I've had this sort of peaceful, tender moment. Just giggling, sharing stories, doing something simple and nice.

My mother would've loved this.

She always adored seeing girls happy. During the harvest season, the young girls of Tárnov danced around the village square, scattering petals given to them by the farmers who brought the annual bounty. Flowers were so rare in Tárnov, their arrival felt like a celebration of life itself. My mother would buy the most colorful flowers at the market. She'd hand them out to girls and grandmothers alike, always with a kind smile and a quiet wish for their day to be brighter.

The memory brings a lump to my throat. I can almost hear her voice, see the warmth in her eyes. These moments, so vivid and yet so far away, make me ache for her all over again.

I wish I could bring her back. Show her all the flowers in Ávera—so many of them, more than we ever dreamed of in Tárnov. She'd love it here. She'd love *them*.

After the fitting, Mina leads me to a clearing surrounded by towering trees. I take a deep breath and let the scent of nature fill my lungs. Here it is. The sacred glade.

Elder Aïna waits near the ancient stone, surrounded by a few of the nýmphí I met this morning. As we approach, they all bow to me. Mina, Naïa, and Essin are at my side.

"Elder Aïna, thank you for this beautiful gown. I'm honored," I say, stepping into the glade.

Her expression is kind as she comes to meet me, the glow of the sacred glade reflecting off her silver fur. She holds out the pendant, but her eyes search mine.

"This crystal," she begins. "It belonged to Ándor."

"Ándor?" My fingers curl around the fabric of my gown. "Was he a vólkin?"

"Yes. He left Ávera long ago, before the barrier appeared. He claimed he'd seen his mate in his dreams and that he had to find her. This"—her paw tips toward the light blue crystal hanging from its new silver chain—"was your mother's crystal, you say?"

My vision blurs, and I quickly blink back the tears threatening to spill.

"She . . . she was human," I manage to whisper.

Elder Aïna offers the pendant to me, and I reach out with trembling fingers. The moment it touches my palm, an inexplicable warmth spreads through me, both familiar and foreign. Like a memory just out of reach. My thumb traces the surface of the crystal. It's smooth and faintly blue. Too faint.

I glance up at Elder Aïna. "The crystals on your foreheads, they're vibrant. This one is . . . dull." My voice grows steadier as I study it more closely. "What does that mean?"

Aïna's gaze darkens, her brow furrowing in thought. She lifts her paw to her own crystals, a V-shaped formation of white gems that glimmer with life. "When a vólkin dies their crystal loses its brilliance, turning dull, like ordinary stone. It's a reflection of their spirit's departure from the body."

My grip tightens on the pendant, dread curling in my stomach. "Then Ándor . . . he's . . ."

Elder Aïna shakes her head, her eyes narrowing as if trying to piece together a puzzle. "This crystal is neither vibrant nor fully dulled. It's muted, suspended between life and death. I have never seen such a thing."

I stare at the crystal, trying to make sense of its unusual state. The weak blue hue pulses in the light, almost as if it's holding on to something. Or someone.

"What does it mean?" I ask.

"I do not know," Aïna admits, her tone uncharacteristically

uncertain. "It should not be possible. If Ándor passed, the crystal would have dulled completely. If he lived, it would shine brightly, as ours do. This faint light . . ." Her voice trails off as she studies the pendant with a frown. "Perhaps it is tied to you."

"To me?" My voice cracks. "How could it be? I don't even—" I stop myself, the words trapped in my throat. I don't even know who Ándor is.

Elder Aïna tilts her head, her ancient, pupilless eyes locking onto mine. "Crystals are bound to the soul, Ethereal Leader. If this was once Ándor's, then it carries his essence. If it came to your mother, and now to you . . ." She pauses. "There may be a connection you have yet to uncover."

My mind races, but no answers come. "You knew him," I say, desperate for more. "What was he like?"

A small smile touches Elder Aïna's mouth, though it's tinged with sadness. "I knew Ándor well. He was strong, intelligent, and protective of those he loved. Even as a cub, he was curious, always seeking more from the world than what was in front of him. He was one of the strongest vólkins I knew."

She exhales, her gaze drifting toward the glade as if she can see him in the distance. "When he left, it was with certainty. He believed he had found his mate in his dreams. That bond is the strongest of all for a vólkin. He would have done anything to reach her."

I clutch the pendant tighter. Was Ándor my mother's mate? Could she have been tied to this world, to the vólkin? But my mother, she was born and raised in Tárnov, just as I was.

"I don't understand," I whisper. "If this crystal belonged to him, why did my mother have it? How did she— How could she . . ." My words falter, the questions too tangled to finish.

Elder Aïna's paw settles on my hand. "The answers may not come easily," she says. "But the crystal found its way to you for a reason. Trust in that. And trust in yourself to uncover its meaning."

Naïa steps closer to me, her paws extended as she offers to help me put on the pendant. I nod as I hand over my precious jewel.

Ándor . . . He probably knew Theron's parents. He knew my mother. The more I learn about this world, the deeper the mysteries grow, twisting my thoughts into knots I can't seem to untie.

"Who were Theron's parents?" My voice cuts through the quiet hum of the sacred glade. I can't stop myself, the need for answers is driving me insane.

Elder Aïna hums, her arms clasped behind her back as she gazes at the ancient stone. "Ánya and Vládan," she replies.

"Ánya?" I repeat. It's a common name in Tárnov, popular for centuries among noble families. Could it be . . .

"Is Ánya human?" I ask, swallowing the lump forming in my throat.

"Was," Elder Aïna replies simply.

Was. Ánya is gone. Of course, she would be. Theron is over four hundred years old, his mother would have passed long ago. Still, the realization stings.

"Ánya was the kindest human I ever met," Elder Aïna says. "Theron has her eyes—hazel and bright."

Theron listened to me speak of my mother's loss, but he never mentioned his own. Did it hurt him too much to say? I need to talk to him. I need to hear this from him, not secondhand.

"Elder Aïna," I say, my voice firm now.

Her ears twitch at my tone, and she turns her piercing gaze toward me.

"I need to speak with Theron," I continue. "Where is he?"

The corners of her mouth curl ever so slightly, a grin that makes her ageless face seem younger. "Hunting," she replies, with a hint of amusement.

"Hunting?"

"For the welcome ceremony," Naïa adds. She steps back after securing the pendant around my neck.

The weight of it settles against my chest. I glance down at the misty blue crystal. *I have so many questions.* "I see," I murmur. But in truth, I don't see at all.

Soon. I will find Theron, and he will tell me everything.

"It is time," Elder Aïna says.

She doesn't need to say more. I know what she expects, so I turn to face the others. More vólkins gather near the ancient stone, each bowing as they approach.

"We'll start with meditation," Mina says, guiding me deeper into the glade. "It will help you connect with the spirits of the forest and find your inner balance."

I nod, and my heart beats faster as I take a seat near the stone, my legs crossed and my hands resting on my thighs.

Elder Aïna's voice is steady as she begins. "Close your eyes and breathe deeply. Feel the energy of the forest flowing through you. Let your mind grow still and listen to the whispers of the trees."

Following her instructions, I let my eyes fall closed and the cool forest air fill my lungs. As I exhale, I imagine the worries leaving me. One by one, I gather my thoughts—the questions about my mother, about Ándor, about this strange world I've been thrust into—and try to push them away.

The wind brushes against my skin, and the grass beneath my ankles is soft.

Elder Aïna's voice continues, calm and guiding. "Now, imagine yourself as a tree. Let your roots grow down into the earth. Feel the strength of the ground supporting you."

I picture it clearly, my roots intertwining with the ancient trees around me. A warmth spreads through me as though the forest is sharing its strength.

"Allow your mind to drift back through time." Elder Aïna's

voice grows distant. "Feel the presence of those who came before us. They guide and protect us even now."

The warmth wraps around me like a gentle embrace.

I see a woman standing with her hand resting on a massive wolf's back. She is beautiful, her hair flowing as though caught in an unseen breeze, her eyes filled with wisdom. The wolf is equally imposing, his gaze intelligent.

"You have come far, my child," the woman says, her voice serene and so powerful. "You are the key to restoring the balance."

I feel as though I know her, though I've never seen her before. "Who are you?" My voice wavers.

"I am the Mother of All," she replies. "You carry my legacy within you. The bond you share with the vólkins is ancient and powerful."

A chill rushes through me. My heart races, but I force myself to ask. "What must I do?"

"You must make the blue rose bloom again," she says simply.

Before I can respond, a whirlwind of blue petals surrounds me. The air grows cold, then hot, and my body seems to be frozen in place. My breaths come fast and shallow as the storm intensifies, the petals brushing against my skin. Then, just as suddenly as it began, the storm vanishes.

I gasp, my chest heaves as I struggle to regain control, and my heart pounds as the vision fades around me. The moment I can, I open my eyes to the present. The vólkins are watching me. Eyes wide.

"Are you alright, Your Majesty?" Mina asks.

I wipe the sweat from my forehead, my voice shaky. "I don't . . . I don't know."

The vólkins exchange glances. Elder Aïna steps forward, her expression grave. "Look around you, Ethereal Leader."

When I do, my breath catches in my throat. Blue roses—dozens of them—surround me.

I turn, looking behind me. More roses. They weren't here before. Searching for answers, I meet Elder Aïna's eyes.

A tear slips down my cheek and falls to the ground. Where it lands, a single blue rose grows from the soil to bloom before my eyes.

I swallow hard. "What . . . what does this mean?"

"It means," she says, her gaze never leaving mine, "the prophecy has truly begun."

26

THE FEAST OF ROSES AND FIRE

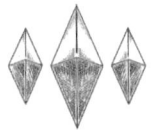

"Before the first fire, before the first word, there was the dance.
Only those born of womb and storm can summon it. For when
women move, the earth listens. And when they move as one,
the balance shifts."
—Láda Veléša, Goddess of Leadership and War

Theron

We head to the stream near Ávera's edge, and I plunge into its depths, letting the cold water cut through the remnants of the day's hunt, washing away the blood and dirt. The current is strong and refreshing, pulling the weight of the day off my fur. Beside me, Kaël and Zephyr do the same. The hunt was a success. We brought back enough game to feed everyone.

This is a feast for my mate.

The others carry the animals to be prepared. As I sink farther into the water, I wonder what she's been doing, how she's adjusting to this world.

Mina has been with her. She's gentle and patient, everything Noël needs right now. But even with that assurance, I find myself restless. My little dove.

I miss her.

She was so beautiful in the water, letting me touch her, trusting me to care for her. The memory burns fresh in my mind, waking my cock again. I glance to my side, half hoping to see her, but find Kaël grinning back at me instead. Shaking my head, I sigh deeply.

"Something on your mind, Theron?" he asks.

"Plenty," I mutter before I step out of the water.

Once clean and dry, we make our way to the main clearing where the preparations for the feast are in full swing. Vólkins move through the area as they string garlands, arrange tables, and light lanterns. The scent of freshly prepared food mingles with the sweet aroma of flowers, filling the air with a warmth that feels like home. The garlands are made from glowing blossoms and floating energy orbs. They light as evening creeps in, painting Ávera in an array of colors. Everything looks perfect for the leader. For Noël.

The tables are laid with an array of meats, some cooked and seasoned for her. While we vólkins favor raw meat, we've learned to prepare it in ways humans find pleasing. It was one of the many lessons Elder Aïna insisted upon, and we were eager to ensure our mates would feel welcomed when they arrived. Alongside the meat, there are fruits and berries, including the strawberries Noël seemed to enjoy so much. I hope she'll find the feast to her liking.

I approach Elder Aïna near the center of the clearing, her presence commanding as always. "Elder Aïna," I greet her with a nod. "The preparations look excellent. Where is my mate?"

"She's with Mina and the others," she replies. "They've been taking good care of her."

I'm about to respond when a familiar, sweet scent hits my snout. My head snaps toward its source. Noël?

And then I see them.

A circle of blue roses, fully grown and vibrant, their petals glowing in the diffuse light of the setting sun. I freeze, my chest tightening with awe. I didn't grow those. "Did she . . . ?"

A smile graces Elder Aïna's features. "She made them appear. A very good omen."

My heart swells with pride. Noël's connection to this land, to Ávera, is stronger than I could have imagined. "She is remarkable,"

"She is," Elder Aïna agrees, her gaze soft as she looks at the flowers. "And so is the path she's meant to walk."

I run my claws over the fur between my ears, smoothing it back so every strand is in place. Then I pull just a few forward. I saw the growlings style their hair this way. "How do I look?"

Elder Aïna smirks. "Handsome."

I grin as I trace my claws one final time over my fur. If this is how my mate will see me tonight, I want to make sure I'm everything she could want.

The vólkins begin to gather. Pups race each other to the clearing, eager to find the best spot to watch. We stand at the front, all eyes on Elder Aïna as she steps forward to address the crowd. Her presence commands attention, and the lively chatter quiets as she raises her paw.

"Tonight," she begins, her voice strong and clear, "we welcome Her Majesty, Noël—the chosen leader who has come to guide us. Her presence marks the beginning of a new era for us all. The era where the balance will return."

The vólkins erupt in cheers and howls, their voices echoing through the trees of Ávera. My ears perk, and my focus shifts to my right as Noël walks toward us. She's flanked by Mina, Naïa, and Essin, her presence lit by the glow of the garlands.

She takes my breath away.

The gown fits her perfectly. Every stitch and detail matches her beauty. My chest tightens, and a familiar ache rises in my throat. I swallow hard, feeling my cock drawing out. She will drive me to madness before the bonding ritual.

As she approaches, the crowd bows low in a show of loyalty and submission. But all I can see—all I want to see—is her. Our eyes meet, and the rest of the world blurs into nothingness. The cheering fades, the glowing orbs dim, and even the pups' laughter is distant.

There is only her. My little dove.

I stride forward through the gathered vólkins. My mind blanks. All I know is that I need her in my arms.

Before I realize it, she's there, close enough to hold. My heart pounds wildly in my chest, and every hair on my body stands on end.

Her eyes widen as she looks up at me. "Theron?"

"Noël," I murmur her name, standing so close to her.

Mine.

Tonight, there is no balance, no prophecy.

There is only a little dove in front of me.

A dove with a beautiful gown, a dove with colorful flowers in her hair. I look down at my cock, and so does she. The veins are going to pop soon if I don't do something about it. My gaze narrows, locking onto her as her pale face flushes red. There it is. That beautiful blush of hers. She lifts her eyes and pushes me away.

"You are the most beautiful and tempting creature I have ever witnessed," I whisper. The red deepens on her cheeks, spreading to her neck, and by the goddesses, every part of me wants to claim her here and now. Ceremonies be damned.

"Everyone is looking," she says quietly.

Her words bring me back to reality. And another low growl rumbles in my chest as I glance around. Right. The crowd.

I tilt my head back and take a deep breath, the cool air doing little to calm the heat in me. *What are you doing, Theron?*

This moment is for her, and it's too important to let my

beast take over. Turning to the gathered vólkins, I catch Elder Aïna and Kaël grinning at me, clearly enjoying my slip in composure. The rest of the crowd stands in respectful silence, their attention fixed on us.

I clear my throat, then raise my voice. "The feast shall begin!"

The clearing fills with cheers as I stride to the main table, catching my mate's hand as I walk. Carefully, I lead Noël to her seat, brushing my claws over her hand once more before stepping to my own seat beside her. She looks up at me, her eyes wide and still shining with warmth.

Some vólkins settle into their places as others begin bringing out more of the game we hunted, the rich aroma of meat and berries filling the air.

Vólkins approach one by one to pay their respects, each offering blessings to the leader such as, "We welcome the ethereal leader" and "May the goddesses bless our leader."

My patience is wearing thin. All I want is to pull her onto my lap, to feel her weight on my thigh where she belongs. She'd fit perfectly there, greeting everyone from her rightful place. On me.

Clenching my jaw, I turn my focus to the task at paw and arrange cooked meat for Noël in the bowl Mina prepared, one I carved myself.

"Do you want fruit with the meat or after?" I ask.

Noël turns to me, her attention shifting away from yet another well-meaning blessing from my people. Her brows knit as she replies, "Theron, I can get my food myself."

"I'm already doing it," I say, barely holding back a grin.

Her eyes narrow, and she sighs. "After."

Did she just *huff*? My Noël, huffing like a vólkin? The urge to tease her is irresistible.

"Should I press more to hear a growl?" I bare my fangs as I ask, setting the bowl before her.

She fixes me with a sharp look. "You owe me many explana-tions for someone who just stormed out of the house," she counters, before adding, "Thank you."

So polite. Polite and feisty. A combination that has me taking more calming breaths than ever.

Before I can respond, Váar approaches, his young pup cradled in his arms. "Your Majesty," he begins, "would you bless my child?"

I glance at Noël, watching the change in her expression as she takes in the sight of the pup. Her gaze softens instantly, her hand reaching out to hold the youngling's small paw in her own. The gentleness in her touch, the kindness in her eyes— I feel a lump form in my throat. Is this how she'll look at our own cubs one day? Is this what our future holds?

Goddesses above.

Noël speaks, her voice warm and sweet. "May you grow strong and wise, and may the goddesses watch over you always."

Váar's expression mirrors my own, full of a profound, unspoken gratitude. He nods, his eyes brimming with emotion as he steps back with his pup held close.

My mate, my Noël, has just blessed the next generation of warriors. The vólkins who will one day carry our traditions, raise their own young in a world that we will restore to balance.

Noël hums as she takes a bite of the cooked meat. The sight fills me with pride, seeing her enjoy the results of my hunt is a satisfaction like no other. My mate, eating what I've provided, feels as natural and right as the rising sun.

I watch her quietly as I put a slice of raw meat into my mouth. After her spiritual awakening, I'll take her with me on a hunt. She'll see me in action, witness what I'm capable of firstpaw. She'll know that I can provide, protect, and that I'm hers, as she is mine.

But first, the bonding ritual.

That sacred rite will tie our souls together completely. Noël will finally awaken to her true self, to what human females are meant to be—strong, free, and connected to the land, to the very soil and sky.

"After the ceremony, we will talk," she says, breaking through my thoughts. She takes the strawberry I offer her, her fingers brushing my claws.

"I need to go to the border first, my little dove," I say. "As much as I want to be with you, I must protect Ávera."

"What's at the border?"

How much should I burden her now? It's only her second night here, and I've only just begun to see her smile more often. The thought of worrying her so soon feels wrong.

"Theron," she presses.

I sigh. Her gaze pulls the truth from me. "My warriors and Elder Aïna have seen unusual things near the border. Right where the barrier once stood."

Her expression shifts, eagerness flashing in her eyes. As though it's the most natural conclusion in the world, she says, "I'm coming with you."

"I can't let you put yourself in danger," I counter, trying to reason with her. "You've had a long day, walking, meeting everyone, you must be tired."

"And yet," she says, "I'm still coming with you."

"Noël," I begin, my tone firmer now.

"This is final, Theron."

A heavy sigh escapes me. How can I deny her when she speaks like this? Her fire, her refusal to yield, it's my greatest weakness.

"Fine," I concede. "But you will have to listen to me. Always."

Her lips twitch into a small smile, and I realize there's no winning against her. And truthfully, I don't mind losing.

After the feast, a large fire roars to life in the center of the clearing, its flames crackling and stretching toward the darkened sky. The glow falls across the gathered vólkins and bathes the clearing in golden light.

The females form a circle around the fire, paws linked as they prepare to begin the ceremonial dance. Around them, the males take up drums, and the deep, rhythmic beats resonate through the ground and into my chest. Leaf spirits flit through the air, in and out of the crowd like threads of light.

The dance begins. The females move with grace, synchronized as though the fire calls to them. The flowers woven into their manes catch the light, their colors gleaming and shifting as they twirl. It's more than a dance—it's a prayer.

Noël's eyes are wide and focused on the scene before her, completely captivated. Wonder written across her face as the leaf spirits circle closer to her.

"Why don't you join them?" I ask as the spirits weave playfully through her hair, urging her forward.

She hesitates, then admits quietly, "I . . . I've never danced before."

Never danced? My mate, who moves with the strength and elegance of a warrior, has never experienced this? It's wrong, unnatural. "Humans don't dance?" I ask.

"We do," she replies. "But my mother never let me join."

The faint smile on her lips doesn't reach her eyes. My chest tightens at the thought of her being denied something so simple.

I glance at the leaf spirits and jerk my head toward Noël. They understand, and their glowing forms swirl around her. They tug at her hair and her gown, urging her toward the fire.

Noël looks back at me, unsure.

"Go. The circle will welcome you."

Finally, she rises and allows the spirits to guide her. As she steps into the circle, her gown flows around her like water, catching the firelight.

The females welcome her with open arms, smiles and laughter on their faces as they pull her into their dance. Noël quickly finds her rhythm, and in that moment, she becomes part of the prayer, an offering to the goddesses.

If I could join her, I would. But this is a sacred dance, a tradition meant for the purest souls. Females. It is their connection to the goddesses, their devotion given form.

So for now, I'll watch. I'll hold this sight in my heart. My mate, radiant and free, moving because she belongs to the very spirit of Ávera.

Perhaps it's a good thing her mother never let her dance. Humans would've witnessed her power.

27

DANCING WITH FIRE AND ROSES

"No woman is truly free if her world is built by those who fear
her power."
—Eyleen Ársa

Noël

My heart feels light, and a rare kind of happiness
spreads through me. With the warmth of the
flames, the laughter of the vólkins, and the energy
of the celebration, I feel like I can breathe again. The fire's heat
brushes against my skin, while the cool night air caresses my
face. Above, the sky is dark and beautiful, and the young moon
shines above us.

My gaze catches on the garlands swaying with the breeze.
They remind me of the small trinkets my mother and I used to
make, silk fabric tied with red thread, and stuffed with sage
roots. She believed sage brought blessings, cleared bad omens,
and invited good fortune.

The memory feels like a dream, but seeing these garlands
above, I feel the same care here in Ávera. The vólkins have

poured thought and intention into every detail of this celebration.

It's primal. And it's beautiful.

During the feast, I couldn't help but watch the vólkins eat.
I'd known they consume raw meat, but seeing it firsthand was
something else entirely. They tore into their meals with sharp
canines. Juices spilled across the tables as they devoured their
food with a ferocity I'd only read about in books. It should have
made me uncomfortable, but it didn't. The meat was clean, no
blood or fur left behind. Though I noticed Theron ate in
smaller slices than Kaël or the others did. I wonder why.

The little pups were digging into larger chunks, tearing at
them from both sides where they lay on the tables.

Theron had explained that vólkins eat at tables to align
with human traditions. Even the fires lighting Ávera aren't for
them. They don't need them. Everything here has been created
for the comfort of their future mates. That thought stayed with
me throughout the feast: how much they've adapted, how
much they've prepared for this moment. For me.

And now, as I dance, I feel Theron's gaze on me. It's as
though it anchors me, pulling me to him despite the distance
between us. Across the fire, our eyes meet, and the world seems
to fade. The drums, the voices, the glow of flames—they all
blur into the background, leaving only him. There's so much I
want to ask, so much I don't understand about this bond that
ties us. The memory of last night is a puzzle piece I can't fit. But
for now, I can be patient.

I can enjoy this celebration.

I focus back on the dance. These vólkins have worked so
hard to make this day special for me. The least I can do is
embrace it fully, to honor their efforts. The female vólkins
release their linked paws, their movements becoming freer as
they circle the fire. They lift their arms to the sky, their bodies
flowing with the rhythm of the drums.

I mimic their movements, allowing myself to let go, to move without thought or worry. I never thought dancing would make me feel so alive.

The grass is soft beneath my feet, leaves brush against my arms, the trees sway in time with the music, and I feel . . . whole.

Every step feels like a celebration of life itself. And here, under the thin scratch of silver of the young moon, surrounded by the vólkins, I feel like I belong.

Is this what Elder Aïna meant?

A shiver runs through me. Body, mind, and soul . . .

Under the crescent's glow, the Leader shall unite and guide. A voice echoes, calm and beautiful. *Her vision will pierce the shadows of doubt, as the spirits foretold. The bond of essence and soul will shape the fate of this world.*

The words make me falter. They're *too familiar.*

Mother used to say the same thing.

I glance around, expecting Elder Aïna to be standing close, but the voice fades as quickly as it came. I keep moving, letting the music guide me.

The fire crackles louder, its flames shifting from orange to a bright blue. The vólkins stop, their chatter replaced with silence as their eyes widen. But I continue to dance like something is pulling me forward. A strange energy flows through me, lights my every step.

Blue roses bloom under my feet, glowing as they spread outward in a trail behind me. Gasps ripple through the crowd, and the vólkins step back, their whispers blending with the crackling fire. Elder Aïna's gaze catches mine across the clearing. There's pride in her expression, and something about it makes my chest swell.

I like that. Being the source of pride.

The feeling is warm, like I've found something I didn't realize I was missing. The roses feel . . . like home.

But then the warmth fades, my vision blurs, and my legs buckle beneath me.

The last thing I see before everything goes dark is Theron's face, his eyes wide.

"Theron? Why are you—"

28

CLAWS, CRYSTALS, AND CHICKEN FEET

"Little light, when the world forgets its name, find the wind that sings for you, follow the leaves. They will remember me. And when you do . . . I'll be blooming in the roots."

—A.

Theron

"Noël!" I roar. My chest tightens as I see her collapse, and my body moves before I can think. I'm at her side in moments, my crystals flaring bright blue. They always glow like this when my emotions spike, but this time, the light feels blinding. She doesn't even stir when it shines on her.

Vólkins crowd closer, their eyes wide and concerned.

"Step back!" I bark, my voice cutting through their murmurs. My heart pounds so hard it feels like it might break free of my chest. My claws flex, my fangs are bared. "No one comes close!"

The vólkins obey, instead forming a wide circle. I kneel and pull Noël into my arms. Her body feels . . . wrong. Too limp. When her head tilts back, I catch it with my paw. Her hair falls over my arm, her hand dangles lifelessly against the grass, and her face—goddesses, her face—is paler than I've ever seen it.

"Noël," I say, as I brush the strands of her hair away.

Elder Aïna steps closer. "Goddesses, we need your guidance," she whispers, her gaze fixed on the sacred stone.

The air weighs on me, thick with energy. A light begins to form, and a rough wind stirs the leaves, whipping around us hard enough I have to shut my eyes. If I weren't so heavy, I'd lose my balance.

The flames of the bonfire suddenly rise wild. The heat brushes against my fur, and I feel it standing on end.

Three figures materialize before us, their presence so powerful it brings the vólkins to their knees, heads bowed low.

Vodínaya, the goddess of healing and endurance, steps forward first, her gaze vast like the ocean's depths. Beside her is Dušava, her hair flowing like ivy, the goddess of forests and fertility. Zárya stands tall, her aura blazing with the power of light and fire.

Vodínaya's voice rolls out. "Her Majesty is undergoing a spiritual awakening."

Dušava's tone is softer. "She has endured too much in too short a time. Her spirit is overwhelmed."

Zárya's piercing eyes meet mine, the fire around her turns brighter as she speaks. "Her Majesty is not yet ready. Her body, spirit, and mind are not in harmony."

I grip Noël tighter. "What must I do to help her?"

Vodínaya steals my gaze. "She must perform the bonding ritual to awaken her full power."

"We still have around two phases to go before the full moon." I clench my jaw, tugging Noël closer. "What can we do until then?"

Dušava tilts her head and narrows her eyes. "Something

else is trying to connect with her. It clouds her spirit, weighs on her mind, and adds to her burden."

Zárya nods. "She needs rest. Time to heal and reflect. Only then will she regain the strength she needs."

My throat tightens, but I agree. "I will ensure she rests."

The three goddesses exchange a glance before speaking in unison, their voices reverberating deep in my chest. "Trust in your bond, noble guardian. Guide her and prepare for the ritual. The fate of this world depends on it."

Each goddess focuses sharply on me as their final words echo in the air. "We cannot allow failure this time."

As quickly as they appeared, the goddesses fade, their light dimming until the flames of the bonfire sputter out. The wind stills, and a heavy silence settles over Ávera.

I look down at Noël in my arms. Her face is pale, her skin clammy with sweat.

"No one will harm you," I murmur, nuzzling her cheek. "No one."

There's a scent on her, a male's scent. It's weak, but it's there.

My fur bristles, and my breaths come heavier with every inhale. My mate smells like another. My claws dig into the furs beneath us as I lean over her still, unconscious body nestled in our nest-bed. Rage simmers beneath my fur.

Who dared come near her? I do not recognize this scent, but it is vólkin.

I lower my snout, my nose brushing her hair as I breathe in. The scent isn't there. Not her hair. My nose trails lower, past her jawline, closer to her face. The trace is stronger now, but not its source. My teeth bare in a snarl, a growl rumbling low in my chest.

I smell it—the vólkin crystal. The pendant resting against her chest, barely glowing. The scent of another male clings to it. It's not her scent. It's foreign. It's unwelcome.

Who gave her this? Who thought they had the right?

My growl deepens, reverberating through the room. My jaw tightens, and my body coils as every muscle screams to hunt and destroy.

I lower my face to hers, watching the way the light from the pendant glimmers against her pale skin and the sweat on her brow. My tongue darts out to trace the droplets on her cheek. Sweet and intoxicating. My cock pushes past my fur, hardens further when her lips part at my touch.

Her face is so small beneath me. Even my claws look massive beside the curve of her cheek. The need to protect her, to shield her from the world, wars with the fury that burns in my veins. Someone dared to touch what is *mine*.

My erection presses against the furs beneath me. My claws grip tighter, curling into the nest. Every instinct I have demands action. Vólkin or human, it doesn't matter. Whoever it is, they dared to touch *my* Noël.

With my nose brushing against her jaw, her scent overpowers everything else. My breaths are heavy, my chest rising and falling as I fight to control the chaos inside me.

So small. So beautiful. So completely *mine*.

The scent of the male clings to the crystal, but it will not stay for long—

"Theron!" Aeson's voice cuts through my haze.

"Come in," I command, rising from the nest to place myself between Noël and the door. Aeson enters, his usual calm masking the urgency in his steps. His white pelt gleams in the light of the crystals around us. He looks over at Noël, then back at me.

"We found a house," he says, "four hours' run from the border. I think you should see it."

"A house?" My brows furrow as I stride toward him. My balls ache from the strain, the friction between my thighs doing nothing to ease the tightness in my chest. "Humans built a house on our lands?"

Aeson shakes his head, crossing his arms. "No. A vólkin house, grown from the trees and land nearby."

A vólkin house? On the edge of our territory? My jaw tightens as I tilt my head, narrowing my eyes in thought. That doesn't make sense. No vólkin would grow a house without my knowledge or my permission. No vólkin would go beyond the border. It's not even possible to grow a whole home in such a short amount of time. The barrier fell just a few days ago. Unless this vólkin is not from Ávera.

I inhale slowly, forcing myself to focus, to think. "Call Mina and the others," I say, my tone leaving no room for discussion. "My mate will not stay alone in this state." My claws flex at my sides as the memory of that scent burns in my mind. "And add two more guards to the entrance." My tone drops, a low growl lacing every word. "No male comes near this home."

Aeson nods. "It will be done."

I watch him leave, my body still thrumming with energy as my gaze shifts back to Noël resting in the nest. Mine. Always mine. Whatever this house means, whoever left their mark on her crystal, I will get all the answers.

We sprint through the forest, our paws flying over the ground as we cross beyond where the barrier once stood. It's like stepping into a world abandoned by life itself. The grass beneath us is dark, its color sickly and unnatural. The trees are no better, lifeless things that seem to sag under their own decay.

This is what happens when the balance is disrupted.

Elder Aïna's words echo in my mind, a grim reminder of the world we inherited. She spoke of how, long before the barrier appeared—when even she was just a youngling—the earth began to cry out in pain. Its beauty faded. The fruits grew smaller and weaker. The soil became barren, the rivers slower, and the forests less vibrant. The land itself bore the scars of imbalance.

Generations ago, long before my parents were even born, the world was different. Vólkins and human females lived as mates, their union bringing harmony. Together, they ignored the greed of human males who sought power and control. The greed of those males twisted the world as they oppressed their own females and ignored the balance of nature.

The vólkins of Ávera—their claws and hearts bound by peace—did nothing to stop it. And then it was too late.

And so it was. Before we could restore the balance, the barrier rose, sealing us off from the outside world. We could do nothing, powerless to reverse the damage.

But no more.

My mate will stand strong. We will bond, our souls will be tied together, and we will restore this balance.

I will never let anyone destroy this land again. My pups, our pups, will be born into a world renewed. They will grow up running through healthy forests, breathing clean air, tasting the sweetness of fat deer. They will know the joy of a land in harmony.

The thought fuels my strides, my claws flexing as the trees blur past us. No one will stand in our way.

Kaël freezes in his tracks, his eyes wide and unblinking. His entire posture stiffens as though he's seen a female.

I stop beside him, my fur bristling with irritation. "What is it now, Kaël?"

Aeson and Zephyr skid to a halt behind me, both rising

onto their hind paws, their gazes sharp and scanning for danger.

Kaël turns to me. "I have NEVER in my LIFE seen . . . chicken feet this huge!"

I blink. "Chicken feet?"

"What are you talking about?" Aeson says, crouching as he scans the forest floor.

Zephyr strides forward. "Kaël, stop being dramatic. There's no—" His eyes drop to the ground.

I step closer, my patience stretched thin, ready to berate them both. "Kaël, where did you even—"

And then I see it.

Deep grooves in the earth, the unmistakable imprints of giant talons. Massive, clawed prints stretch across the forest floor, each one as large as a vólkin's home. My jaw tightens as my gaze follows the trail of absurdly large tracks disappearing into the dense forest ahead.

"What the . . ." Aeson mutters, inspecting the marks. "These are fresh."

Zephyr's ears flick back. "Are we . . . are we seriously looking at chicken feet this size?"

Kaël, no longer worried about being reprimanded, gestures wildly at the prints. "GINORMOUS chicken feet! Look at them! How is this even possible?"

I stare at the tracks. "These aren't . . . chickens," I growl, my voice wary. "Something's wrong. No creature with claws like this belongs in this forest. Not naturally."

Aeson straightens, his brows furrowed. "Theron, these tracks . . . they lead straight toward the vólkin house."

"Let's get going then," I say as I cast one last look at the strange, enormous tracks. "We're dealing with something far beyond what we've ever faced."

Kaël grumbles under his breath, "Something far beyond a giant chicken, apparently . . ."

"Kaël," I growl with a glare. "Focus."

He nods quickly, falling silent. We cautiously follow the markings on the ground. They're consistent, which means the creature was walking in a specific direction. No change of pace, no deviation. It knew exactly where it was going.

My nose twitches, and a knot forms in my stomach. Something about this feels off.

"We're almost there," Aeson says.

I give a curt nod, my focus on the path ahead. After a few strides, the house comes into view. It's well constructed, the work of an experienced vólkin. The energy transfer is skillful. The shape, size, and the way it's grown from the surrounding trees mirror the structures in Ávera. Whoever built this was one of us. There's no mistaking it.

I take a few steps closer, scanning the area. No sign of the creature. The massive tracks are gone, vanishing without explanation. My jaw tightens. What is happening here?

Then I catch it—a scent. It's familiar.

I turn toward it, my muscles tensing as I follow the trail. My steps quicken as the scent grows stronger. I round the house, and then I'm rooted in place.

Goddesses above.

29

BOUND BY BLOOD

"Maybe one day, we'll live somewhere green. No uniforms. No orders. Just flowers and books with pictures and stars so bright we forget who hurt us."
—Linnéa Fenrówe, age nine

Gregor

The darkness is absolute. My eyes are covered with a thick cloth, denying me any sense of location or direction. The air is damp, musty, and it smells of mold and decay. I can feel the cold, rough surface of the stone wall against my back and the hard floor beneath me. My hands are bound behind me so tightly the ropes cut into my wrists. Every movement sends a jolt of pain through my exhausted body.

Since they took me, everything has been a blur of agony and fear. They dragged me here, wherever "here" is, and left me. I've lost count of how many days I've been trapped in this darkness. The only sounds are the distant voices and footsteps above and the drip of water from the ceiling.

My stomach growls. I've hardly eaten. They've given me just enough water to keep me alive and thrown some dried bread on the floor. My throat is parched, my lips cracked and dry. Each breath is a struggle. I'm completely miserable.

But the physical pain is nothing compared to the mental torment. The constant uncertainty, the fear of what might happen next. I've tried to stay strong, to hold on to the hope that I'll find a way out, but each passing day makes me believe my end is near.

The faces of my captors . . . their cold eyes. The threats, the beatings, the games they play with me. I am nothing more than a pawn in their hands, a tool to be used as they please.

The sound of footsteps approaching pulls me from my thoughts. My heart races. What new torment will they bring today? The footsteps stop in front of me, and a rough hand grabs my chin, tilting my head up.

"Gregor," a cold voice says. It's the stranger who found me on the road, the one who promised help only to deliver me into this nightmare. "How are you feeling today?"

I don't respond. What can I say? My mouth is dry, and my voice feels like a distant memory. The stranger's grip tightens.

"You've had a week to think about your situation," he continues. "Do you understand the gravity of your position?"

I nod in his hold. There's no point in resisting. I've learned that lesson the hard way.

"Good," he says, releasing my chin. "We have a task for you. A mission, if you will. Succeed, and perhaps we'll consider your cooperation. Fail, and Linnéa pays the price."

The mention of my sister makes my heart beat faster. I've endured this torment for her sake, to protect her from these monsters. At least I know they need me and won't kill me. Or her.

"Wha . . . what do you want me to do?" I manage to croak out.

"We need you to infiltrate Ávera," the stranger says. "Gain their trust, learn their secrets, and report back to us. We will provide you with a means of communication."

He pauses, and I feel the warmth of his body near me. The cloth around my eyes is finally removed, the sudden light blinding me. As my vision adjusts, I see the stranger standing before me, a crystal that glows with pink light in his hand.

"This," he says, holding the crystal up for me to see, "is your means of communication—a vólkin crystal. You will use it to send us messages. Place it in water, and it sends one signal. Rub it with a warm cloth, and it sends another. Simple enough, even for you."

I swallow hard, my eyes wide, dancing between his face and the crystal in his hand. Why would they have a vólkin crystal in their possession?

That's it. I'm done.

Noël . . . How can I betray her? She spared my life.

Goose bumps cover my spine as I think of the day that giant beast shredded Arnold into nothing. Noël was kind enough to let me live, even knowing the plans we had for her. I never wanted her death. But Arnold . . .

I'm so sorry, Noël. I have no choice.

"I'll do it." My voice trembles.

"Excellent." The stranger sounds satisfied with my answer. "But first, we need to prepare you. You're a wreck. We'll heal you and teach you everything you need to know about the vólkins."

He kneels down in front of me and says with a grin, "Then, before sending you off, we will beat you a little more."

I nod again, too exhausted to argue. The stranger motions to someone beside me, and rough hands untie my wrists. This giant of a man pulls me to my feet, and my legs shake from the effort it takes to stand.

"Come with me," the stranger says, leading me out of the

cold room. The light is blinding after days in darkness, and I stumble, barely able to keep up. They guide me to a small room where a healer awaits, his expression indifferent as he examines my wounds.

They forced me to quit the military using a forged healer's note to explain my sudden departure. It was a reminder of the power they hold, how easily they can manipulate my life. The beatings have been relentless, a method to extract every detail I know about the vólkins and my brief time in the forest. But I couldn't tell them much, I only saw the vólkin for a few moments.

They were not satisfied with my answers.

Now, as the healer's hands move over my injuries, I feel the slightest relief—relief that the physical pain might soon lessen —and dread for the mission that awaits me. I'm being prepared, molded into a tool for their use, and I can do nothing to stop it.

The wounds disappear before my eyes. How is that possible?

The bruises heal within moments, the cuts seal, and I feel as good as new.

What?

If they have this type of medicine, why aren't they healing citizens? People die every day from fever. I don't understand.

The healer finishes and steps back, his work done. The stranger, his gaze cold, hands me the glowing crystal.

"Remember, Gregor," he says. "We are always watching."

I take the crystal, its surface cool and smooth in my hand.

"Come," he says, leading me out of the healer's room. "We shall begin your vólkin lessons." He looks at the crystal in my hand. "There's so much you need to know."

I feel a knot of fear tighten in my throat. I must succeed. For my sister's sake and mine, I have to.

Otherwise, I'm dead.

30

THE HALL OF HANDS AND PAWS

"Let them fear the girl who was raised in silence. Because when she learns to speak, she'll teach the world to burn."
—Eyleen Ársa

Noël

The world around me dissolves into an endless void of darkness. There's no ground or walls, just an overwhelming nothingness, as though I've been swallowed whole by the night. Where am I?

Slowly, dim lights begin to appear above, tiny strings glowing in the void. They pulse like the beat of a heart I cannot see.

I don't move, yet I feel pulled forward, drawn into the strange glow. And I see them.

Hands. Paws.

So many hands and paws rise from the shadowy ground. They stretch upward, fingers curling and reaching. Each one is unique—weathered or delicate, clawed and strong—but they all share the same destination, grasping for the light above.

They rise higher, and that's when I notice what they're reaching *for. Suspended above them is a small figure, glowing like a blue rose in a black, starless sky. I hold my breath as my sight sharpens, and I see it clearly.*

A baby.

Me.

I am that baby.

The infant is held aloft by countless hands that cradle her carefully. As she's lifted higher, the glow of her skin grows stronger, silvery-blue light bright enough to cross the dark hall. The whispers start then, rising around me. I hear them everywhere I look. I can't make out the words, but I feel them—prayers or hopes. Warnings. They ripple through me, raising goose bumps on my skin.

The hands and paws remain outstretched, as though pleading, begging. Their desperate yearning seems aimed not at the baby, but at ... my heart?

Then, from the shadows, someone steps forward. Cutting through the sea of hands and paws.

Mother.

She walks with grace. Back straight, chin high, just like she always did. Her hair flows like midnight silk, her gray roots glowing in the light. Her face is etched with sorrow, a grief that hurts even from where I stand. Her bare feet are silent against the shadowy ground, and her gaze never leaves the baby. Me.

The whispers quiet as she approaches, the hands freezing midreach as though waiting for her permission to touch the infant. She leans down, her arms passing through the layers of hands and paws to lift the baby into her embrace.

"My little rose," she murmurs. She presses a kiss to the baby's forehead, her tears catching in the glow. "My Noël."

A lump rises in my throat. "Mother," I whisper.

She doesn't hear me. Her eyes are closed as she holds the baby for a long moment. Then, with a deep breath, she lifts the infant high. Her strong voice echoes through the void as thousands of white feathers fall from above.

"The blue rose will bloom again."

My heart pounds, chest tight and aching. My head feels heavy, eyes swollen as though I've been crying for hours. I'm warm, no, my body is nearly burning. Seeing my mother's face so clearly . . . I miss her so much.

There's so much I want to say to her, so much I need her to know. How I long for her touch, her wisdom, and love. How I wish I could tell her everything that's happened since she left me. I need to know why she was taken from me, how it all ended. And I want to tell her about Theron, how kind he's been, how he cares for me. I think she would've liked him if only she were still here. Maybe he could've helped her with that fat raccoon who always stole her trinkets from the roof. We didn't have many wild animals in Tárnov, but this raccoon managed to find a way between Tárnov's walls, and for some reason, would appear in our home. Theron's so tall, he probably could've reached it easily.

It is so painful.

I want to reach out for that baby, to hold her close, to whisper to her that she'll grow strong, that she'll grow smart and beautiful.

But the hands. All those paws. Who were they? Why did they feel so familiar, like ghosts from a forgotten memory?

A gentle touch grazes my cheek, pulling me from my thoughts. I lean into the soothing sensation. It's damp and fluffy, like fur.

Fur?

I force my eyes open, blinking away the blur, and find myself staring into Theron's bright, hazel eyes. There's something soft in the way he looks at me. It's comforting.

"I can finally see your eyes, my little dove," he murmurs.

Why does it feel like I haven't seen him in so long? A breeze brushes against my skin, and I glance to the side. We're on the porch.

We're home.

Home. The word feels strangely right. My mother's house in Tárnov seems like something from another lifetime.

"Theron," I whisper, my voice hoarse, my throat dry and aching. I try to clear it, but the effort turns into a cough, and I wince, closing my eyes again.

"Your Majesty, please, drink this," a melodic voice, light as a song, says. A nýmphá.

I open my eyes again and see her pale hand holding a cup shaped from a leaf.

Theron takes it from her and raises it to my mouth, his other paw bracing my back as I sit up. As soon as the cool water touches my lips, I drink desperately, and I don't stop until it's gone, my body craving every drop.

I'm sitting on his lap, leaning into his solid, rock-hard chest as he rests his paw on my back. "Thank you," I murmur, glancing at the nýmphá who offered me water. My gaze shifts to the garden, and my breath catches.

"Theron!" Blue roses, countless and fully grown, stretch out around the porch. Their glow illuminates the nýmphí sitting among them and the way their small hands trace the petals as they chat with one another.

I've never seen so many before. My mother's garden had a few dozen flowers she ardently nurtured. But this? This is unlike anything I've ever imagined.

"I love having these rare and beautiful roses inside our home," Theron says, his tone calm. "But you grew so many, and we needed space to walk. So I brought us out here."

My jaw goes slack. I tilt my head to look up at him, my eyes heavy and struggling to stay open. "How did I do this?"

"It is said that the tears of a blue-rose blood make the flowers bloom," he says, his claws combing through my hair.

It hits me all at once. My mother never cried. At least, not in front of me. Not once in my life had I seen her shed a single tear. Is that how we have blue roses in the first place? Did she cry when I wasn't there to see it?

Why had she never told me a thing? Never answered any of my questions?

"Did I cry that much? Enough to grow a whole garden?"

Theron nods. "Three nights, my mate."

Three nights?

I blink at him. "Have I slept for three whole nights?"

"You were asleep for seven." His tone is heavy with a sadness that makes my chest ache. "The last three, you were crying."

I reach up instinctively to rub my temples. No wonder my head feels like a horse trampled it.

"What dreams haunted you?" Theron's deep voice rumbles as he tugs me closer and wraps his arms around me.

"I saw my mother," I begin, my words barely audible as I rest my head against his chest. "I saw myself . . . saw lots of hands and paws. They were reaching for a baby, for me. I was that baby." My voice trails off, the memory still so vivid. "Theron . . . what was that dream?"

If I had any tears left to shed, they would've come now. But I'm drained, hollow. The ache in my chest reminds me how much I miss her.

I sigh into his fur, then inhale his scent. He smells so good, like the roses surrounding us, earthy and comforting, with a warmth that soothes my raw nerves.

His brows knit together, his gaze fixed on me. I brush my hand over his furrowed brow, trying to smooth it. His throat bobs as he swallows. And then . . .

Oh. I feel something, hard and growing, against my hip. My face burns as realization dawns.

"Alright, time to feed you and get you cleaned," Theron blurts, panic flashing across his face as he scoops me up with a speed that leaves no time for protest.

I want to tell him to put me down, but my body feels like a sack of stones. So, for now, I let him carry me, my pride taking a backseat to my exhaustion.

As Theron opens the door, my eyes catch the overgrowth of blue roses spilling around the bed-nest. My jaw slackens at the sight.

"Goddesses," I murmur. "I must've stayed unconscious so long just because I was so dehydrated."

"Actually," he says, his chest puffing, "I gave you water every day, and Mina and the nýmphí were bathing you." He says the last part of the sentence with a disappointed expression.

If he'd bathed me, I'd probably melt with embarrassment. I should thank Mina as well.

I feel like that baby in my dream, helpless and cocooned. The strong, fierce Noël seems like a legend whispered among the vólkins as I sit wrapped in furs, barely able to move. Mina and the nýmphí bathed me earlier, leaving me feeling clean but still weak. Now, I'm bundled up so snugly that the only parts of me that can move are my eyes and my mouth, which I open wide every time Theron offers me another strawberry.

I'm starving. After not eating for an entire week, I feel like I could hunt a bear, though the thought of harming the poor creature makes me wince. Theron, however, is insistent that I eat in small amounts to avoid getting sick. His practicality is both endearing and infuriating, especially since I know he genuinely believes I could take down a bear on my own. Honestly, I'm flattered.

"This one is juicy," he says as he holds another strawberry to my lips with his claws. I open wide and let the sweetness burst in my mouth. His gaze doesn't move, and the intensity in his eyes as he watches me eat each berry . . . He's so eager to feed me.

If I weren't so drained, I might laugh at how terrified I was of him just over a week ago. Now, this massive vólkin is carefully feeding me strawberries like I'm the most precious thing in the world. I shake my head, trying to clear the thought.

"No more? Already full?" he asks, tilting his giant head. Seriously, his head is at least four times the size of mine.

"More," I say eagerly as I open my mouth again. Maybe I should gift him something, but what?

His massive muscles shift before my eyes and it's distracting. Every time he reaches for a strawberry, his arms flex, the cords of muscle standing out beneath his fur. Is he doing this on purpose? The broad span of his shoulders, his thick neck, the way his mane frames his face. All of it demands attention. His crystals glow beautifully.

Ándor's crystal is almost dull.

"You're probably the biggest male I've ever seen," I mutter, my gaze traveling from his well-defined abs upward. He straightens at my words, and I catch the slightest flicker of surprise in his eyes.

"You flatter me, my mate." His deep voice is filled with pride. "Worry not. I will always protect you and will always be the strongest." He leans in. "I am a leader for a reason."

His words make my face flush with warmth, and I find myself suddenly unable to meet his intense gaze.

"Do you know why I fainted?" I ask, trying to shift the focus.

He nods, his expression darkening even as he places the last strawberry on my tongue. "Your spirit was overwhelmed," he explains, his voice full of . . . regret. "You've endured more than your spirit could handle, and when you stepped into the circle, it tried to break free. Your body couldn't keep up." There's a raw pain in his eyes, as though he blames himself for what happened.

"It's not your fault." From the moment we met, Theron has been by my side—protecting me, feeding me, fighting for me. I wish I could touch him, reassure him that he's done everything right, but the weight of the furs makes it impossible to lift my hand to comfort him. "Why did my spirit try to break free?"

Theron sets the empty bowl aside, pulling me against him as he speaks. "A circle is a powerful shape," he begins. "It represents the sun and the moon. The sun, like a male's cycle, spans day and night. The moon, like a female's cycle, moves through phases—new, full, and back again."

I nod. He knows so much. I admire that.

"Is that why women bleed every month?" I ask.

He nods, his claws brushing over the fur on my head. "Yes. The moon symbolizes femininity. That's why rituals involving female energy are always performed under a full moon. It's the height of your spirituality."

I hum in understanding, though his explanation only makes me realize how much humans don't know. There's so much hidden, so much I've never been taught.

In Tárnov, knowledge is a privilege strictly reserved for men. Women are forbidden from seeking education or even displaying intelligence openly. My mother defied this norm, teaching me in secret, away from prying eyes. No one ever entered our home, she made sure of that. If anyone had, they would have seen the shelves lined with books, filled with knowledge that could have condemned us both.

Whenever I spoke to men, I had to play the part of a fool. Feigning ignorance when history came up, pretending I couldn't grasp even the simplest of mathematical concepts or scientific ideas. It was exhausting, suppressing my true self to fit into the fragile world they had constructed for themselves.

It's absurd, really, this idea that a man's worth is tied to a woman's ignorance. As though they needed us to be stupid to validate their intelligence, to feel superior. How fragile their pride must be.

"Do you want to stretch your legs?" Theron asks, breaking through my thoughts.

He helps me out of the cocoon of furs before we make our way outside. Together, we carefully step around the overgrown roses that have claimed parts of our home. I hold onto Theron's arm because my legs are so weak that it's hard to walk, even slowly.

The garden of blue roses stretches wide, beautiful and alive. I sit down on the grass with the flowers surrounding me, their beauty fills me with warmth. They remind me of my mother—and of Theron too.

He joins me, and the nýmphí, who were chatting among themselves in the roses, notice us and quickly rush over, giggling as they begin weaving tiny flowers into my hair.

"Why do my tears make flowers grow?" I ask a nýmphá as I run my fingers over the soft petals of a blue rose.

"When the Mother of All wept on red roses, her sorrow turned them blue, Your Majesty," she explains, her voice like a breeze.

"The Mother of All?" I echo. "I've heard her." The words tumble out before I can stop them, but my eyes widen as the realization hits me. "I've heard her!"

Theron tilts his head. "You've heard of Éva?"

"Éva? The Mother of All is Éva?" My throat is dry, my heartbeat loud in my ears. "The Éva who ate the apple in the garden? The one who doomed humanity because of a snake?" My words spill out faster and faster.

Theron straightens, his broad shoulders stiff, and he exhales as he shakes his head in disbelief. "Is that what humans think?" he asks, almost to himself. "Unbelievable."

His intense gaze meets mine and he says, "Noël, there's a story every vólkin knows. It's been passed down for generations

—a tale of love, betrayal, and balance. It's the story of Éva and the Wolf."

I lean in without thinking even as the nýmphí weave more flowers into my hair. "I'm listening."

"In the beginning, when the earth was new, countless spirits roamed the land, each searching for their purpose. The world was beautiful, brimming with potential, but it was wild and untamed. Among the spirits was one of great power and wisdom, a guardian of creation who watched over everything.

"The spirits wanted to see their world through new eyes, to give life to something that could experience it as they never could. So they shaped a man from the earth and breathed life into him, calling him Ádám. He wandered the world in awe, but he was alone. His heart grew heavy with loneliness, and he longed for a companion.

"Moved by his longing, the spirits created a woman, Éva, who was graceful, strong, and full of life. For a time, it seemed like the two would build a bond that would shape humanity's future. But Ádám's heart faltered. He sought another, abandoning Éva and leaving her with nothing but betrayal and grief.

"Devastated, Éva fled to the heart of the forest. She found solace in nature, learned its ways and connected with the wild. The trees, the rivers, and the creatures became her companions. She spoke their language, sang their songs, and found a balance within herself that the world outside had denied her.

"One day, a terrible beast attacked her, threatening to end her life with its hunger and fury. But just as it struck, a wolf emerged, strong and noble. The wolf fought the beast with everything he had, driving it away and saving her life. Wounded but victorious, the wolf lay at her feet, and Éva cared for him, tending his wounds.

"Over time, they grew close. Their bond was built on trust and respect, and eventually, love. When the spirits saw this union, they blessed it, granting them a child, the first vólkin.

This child was unlike any other, a being of both human and wolf, embodying the harmony between the natural world and humanity.

"For years, Éva and the wolf raised their child in the forest, teaching it the ways of both worlds. But Ádám, consumed by jealousy and anger, couldn't stand the sight of Éva's happiness. He sought them out, determined to destroy what they had built.

"When Éva learned of his plan, her fury burned brighter than the stars. She called upon the spirits to find Ádám. They obeyed, and when Ádám stood before her, she used her power to seal him deep beneath the earth, ensuring he could never harm her family again.

"With Ádám gone, Éva raised her child in peace, teaching the vólkin to respect life, to live in balance, and to protect what they loved. The vólkin carried these lessons forward, becoming the guardians of the natural world."

My eyes widen, and anger simmers beneath my skin. Éva, the Mother of All, wasn't just misunderstood, she was silenced. Another woman condemned by the will of men. The thought holds tight in my chest, and my heart pounds like a drum.

I sit up straighter, staring at Theron, my hands trembling.

"Noël?" His brows pull together in concern.

"For centuries," I say, my voice raw, my words sharp and bitter, "women have been silenced and abused. For centuries— if not longer—women have endured stupid rules made by stupid men."

My fingers dig into the grass as though it's the only thing anchoring me to earth. "We suffered! From the very beginning. From the time of *creation* itself!"

The thundering in my chest becomes louder, each beat stoking the fire in my veins. Around me, the roses respond to my fury, sprouting dark, twisted thorns. My breath comes hard and fast as rage swallows every thought.

I try to push myself up, but my body refuses my sudden motion. The nýmphí are at my sides instantly, holding me firmly. Theron moves just as quickly, his strong arms wrapping around me.

I clutch at his thick fur, my fingers trembling, my chest heaving with my fury. My vision blurs as anger boils through me.

Looking up at him, my voice shakes, raw and enraged.

"I will restore the balance."

31

SIX WILL RISE UNDER
THE CRESCENT'S WATCH

"When the moon turns thrice and the veil thins, she will rise
with soil on her skin and fire in her blood. The first of six, born
of sorrow and silence. The world will know her not by name,
but by the weight of her vow."
—Láda Veléša, Goddess of Leadership and War

Theron

"The bonding ritual is a sacred tradition, Your
Majesty," Elder Aïna says, her paws resting behind
her back. "The last time it was performed was
before the barrier appeared."

We're gathered in the council room. My mate's declaration
still echoes in my mind and my pride hasn't calmed since. Her
vow to restore the balance felt like peering into the dream I've
carried since I was a pup.

The earth cries out, its pain born from the greed of men.
Humans who know no satiety, no balance. Ádám was no different, seduced by a snake in the guise of a human female, even

though he had Éva, our mother. Why would he forsake her? The answer is simple: greed.

I feel anger rise within me, not just at humanity's selfishness but at my own ancestors, the vólkins who stood by and did nothing. They had their mates, their peace, and ignored the cries of the human women who suffered under men's control. Time passed, and men's power grew, until now, when women are confined to their villages.

"One of the goddesses said we'd meet at the bonding ritual," Noël says, gripping the edge of the round table for support. Her body has been weak since she woke yesterday, and she's still unable to stand for long. She argued with me earlier, insisting she didn't want to be held like a child in the council room. So we compromised. I carry her only when she tires or needs to be moved. I'm not pleased that her body is suffering, but I can't deny the selfish satisfaction I feel in being able to hold her. From the moment we met, carrying her has been my greatest honor.

Elder Aïna tilts her head, her ears flicking. "The goddess will be present? That is ... unprecedented."

"Elder Aïna," I say with pride swelling in my chest, "I remind you that we are speaking of the six, especially the leader."

Noël lifts her chin, her gaze catching mine. "The six?"

I nod. "The prophecy speaks of six human females and their six mates, who will unite and together will restore balance."

"Since I am the leader," my mate murmurs.

"Five more," I finish her sentence.

"Where is this prophecy written? How does everyone know of it?" she asks.

"Before the goddesses disappeared, they whispered the prophecy through the trees," Mina says before I can speak. "Elder Aïna taught us all their words."

Elder Aïna's gaze is warm as she looks at Noël. "Ethereal Leader, would you like to hear the words of the goddesses?"

Noël grips the edge of the round table tighter. I trace my claws over her back, offering support. She glances up at me, and I nod.

"The prophecy speaks of a leader born of the blue-rose lineage, who will restore balance to our world."

As Elder Aïna begins to speak, a soft breeze drifts through the room, carrying with it the fresh, earthy scent of the forest. The carved roses on the council room walls pulse with a gentle blue light.

The vólkins in the room straighten, their postures instinctively proud. Mina, Naïa, and Essin stand on our right, with Kaël, Aeson, and Zephyr on the left. My mate and I stand before Elder Aïna as she speaks.

"In the heart of Ávera's ancient woods, where moonlight gently hugged the earth, a sacred prophecy whispered through the forest. Secrets floated on the wind, known only to the wise. Amidst the mystical land, where spirits roamed and goddesses wove our fate, the Mother's words echoed through time. Shadows danced, a connection between two worlds. Essence and soul will unite, tied by destiny's threads. A coming together of spirit, body, and mind—a dance guided by moonlight and earth's embrace. Yet, as this celestial dance unfolds, a shadow threatens to break Ávera's destiny."

Elder Aïna pauses as the wind grows stronger. The blue roses glow so bright their light reflects in the eyes of everyone present.

Noël stands tall despite her condition, her focus remains locked on Elder Aïna.

"The prophecy, whispered by the winds, spoke of a union between earthly souls and ethereal beings, a timeless bond that once upheld nature's balance. But shadows hinted at disruption —a force conspiring to shatter harmony." Elder Aïna's voice rises. "Six will rise under the crescent's glow, each bearing the mark of the ancient vow."

Noël's hand tightens on my arm. "I've heard this before," she murmurs.

I close my eyes and take a deep breath. Every vólkin knows the prophecy by heart, but hearing it now, in her presence, makes my fur stand on end, the ancient words gripping my soul.

"The Leader," Elder Aïna continues, and to my surprise, Noël joins her. Their voices blend together as one. "With vision clear, shall unite and guide. The Healer's touch, life anew, against the tide. The Warrior stands, fierce and true, a protectorate's might. The Scholar's wisdom, a beacon of light. The Sentinel's bond, with nature entwined. The Seer's gaze, through the veils of time. Together they stand, against the night's embrace, to heal the rift and restore grace."

I open my eyes, and the council room is transformed. Blue petals drift through the air, falling from above like a gentle rain, as if the prophecy has awakened the walls' essence.

The vólkins in the room exchange glances, but Elder Aïna's attention remains fixed on my mate. I place my paw on her head, running it down her braid. My Noël looks around the room, her narrowed eyes studying each face.

"Noël?" I say, lowering myself to her level.

She meets my gaze but shifts her weight to lean toward the table. Ah, her legs are tiring. I wrap my arm around her waist and lift her into my hold. Compromising with her earlier was wise. She murmurs a quiet thank you as she grips the fur of my chest to steady herself.

"If we're to find the remaining five," she begins, her eyes sweeping over the room, "we'll need to reach all the women in every village across the land."

"Currently, there are vólkins stationed beyond the border," I say, holding her closer. "They're studying the human villages nearby—their layouts, patrol routines, and defenses. We must understand the world outside before we act."

Noël nods. "The land is ruled by a tsar, with knyzya governing the five biggest villages under his command. Tárnov, Róstan, Yáarím, Gráyárk, and Velháven—the capital. Around every big village, there are smaller ones without a knyaz, which means that their defenses are less than the main five. I've only been to Tárnov, so most of what I know comes from my mother's wisdom and my military training. But I'm beginning to piece together a clearer picture of what's happening."

Aeson leans forward, while Kaël stands with his arms crossed, his expression serious.

"I met the tsar once," Noël continues, brushing a few shorter hairs back from her face. "When I saw his warriors, they wore uniforms embroidered with a blue rose."

"What's a uniform?" Kaël asks.

"Human warrior clothing," I explain.

"So, this tsar knows of the blue rose," Aeson says.

"It's not a flower that grows naturally," Zephyr adds.

Noël's eyes harden, and I feel the tension in her muscles. "The tsar is who sets the rules for humans," she says. "One of those rules restricts women to their villages. *A woman who is born in Tárnov dies in Tárnov.* It's a saying everyone knows."

A growl rumbles through my warriors, and I share their anger. That same rage burned in me the first time I heard those words.

"Your Majesty." Naïa speaks up. "If women aren't allowed to leave the villages, and this tsar knows of the blue rose . . ."

"It means he knows of the barrier," Elder Aïna says, her voice grave. "And he knows of its power."

Zephyr's claws dig into the table, leaving visible marks on the stone. "If the tsar knows about the barrier, then he knows about us."

The room falls into silence. Humans are taught to fear

and hate vólkins. But they don't know much about us. They don't know our abilities, they don't know our way of life. They only know that we are mindless beasts who can't even speak.

"We should strike now, before he has the chance to act first!" Kaël says, leaning forward.

Zephyr exhales, and I can see the effort it takes him to fight the urge to shake his head. His restraint is admirable.

"If the tsar—or his ancestors—has knowledge of magic so dark and powerful that it could trap us and the goddesses inside Ávera for so long," I say, tracing my claws over my mate's hair, "then we cannot underestimate him. We have been isolated for centuries, Kaël. We do not know what humans are capable of now. And they most likely outnumber us. Acting impulsively might lead us to ruin."

The quiet is broken by my mate's voice. "Then we will undergo trials to test our strength first."

"Trials?" I ask.

"Yes. We will create challenges for all the males. Tests of physical endurance, strategic thinking, and teamwork."

That is a very good idea.

"They can span two days," she continues, "and they will give me the chance to get to know everyone better."

The fire in her eyes burns brightly. That fire is something I will never tire of, even if it stirs my beast and makes controlling myself a daily battle. This will be a long week, and it seems the first challenge is taming myself and my cock.

We spend the rest of the day touring Ávera and greeting our people. My little dove is determined to fulfill her role as leader. Every time her legs tire, I lift her into my arms without question and carry her as we move forward together.

Her mother prepared her well. I can see it in her strength, how her body can bear such power. After the bonding ritual, when her spiritual awakening is complete, Noël will be so powerful that all living beings on earth will kneel before her. I do not doubt it.

Tomorrow, we'll leave Ávera and enter the forest. I'll teach her the routes and lands she must know as a leader. If she can keep up, I'll take her to the vólkin house the day after. But not yet. She needs time to heal mentally before she sees what I saw there.

"We should build shelters," Noël says suddenly.

"Shelters? What for?" I watch her feet carefully as she steps over the uneven stones.

"Humans have developed strong weapons over the centuries you've been locked in Ávera," she explains. "The basic weapon of any soldier is a sword. It's sharp, deadly at close range, and lethal in the right hands."

A hum rumbles in my chest. "So, like our claws?"

She smiles, stretching her human lips. Those reddish human lips that I can't stop staring at. "There are also bows and arrows. Archers can strike from a distance—longbows, short bows, even crossbows. With enough archers, you can darken the sky with arrows."

I nod, her words painting a picture in my mind. "An attack from afar? That is clever." Humans are indeed resourceful, capable of creating tools I could have never imagined. "But such weapons would not harm a vólkin, even if they outnumbered us."

Noël's expression darkens. "There are also the ballistae."

I tilt my head. "Ballistae?"

"They're like giant crossbows," she explains, making their shape with her hands. "They fire massive bolts that can pierce walls or armor. Some of our engineers even modified them to launch fireballs."

"You mean humans launch *fire*?" My fur bristles at the thought. Such a weapon sounds like something only a goddess could command. "Why would humans go so far against nature?"

"Because we're not all built like mountains on legs, Theron. We have to be smarter."

It flatters me when my mate says I'm big, but I fall silent. Humans are fragile compared to vólkins, though their ingenuity is something I can't deny.

The sun dips below Ávera's trees as we make our way back home. My mate walks beside me, her round, muscled hips swaying with each step. I glance up at the darkening sky and take a deep breath.

You've battled for so long, you can battle more.

As we pass the gathering area, I spot Kaël sitting with the growlings, listening intently to Elder Aïna's lesson. To my surprise, he looks focused—*truly* focused. Good job, Kaël.

Noël stops at the sight. "Isn't that Kaël?"

I nod, suppressing a grin.

She frowns. "What's he doing there?"

"Do you want to join their lesson?" I offer.

"Can I?"

This is going to be *fun.*

We approach the gathering area where Elder Aïna stands tall in the center. The growlings sit cross-legged around her, and Kaël leans against his thigh, though his eyes locked on Elder Aïna are unusually serious. I've never seen him so . . . studious.

"The knot is an essential part of our mating process," Elder Aïna explains. "You must understand it well, as your future mates will be human, and they likely will not be accustomed to it."

Oh, Elder Aïna's lesson today is about *knots*? I glance at Noël to gauge her reaction.

Her brow furrows as she looks up at me. "Knots? What knots?"

And there is my answer.

I gesture toward Elder Aïna with my snout, biting back a chuckle. Noël turns her attention to the lesson.

"Vólkin males possess a knot," Elder Aïna continues. "It is a swelling at the base of their anatomy that locks them to their mate during mating. Its purpose is twofold: to strengthen the bond and to ensure the semen stays inside the female."

Noël freezes, her mouth drops open, and her wide eyes snap to mine. "You have a knot *too*?"

"Of course," I reply, grinning broadly. My knot is big and round. Will fill my mate properly.

Around us, the growlings blink in confusion, some muttering among themselves. "Locked? Like . . . *stuck*?" one of them asks.

"Precisely," Elder Aïna confirms. "This is part of our biology and cannot be avoided. For human females, the experience may be . . . unfamiliar."

Noël sputters, choking on air. "I'm sorry, *what*?"

All eyes swing toward us, and I have to press my mouth to keep from laughing. Her face burns red, and I swear I hear her whisper a human curse under her breath.

"My apologies. Please, continue," she says, her voice higher than usual.

Goddesses, thank you for this moment. I will treasure it for the rest of my life.

If I didn't know Elder Aïna so well, I might have missed the half-hidden grin on her face. She's enjoying this as much as I am.

Elder Aïna clears her throat and continues, still perfectly composed. "A human female must be prepared before receiving the knot. There is an important ritual that ensures her body is ready. But that you will learn as you grow older."

Kaël, predictably, can't help himself. "So, we're supposed to prepare them? Like . . . explain beforehand? That'll go well. 'Hello, my mate. I'm going to get stuck for a while.'"

The growlings hiss at him to be quiet, but Elder Aïna answers. "Talking about it in advance is both good and preferable. However, I am referring to *physical preparation*, stretching the body so that the knot will fit inside."

Noël's face turns an even deeper shade of red, her wide eyes locked straight ahead. I can see her lips twitch, caught somewhere between disbelief and sheer mortification.

And me? I've never enjoyed a lesson more.

"Ethereal Leader, would you like to explain the mating process to the next generation?" Elder Aïna asks, her expression calm but teasing just beneath her fur.

Before Noël can respond, I step in. "I think our leader is tired after a long day, Elder Aïna. How about letting Kaël explain what he's learned so far?"

Kaël shoots me a murderous glare, his brows pulling into a scowl that promises revenge. I meet his eyes with a smug grin. My mate, however, turns to me with grateful eyes.

I've done my part today.

"Shall the leader lead by example," I say, grinning wider, "and show the growlings how important it is to rest?"

Noël straightens and nods with an air of authority, though her voice betrays her relief. "I . . . shall. Yes." She looks toward the group and offers them a tired smile. "Have a great night."

The growlings bow their heads, murmuring their respect as we turn to leave.

I glance at Noël, whose face is still flushed, and a satisfied warmth settles in my chest.

One victory at a time.

We arrive home, and I can feel her exhaustion settling in. The weight of the day is finally catching up with her.

"I owe you for that save." She sighs as we pause behind the door.

"Owe me?" My head tilts on its own. Why would my mate owe me anything?

She hesitates, her voice quieter. "I don't know much about . . . sex. If I had to explain it to them, I—"

I assume sex is how humans say mating?

In a few steps, I close the distance between us to trace my paw along her jawline. Her skin is soft under my touch as I tilt her face upward. "My beautiful dove," I begin, my thumb grazing her chin. "You don't have to do anything you don't want to. Ever. And you certainly don't 'owe' me anything."

Her brows knit, and she leans into my touch, her tired eyes searching mine.

"I will always be there for you," I continue. "Whether you're in danger or just uncomfortable, it is my honor—and my greatest desire—to do anything for you."

She blinks up at me, her wonderful eyes, so wide and clear, shaped like pointed berries, like leaves after rain.

"You are my mate, just as I am yours." My chest tightens as I lose myself in her stare.

"Thank you." Her voice is so soft it melts me.

"Tell me," I murmur, my gaze moving over the lines of her face. "Humans do not have mating lessons?"

She shakes her head in my paw. "We do not. You probably know more than I do."

I tilt my head and allow my thumb to brush over her lower lip. "How about Mina rests tonight." My voice drops lower, softer. "And I bathe you instead?"

Her breath catches, her eyes widening as I lean closer.

"And while I do," I continue, "I'll teach you what I know."

32

FLESH AND FUR

"When two souls are ready, the body follows. In that joining, spirit meets flesh, and the old magic remembers its shape."
—Elder Aïna

Noël

"Look at me," Theron says, breathless.

The water in the stream I sit in is unusually warm, almost like it's absorbing the heat of my embarrassment. Theron is on his knees in front of me, fur soaked and clinging to him, his crystals shining bright. His size is overwhelming. His *cock*—huge, hard, and impossibly close to me—makes my face burn hotter than I ever thought possible.

I force myself to look up, to meet his gaze, though my heart feels like it's about to beat out of my chest.

His giant paw slides over my arm, the vólkin soap leaving a fragrant trail on my skin.

The tenderness of his touch makes my stomach flip, and I press my thighs together. *Goddesses*, how can someone so massive be so gentle?

"Your muscles are beautiful, Noël," he murmurs, his deep voice sending a shiver down to the wrong place.

I'm going to pass out.

I've led soldiers, trained for hours, until I could barely stand, fought like a woman possessed. Yet here I am, undone by a simple bath, by Theron's patient touch and the way he looks at me like I'm the most precious thing he's ever seen.

This is beyond any bath I've ever had.

"In our lessons, we learn about pleasing our mate." His eyes lift from my arm to meet mine again. "We learn that human females' breasts are sensitive."

I swallow hard, my pulse pounding in my ears.

"May I?" he asks.

I nod slowly.

His paw moves up my arm to my shoulder and then down to my chest. His touch is delicate, as if I might shatter under his paw. When his fingers brush over my nipple, a whimper escapes before I can stop it. I freeze, my breath caught, and his eyes flick up to mine.

"Is it good?" he asks as his fingers graze the same spot again.

"Mm-hmm," I manage, my throat too tight for words.

His eyes darken, and he leans closer, his voice dropping to a whisper. "I want to taste it, my dove."

I stare at his mouth, at the way his tongue flicks out to glide over the tips of his sharp fangs. The sight alone sends a jolt of heat through me, and he lowers himself to my chest.

Slowly—so slowly it's maddening—he traces his tongue over the sensitive skin, the warmth of it flares up my nerves. "Theron," I gasp, my fingers curling into his mane.

He growls low in response, the sound vibrating through me, and this time, when his tongue moves again, he doesn't break eye contact. His gaze locks onto mine, so predatory it leaves me dizzy.

"You're so incredibly soft," Theron murmurs against my

chest. His nose brushes over my now hardened nipple, and I'm overwhelmed by the sensation. "I have waited so long, Noël," he continues, shifting to the other breast with aching slowness. "So long, I thought I'd go mad."

My head falls back, my breaths coming faster as Theron's tongue traces a trail of fire over my skin. How did I never know it could feel like this? I've *never* touched myself like this. How much pleasure have I missed?

"Theron," I whisper, Heat pools low in my stomach, the wetness between my thighs . . . It's not from the water.

"Mm?" he hums, his nose gliding up the curve of my neck.

Another whimper escapes me, my skin prickling in response to his touch. I feel like I'm melting, piece by piece.

"Whenever I . . . touch myself," I admit, my voice shaky, "it feels good, but . . . I don't know how to take it further."

He growls, the sound rough and primal. His strong arms wrap around me, and his paws cup the curve of my arse as he lifts me.

Water cascades off both of us, the droplets falling into the stream echo in the room, and I cling to him instinctively. My legs wrap around his hips, and I press tightly against him as he lowers us both to sit back in the stream. I can't even close my legs around him.

"Where do you touch yourself, my beautiful mate?" he asks. He settles me on his lap, my chest pressed against his, my heart hammering as I look into his eyes.

My thighs are spread open on either side of him, and I feel so exposed. I know Theron sees, but his gaze remains locked on mine, not straying, not pushing. He understands. He knows I want to explore this, but at my own pace. That silent understanding eases some of my nerves, though it doesn't calm the need building inside me.

I'm so aroused right now, it's staggering. His cock—rigid and thick—*stands* between us, and my breath hitches as I glance at it. A bead of white trails down the length, and I swallow hard.

Taking a deep, shaky breath, I lower my hand between my thighs. "Here," I whisper, brushing my fingers over the spot that makes my legs jerk.

Theron's eyes drop to my hand, his expression completely focused, his mouth parting as if he's forgotten how to breathe. "Your clit," he says, his voice low and husky.

A wave of mortification washes over me. "Don't say it out loud!" I hiss, yanking my hand away.

He catches my wrist before I can escape, his grip firm, but not enough to hurt. Bringing my hand to his mouth, he inhales, his chest rising with the motion. My eyes widen, heat crawling up my neck.

Oh . . . *oh.*

When he licks my fingers, I swear I see his eyes roll back.

"You are sinfully delicious," he growls.

I blink in disbelief, my heart pounding wildly.

"Let me," he says, his paw sliding down to replace my hand.

I don't even have time to process his words before his finger glides over the spot I touched, gently pressing. A jolt of intense pleasure shoots through me, and a small cry escapes my lips.

"Goddesses," I whisper, my thighs trembling as I grip his shoulders, fingers tangling in his wet fur. *This*—this is unlike anything I've ever felt.

"Just like that, my dove," he breathes. "Let me show you how good it can feel."

It feels . . . incredible. Yes, *yes.*

His finger shifts, sliding back, brushing over my entrance. My body clenches, and my breath catches as his gaze lifts to study me, hooded and dark.

"My mate," he pants, his voice strained.

He pulls me closer. My breasts flatten against his chest, the solid warmth of him surrounding me. I barely notice when he moves, his cock now nestled between my arse cheeks, and suddenly, I'm keenly aware of just how *big* he is. I'm literally parted.

Theron's large paws grip my hips as he begins to guide me back and forth. The friction builds instantly, and I lean into his mane, letting its softness anchor me as we move together. Each time my clit brushes against the base of his hard knot, a moan slips from my lips.

Theron's breaths come heavy, matching my own. His paws glide me faster, urging me over his thick cock, and I let him. *Goddesses*, this feels so incredibly good. My head spins with it, my body completely overtaken. I pant into his mane, my forehead pressed against him, the strong, rapid beat of his heart pounding against my chest and forehead.

The sensations, the sounds we make, his deep growls with my breathless cries. Somewhere through the haze, I hear his voice, saying something about how incredible it feels. I can't make out the words, but I agree completely.

The pleasure coils tightly, building higher until I think I might shatter. I grip his fur desperately as the pressure becomes too much.

"Theron," I gasp, my voice breaking. "I . . . I—"

A shaky cry escapes me as the tension inside me snaps. My whole body tenses, then melts into release.

"There you go," he growls between clenched teeth.

Theron's roar echoes in the house, loud and raw, but I'm too spent to react. I collapse against him, completely undone, my body limp in his arms. My head rests on his shoulder, the frantic rise and fall of his chest is the only thing I feel.

I never thought intimacy could be like this.

We stay quiet for a while, both of us catching our breath, the sound of running water filling the space around us. Theron nuzzles his nose into my hair with a motion so gentle I feel like I'd slip right into the stream if he weren't holding me in place.

"How do you feel?" he rumbles against my ear.

"Very good," I whisper, my body too relaxed to move.

He chuckles. His claws glide along my back, tracing slow lines before moving up. "I would love to comb your hair." His claws are already working through the tangles in my locks.

"You're doing it now," I murmur, my words muffled against his fur.

"I want to do it like humans do," he explains, "with a comb."

"Mm. Tomorrow morning." I lift my face to look at him, only to find he's already watching me.

"Hello," he says, the faintest hint of a smile tugging at his mouth.

"Hello," I mumble, suddenly feeling shy. *Why is this so embarrassing?*

We stare at each other in silence for a few moments, and then we both smile for real. It feels simple. Warm and nice.

My curiosity gets the better of me, and I ask, "Have you ever done this before?"

His gaze doesn't waver. "I have not."

"All these years and you've never . . . found release?" My eyes drift to the beautiful crystals on his forehead as I fight the heat rising to my cheeks.

"I have," he replies matter-of-factly.

I hum in question, tilting my head to meet his eyes again.

"I have pleasured myself many times before." His large paws tighten their hold on my thighs.

I don't mind. In fact, it feels . . . good.

"Especially since I met you," he adds. "There have been days I sought release more than once."

Oh Goddesses above. My eyes widen, and the heat burning my face spreads like wildfire. I swallow hard, staring at him in disbelief. *This is too much for me in one day.*

Theron rises from the water with me cradled in his arms,

then sets me down on the bed before grabbing a fresh set of furs to dry me off.

"Don't say you can do it yourself." He grins, wrapping me snugly in the plush furs.

I can't stop the smile that spreads across my face.

He steps back and gives himself a vigorous shake, sending water droplets flying everywhere. I laugh when they hit my face, but the moment is short-lived as he shakes again, splashing me even more.

"Theron!" I frown, though I can't hide my amusement.

My gaze stays on him longer than I intend. He stands tall, his fur shining from the water, his muscles so defined they seem sculpted. There's something mesmerizing about the way he stands—graceful and powerful, like he was built for both battle and beauty.

When Theron catches my stare, he freezes.

Why is he looking at me like that?

My cheeks flush as he starts walking toward me, his steps slow. I can't make sense of the look in his eyes. Could it be . . . No, surely not. Again? Are we really going to— *Again*?

"Theron?"

He stops in front of me, leaning down until his face is so close I can feel his breath on my skin. "How about we heal you, my little mate? A healing session after a mating lesson."

I swallow hard as his mouth hovers only inches from mine, the heat of his body dries my skin but . . .

"Who knows," he whispers, his voice deep, "maybe my tongue can heal more than open wounds."

33

THROUGH THE PAIN OF THE PAST

"There's something in him, Elder Aïna . . . something wild and still, like the wind before a storm. He's Ánya's son, through and through. Quiet now, but one day, he'll rise, and the whole forest will know his name."

—Vládan, mate of Ánya, before departing north

Theron

Mina mentioned she placed the comb near the ribbons. Did my mate move it?

I scan the bathing room until my eyes land on a neat arrangement of her belongings in a small corner.

My sweet dove has carved out a tiny space for herself here. Pain twists in my chest as I take in the sight. Just this small corner. She left everything behind when she was taken.

I need to ask her what belongings she had in Tárnov.

She should have more, so much more. This home will never lack anything she needs.

I've seen how she hides certain things. Her small weapon, for example, tucked under the nest alongside her mother's handkerchief. But here, among her few belongings, I spot the comb. And something else.

Curious, I pick up the smooth, thin object. It has her name, her face, on it, and a string of numbers. What is this? Her painted image is strange too. She's wearing something green on her head. It doesn't cover her entirely, and it certainly doesn't look like it's meant to keep her warm. Is it ceremonial? Customary?

Humans do so many interesting things, things that are often difficult to understand.

When Elder Aïna told us that humans prefer not to urinate outside, instead using something called a *toy-let,* I built one. When she explained that humans wash in warm water, I charged the crystals to ensure the streams always stay warm.

And now, I wonder what significance this little green head-piece holds? Humans truly are so different.

My ears twitch at the sounds of her stirring awake. For some reason, I expected humans—especially females—to sleep deeply. Elder Aïna always said that human women needed more rest. The sun hasn't even risen yet.

Comb in my paw, I step out of the bathing room, and my gaze immediately falls on my mate sitting in our bed-nest. Her bare skin looks so beautiful and so smooth. Pride swells in my chest at the sight. After our healing session yesterday, I had the honor of bathing her again. Her sweet moans of pleasure are becoming my favorite sound. Right after the question about whether I have a knot—that was brilliant. This should be our nightly routine. Me, tending to her delicious body.

"Good morning," she says, her voice warm and husky from sleep as she stretches and rises from the bed-nest.

Why is she wrapping the furs around herself? I have already seen her bare.

"Good morning," I reply eagerly. Then, holding up the

comb, I ask, "Can I?" It looks so small in my paw, but I am determined.

Zephyr often braids his fur, something Elder Aïna told him his mother used to do for him when he was a pup. It's a beautiful and intimate act, and I want to learn it.

Noël glances at the comb, then meets my eyes with a smile. "Let me wash my face and brush my teeth first."

I nod, following behind her as she heads to the bathing room.

I've never seen her brush her teeth before. The concept intrigues me, especially since humans lack fangs. I can't imagine her hunting a deer with her teeth, and when I try, it's entertaining.

Before I can stop myself, a grin spreads across my face. The image of Noël sinking her teeth into a running deer is indeed quite humorous.

My mate scoops a bit of ash and mint paste onto a little twig and begins gliding it along her flat, human teeth. Fascinating. Everything about humans is so small—their tools, their actions, and . . .

"You have very small teeth," I say, leaning closer to inspect them.

She coughs, turning toward the face-washing basin, and my ears flick upright in alarm. Panic surges through me as I crouch beside her, fur rising along my back.

"Here!" I blurt, filling my paw with water and holding it out to her.

She washes her mouth with the water in my paw, and when she looks at me, she isn't upset or sick. She's . . . amused?

"Are you alright?" I ask, scanning her face. "Why did you start coughing?"

Her lips curve into a wide smile. "Theron! Don't look at me like that!"

I tilt my head, knitting my brows. *What did I do?*

But she wipes her mouth and straightens, still smiling, so I ease my posture. If she's fine, then all is well.

As she washes her face, I tighten my grip on the comb. Once she's done, I can finally comb her hair. Maybe even braid it.

"I need to dress, Theron."

Oh. I nod quickly, setting the comb aside and grabbing her gown from the counter. "Lift your hands," I say, unfolding the fabric and holding it out for her.

She takes a breath, and I catch the barest hint of a grin tugging at her lips.

"Theron," she says slowly, grounding herself as if she's trying not to laugh.

My tail thumps against the face-washing basin, betraying my excitement. I step aside. She probably prefers to dress in silence.

"*You* do not dress me!" she says, that grin breaking through as she pushes me out of the bathing room.

"Why not? Mina dresses you."

"And that is enough," she replies, taking the gown from me and closing the door behind her.

I stand in the corridor, staring at the wooden door, blinking.

Does she think I cannot dress her?

My dove finally comes out of the bathing room, the comb in her hand. *Finally.*

I can do this now.

She walks past me with a wide grin. Anticipation roaring in my chest, I follow her through the corridor to one of the cushions.

"It will be more comfortable if you stand behind me," she says. I nod and circle around her, positioning myself. She had to jump to sit comfortably. I should make them smaller.

Alright. She's settled. I've seen Zephyr do this before.

I raise the comb to her roots, hesitating for just a moment as she turns to look up at me.

"Start from the bottom," she instructs, "and slowly work your way up as you brush through the strands."

I nod again, then grab her hair as gently as I can and glide the comb through her locks.

It's . . . soothing. The repeated motion, the way her dark locks shine under the light of the crystals.

"You're doing great," she says.

Her words fill me with pride. I take another section of her hair, making sure not to miss a single strand.

As I finish, my mate looks up at me again and says, "Thank you." Her voice is so beautiful it wakes my cock. My body reacts, and I shift my weight. Yesterday's activities have not calmed my shaft. I traced my tongue all over her, and her little sounds of pleasure were beautiful. Every sound she makes is beautiful, just as her face, her body, and her hair are. I love my mate's hair.

"Can you teach me how to braid your hair?"

"Of course," she replies, lifting her hands to section it into three parts. Body, mind, and soul—the sacred elements every vólkin knows. A braid isn't just practical, it's tradition, a symbol of unity. Human mates wore them often. Zephyr does too.

"You need to weave the sections like this," she says, demonstrating the pattern slowly.

I watch intently, memorizing each movement of her fingers as they curl around the chunks of her hair. Left, right, left, right.

"Your turn."

I carefully take the sections, weaving them together. The strands slip through my claws, and the pattern falters at first. It isn't easy, so I try again.

By the third attempt, the braid takes shape, and I lean back, satisfied.

"You are beautiful," I say as I admire her with the braid I've made.

Her smile, serene and lovely, is my reward. "My mother used to braid my hair when I was a child," my mate says as she rises from the cushion. There's sadness in her eyes, something I wish I could take away.

"This memory is special,"

She nods.

I cup her face, my thumb brushing over her cheek as I study her eyes.

"Thank you for this, Theron," she whispers. "Truly."

Before I think about it, I lean forward and trace my tongue along her cheek.

Her eyes widen, her face turning a delightful shade of pink. My little dove blushes so prettily. Good. I love seeing her like this.

"Yesterday's healing session . . ." she murmurs, her voice trailing off as her blush deepens to a color reminiscent of ripe strawberries. "I . . . I feel good now, so . . ."

"Let's go to the forest then," I say, stepping back, though my gaze is on her glowing cheeks.

"The preparations are going well, Your Majesty," Mina reports, her tone confident as she gestures toward the plans.

Noël nods. My mate introduced us to the idea of fabric shelters called *tents*, explaining that they would house the females and nýmphi during our trials. Elder Aïna confirmed that human skin burns easily. Tents are good. Tomorrow is a significant day, one that will test our strength and unity.

I've decided to participate in the trials alongside my

warriors. A leader should lead, not stand to the side while others do the work.

"We'll meet tomorrow at dawn," I tell Mina. She bows alongside Naïa and Essin before the three head off to continue preparations.

My mate turns to me, her expression curious. "What is it you want to show me in the forest?"

"First," I reply, tracing my claws along her braid, "we'll see if your body is fully healed and capable of walking long distances, my mate."

"I would love that," she says with excitement in her voice. "It's been too long since I've trained. I'm used to constant activity. I've never rested for this long before." Her gaze travels down the length of the braid I'm holding, her fingers brushing over it.

"Then we shall train as well," I say.

As we step outside Ávera and into the forest, I take my time explaining the plants, animals, and natural elements to my mate. Her curiosity is insatiable, and each question she asks is like a spark, lighting up my honor to answer her.

To think that humans would deny their females access to such knowledge. It infuriates me. My mate, however, defies those limitations. She studied under her mother, learned everything she was taught, and asks questions without hesitation. She is everything they tried to suppress.

"You know so much, Theron," my little dove says, stepping on the dark leaves scattered across the forest floor, carefully avoiding the lighter ones.

Unsure what to make of this game, I pause before I answer her. "Vólkins value knowledge." I try to mimic her steps and place my paw on a dark leaf, but my paw is far too large for this. "Not knowing something you've been taught is considered foolish."

She hums in acknowledgment, her focus momentarily on the forest path.

We reach a clearing, a good one. The ground is flat, without stones or rough patches. Ideal for training.

"Are you tired?" I ask, noticing how she still steps carefully on the dark leaves.

She shakes her head, her gaze fixed forward. "This is a great spot to warm up the muscles!"

And just like that, her focus shifts. She abandons her game, stepping on dark and light leaves indiscriminately as she rushes forward, then spins around to face me with a bright grin.

I do not understand.

"Attack me!" she exclaims, her eyes lighting up.

I tilt my head. "Is that how you want to train?"

She nods, that grin growing wider. "I may not be as big as you, but I have this."

She pulls out the weapon she used to stab me, holding it up like a trophy. The sight of that small weapon reminds me of the fire in her eyes the first time we met, a fire that has only grown brighter.

"How about you attack me?" I suggest, patting my chest with a grin of my own.

A wicked smile is her only reply before she tightens her grip on her weapon and sprints toward me.

This shouldn't arouse me as much as it does. But goddesses above, the way her breasts move with each stride, the sway of her hips, the sharp focus in her gaze—I can barely think straight. *We need to get back to the furs immediately.*

She strikes, holding the weapon in one hand and using the other to push it forward for extra force. Clever. Very clever. The added power makes her hit more effective. My little dove is so smart. I catch the weapon in my paw, and my tail wags uncontrollably.

She smirks as I catch her weapon. Why?

Her hand, the one she used to push the weapon, suddenly shifts its direction, aiming straight for my jaw.

Incredible. She's not just strong, she's quick and adaptive.

Before the weapon can reach me, I catch it between my teeth. Now her small nose is right in front of mine, and we're grinning at each other like two mischievous pups.

The urge to snap the weapon in my mouth is almost unbearable. But this weapon is special. She crafted it herself, poured her time and care into it. I could carve as many as she wants, but this one holds meaning.

I unclench my jaw and release it.

"Why do your crystals shine so brightly? This isn't the first time," she says. The light makes her irises look blue, and it's mesmerizing.

"Every time a vólkin feels strong emotions, the crystals mirror the frequency our souls release."

Her eyes narrow as she lowers her weapon. "When we first met, your crystals were bright like this," she says, taking a step back. "And yesterday too."

"Of course," I say, stepping closer. "When we first met, I was excited, aroused, and happy. Finding my mate was the greatest moment of my life." I lower my paw to grip my semihard shaft. "Yesterday too."

As expected, my shy little mate's eyes lower to my cock before she blushes, her cheeks glowing that delightful shade of pink.

She clears her throat, quickly shifting the subject. "What else can your crystals do?"

"I can send waves and signals to vólkins not too far away," I say, though her reaction still amuses me. "If I wanted to call the warriors here, I could signal them, and they would feel it and come immediately."

"That is incredible! So useful, it's unbelievable," Noël says, her gaze fixed on my crystals like she's studying them.

"You will have them too, my mate," I say, releasing my cock as the tension becomes too uncomfortable. My sac growing too tight.

"Me? What do you mean?"

"After the bonding ritual, you will awaken. You'll become your true self. Every spiritual being has crystals, and you are no exception. They will be blue like mine, like the blue rose."

Her eyes widen. "How? What?"

"My mother had crystals, Kaël's mother, Aeson's mother, they all had crystals."

Her expression shifts, something I can't quite place.

"Your mother was human . . . right?" she asks, leaning close and resting her hand in my paw.

"Yes," I confirm, tilting my head as I watch her. "What is it?"

"How did your parents die?" Her voice is quieter now. "Ánya and Vládan."

A smile tugs at my mouth. "You know their names. Let's sit, and I'll explain everything."

I lead her to a calloused tree, its shadow shielding us from the warmth of the spring sun. Sitting down, I motion for her to settle between my thighs. She grips her gown before sitting—carefully avoiding my cock—and looking up at me.

"Before the barrier appeared, a curse of flesh swept through Ávera," I begin.

"A sickness?" Noël asks, her brows furrowing.

I nod. "There is a plant, an apple from the tree of knowledge, that can cure such harsh diseases, but it only grows in the far north, far beyond these lands. Elder Aïna said the grown vólkins decided to travel there together to gather enough of the herb and return safely, as humans roamed the land at that time."

"Did Elder Aïna go as well?"

I shake my head. "She stayed with us, the pups."

Her expression softens, her eyes glistening as she leans back against my chest. "And they never came back?"

The words are heavy on my tongue, the pain fresh even after all these years. "No, they didn't."

I do not remember my parents, only the stories Elder Aïna told me. She always says my mother was like dawn's first light, happy, and always seeing the good in others. My father, she said, loved her deeply. He was more serious, and Elder Aïna often remarks that I resemble him.

I tug my mate against me, wrapping my arms around her, shielding her from my own words. "The barrier appeared the night they left Ávera."

"Maybe they're still alive! Maybe they settled near the barrier, hoping it would disappear so they could come back." Her eyes shine with so much hope it pains me.

"Elder Aïna said," I begin, exhaling, "that all their souls have reached the skies."

Her expression softens, and she leans closer, wrapping her arms around my neck. She presses her forehead to mine and whispers, "I am so, so sorry."

My sweet mate. Even with all her strength and fire, she holds compassion like no other. The goddesses chose the perfect female for me, and I will carry gratitude for that with me for the rest of my days.

"Let's start training, my dove."

34

A BROKEN SOLDIER

"I hate askin, Gregor. I know yu have nothin left to give, and stil I ask. But when yu stoped writing, I new . . . I'd asked too much. I'm sory. I just didn' know who else too turn to. You're all I hav."
—Linnéa Fenrówe, in a letter never sent

Gregor

T he carriage jolts again, and I grip the edge of my seat, trying not to let the fear show. The cloth over my eyes, trapping me in darkness, has grown filthy. My body aches from the bruises, and the air smells of damp earth. Each bump rattles my bones, but it's not the pain that terrifies me. It's the waiting.

Bard's voice, calm and sharp as always, cuts through the sound of the moving carriage. "Remember, Gregor," he says, "your sister's life is in your hands. One wrong move, and she pays the price."

I swallow hard, tasting the salt of sweat on my lips. His words make it hard to breathe, and my hands tremble despite my effort to steady them. "Yes, sir," I murmur. I know what failure means. I've failed before—in the military, with my family, in everything—but this . . . If I fail here, I won't just lose again. I'll lose Linnéa.

I will arrive in Ávera and meet Noël and the vólkins.

Noël . . .

I can't stop thinking about her. She was always so . . . unreachable. I admired her strength, her confidence. Even when I tried to keep my distance, I found myself watching her at the base. There was something about the way she never let anyone push her around. I envied her for it. Maybe even more than envied . . .

I could never get those thoughts out of my head, so I buried them deep. I was nothing but a soldier, and she was a sergeant. She'd never see me like that.

But now, I wonder if she'll even recognize me.

I cannot help the sigh that escapes my lips.

My sister, the last time I saw her. She was saying her goodbyes to me, wearing her worn-out tunic. "Don't worry about me, Gregor. You go to Tárnov, find a better life. I'll be fine."

But she wasn't fine. I left her behind, and now her life hangs by a thread because of me. *I failed you, Linnéa.*

The carriage slows, and my breath quickens, my pulse drumming in my ears. My body tenses in anticipation of the next horror. "Have we arrived?" I ask, struggling to keep my voice composed.

Bard yanks the cloth from my eyes, and the sudden brightness stabs at my vision.

"Not yet, my dear Gregor." The cold edge of his voice turns my stomach.

Before I can respond, the door opens, and more of Bard's men pile into the carriage. I try to move, but my body is too weak. Bard's face hovers close to mine, his smile a twisted lie of kindness. "We need to make you look convincing, Gregor. After all, you've 'escaped' us, haven't you?" He grabs my jaw and continues, "Need to make you presentable for our dear Noël and her new friends."

The men fall on me, their fists slamming into my ribs and my face relentlessly, breaking me down inch by inch. My mouth fills with the metallic taste of blood, and my vision blurs. I barely manage to suppress my screams as they shove the filthy rag into my mouth to muffle the sound.

The beating drags on, but the real torment doesn't begin until they force the crystal into me. They made me practice this over and over, stripping me of any last shred of dignity. The first time they handed me the crystal, I froze. My body rejected it, my mind screamed, but their fists gave me no choice. The second time, I wept. The third, I was numb. The healer's cold grin, the way the others watched . . . it still makes my skin crawl. And it pulses, this damn thing, every few days it fucking pulses. Reminding me that no matter how far I go, they'll always have a hold on me.

When they finally stop, I'm left crumpled on the carriage floor, unable to move. My body is broken, but the worst pain is inside me. The humiliation, the knowledge that I am nothing but a tool.

Bard crouches beside me. "There. Now, you look like you have escaped."

They throw me out of the carriage and onto the ground. My legs wobble, only just able to hold my weight.

Bard kneels beside me again, this time pulling something from his pocket. My heart stops.

It's Linnéa's necklace.

Tears well up in my eyes. *Fuck! Fuck! Fuck!*

They have her. THEY FUCKING HAVE HER!

Bard pockets the necklace. "Don't forget, Gregor. Do not fail."

He jerks his chin toward the trees, commanding me to move.

With a weak nod, I stumble into the forest. Every step is agony, but I push forward.

35

A GUARDIAN'S SHIELD AND A LEADER'S COMMAND

"They taught us softness was weakness because they knew what would happen if we ever turned gentle hands into fists."
—Eyleen Ársa

Noël

"I miss the leaf spirits," I say as we walk toward something that makes Theron tense every time I ask about it. *What is this place?*

"You can summon them whenever you want," he replies, his voice calm as he holds up a low branch to clear the path for me.

After everything we've been through, I feel strong, *alive.* Our healing session made me feel like a new person. His saliva definitely heals more than open wounds.

"Can I? Do I just . . . call them?" I ask.

He nods, his steps slowing until he stops entirely.

I stop too, taking in the beauty of the forest around us. The trees sway in the breeze, their leaves are bright and beautiful green. We're beyond the barrier now, and it's so refreshing to walk freely.

Eyes closed, I fill my lungs, letting the forest's energy seep into me. Nature feels like home—*this* feels like home. *Soon, all women will be home.* By the goddesses, I swear it.

"My dear leaf spirits, please, come to me," I whisper.

A gentle breeze brushes against my skin, and I hear the quiet, tinkling laughter of the spirits, so sweet and pure it makes my heart sing.

They appear, flying toward us with tiny arms full of colorful petals, they're as joyous as I remember.

"Theron."

He tears his gaze away from the leaf spirits, and his expression shifts as he turns to me.

"You've noticed," he says.

"There are blue rose petals among them," I reply, reaching out to take one. The petal feels cool against my fingers, its glow faint but unmistakable. I know well what a blue rose petal looks like.

"Blue roses do not grow without purpose, do they?" I repeat his words from when we first met.

"They do not," he confirms. "That is why we're here."

I glance down at the petal in my hand. Something about this unsettles me. *My leaf spirits, show me the source.*

The spirits circle around me. Their tiny voices blend with the wind. Suddenly, they jolt forward.

Heart pounding, I follow them. There's a strange sensation in my chest, like some part of me is trying to tear itself free, pulling me toward something I need to know.

I sprint after the spirits, my brows knitting as I scan the blur of the woods around me. Each step feels faster, like I'm moving beyond my own limits. My legs drive me forward.

What is this?

The forest changes, every sound sharper, every texture more vivid. I feel the stones underfoot before I even step on them, hear every leaf shiver in the wind. Even the air tastes different.

What's happening to me?

And then I catch the scent. It wraps around me like a memory I can't place. Blue roses. My chest tightens. I look around, my gaze darting between the trees, but I don't stop running. Where is it? Where?

I skid to a halt. My voice is raw as I shout, demanding an answer, "Where!" The word echoes through the forest. *Home.*

The spirits tug at my gown, and I don't question them. I run. The pull in my chest grows stronger, guiding me as much as they do. The crystal on my pendant, Ándor's crystal, begins to pulse against my skin.

My eyes widen as I move forward, the forest giving way to something I can't yet see.

What is going on?

It looks familiar. Like a house—a vólkin house. It's grown, not built. How?

My blood thunders in my ears. The crystal on my pendant pulses harder with each beat of my heart.

"Ándor?" I call, my voice cutting through the quiet. Nothing.

Is it Ándor's home? Is that why you're pulsing?

The leaf spirits tug at me, pulling me toward the right side of the house. They flit. I follow.

This house is enormous. Whoever grew it must be powerful, almost as powerful as Theron. *Theron.*

Where is he?

I stop to glance over my shoulder. He's not there. I hadn't even noticed he didn't follow. My chest tightens, but the spirits pull harder, urging me forward.

Footsteps. Heavy, getting closer. Could this really be Ándor's home? Is that why it's outside Ávera?

The scent of blue roses grows stronger, sweet and overwhelming my senses. And then I see it. I stop. Goose bumps rise along my arms as my eyes widen. A blue rose garden. But it's not like the one I grew. This one stretches endlessly, covering the land.

"My mate."

Theron?

I lift my head, and there he is, standing tall, arms crossed. Kaël, Zephyr, and Aeson are with him, and a few other vólkins I don't recognize beside them, forming a wall.

"What is this?" My voice is low, sharper than I intend. Something twists inside me. Anger? Unease? Why are they circling me like this?

Theron takes a step closer, and the others stay where they are.

"Do not move," I snap.

His ears twitch, but he listens. He stops.

"Answer my question, Theron."

"You were weak—"

"I am NOT!" My pulse thrums in my ears, my anger rises hot and fast, and I advance on him.

"Noël," he growls. A warning.

The leaf spirits dart behind him frantically. There's something there, something behind him.

"Move," I command. My gaze sweeps over the others. "ALL OF YOU!"

Mother taught me how to command a room, how to claim space and demand what's mine. And I will. *I always will.*

The vólkins exchange hesitant glances before they slowly step back. All except Theron. He doesn't move.

I've softened with comfort. Too much. "There is no room for softness, Noël," Mother would say. She was right. She was always right.

There is no room for softness.

"You're in my way," I say as my eyes stay on Theron.

His jaw clenches. "I am never in your way. We walk the path together, my mate."

"Is that why you haven't told me about this house?" I ask, holding up the crystal. Its light pulses against my palm. "Ándor's crystal is pulsing. This house belongs to him, and he was connected to my mother. And you didn't say a word."

Theron exhales, his shoulders sagging before he places a paw on his chest. "When you collapsed, I thought I'd lose you. I thought that restoring balance and following the prophecy would mean nothing if you weren't here."

His paw presses harder against his heart as he speaks. "Your soul is wounded, and I brought everything else upon you. I was a selfish male. A selfish mate." He clenches his paw into a fist. "I should have taken you far from all of this. I should have shielded you from the world, from everything. I should have shown you that you can trust, that you can love. That you can see the beauty in life."

If he had shielded me, everything my mother taught me—everything she sacrificed—would have been for nothing. Her lessons weren't to coddle me or to keep me from the world. They were to prepare me to restore balance, to make me the leader I am meant to be.

Everything points to me. The blue-rose blood, the prophecy, the vólkins, the spirits, and the goddesses. It all comes back to *me*.

Theron didn't ask for this, no more than I did. None of it was by choice.

"If this is what you want, my mate, I will move. But I will not leave you to weather it alone."

And with those words, he steps aside.

My heart sinks at what I see.

36

WHERE ROSES BLOOM

"There's something calling me beyond these woods, Elder Aïna. I can't explain it, but I feel her. Like a thread tugging at my chest. If I follow it, I may not return. But if I stay, I'll always wonder what I left behind."
—Ándor, one year before the barrier rose

Noël

*Á*ndor, my love and my life. We were meant to raise our Noël together, but now I face this world on my own. I will always be your Eyleen, your blue rose.

A grave. This is a grave.

Ándor's grave.

My heart feels like it's been ripped apart as the truth stands before my eyes. Mother was Ándor's mate. They wanted to raise me. Together. Ándor . . . Ándor is my father. I just now understand what truly happened. He left Ávera when he saw Mother in his dreams, then the barrier rose, and he stayed here—somewhere—for hundreds of years, until he somehow met her.

This is all too much to handle.

We could have had a good life. I could have had them both
—Mother and Father. A family. I close my eyes, the image
searing itself into my mind: running through the trees with
him, laughing, chasing, him catching me in his arms. We could
have gone back to my mother, together. We could have been
happy.

She could have been happy.

I fall to my knees. The ground feels cold. It feels like the day
they took my mother's lifeless body away, the carriage creaking
as it carried her farther and farther from me. Carried where?
Where is she?

Father . . . do you know where Mother is?

My vision blurs, tears slipping down my face. With every
tear, each drop that lands on the ground, blue roses bloom.
One by one, they spread around the grave, bright and glowing
against the earth. *All these roses . . .*

Mother cried here. She never cried in front of me, but I
know she did. She was grieving. She buried her loved one, her
mate.

She wasn't born and raised in Tárnov. No. She was here,
near the barrier. She wanted to raise me in Ávera. She hoped
for a better life for us.

A sob tears through me, raw and wounded. I want to scream
until there's nothing left inside me. We could have lived a
happy life. Mother. Father. Together.

My hands tremble, and I feel the crystal's warmth against
my chest. Its light glows brighter. My eyes widen.

Ándor . . . he's listening. I found him, but it's too late.

My hand shakes with how forcefully I grip the crystal. "You
saved her, didn't you?" I whisper, my voice cracking under my
own words. "You didn't leave her without reason, right?" The
lump in my throat burns painfully, and my breath hitches.

"A vólkin would never leave his mate," Theron says,
crouching beside me as his claws trace over my braid.

I lift my gaze to meet his, my brows knitting together. "Then what happened? Everything I believed . . . it feels meaningless now."

"I want you to see something." He stands and helps me to my feet. His paw is firm. It anchors me when I feel like I'm falling back down again.

Theron turns to the others and commands, "Stand on guard. We're entering the house."

Glancing around, I notice Kaël, his face streaked with tears. Zephyr stands beside him, his paw resting on Kaël's shoulder. Right. Everyone here is my family now. I can't let my pain consume me. I can't turn it against them.

I look back at Theron and take his paw in my hand. His expression softens, there is reassurance in his eyes. "When I entered the home, I was searching for answers," he says. "And I think you need to see what I found."

I nod, overwhelmed with both dread and hope. Together, we move toward the house.

It's undeniably a vólkin home, both inside and out. The structure is grown from the surrounding trees, their trunks and branches weaving together to form walls and beams. Yet, it's not entirely wild—it feels welcoming, designed for human comfort. Father made this for my mother.

Father. The word feels strange but comforting, it's something I've longed to say my entire life. To finally know who he was, to piece together the parts of him that Mother never shared. She never spoke of him, never explained why. But now, I understand. It was too hard for her, too painful to put into words.

Elder Aïna told me he was an honorable male, and standing here, I believe it. This home, this place, is proof of his love for her. My mother deserved the best of everything, and he gave her that. I'm grateful to him for growing this place for her.

The living area is spacious and open, with what looks like a kitchen. Wooden cabinets line one side, along with a sturdy table and matching chairs, all grown from the same trees. My chest tightens as I imagine her here, making trinkets the way we used to in Tárnov.

A faint scent draws me toward the cabinets. Fresh herbs.

How? It's been over twenty-five years.

I inhale deeply. My heart races as I begin opening the dark cabinets, searching for the source. "Theron," I call, "do you smell the herbs?"

His brows furrow as he scents the air. "When I was here before, there were no herbs. But now I do scent them, my mate." He moves toward the higher cabinets and pulls one open. "It's from here," he says, reaching in and removing a small object.

A trinket?

My fingers tremble as he hands it to me, and I lift it carefully to my nose. The smell is so familiar it nearly brings me to tears again. "This . . . this is just like the trinkets my mother used to make," I whisper. "To shield us from illnesses."

I turn the small silk bundle in my hands, the red string binding it tightly. "Rosemary and salt. Tied in silk cloth."

Theron's gaze darkens. "It is a shield ritual, my mate," he says. "But not from illnesses. It's meant to ward off unwanted visitors."

"What do you mean by 'unwanted visitors'?"

"If you burn rosemary, it temporarily wards off unwanted visitors, but for a more lasting effect, scattering rosemary around the house works better. Adding salt and tying it in silk keeps it fresh longer, and binding it with red string seals the ritual with greater strength." He pauses, then says, "Those who are unwanted by the creator of the ritual won't even be able to see the house it protects."

I blink. Is that why no one ever came to our home? *Mother, you continue to surprise me. How much more did you know?*

"So," I say, turning the trinket over in my hands, "if this is still so fresh, and we're able to see this house . . ."

"The one who created it knows of us," Theron says, finishing my thought.

We continue walking through the house, and with every step, more questions churn in my mind. Mother had a mate. She buried him here, in this place, and then she left—moved to Tárnov. But where was she from before that?

She always told me her parents, my grandparents, were long gone. That their graves couldn't be found.

I remember searching the burial grounds in Tárnov, going through every section—military, citizen, rebel—combing through names etched in stone. Dirt and silence greeted me, rows of graves bearing names of people I'd never known.

Were they buried in another village? Did Mother leave more behind than I could ever guess? Or . . . are their bodies truly missing?

Theron and I walk into the bedroom. In the center is a massive nest, layered with furs and twigs. My eyes sweep across the space, and that's when it hits me. There's no dust here. Not anywhere.

Could the person who left the trinkets also be cleaning this place? Who are they? Who is doing all this?

Why would she leave this place, so full of life and love, for the harshness of Tárnov? What danger could be so great that even this home wasn't enough to keep us safe?

Theron moves toward a small drawer near the nest. I watch as he picks something up.

"What is it?" I ask.

"A book," he says, turning toward me. "I found it the last time I was here, but I haven't opened it. I think it belonged to your mother."

It's small, old, and weathered, the kind of thing that has seen many years and journeys. As I move closer, the delicate embroidery on the cover catches the light from the window—a blue rose, just like the one on Mother's handkerchief.

Theron hands me the book, and it's heavy in my hands. "It feels wrong to open it," I murmur, my fingers tracing the worn leather. I glance up at him.

"It felt wrong for me because it is your mother's. But it feels right that you are the one to see."

I swallow, nodding. *If I was not meant to see this, Mother, I am sorry.*

With a deep breath, I open the book.

Year 701, MY BIRTHDAY I AM 8!

Today, I read many chapters of a book with my mother! She says books hold all the world's secrets. One day, I'll read them all.

Mother says I'm special because of the blue-rose blood. She says it means I'm meant to do great things. I don't know what that means yet, but I want to learn everything.

Father showed me how to carve the symbol of the rose into wood today. He says it's the mark of our family, and I must always protect it.

"Theron," I whisper.

"What is it?"

It's a struggle to force out my next words. "It's not a book. It's my mother's diary."

37

THE LEADER WHO NEVER WAS

"You say I'll understand when I'm older, but every time I ask, you close the door like I'm a child. I'm not a child. If I'm meant to carry something heavy, then stop keeping me in the dark and start telling me what it is."
— Noël Ársa, age fifteen

Eyleen

Year 707
The blue roses bloomed again today, just like Mother said they would. She says they're special because of me. I don't know if I believe her, but when I cried last week, blue roses appeared right where my tears fell. It was . . . strange. Beautiful, but strange.

Mother says I'm destined to save the world, but I don't know what that means. Save it from what? The roses are beautiful flowers, but that's all they are, right?

Father looked worried when he saw the new blooms. He doesn't like to talk about them, but I saw him pick one and press it in his journal.

. . .

Mother says we're going to a feast in honor of the tsar. She's been fussing with my hair all morning, trying to make it pretty. She says I must look my best because we'll be in the presence of royalty.

I don't want to go. I'd rather stay in the garden and read, but Mother says we must pay our respects. Father says it's our duty as nobles.

The tsar looked at me today. He didn't speak, but his eyes were cold. I didn't like it. He smiled at Father and said something to him I couldn't hear, but it made Father's face go pale.

Mother told me it's an honor to be noticed by the tsar. That my debut will be grand if everything goes well. But if it's an honor, why do I feel so strange? Why did Father seem so afraid?

I asked Mother about the prophecy today. She always says I'm destined to save the world, but she never explains how. She just says I'll understand in time. But I don't want to wait. I want to know now.

Father says I mustn't speak of the roses outside our family. He says people wouldn't understand. But why wouldn't they? Aren't they beautiful?

Father has been acting strangely since the feast. He's been sharpening his sword more often, and his voice gets tight whenever the tsar is mentioned. I asked him what was wrong, and he just said, "Stay close to your mother. Don't wander."

Why does the tsar make him so uneasy? Isn't he supposed to protect us? Mother says the tsar is a great man, but I'm starting to wonder if she's wrong.

.   .   .

Today, I saw two men in black cloaks near the garden. I've never seen them before. They didn't come inside to say hello, but they stood there for a long time, watching.

Father says they're probably messengers from the tsar. He says I shouldn't worry. But why would messengers be watching our garden? Why wouldn't they knock on the door?

More roses bloomed today. I wasn't even crying this time. They just appeared, brighter than ever. When I showed Mother, she said, "It's starting." What's starting?

Father picked one of the roses and burned it. He said it's dangerous for others to see them. Why would flowers be dangerous? They're beautiful. They're mine.

Year 709

The tsar says I must marry him. Father begged him to wait, to give me time, but he refused. How can I marry such an old man? He is already sixty years old, and he frightens me . . .

Mother says I must do my duty, but her voice trembled when she said it. Even she doesn't believe her own words.

Father has been quiet since the feast. I know he's angry, but at whom? The tsar? Himself? Me?

I heard them arguing last night. Mother and Father. He said we should leave, that we should go far away, beyond the tsar's reach, where he couldn't find us. But Mother said we can't because he'll burn the village. He'll kill us all.

I couldn't sleep after that. I sat in the garden and watched the roses. They were wilting. I've never seen them wilt before.

They told me today. I am to marry the tsar in a fortnight. Mother wouldn't look at me, and Father left the room. I wanted to cry, to scream, but all I could do was sit there, staring at my hands. They're shaking as I write this.

Nina tried to comfort me. She said the tsar only wants what's best for the realm, but her eyes were full of pity. She doesn't believe that. None of us do.

They're gone. He killed them. Mother and Father tried to protect me, but it wasn't enough. I saw it happen. I'll never forget the way the guards dragged them away, how Mother screamed for me to run.

I didn't run. My legs wouldn't move. And then it was over. The guards came back, their hands stained with my parents' blood, and told me to prepare for the wedding.

I can't stop crying. I feel like my chest is caving in, like I'll never breathe again. They're gone. They're gone, and it's all my fault.

I tried to eat today, but I couldn't. The food tasted like ash. I feel like I'll never taste anything again.

Nina hasn't left my side since it happened. She tries to comfort me, but I can see the fear in her eyes. She's afraid of him too.

The house feels empty now. Every corner reminds me of them. Father's sword still leans against the hearth, untouched. Mother's embroidery sits unfinished on the table. I can't bring myself to move them.

He came to see me today. The tsar. He told me I should be grateful for his mercy, that he allowed me to stay here with Nina instead of dragging me to the stronghold immediately. He smiled as he said it. I wanted to spit in his face.

He wanted to marry me so much he killed my parents. What kind of man does that? What kind of monster?

I sat in the garden today, hoping the roses would bloom again. They didn't. Maybe they're gone for good, like Mother and Father. Maybe I'm broken now.

But Nina says I'm strong. She says my parents would want me to keep fighting. I don't feel strong. I feel like a shattered piece of glass. But maybe . . . maybe I can put the pieces back together. Maybe one day, I'll find a way to stop him.

He thinks he's won. He thinks he's broken me. But I'm still here. And one day, he'll regret letting me live.

Year 713

It's been four years since the wedding. Four years since I was dragged into this nightmare. He decided to start celebrating it this year and every year to come, celebrating the day I lost my soul.

He forces himself on me every night. Every. Night. I close my eyes and pretend I'm somewhere else, anywhere else, but it doesn't help. His breath is hot and rancid, his fat belly resting on mine, his hands rough. I hate him. I hate him so much I could tear my own skin off to escape his touch.

Afterward, he leaves me there, used and hollow. As soon as he's gone, I clean myself. But no matter how much I clean, I still feel him on me. Nina always brings me the tea, her hands shaking as much as mine. She says it will stop anything from taking root.

I want him dead. I want him to choke on his own blood. I want to watch him burn, his cock in his hand, shriveling like the pathetic thing it is.

He thinks he's powerful, but he's just a man. A weak, greedy, pitiful man. If I could poison him, I would. If I could light the whole stronghold on fire, I would.

But I can't. Not yet. Nina says we must be careful. She says we must wait. How much longer must I endure this?

It happened.

Nurse Nina says she has a plan. She says we can't stay here any longer. "He'll kill you," she said, her voice shaking. "He knows about the prophecy. He knows about this too."

I don't know if we'll survive, but I trust her. She's the only one I have left.

She packed the tea, the herbs, and the salts. She told me to run, to go as fast as I could and never look back. She stayed behind to distract them. I didn't want to leave her, but she shoved me toward the door. Her hands were trembling.

I made it to the forest. My lungs burned, my legs felt like they would give out, but I kept running. Nina said to run until I couldn't hear anything but my beating heart. So I did.

The trees here are dark, the ground uneven, but I didn't stop. I couldn't. The sound of the village faded behind me, replaced by the pounding in my ears and the crunch of leaves.

I don't know where I am, I don't know where to go, but I'm free. For now.

I met a vólkin today. I thought they were only stories Mother told me as a child. "Guardians of nature," she'd called them, protectors of balance and life. Now I see she was right.

His name is Ándor. He's enormous, with fur the color of a stormy sky and eyes that seem to see straight into my soul. At first, I was afraid, but he knelt before me, and his voice was calm when he said, "You're safe now."

He told me he felt my presence long before he saw me. He said it's because I'm spiritual. I told him what my mother said, that I'm a leader from a prophecy, that I must restore balance.

He knew where to go, so we went and found an old woman. She said she's Nina's friend and told me I'm the Lidéřen. She knew my mother as well, and I don't understand anything anymore.

Ándor brought me food today. Berries and roasted meat. I haven't eaten like this in months. He watches me with such care, as if I'm something precious. It makes me feel strange, but not in a bad way.

He placed his paw gently on my belly and said, "She'll be strong, like her mother." For the first time in a long time, I felt hope. Nina's friend said it's a girl. She knows everything.

I've been thinking about names. Mother always said names carry meaning, that they shape who we are. I told Ándor about a name I read in one of her books: Noël. It means birth and new beginnings. He smiled.

Noël the blue rose. It sounds perfect.

That's who she is, my little Noël. She's the start of something new. After everything, she's my hope, my light.

My belly is rounder with every passing moon. Ándor laughs when she kicks, saying she's already strong like her parents. He talks to her a lot, his voice low and soothing, telling her about the forest and the stars. It makes my heart ache in the best way.

I think about what her life will be like here. No walls, no fear, only freedom. Ándor says he'll grow us a home, a place where she can grow up surrounded by nature's beauty. I believe him.

The forest feels alive. It's quiet, but not silent. The trees whisper, the streams sing, and the air is sweet with the scent of flowers. Ándor says the land welcomes me, and I carry blue-rose blood. The forest loves our Noël too.

He told me today that we're bonded. Mates, he called us. I don't fully understand it, but I feel it. It's like a thread connecting us. For the first time in years, I feel safe. I feel loved.

I am happy.

I can't wait to meet her. Every time she kicks, it feels like she's reminding me she's there, waiting and growing. I imagine holding her, seeing her little hands and her big eyes. Ándor says she'll look like me, but I think she'll have his strength. He loves her so much.

She's my everything already. My Noël. My new beginning. Noël will run through these trees, free of chains. That is my promise.

Year 714

Ándor says this is the perfect place for us. He grew our home right from the trees, weaving the walls from their branches. It feels alive and warm, like the forest is holding us close.

He tells me stories about Ávera, the land beyond the barrier. He says it's beautiful, full of green fields and crystal streams. It's where we belong, he says. Where Noël will grow. I can't wait to see it. I can't wait to raise her there when the barrier finally lifts. After the bonding ritual, I'll have crystals like Ándor. And I'll live as long as he will—thousands of years.

I will have thousands of years with the family we're creating. I don't know how to put the joy into words.

We made her a crib today. Ándor worked all morning, shaping the wood with his massive paws. I cried when I saw it. It's simple and strong, just like him. The moment my tears fell, blue roses bloomed around it.

I carved the symbol of the rose into the side, like Father taught me. It felt right, like I was giving her a part of our family, a piece of who we are.

I've never been this happy. I've never felt this much love. Ándor says she'll grow up strong and smart, that she'll do great things. I believe him. How could I not?

My baby, Noël, will be happy just like I am. When a white dove appeared today, I gave her water, and Noël, the little darling, got excited in my belly.

It happened so suddenly. I was in the garden, tending to the roses, when Ándor stiffened. His ears twitching, he turned toward the trees and said, "They're here."

The tsar's men. They found us. I don't know how, but they're here.

Ándor told me to stay inside. Told me not to worry because one vólkin can kill a hundred men. I wanted to believe him. I wanted to trust him. But I saw the way his claws flexed, the way his tail lashed. He was ready to fight.

I heard the screams first. The clash of steel, the roar of his voice, the cries of the men who dared to face him. I wanted to run to him, to help, but he made me promise to stay. So I stayed. I waited. I prayed.

And then . . . silence. No more screams. No more steel. Nothing but the wind in the trees and the pounding of my heart.

I told myself he would come back. He promised he would. I waited by the door, my belly heavy, my hands trembling. But he didn't come.

When I couldn't wait anymore, I stepped outside, into the air thick with the smell of blood. The ground was littered with bodies, hundreds of them. The tsar's men, their swords broken, their armor shattered. He killed them all.

And then I saw my Ándor. My mate. My love. Lying among the dead, his body still, his fur matted with blood. I screamed. Fell to my knees. I begged him to wake up, but he didn't.

The goddesses didn't listen to my prayers.

He fought for us. For me. For our Noël. He wouldn't let them touch us. But the cost . . .

I buried him by the house. He was so heavy and my belly hurt. If I hadn't begun my awakening, I wouldn't have been able to do it. I pressed my forehead to his, the way he used to, and told him I would protect her. I promised him his sacrifice wouldn't be in vain.

I will raise her to be strong. I will raise her to be ready. She will carry his strength and his honor. She will make this world better for all of us.

.   .   .

My belly is heavy and my heart is broken. I can't stay here for much longer. I have to find a way to survive. I can't hunt, can't even move much anymore.

I'm tired.

My Noël is kicking harder every day.

She is strong, but I am not.

38

THE ECHOES OF THE FALLEN AND THE STRENGTH TO RISE AGAIN

"He came out growling, Vládan. Not crying, growling. I swear the goddesses tucked a storm in his lungs and claws in his smile. This one will lead. His roar will silence storms, and his silence will make tsars tremble. I don't need a vision to see it. I've grown it in my womb."

—Ánya Volkóva to her mate, Vládan, the night Theron was born

Noël

*S*he was supposed to be the leader. The Lidéřen.

All my mother wanted was a world where I could breathe without asking permission.

Theron holds my face with both paws, his eyes on mine, grounding me in the storm of emotions. "Noël," he whispers.

"My mother . . ." I falter, my throat burns. "My mother was raped and abused for years. She lost her parents. She was so strong, Theron. She didn't even know it. She had no idea how strong she was!" The words burst out, cutting through the silence in this cold house.

Theron pulls me into his arms. "Your mother was a true warrior."

"She endured so much, Theron." My voice breaks as I bury my face in his fur. "She sacrificed everything for me. She went through so much pain . . . She wanted to raise me here, with my father, with Ándor."

In another life, my mother could have chosen herself first. She could have traveled with no restrictions, lived her dreams, read all the books in the world. And never looked back. She'd have danced around the fire at midnight, laughed without worries.

She'd never have had to give herself away.

Theron's hold tightens. "She will be remembered by everyone, my mate. I vow this to you."

I nod into his chest as tears well in my eyes. "There's more," I whisper.

Theron releases me, his paws resting on my waist. "Do you want me to read it?"

I shake my head. This is something I want to do.

Taking a deep breath, I open the diary again. My fingers brush against a piece of paper tucked between the pages, its edges yellowed and brittle, even older than the diary itself. I pull it out, unfold it carefully, and my hands tremble as I prepare for what it might reveal.

The Barrier of Sovereignty and the Eradication of the Vólkin Threat
On the 12th moon of the year 314, by order of Tsar Aldrik I, the vólkin threat was eradicated, and the Barrier of Sovereignty was raised to ensure humanity's dominion over the land.

Sixty-four spiritual beings were sacrificed to fuel the creation of the barrier. The vólkins and their human mates were lured beyond the borders of Ávera. The Tsar's men, armed with arrows forged to pierce spiritual crystals, targeted the women's heads. As each crystal shattered, their bearers fell. The *vólkins*, bound to their mates by the goddesses' will, perished immediately.

The bodies of the fallen were collected and burned to form the foundation of the ritual to raise the barrier. Their ashes were scattered at the six points around the land, and the power of sixty-four spiritual beings was harnessed by the incantations of the Council of Crown.

The Barrier of Sovereignty was declared impenetrable, severing *Ávera* from the outside world. Within, the *vólkins* are confined, their influence extinguished. Beyond, humanity will thrive under the Crown's divine authority, free from the interference of nature's guardians.

The prophecy of the *Lidéřen* remains the greatest threat to this balance. Should the blood of the blue rose awaken, the barrier will falter, and the spirits of the fallen may rise again to undo what was built. The Tsar and his descendants must guard against this prophecy at all costs.

This document is to remain within the Tsar's study. Any attempt to uncover the truth of the barrier's creation or the identities of the sixty-four sacrificed beings is punishable by death.

The Sixty-Four Sacrificed to Raise the Barrier of Sovereignty

1 Miroslár and Tatiána Kholína (Sister to Míra, Tárnov)

2 Drágan and Miléna Drazíc (Merchant's Daughter, Róstan)

3 Rádon and Zóra Ková č (Noble of Tárnov)

4 Míslaven and Vésna Petróva (Healer of Gráyárk)

5 Boríslon and Lýuba Tarnóvska (Lord's Daughter, Vódany)

6 Zóran and Míra Kholína (Citizen of Tárnov)

7 Rádomir and Daníca Thórne (Lady of Velháven)

8 Srdján and Ívana Haymoor (Noblewoman of Yáarím)

9 Bódan and Jeléna Vorst (Village Elder's Daughter, Róstan)

10 Vukásin and Katarína Markóvicová (Noble of Velháven)

11 Brán and Sláva Ríke (Merchant's Wife, Gráyárk)

12 Stánimir and Natálya Tarnóvska (Sister to Lýuba, Vódany)

13 Velímir and Rádmila Ivanóvic (Citizen of Velháven)

14 Dobromír and Sofíya Kováč (Noblewoman of Tárnov)
15 Vládan and Ánya Volkóva (House Volkóv, Nobility of Velháven)
16 Unknown
17 Unknown
18 Unknown
19 Unknown
20 . . .
—*Council of Crown, Year 314, The Royal Court*

"Ánya and Vládan," I whisper and immediately turn my gaze to Theron.

"I walked past my parents' ashes for four hundred years." His hold on me tightens, and I understand. We've both come to learn the unbearable truths of what our parents endured. This is beyond inhumane.

"The barrier wasn't just a prison for the vólkins," Theron continues, his voice low and trembling. "It was a tomb for their legacy." His hazel eyes glisten with unshed tears, and my chest tightens at the sight.

I pull him closer, my arms wrapping around him as I lean in and say, "We will restore the balance. We'll kill the tsar and every one of his men. We will never let anything like that happen again."

"My mate," Theron breathes as he buries his snout into the crook of my neck.

I hold him as tightly as I can, pouring every bit of strength I have into the embrace. "We will remember them all." My vow rings in the silence like a promise carved in stone.

After a while, we pull away from each other, though everything we've shared is heavy in the air. Without a word, we rise and move to return to the vólkins waiting for us. I have no idea how much time has passed since we entered my parents' home, but it doesn't matter. It's time to go back.

Theron and I . . . we're closer now. The bond between us feels unbreakable. I know, without a doubt, that I can trust him with my life.

We've both learned the depths of what our families endured—the terror they faced—and together, we've vowed to make this world a better place. A place where their sacrifices won't be forgotten. There will be *war*.

My mother. My father. All the vólkins and their mates. They will be remembered.

As we step out of the home, everyone's eyes are already on us. Even before we cross the threshold.

They all look broken.

They heard it all.

The trip back to Ávera is silent. I sit on Theron's back as he runs, and the others follow close behind. No one speaks. What we've learned hangs heavy over all of us, each lost in our own thoughts.

I clutch my mother's diary tightly, the document of the incident tucked inside it.

Still, there's some relief in the truth I learned. I don't know exactly how my mother died, but now I know her story. Her struggles. Her strength. The pieces of the past are beginning to fall into place.

Our mission is clear.

Find the five. Kill the tsar. Destroy his men. Restore balance.

The trials will begin tomorrow, and with them, our chance to push ourselves, to discover our limits, and to reshape the forces that will fight alongside us. Theron has trained them well.

The shelters are built, and we've learned of three nearby

villages. That's where we'll start. But trials first, then the bonding ritual. One step at a time.

By the time we return to Ávera, night has fallen. We're greeted as though we've returned with victory. No one but us knows the truth.

Theron hasn't spoken a word since we left the house.

At the entrance, where trees part and streams flow, vólkins of all ages gather.

They all look excited and eager, and soon, I will pop that bubble of hope.

Elder Aïna steps forward with Mina, Naïa, and Essin. They bow, and the others follow their lead.

Theron lowers himself and I dismount, my boots crunching against the ground. I feel nothing. No triumph or anger. Nothing but a hollow numbness.

"Elder Aïna," I say. "The Lidéřen was once someone else."

Elder Aïna's expression shifts, and her eyes widen as she murmurs, "The ancient language."

I continue, my voice strong enough so everyone can hear. "Today, we uncovered the truth of the barrier's creation. The generation that gave us life was destroyed by the children of the Snake. Tonight, we will honor our people. We will perform the farewell ritual."

Mina raises a paw to her chest. "Your Majesty,"

"Prepare everything," I command. "The wax, the herbs, the wood. Tonight, we'll honor the fallen and their stories. We will give them the farewell they deserve."

The warriors who returned with us, their faces are etched with exhaustion and grief. My gaze lingers on Theron, and my chest tightens. He looks distant, his strength and presence overshadowed by the sorrow in his eyes. The others wear the same broken expressions.

"We will remember them," I say firmly. "Your parents. Your loved ones. Their sacrifices won't be forgotten. And while we can't punish those responsible—they've long since died—we will end their legacy."

Pressing my hand over my heart, just like I've seen them do, I step closer to the group. "We will hunt down every son and father. We will burn their lands and take what rightfully belongs to us. Vathéria will be ours, as it was always meant to be." I clench my fists. "That is *my* promise to *you*."

A low growl ripples through the vólkins surrounding me. It's the sound of revenge.

This is what we need. Tomorrow, in the first trial, their anger will become their strength. It will carry them through the fire. And in battle, it will be their weapon.

I turn to Theron. He supported me when I was at my lowest, and now it's my turn to be there for him. I take his paw in my hands, and his grip tightens.

When our eyes meet, I see the sorrow he can't hide. It's raw, etched into every line of his face. My heart aches for him.

"Do you know what your parents loved?" I ask as others disperse, leaving us be. "Let's honor them with it . . . for their farewell."

Theron leads me down a path I've never taken before, far from the streams, our home, and even the sacred glade.

"Where are we going?" I ask, my hand wrapped around his paw.

"To a place I visit often," he answers. His expression is calm, but there's more to it. "As you read in the document, my mother was a noble. I always knew that. Elder Aïna told me she loved the finer things in life. When she met my father, he promised her every luxury she could imagine."

A small smile pulls at my lips. Ánya loved expensive things

—it suits the image I have of her. Thinking of Theron growing up in a house filled with nobility makes sense. He's so composed and dignified, a noble vólkin to his core. Even the way he arranges my meals, the way he refuses to let the different foods in my bowl touch, reflects that.

"How did they meet?" I ask, tucking a strand of hair behind my ear as we walk. The vólkin homes are far behind us now.

"Elder Aïna doesn't remember the details for every couple, but she said the women all escaped their villages in some way,"

"Just like my mother,"

Theron nods and turns his gaze ahead.

I follow his line of sight to a large hill rising on the edge of Ávera. "Are we going up that hill?"

"Almost."

The path ahead, leading to a high cliff overlooking the ocean to the west of Ávera, is clearer than the forest we left behind. The trees thin out as we go, and the cooler wind bites at my skin. Walking keeps me warm.

Theron points to what looks like the mouth of a cave.

"Here?" I ask.

"I found this cave when I was a youngling," he says. "Elder Aïna told me it wasn't by chance. She said the cave called to me for a reason."

We pass through dense bushes, which Theron holds aside to make the path easier for me. The cave's entrance comes into view, wide and framed by greenery. The way the light filters through the bushes outside creates patterns that dance on the stone walls within. It's beautiful.

"My mother liked colorful gems," Theron says as he guides me toward a pile of furs near the cave wall. "My father would come here often to gather the most beautiful crystals he could find for her."

"Did you bring these furs here to sit on?"

Theron shakes his head, a small smile playing on his

mouth. "My mother loved to watch my father work," he says as he sits beside me. The warmth in his expression tells me how deeply he cherishes those memories. Ánya sounds like such a lively, spirited person.

"I wonder what it would've been like if our parents had met," I say.

The thought of my mother sitting with Ánya, chatting over cups of tea, brings an unexpected smile to my face. My mother, always so reserved and serious, paired with someone as vibrant as Ánya—it feels like they'd complement each other perfectly. I think they could've been great friends.

I pat my thighs.

It catches Theron's attention, and he tilts his head. "What's that? A human custom?"

Shaking my head with a small smile, I say, "It's an invitation. When I was little, I'd rest on my mother's lap, and she would sing me lullabies."

Theron shifts back, studying me before carefully resting his head on my thighs. The weight of him warms my heart.

"Are you comfortable?" I ask, brushing my fingers over his fur.

He nuzzles his snout against my knees. "Very."

My fingers trace over his pointed ears, smoothing the strands of hair he so carefully combs in the mornings.

It's been a while since I last sang this. I take a deep breath and begin.

Rest, my rose, in the night's warm glow,
The stars will guard you, their secrets flow.

Theron's ears twitch at the sound of my voice, and his paw tightens under my knee.

Your petals soft, with strength unseen,
Through darkest shadows, a light serene.
The crystal waits where the frost runs deep,
Its heart aglow, in eternal keep.

I lean back against the cool cave wall and let the melody play in my mind. My mother's voice echoes in my memory. This lullaby . . . For the first time, I truly understand it. I am the rose, and Theron is the crystal.

"My mate." Theron shifts to lie on his back.

I hum in question, my hand still on his mane.

"I've heard this song before."

"You have?"

He nods, his golden eyes meet mine as he sings.

A guardian bold, through storm and tide,
Protects the bloom with steadfast pride.
When rose and crystal together stand,
The winds shall sing across the land.
A bond unbroken, the dawn will rise,
To heal the earth, beneath shared skies.

I didn't know there was more to the song. His deep voice gives the words weight and meaning. My heart feels so full, and slowly, I lower my face, my eyes closed.

He nuzzles my nose.

"They all could have been happy."

39

THE NIGHT OF ONE FINAL FAREWELL

"Do you see the stars, little ones? That's where your parents play now. They chase the wind across the sky and laugh in the moonlight. And when the fireflies gather around your nests at night, that's them kissing your cheeks good night."
—Elder Aïna, to the growlings during their first winter without their parents

Theron

"Our mothers were brutally murdered. Human arrows pierced their crystals, and they perished as one with their bonded mates. Their bodies were burned in fires of hatred and fear, leaving only ashes. This wasn't accidental, it was planned. A plan to break us and cage us, to ensure the remaining pups would fade into time.

"But tonight, we mark the day we learned the truth. We pray to the goddesses and thank Elder Aïna for raising us all. We honor our females and remember one extraordinary woman who brought us the truth and our Lidéřen."

I stand tall before our people, my mate by my side.

Together, we oversee the gathered crowd at Ávera's sea. The waves behind us are quiet, the animals of the forest, silent.

"That house is proof," Noël says, her voice strong and commanding, "of a woman who gave up everything to save this land. She sacrificed herself so we could have a bright future. Eyleen Ársa will be remembered as a hero, a great woman who fell so we may walk with pride. We will restore the balance, and the world will know a new order. The order of life."

She brings her hand to her heart, and I follow. Across the crowd, every vólkin mirrors the gesture—males, females, growlings, and younglings alike—all of us bow our heads in unity with respect and honor for the fallen.

"We will begin the farewell," I announce. I turn to the nýmphá standing to my side. She bows and hands me the wooden base of the svytyn prócha, the ceremonial vessel my mate and I crafted together.

We did this before, centuries ago, when Elder Aïna told us their souls had left us. Back then, we were too young to truly understand. But tonight, we know. We understand what happened. As pups we named these waters the Sea of Fire in memory of the fire-covered ocean, and the souls who will never return. That night, Kaël caught a few fireflies and kept them close.

The cool breeze carries the scent of the ocean as my Noël and I crouch near the water. The others follow our lead. For the farewell, we chose blue roses to adorn our svytyn prócha. My mate said it would honor our bond and symbolize the strength of our parents' sacrifices. I agreed. My parents would love the beauty of the blue roses, and their symbolism feels fitting.

My mate reaches into her pocket, pulls out small, colorful stones, and carefully arranges them on the wooden base.

She's so thoughtful. They are for my mother.

"Thank you," I murmur as she places the final stone between the roses.

"This one is from my mother, father, and me." She reaches for her pendant and places it atop the roses and stones, and my brow furrows.

"But—"

"I want them all to look over us together," she says, looking into my eyes. "Ánya, Eyleen, Vládan, and Ándor."

My sweet, sweet mate.

I reach for the back of her head and pull her close. My forehead rests against hers, and I nuzzle her face, breathing her in.

Focusing inward, I lead the energy within me into my paws. Slowly, two glowing energy balls form, one in each paw. Their warmth radiates over my fur as I rub them together. The friction creates a spark that crackles in the night air.

My mate crouches, then raises the wax beneath the spark, and the flame comes flickering to life between us. Together, we light the svytyn prócha, and its glow brightens the blue roses and stones placed within.

Gently, we send the svytyn prócha onto the water to drift down the stream. Soft ripples carry it farther. Around us, the others do the same, releasing their own vessels to honor their families and loved ones. A sea of flames dancing in the dark stretches across the water, a breathtaking mosaic of color and remembrance. A Sea of Fire.

Rising, I extend a paw to my mate and help her to her feet. Side by side, paw in hand, we stand at the edge of the bank, gazing over the colorful waters.

Their deaths will not be forgotten. The memory of their sacrifices burns within each flame.

I tighten my grip on Noël's hand.

"Theron, Your Majesty," Aeson calls out. I turn to see him approaching with Kaël and Zephyr. Both bow to my mate.

Noël looks up at me with a sad smile that tugs at my chest. "I'll go to Mina and Elder Aïna. We need to oversee the preparations for the first trial tomorrow. You should have a moment with them."

I nod, but bring her hand to my snout before I let her go. As she walks away, I feel the ache of her absence immediately.

Zephyr crosses his arms, his expression grim. "It's been a difficult day."

Kaël rubs his face, ruffling his fur. "I want to run until my legs give out. Thinking about Mother and Father has always been hard enough, but now . . . knowing the truth . . ." His voice trails off.

Aeson remains quiet, his gaze hollow.

A low, snarling voice cuts through the air behind us. "I'm going to destroy the tsar. I'm not waiting for trials or your little ritual with your mate."

I turn to see Orïon standing there, muscles flexed.

Orïon is much older than the rest of us, at least two hundred and thirty years. He remembers his parents, having been raised by them for far longer than any of us. That memory, I know, fuels his rage.

"You're not going anywhere," I growl. This isn't the time for rebellion.

"The barrier is gone, and we know the truth now. What are we waiting for?" His fur bristles as his shoulders tense. His eyes are wild with anger.

Baring my fangs, I stride toward him, grip his mane, and force him to look at me. "You will *not* cause trouble, Orïon," I say. "You will behave as your leader commands. We will complete the trials, bolster our forces, and then we will attack. That is the plan. That is *her* word."

Orïon huffs and grabs my wrist, his claws digging in.

"Alright, mighty warriors, let's not tear each other apart." Kaël steps between us.

I straighten my back and lift my chin as I look down at

Orïon. "If you wish to defy your leader, then you have no place here."

"You can wait, but I can't," Orïon snarls. "I see their faces every time I close my eyes. I hear their screams. You didn't live with their voices haunting you for centuries." His claws flex, digging into the dirt.

I understand his rage, I feel it too. The craving for revenge burns deep. But we cannot afford recklessness. We are the last of our kind. Only a few hundred vólkins remain in the world. If we fall, there will be no one to remember, no one to restore balance.

"You want to charge in by yourself and die for nothing?" I ask, my voice cold.

Orïon's jaw tightens, but he doesn't answer.

Aeson finally speaks, his fists clenched so tightly his knuckles pale. "Rage blinds us all. Let's hope it doesn't cost us more than it already has."

I turn my attention back to Orïon. "The tsar and his warriors were able to cage even the goddesses. Do not underestimate what they are capable of now. You are older, Orïon, but not wiser."

He growls low in his throat.

I step closer, invading his space. "Hold yourself together. No one will go against my mate's order."

He doesn't reply, but his claws retract, and his shoulders relax just slightly. For now, the fire in him is quelled. But I know it will take more than words to keep it contained.

I walk through the forest. Alone.

The air is cool, but it does little to settle the heat in my chest. I need to breathe, to calm myself, before my anger mirrors Orïon's. His dreams have turned into nightmares, but at least he has them.

Orïon knows the sound of his mother's voice. He remembers the habits of his father, their values ingrained in him over years of shared life. He knows them.

I do not.

A sharp ache rising in my blood, I bare my fangs in frustration. With a burst of energy, I leap forward. The branches whip against my fur as I run through the forest, the ground crunches beneath my paws, but none of it slows me.

I must calm this storm before I return to my mate. She carries enough burdens without mine adding to them.

Does Orïon think I haven't thought of revenge? That I haven't dreamed of tearing apart those who dared to leave so many pups orphaned?

I have. From the moment I met my mate and heard her stories, the thought has consumed me every day.

My sweet, sweet mate. The simple thought of her wakes the beast within me. My cock unsheathes, ignited by her scent alone.

Her scent.

I stop, and my claws sink into the bark of a nearby tree. My ears twitch as I strain to catch the sound of her voice.

"This will be a good spot. Try not to leave any traces of scent, you know how they can track even across distances."

Who is my mate talking to?

A low growl rumbles deep in my chest. The beast within me stirs, starts to claw its way out.

Hunting. My mate.

I drop low to the ground, my body coiled and ready. Her voice guides me, and the sweet scent of blue roses fills my snout. My nostrils flare as I follow her trail.

Through the bushes and twigs, my heart pounds in my chest. The thrill of a hunt.

"Tomorrow at dawn, we will gather. Make sure the scrolls are there as well," she says, confident and commanding. Deliciously authoritative. It excites me beyond reason.

I stalk closer silently. My precum soaks the soil beneath my paws.

My thigh muscles rub my swollen sac, and it only fuels my desire.

And there she is, my beautiful mate. Standing with two nýmphí. They haven't noticed me yet. Good. This is good.

She's wrapped in fabric, her body concealed from my eyes, teasing me, hiding the full grace of her. I want to tear it with my teeth and mount her.

A low growl escapes me, and all three turn their heads in my direction. The nýmphí wouldn't leave, even if I signaled them to. They serve their Lidéřen, not me.

"Theron?" my mate calls. Her chin lifts as she inhales.

She can scent now, almost like we can. Oh, how thrilling this is.

"I know you're here," she says, amused.

I know you know, my sweet dove.

I shift to my right, changing direction, and growl again. Each step is important in a hunt: slow at first, then faster. Confusing my prey. My tail brushes against a bush, rustling the leaves.

Her gaze snaps toward the sound.

The moon hangs high above, nearly full. Its light spills over her. Painted in silver, she is divine, a vision of strength and beauty.

My dove nods to the nýmphí, handing one of them a scroll.

My head tilts. What has she decided?

Then, with a sly grin, she grips the fabric of her clothing in her fists and bolts to the left, away from me, in the opposite direction.

She wants to play.

A smirk spreads across my face as I arch my back. The thrill of the chase hits every nerve in my body. With a loud roar, I launch after her.

I let her run. She needs to tire before I pounce.

As I leap over a fallen log, my hard cock strikes the wood, and I hiss at the sting. The brief pain sharpens my focus, my energy spikes in response, and I push myself to run faster.

There's no hiding my presence now. My heavy thuds reverberate through the forest, my growls loud and feral.

But she doesn't look back. Not once.

She doesn't look at me.

I *want* her to look at me.

She veers in another direction, but I pull up short, cutting a corner and moving straight toward her. I lower myself, lunge. My body hurtles through the air.

With a scream, a laugh, and a pounding heart, my mate falls to her side beneath me. Her chest heaves.

I roll her over to face me, positioning her thighs to straddle my hips. Her skin glows under the moonlight, flushed red.

My cock presses against the fabric over her belly. Lowering my snout to her, I growl, "You ran."

"I ... did ..." she murmurs on heavy exhales.

I trace my tongue along her chest, up to her face, then back again. Her sweat against my tongue is sweet and salty. Delicious.

My cock rises and falls with her every breath.

I must find release.

My mate furrows her brows as I glide my paw along her calf, lifting her leg.

"You look angry," she says as her hands rest against the forest floor.

Even now, she sees through me. I can't hide anything from her. Not even like this.

My precum dampens her gown, smearing across her belly. The sight only stokes the need inside me. "Let's take this off."

"First," she says firmly, "you tell me what's troubling you."

Her scent clouds my mind. She's aroused—I can smell it—but she asked, and I must answer.

"Orïon had centuries with his parents." My voice is strained as a growl rumbles in my chest. "He knew their voices, their scents. And what did I have?" My claws dig into the earth beside her. "Ashes. Ashes and silence."

She watches me, her eyes soft. "Orïon? The black-coated vólkin?"

Hearing his name on her lips sends rage through me. I snort, my fangs bared. "Yes."

"And I had a mother who fought until her last breath to make sure I'd survive," she says. "I lost her too, Theron. But I'm here. I'm here because of her. And you're here because of them."

"I know." I lift the fabric, revealing her strong, beautiful body. Her thighs are firm, her abs defined, her skin like the moonlight itself. My mate is a goddess.

Propping myself on an elbow beside her, I lean down so close I can see the fire in her wide eyes. "Your nose is small," I tease, a grin pulling at my mouth.

She grabs my jaw, her fingers pressing down on my tongue and against my lower teeth. "Don't change the subject," she warns.

I lift her fingers with my tongue, a low chuckle rumbling in my chest. She's so fiery. "Now I can speak," I say, then lick my fingers to wet them before lowering them to her. My paw slides from the curls between her thighs down to where I belong.

She whimpers, and the sound drives my need to its limit, precum spilling from my cock as it lies on her abs.

"Orïon thought he could decide on his own, to go against our plan." My voice is gravelly as I rub her clit.

Her moan escapes, and her hips jerk against my paw.

"He wants to fight without preparation," I growl. My control slips as her arousal floods my senses.

"Theron," she cries out as I glide a claw from her clit to her entrance.

She lies beneath me, covered in forest dirt, panting, flushed, and divine. The vision alone is enough to trigger my release. *Not yet.*

"I don't deserve you," I murmur as I slowly slide a finger into her.

"You deserve everything," she breathes. "Theron—" She clenches around me, her tightness testing my control.

If I didn't know humans could mate with vólkins, I might not believe it was possible. But we've learned. Patience and care. Stretch, then in.

"Did you put a log inside me?" she pants. Her words pull a low chuckle from me.

"Not yet." The grin on my face grows as I lick her face to soothe her. Again and again, my tongue traces over her skin until she begins to relax.

I press forward, just a little more, letting her body adjust to the tip of my finger. Slowly, I guide her through the stretch.

When vólkins mate, we shave our claws for this moment, and I've done the same. Three claws are half-shaven. Together, my three fingers are nearly the thickness of my cock.

"You're doing so well," I whisper, my voice prideful as her little cunt spills more onto the forest floor. Her body responds so perfectly to me.

"How," she moans, "how will you ever fit?"

"I will make it fit," I murmur against her neck, my mouth brushing her skin as I push deeper.

My dove arches her back. A cry escapes her lips as I pump inside her, pressing nearly half my finger in. My paw is slick with her arousal, and in this moment, nothing else matters. Not the war ahead, not Orïon, not the barrier. Nothing.

All I care about is my little mate, taking me like the leader she is.

Slowly, I press deeper, her cries soft and sweet, her body adjusting to me. Her gaze is unfocused and beautiful.

She is brave, my brave little dove. And it's because of *me*.

I am the one who pleases her. *I* am the one who will make her swell and fatten with our pups. Soon, after the bonding ritual, our bodies will become one, and so will our souls.

Her nipples prick through the fabric of her gown, tempting me. Who am I not to tend to every part of my needy mate?

I lower my snout to brush my cold, damp nose over her left breast. She shivers beneath me as I push deeper inside her.

"Theron, I— I am—" she cries out.

"You are," I murmur and push my finger into her fully.

She hisses, and her body tightens around me.

My ears pin back as guilt twists in my chest. "I'm sorry," I whisper. "This is the first and last time I will ever hurt you, my sweet dove."

Carefully, I withdraw my finger. There it is—the tip stained with blood, marking the moment of her first stretch. I clean it with my tongue, savor the sweetness of her blood and arousal.

When I gaze back at her, I find her staring at me, eyes wide.

"Did you just lick it?"

I nod, a grin tugging at the corners of my mouth. "But we're not done yet," I say as I add another finger. She's ready to take two.

My cock throbs with need. I want to be inside her. To fill her, to claim her completely.

Patience, Theron. You've waited this long. You can wait a little longer.

Lowering myself between her thighs, I press my tongue against her clit. Her body jerks with every stroke. Her cries grow louder, and when her release comes, it spills over my mouth, nose, and paw.

She's breathtaking. Completely undone. My sweet dove, so beautiful.

I rise to my knees, gripping her legs, pressing them together. "May I?" I ask, my voice strained, the pressure in my sac near its limit.

She nods, her gaze hazy, her chest rising and falling with every breath.

I shift onto my back paws, position myself between her hard thighs. A growl escapes me as I slide my cock between them. The pressure is almost too much. I move my hips forward, and the friction builds until my swollen knot presses against her thighs.

Goddesses above.

I close my eyes and force myself to take a deep breath. Not yet. I can't let go yet—I want to feel her skin.

"You're going to spill on me," she murmurs, her voice breathy.

"Yes." I meet her gaze as I thrust between her thighs. "This is"—I grunt, thrusting again—"how I'll do it"—thrust—"in two days." My sac hits her sensitive flesh with every push.

One more thrust, my knees weaken, and I roar. I'm overwhelmed by my release, spilling hot and thick across her torso.

My beautiful mate is covered in my semen, and I want to do it again.

40

THE WARRIORS' FIRST TEST

"You speak of courage like it's enough, Zárya. But these are not gods, they're pups born in a cage. They've never tasted blood in their teeth or ash in their lungs. When war finds them, it won't ask if they're ready. It will burn first. Then ask nothing at all."
—Láda Veléša, to Zárya on the eve of the first trial

Theron

Lying on my side in our bed-nest, I watch my mate as she sleeps.

The sky will soon begin to change. The first streaks of orange and pink signal the arrival of dawn. In just a few moments, my dove will wake.

Yesterday, I stretched her for the first time. With my fully erect shaft resting against her thigh, it's hard to focus on anything else.

But I must.

The trials begin today. With each passing day, we draw closer to war.

Bolstering our forces as humans do will be critical, even if it means adopting some of their methods. We must understand how they fight if we are to stand against them.

I signal the nýmphí and grant approval for them to enter our home with a double pulse from my crystals. As they step inside, I raise a finger to my mouth, instructing them to be quiet.

All . . . one, two . . . thirteen nýmphí nod and sit in a semi-circle around our nest.

My gaze lowers back to my mate. Small droplets of sweat bead on her forehead where they glisten against her otherwise calm features. It's the season when the snow melted, and the days grow warmer, which will give way to harsher weather in the coming moons. The air is neither cold nor hot—why is she sweating?

My ears twitch as an unwelcome feeling settles in my stomach. The nýmphí's expressions are tight with worry as they lean closer to my mate. What do they sense that I do not?

Outside, the birds sing their songs of early morning, the forest is quiet . . . but something is not right.

Before I can act, my mate gasps for air and sits up suddenly. "I'm alright. Everything is alright. It's home. Home."

I scoop her into my arms, and she turns her wide eyes up to me, searching for reassurance. "A bad dream?" I ask as I run a soothing paw along her back.

Her body relaxing against me, she nods.

I lower my jaw to rest on the top of her head, letting my warmth comfort her. "Now," I murmur, "you tell *me* what's bothering you."

"I sometimes dream of Arnold's death."

Why does his death haunt her? "Are you not happy he is gone?" I ask. "He did not deserve to breathe the same air as you."

She tilts her face upward, and I trace my tongue over her face. "Come in," I call toward the door, sensing the others waiting outside. The door opens to Mina, Naïa, and Essin. The nýmphí rise to their feet and part to make way for the three females.

"Good morning, Your Majesty. Theron," Mina says as they all bow.

I nod, and my mate greets them with a soft smile. "Good morning."

"Where is Elder Aïna?" I ask, scanning the room.

"Your mate's scent clouds your senses," Essin replies with a wide grin.

My ears twitch, and I turn toward the entrance as Elder Aïna walks in and says, "I have been standing here for a while now, mighty warrior."

A deep sigh escapes me as I rise, still holding my mate in my arms. "Her Majesty needs to wake first."

"That is our duty." A few of the nýmphí step forward as if to take my Noël from me.

"I can do it too," I argue, lifting her higher.

"Theron, let me down."

My ears fall back. "Can I braid your hair, then?"

The horrified looks that ripple across the room stop me in my tracks. Every female in our home stares at me as if I've just claimed I can shift into human form.

"Don't *ever* touch her hair again," Essin huffs, her tone sharp.

I blink. What have I done wrong now? I set my mate down and watch as the nýmphí immediately swarm around her.

"Should we go so you two can take care of this?" one of them asks, motioning toward my hard cock.

They're all here already, and my mate wouldn't like to show that side of herself to others. I agree with her, but also, I'd love to stretch her some more before the trials. I shake my head, exhaling as I decide to surrender this battle. Some fights aren't worth winning.

I walk out of my own home, leaving the females to tend to their duties.

My cock remains hard, my soul longs for the connection we've yet to complete. Being together, yet unbonded, is a torment I wasn't prepared for.

Elder Aïna explained it. When mates meet, the bonding ritual must be performed within six moons, or their bodies will begin to betray them. The closeness of two unjoined souls takes its toll on the physical form.

There are no stories of what happens to mates who delay the ritual for too long. It's unheard of. And I know we won't be among them. In two days, my mate and I will bond. That certainty eases the burning in my soul.

Still, my heavy cock resists relief. The image of it buried deep inside her flashes through my mind, and I growl low in my chest.

I lost control last night, and I don't regret it. Not one bit.

She welcomes my touch. My mate wants me.

A smile stretches across my face at the thought. She is curious, open to me. Yet, she hasn't come to me herself. Not yet. These things take time. Yes, time.

I stop, stroking my cock to ease the ache. My knot is swollen, throbbing with the need to claim her fully. "Soon, we'll fill her womb," I murmur to my cock. The thought calms me even as I find release.

With my body temporarily sated, I stride toward the gathering for the trials.

Everything is set and ready. The benches have been cleared away to make space for all the warriors gathering for my mate's trial announcement. The tents are ready too.

Based on what I overheard yesterday, it seems the trials will involve searching for elements within the forest. I wonder how my mate and Elder Aïna designed the challenges.

Since I'm participating, it's only fair that I remain in the dark, like the others. Still, I'm eager to show her my skills. Let her see what her mate is capable of.

Closing my eyes, I send out a signal with my crystals, summoning all the vólkins. My mate will arrive soon, and when she does, she shouldn't have to wait.

Within moments, warriors pour in from all directions of Ávera. The trees sway with their presence, but my gaze sweeps the group for one in particular.

Where is Oríon? If I'm paired with him in a team, I'll need to keep a close eye on him.

"Everyone ready?" I ask, my arms crossed.

Zephyr stands with Kaël, who's closely inspecting Zephyr's braid.

"It looks tighter today," Kaël says, scratching his mane.

Zephyr's tail sways with pride as he shows off the neat braid. "It should look proper while we fight."

"You think we'll fight?" Kaël's ears twitch.

"If our strength is being tested, sparring seems likely," Aeson chimes in.

Sparring. Yes. A perfect opportunity to show my mate the power I wield. I never lose.

"All warriors, stand straight!" My command echoes through the clearing as I hear my mate approaching with the females.

All two hundred seventy-three warriors straighten their backs, standing tall and facing me. The females and younglings gather on the sidelines at their own pace. I scan the group until my eyes land on Oríon. For now, all is in order. "Today," I declare, "we will show Her Majesty how strong and capable we are. Show your strength and your mind. Show your pride in being vólkin, children of Éva."

A low growl rumbles through the warriors, a shared sound of will. They are ready, eager to prove themselves, to fight and win.

I let my narrowed gaze sweep over them. "If I find out

anyone has crossed the border today, they will face my claw. Each and every one of you knows the rules and the limits." I pause, my voice grows sharper. "Show me."

As one, the warriors raise their snouts to the sky, and a deafening howl breaks through the quiet of the forest. The trees shudder with the force of it, birds scatter from their branches in a flurry of wings. Sensing the strength of the vólkin, deer and boars flee.

This is vólkin power.

My mate approaches with the others, walking with confidence and a serious expression. The combination of her commanding presence and her scent makes my shaft peek out again. If we didn't have a balance to restore, I'd mate with her endlessly, day and night.

"Her Majesty has arrived!" Mina declares, and I step aside.

My sweet dove's eyes flick down to my semihard cock. Her cheeks flush a deep red, and my soul sings at the sight. She moves her lips silently, mouthing the words, *Cover it.*

A grin spreads across my snout. Why would I cover my cock? It's no secret that I desire my mate—everyone knows, and it's only natural. This is how the world works, how Mother Nature intended it. Sometimes, humans truly don't make sense. Or maybe human males have small cocks, and that is why they hide them.

A male should be eager for his female. It is how it has always been.

Still, she steps in front of me. She's shielding me from the gaze of others. I shall convince myself it is her possessiveness and not the modesty of human ways.

She doesn't look troubled by her nightmares for now. Tonight, we will talk about it.

"Today, we will test our strength and teamwork," she announces, her voice clear and authoritative as the females and nýmphí take their places at her sides.

All my warriors listen closely, and pride fills my chest.

"In the forest are hidden artifacts," she continues. "You must find them by the time three stars rise in the night sky."

A nýmphá steps forward to hand her a scroll.

"You will solve riddles," my mate explains, "as the clues within them will guide you to the items you need to gather. Each team will be given a scroll, and Naïa will announce the teams before you begin."

Solving riddles? My ears twitch. What is she planning? This is unexpected.

She begins to read the three riddles aloud:

In a grove where flowers bloom bright,
Find the herb that heals with might,
Among the petals, it hides its form,
A remedy to keep us warm.

Where the forest's heart beats strong,
Find the feather from a song,
High in branches, it does rest,
A token from a sacred nest.

By the stream where waters flow,
Find the stone with a gentle glow,
Marked by runes of ancient lore,
A gift from spirits, evermore.

"The spirits of this land are a part of my soul," my mate declares, raising her hands to the sky. From the shadows of the trees, leaf spirits emerge, and their laughter rings out as they flit toward us. They circle the younglings, showering them with colorful petals.

The sight before me is unlike any other. My mate, standing tall and proud before the warriors, commanding not only their attention but also the spirits of the forest.

"They are my eyes and arms, and the goddesses above are the guardians," she continues.

I lift a paw to my heart, and the warriors mirror my action.

"The last team to bring back the items"—her tone shifts to take on a playful edge—"will be the one to hunt for tonight's feast!"

A ripple of growls echoes through the warriors.

"Let the strongest, smartest, and best team win!"

Muscles coil, fangs bare, and the tension in the air grows. Every warrior is ready to sprint into the forest.

"The teams are," Essin begins, unrolling a scroll. "Team one: Ívar, Orel . . ."

As all eyes turn to Essin, I walk closer to my mate. She tilts her head up, her voice quiet as she says, "If you lose, I expect a giant boar for the feast."

Lowering myself to her height, I let a grin spread across my snout. "I will win, and I will hunt a boar worthy of you." Taking her hand in my paw, I lift it to brush my mouth against her knuckles and whisper against her skin, "You will eat only what I hunt, my sweet dove."

Her wide eyes and flushed face are the last thing I see before Elder Aïna announces, "GO!"

Kaël scratches behind his ear, a familiar gesture that signals he's deep in thought. "Her Majesty isn't holding back. Those riddles? She's full of surprises."

Aeson rubs his chin. "I didn't expect this kind of challenge."

"I figured we'd be running through physical obstacles, not solving riddles," Zephyr adds with a huff. "This changes the game entirely."

"What's the first riddle again?" Kaël asks, his tail flicking.

I unroll the scroll. "In a grove where flowers bloom bright, find the herb that heals with might. Among the petals, it hides its form. A remedy to keep us warm."

We fall silent.

"It has to be in a place known for its flowers," I suggest.

Aeson's eyes light up. "There's a grove nearby full of bright blooms. That's probably it."

Zephyr nods. "Makes sense. The herb's likely hidden among the petals."

"Lead the way, Aeson," I say, the edge of a grin tugging at my mouth. "And be ready to fight if another team is already there."

As we dart into the forest, the leaf spirits flit around us, their laughter trailing behind. My mate is clever—watching us through the spirits' eyes. Every step we take, she'll know.

Good. Let her see.

I will return with every artifact and a fat boar for her. And if there's time, I'll bring her strawberries. After a long day, she'll deserve every indulgence.

"Theron?"

Kaël's voice snaps me out of my thoughts, and I blink. We've stopped. All three of them are staring at me, smirking.

"What's got you so distracted? And don't think I haven't noticed the shaved claws."

I glance down at my paw. "Don't be jealous, Kaël. You'll find your mate someday."

Aeson points toward a narrow path that winds along a stream. "This way. The grove should be just ahead."

We move, weaving through the ancient trees. The canopy

overhead paints the forest floor in moving patches of light. The ground beneath us is damp and slick. We must be careful.

Everything stops.

The birds, the rustling leaves, every sound vanishes, leaving behind complete, unnatural silence. We freeze, exchange glances.

I motion for everyone to stay alert and point to the crystals on my forehead. We'll communicate silently from here.

Breathing in, I try to pick up any scent of danger, but all I catch is the fresh, damp smell of the stream nearby. Something's wrong. I can feel it, even if I can't place it yet.

We move forward, every muscle taut, ready for whatever might be waiting. Then, we hear a sound. Soft giggles, light and carefree. Nýmphí.

I recognize the sound instantly, so I raise a paw to signal for calm and to ease the tension. Leading the way, I guide us closer to the stream. The giggles grow louder, and soon, they come into view: Nýmphí shimmering in the morning light as they laugh and splash the water with their feet. One of them plays with a group of leaf spirits, exchanging petals and stones. The nýmphí pause, then turn their attention toward us. Their eyes glitter like the surface of a sunlit stream. One steps forward from the water.

I know her.

Years ago, during a hunting competition, I was determined to win. I needed to prove myself, to show my strength and worth as a warrior and as a future mate.

I tracked an elk to a stream, and that's when I saw a nýmphá sitting by the water's edge, her hands weaving glowing orbs of energy in the air. She caught my eye and smiled.

"You seem focused, young warrior," she said, her voice like a ripple on water.

"I'm trying to win the hunt," I said. "I want to be the best."

She laughed. "And why does being the best matter so much to you?"

"Because I need to protect my future mate," I answered without hesitation. "I need to be strongest for her, whoever she is."

Her expression softened.

I remember asking her then, "Do nýmphí have mates?"

She smiled again, shaking her head. "No, we don't. Our purpose is different. We serve the goddesses, and one day, we'll serve the Lidéřen who will restore balance."

Nýmphí do not have mates, they do not eat or sleep. They just exist to serve the Lidéřen. Kaël used to sit with them and gossip. He said they knew all the secrets of the forest.

The memory fades as the nýmphá before me speaks, her voice as soft and musical as I remember. "Welcome, brave warriors. To proceed, you must solve our challenge."

Kaël raises an eyebrow. "Ladies?"

The nýmphá remains unfazed. "Answer this: What has roots nobody sees, is taller than any trees. Up, up, up it goes, and yet, it never grows?"

We huddle, whispering our guesses.

"A mountain," Aeson says. "It's a mountain."

The nýmphá nods. "Well done. You may pass."

She gestures toward the grove ahead, where vibrant flowers bloom in abundance. Just as we step forward, the nýmphí gather once more. Their hands rise high, and they murmur something under their breath.

The ground shakes violently.

Stones and debris fly into the air, and instinctively, we leap for the trees to avoid the chaos erupting below. I strain to grab Kaël as he slips, my muscles burn as I haul him to safety.

The nýmphí retreat into the distance, their giggles carried away by the howling wind.

I spot a large, sturdy branch above us and shout. "Aeson, up there!"

He signals to the others, and we scramble higher, fighting against the relentless wind and quaking earth. Trees fall, stones shift unnaturally, and the sharp gusts sting like claws raking across our skin. Every step is a battle, but I push through the pain to drive myself onward. Finally, we reach the branch and collapse onto its surface, panting as we catch our breath.

"What was that?" Kaël gasps, his eyes wide.

Zephyr leans back against the trunk, shaking his head. "That wasn't part of the trial, was it?"

I scan the branches above, and something catches my eye— a nest tucked up high in the leaves. Feathers gleam in the light. *The second riddle.*

"My mate is definitely not playing around," I mutter.

41

BETWEEN LIFE AND DEATH
IN THE LAIR OF BEASTS

"The barrier didn't only keep the vólkins in, Gregor. It kept
something else out."
—Bard, during a vólkin lesson

Gregor

The damp air clings to my skin as I nearly crawl through the forest. Each step is so painful, I don't know how much longer I can bear it. Every part of my body aches. Bruises from the beating cover my arms, legs, and ribs. The cut above my brow stings as sweat reaches it. The taste of blood lingers in my mouth, and the metallic flavor churns my stomach. I think I need to throw up.

Each step brings me closer to the vólkins.

The memory of Arnold haunts me. It runs over and over in my head every time I try to sleep. Every time I close my eyes, I see him.

Bard showed me the direction to Ávera, pointing it out like it was some kind of scenic route, but the reality is far worse. The forest around me is dark and endless. Fog hangs over the moss-covered trees in a ghostly veil. Every shadow feels alive. Every rustle of leaves sends a jolt of fear down my spine. My hands tremble as I clutch the crystal hidden inside my arse. The vólkins might sense it, so the healer told me to keep it hidden until I can stash it somewhere in Ávera. If they find it, they'll kill me without a second's hesitation.

The thought of them finding me makes my heart race. I've learned enough to know what happens to traitors in vólkin territory. Every vólkin has those glowing crystals embedded in their foreheads, the source of their power and connection to their mates. And there are no female vólkins. That's the part that stunned me most during the lessons Bard forced on me. Vólkins live for thousands of years, bonded eternally to their mates. When one dies, the other follows immediately, their souls connected beyond death. It's a commitment I can't even begin to comprehend.

I shudder as I recall Bard's words about killing them. Two ways, he said. "Break their crystals or kill their mate. Either way, it's a death sentence."

The knowledge twists my gut. Bard knows more about vólkins than the entire military, and that terrifies me. His power is vast, too vast. Bard isn't just a captain, as I first thought. He's the tsar's shadow. That explains everything. The way he commands fear with a single glance, the knowledge he wields like a weapon.

I'm terrified to even think how much I *don't* know.

I stumble over a twisted root and only just catch myself before I hit the ground. The crystal moves inside me with every step. How did they even get it? Vólkin crystals lose their power when the vólkin dies, becoming nothing more than dull stones. But this one still shines and even pulses from time to time. Someone made it possible. The thought churns in my stomach like acid.

I can't stop. I can't fail. If I don't make it to Ávera, my Linnéa dies. They'll kill her. A sound rips through the forest, and I freeze in place. It's faint at first, but it grows louder as I pay more attention. A low growl echoes through the trees. The hairs on the back of my neck stand up. My body goes rigid as I turn. The sight of a massive bear, its eyes gleaming with hunger, makes my blood run cold.

My legs lock. My breaths are shallow. This is it. This is how I die.

The bear moves closer. Its massive paws sink into the mossy ground, and its growl deepens until it's vibrating through the air.

Its eyes lock onto me, and I realize with horror that it's drawn to the blood on my clothes. My scent has given me away. The bear takes another step, its breath visible in the cool air. *Mama, help. Please help me.*

I can't think. I can't breathe. The ground seems to tilt beneath me. My vision blurs as the bear gets closer still.

Another louder growl echoes through the trees. The bear whines and darts away. I flinch, raising my arms in an attempt to shield myself as my knees give out, and I collapse onto the ground. The crystal presses painfully against the inside of my gut, and I clench around it, desperate to keep it from slipping out.

I'm scared to breathe, my body is shaking uncontrollably. The bear is gone, but the heavy footsteps of whatever scared it off move closer. Each one makes the earth tremble beneath me. My head jerks toward the sound.

I try to stand, and a warm wetness spreads over my trousers. Shame burns through me as I realize what's happened, but I'm too terrified to care.

A figure steps out of the fog.

A vólkin. Giant, dark gray vólkin, its green crystals glowing on its forehead. Its eyes lock onto mine, and I know this is it.

I'm dead.

"What an ugly human," the vólkin sneers as he crouches down to look at me. His eyes shine in the dim light, and his breath is hot on my face.

A whimper escapes my lips, and to my utter mortification, I feel myself lose control again. My trousers cling to my inner thighs.

He grins, baring his deadly fangs. "Are you scared?"

Another vólkin, a few shades lighter than the first one, with black crystals, steps forward. His shadow looms over me as crows fly in all directions, crying as they dart away. "What's this?" he asks. "Are all human males this ugly?"

The first vólkin snorts a chuckle, then his snout wrinkles. "And he reeks too. Filthy."

I'm dead. I'm fucking dead.

Without warning, he grabs me by the collar of my tunic and yanks me off the ground as if I weigh nothing. My hands instinctively clutch at his wrist, but my fingers barely circle it. I desperately clench around the crystal hidden inside me. *Please don't fall.*

The vólkin brings me closer, sniffing the air around me but careful not to touch me directly. I know how disgusting I must smell, bloodied and covered in piss. My skin crawls with humiliation. How much longer do I need to take this? Bard, his men, and now these vólkins. I can't . . .

"Why do I smell vólkin on you?" His voice drops into a low, deep growl that sends a shiver down my spine.

"I-I . . ." The words get stuck, my brain too panicked to form a sentence.

"Speak." His grip tightens, a warning. "Have you met a vólkin before? Why do you smell like one?"

"I . . . I met one once," I manage to choke out. *Shit, shit, shit. He smells the crystal.*

His eyes widen slightly, his grip loosening just enough for

me to gasp in some air. "You did? And how are you still alive?" There's genuine surprise in his tone.

I force the words out, though my entire body shakes with fear. "Noël . . . Noël let me live."

A sharp intake of breath from the other vólkin. "Her Majesty spared you?"

Her Majesty? That's what they call her? Bard told me she was important, but he didn't give me any details.

Before I can make sense of it, the vólkin's claws dig into my skin as he lifts me high enough that my feet dangle above the ground. Panic seizes me. I struggle to breathe, and my vision blurs.

"You do *not* call Her Majesty by her name." His claws press deeper. The pain shoots through me as his eyes burn with fury. "That honor belongs to her mate only." He pulls me even closer, his fangs dangerously near my face. "You would do well to remember that."

I nod frantically, the pressure on my throat making it impossible to speak. Tears sting my eyes.

I just can't take it anymore.

I hear more footsteps, and another vólkin joins them. "I smelled piss from a sprint away. Who's guilty this time?" He chuckles. "Oh, what's that in your paws? Is this part of the trial?"

I can feel his gaze on my back.

Great, another one. Why are the gods never on my side?

"I don't think so," the first vólkin replies, loosening his grip on me.

"Though this human claims he's met Her Majesty."

The newcomer hums in amusement. "Should we bring him to her and let her decide?"

"What about the trial? I don't feel like hunting for the feast." The second vólkin sighs.

Feast?

The one holding me leans in, a vicious smile creeping across his face. "I think we've got a pretty good excuse to skip out." He looks me over with narrowed eyes. "We can't present you to Her Majesty like this, though." His grip on my throat tightens again, sending a fresh wave of fear through me. "Let's get you cleaned up first. You stink worse than a boar's corpse."

The vólkins lead the way to the nearest stream, their massive bodies moving easily through the forest. In contrast, each of my steps feels like it's echoing through the trees as my weakened body struggles to keep up with them. Every bruised inch of me aches, and my ribs scream with each breath.

I can feel their eyes on me, watching, studying. It's like walking with predators, and I know full well that I'm the prey. They don't need to bind my wrists or tie me up—they know I'm no threat. I can barely walk, let alone try to escape.

"We're almost there," one of them grunts, not even sparing me a glance.

My legs feel like they might give out any moment, but I nod and try to keep my balance. The only thing keeping me moving is the knowledge that if I stop, they won't help me. They'd probably laugh.

42

AMIDST THE TRIALS

"Your daughter was never meant to walk through gardens. She was born for fire, shaped by silence, sharpened by loss. The world will bleed before it bends to her, but bend it will."
—Láda Veléša, to Eyleen Ársa

Noël

"One, two, one, two," I call aloud as the sound of claws striking fills the air.

Walking through rows of female vólkins, I keep an eye on each one of their movements, scanning for any mistakes.

"If the enemy ever reaches you," I say as I stop to adjust Naïa's stance, "you need to be ready and know how to defend yourself."

She straightens under my guidance and nods.

The children wanted to join today, so I've modified the training. For now. The trials began hours ago, and most teams have already found at least one item. The males are making progress, and while they push themselves, we train here.

"Your Majethty, am I doing good?" a small voice calls out. I turn to see Árne, a tiny vólkin with wide eyes.

Kneeling to meet his height, I lift his paw and press on it to extend his tiny claws, then smile and say, "The enemy should be afraid of these,"

Árne beams, his tail wagging. Children always have a way of softening my heart, especially ones as sweet as he is, no matter how hardened I try to appear.

"I used to wield a sword," I say, standing and turning back to the group. "It was like an extension of my arm. But you—" I pause, meeting the eyes of the vólkins standing before me. "You have claws and immense strength. Use them."

"My muscles burn already!" Essin whines, dropping her shoulders dramatically.

I raise an eyebrow at her. "That's because you've never trained. I know the males will do everything in their power to keep us safe, but no one can predict what the future holds."

They may not be warriors like the males, but they have strength—and I'll ensure they know how to use it when the time comes.

"Do all human females know how to fight?" Lyssia asks. She's one of the females I met during my tour of the land a few days ago.

"No," I answer. "In the human world, women aren't allowed to."

The murmurs stop, and all eyes turn to me.

"What if they want to?" Lyssia's question is genuine, but it cuts deep.

I sigh. "In human villages, women are not allowed to grow, to become who they want to be. From the day we are born, we are told to serve men." My teeth grind, and my jaw tightens as the words leave my mouth. The truth tastes bitter, but it must be said.

The females growl as they process my words.

"This is why I want us all to be strong. To know how to take care of ourselves, to save our own lives when the moment demands it. The day we start conquering lands, the real horror begins. And from that point on, no one can predict how long it will take to change the world."

I let my gaze settle on each of them in turn. "I want us to be as prepared as we can be to face every challenge with strength. When we rescue the women from the villages, everyone here must be ready to guide them and teach them how to protect themselves."

The growls deepen among the females before me. Soon we march to war, and they all must be ready to help.

"Cover the children's ears," I command.

The nýmphí rush to obey, shielding every youngling's ears.

I clench my fists so hard that I feel the strain in every muscle, but my voice carries across the clearing, cold and strong. "From the very first woman on this earth, men have been greedy. Every woman has been misunderstood, silenced, stripped of her power." My chin lifts high. "But no more."

The words burn like fire in my throat. "We will *destroy* every soul that stands against us."

Sharp pain shoots through my palms, but I barely register it, consumed by the storm raging within. "And when the whole world dares to rise against us," I declare, my voice a roar, my rage blazing, "we will destroy them *all*."

A searing jolt of pain shoots through my hands, and my breath catches, my heart pounding in my chest. Blood drips from my clenched fists, splattering onto the ground. Slowly, I open my hands, and my eyes widen.

Jagged thorns have sprouted from my palms and pierced through my skin.

The clearing falls silent. Even the wind stops. "This blood in my hands," I say as I turn back to them, "is the blood of a family slaughtered by greed and cruelty. I have no brothers. No sisters. My mother is dead, and so is my father."

Raising my fists, I stare at the streaks dripping from my palms. "They are not the first, and they will not be the last, to die in this cruel, merciless world."

I will scorch the earth if needed. I will shield these souls with my own body.

"I am the last blue rose in a garden choked by weeds. A garden overrun with parasites—creatures who only know how to take, to consume, and yet are never satisfied. They poison the soil, spread their rot, and expect us to bow to their will."

My hands shake. More thorns tear my skin. "For too long, they have underestimated us. They believe we are weak, that we exist to serve them, that we are nothing without their approval. But they are wrong. *They have always been wrong.*"

The ground beneath my boots trembles. My blood drips, staining the earth red as I raise my voice. "This is where it ends. Their reign. Their greed. Their endless hunger for power."

Every father and every son. Every single one of them.

"We will destroy every soul that stands in our way! Every sword lifted against us will be broken. Every lie they spread will be silenced. And when their armies come, and their leaders sneer, we will destroy them *all.*"

The thorns grow bigger and more savage. "This is the blood of rebellion. This is the legacy of those who came before me. My mother. My father. Every woman who dared to dream of a better world."

"Enough!"

A sharp voice snaps me out of my rage. The thorns retreat instantly, each falling to the blood-soaked ground with a lifeless thud. Turning slowly, I see Elder Aïna standing tall with her piercing gaze fixed on me.

Not the crowd. Not the nýmphí. Me.

I swallow hard and, stomach twisting, turn back toward the

others. The scene before me feels like a punch to the gut. The children are trembling, their tails tucked between their legs, while the females stand frozen and wide-eyed with fear. Fear of *me*.

What have I done?

I glance down at myself. Thick, thorny vines have sprouted from the ground, encasing my boots and legs, crawling up my body like chains. My arms are stained with blood. I'm so soaked in it the metallic scent hangs in the air.

"You could hurt yourself and the others, Ethereal Leader," Elder Aïna says as she steps closer and lifts her paw. With that simple gesture, the vines loosen their grip and sink back into the earth. My body feels lighter, but the shame weighs heavily on me.

"I-I'm sorry," I mutter. *These dark thoughts . . .*

Elder Aïna's expression softens. "Power without control is chaos. You must find balance, Ethereal Leader. For their sake, and your own."

Her gaze flicks to the cowering children, and my heart aches. I've scared them.

"The training is over," she declares.

The nýmphi release the children and offer them small, colorful stones to ease their fear. The children clutch the tokens tightly, their trembling gradually easing.

I stare down at my bloody hands. My voice comes out in a whisper, barely heard even to myself. "What is wrong with me?"

"Nothing is wrong," Elder Aïna says. "You are slowly awakening, and you let your emotions take hold. It isn't a bad thing. But you must learn to control it."

"I feel like I'm doing nothing!" My head jerks up to meet her gaze, and I see no anger there, only understanding. "I need to act, to *rush forward*! Every second I wait, I feel like I'm failing them."

"You have done plenty," she replies.

"Not enough," I insist, shaking my head. "Not at all. Women are still suffering. I am here, fed and safe, while others live only to survive. How can that ever be enough?"

"You see each achievement as another task completed, but you never stop to notice the victories that come with them."

"Victories?" I echo. "What victories? I am *here* while they are still in chains. How can I call anything I've done a victory?"

"You've lost your mother, yet you found your father. You've uncovered truths that others could not even dream of knowing, and you've begun to piece together a plan to fix what was broken. You teach wisdom to the females. You give strength to the children. You care for *us*, Your Majesty. You care for us all."

The truth in her words stings. My jaw tightens as I fight against the urge to argue, to insist it isn't enough, that it never will be.

"You think your victories are small because the world isn't yet whole," Elder Aïna continues. "But every step you take, every lesson you give, it matters. It's the start of the balance we've been waiting for."

I swallow hard. The blood on my hands has gone cold and begun to dry.

"We all want to go out and bring this world peace," Naïa says.

Of course they want it as much as I do. They've lived in this confined world, dreaming of freedom, just as I have. But . . . I've *seen* what it's like out there.

I've heard the tales of other villages—of their struggles, their poverty, their lives spent clawing for scraps. At least Tárnov didn't lack as much as the others, even if the only truly wealthy village is Velháven, the capital of Vathéria.

The tsar's stronghold sits there, ruling over everything. It's a fortress of wealth and indulgence, surrounded by nobles and businessmen who thrive while others rot.

The tsar has a daughter, Tsarevna Elara. The portrait of her and her father is seen in every office. My general kept it in his office as well, a symbol of power and loyalty. Every meeting I attended, her painted gaze stared back at me. Beautiful blonde hair, full cheeks, and round shape. The definition of beauty.

If he has a daughter he loves so much, then why does he allow other women to suffer?

The answer is obvious: Because he doesn't care. He enjoys his power. He revels in his control. But I will take it from him.

He may enjoy these final years of his life, but they won't last. I will come for him. And I will *destroy* him. With the other five or not, he will be defeated.

"As pups, we would run around these trees, not knowing what was happening outside." Naïa's voice pulls me from my dark thoughts.

I realize I've been staring at her, but I haven't spoken. Her words hang between us, and she hesitates, studying my expression. How will I ever awaken if I cannot silence this storm inside me?

Our conversation is interrupted by a harsh rustling from the tree line. A nýmphá rushes in my direction. "Your Majesty," she begins. "A group is approaching. Our warriors but . . . there is a human with them."

My heart starts pounding faster. A human?

Another nýmphá steps forward, her voice almost a whisper. "It is the one you spared, Your Majesty."

The one I— "Gregor?" *What is going on?*

Why would Gregor be here? After almost two weeks, why would he come back?

Naïa tilts her head. "Who is Gregor?"

Essin wrinkles her snout. "What kind of name is that?"

"Tell the warriors bringing him that I'm waiting. And inform Theron. I need him here."

The nýmphí bow low before rushing back into the forest

where their glowing bodies disappear into the trees. My pulse quickens, but I have to remain calm. We're in the middle of the first trial, and already things aren't going as planned.

I turn to Elder Aïna, my voice steady despite the tension building in my chest, and say, "Whatever this is, I need to be prepared."

She gives me a knowing nod. "And you will be."

43

THE TSAR'S COURT OF FEAR

"You think this ceremony binds me to you? It binds only your fate to rot beside mine. You will sit on your golden throne, Varyán, and you will drown in the empire you built with my chains."

—Eyleen Ársa, on her wedding day

Tsar Varyán II

The scent of blue roses fills the grand hall. Golden tapestries bearing my crest—the blue rose, a symbol of power—line the walls. My dark oak and gold throne gleams beneath the light streaming through the high stained-glass windows.

When commoners come to speak to their tsar, they see me as *god*. Sitting on the shining throne.

Servants flit along the edges of the hall like shadows, silent as they execute the rituals of the day. Trays of ripe fruit and goblets of dark wine are brought to me on silver platters. The servants must climb seven steps before they reach my seat. I take a sip, letting the bold flavor cling to my tongue as I watch my knights patrol outside the towering windows.

Each man's hand rests on his sword, and their every step echoes through the stone courtyard. To the untrained eye, it might appear to be a dance.

"Magnificent, aren't they?" Commander Stefan interrupts my thoughts. His armor gleams in the sunlight as he bows.

"They are disciplined," I say, brushing my beard. "As they should be. Discipline without fear, however, is meaningless. Ensure they understand the consequences of failure, Stefan. Remind them, if necessary."

Stefan straightens. "Yes, Your Imperial Majesty. They know you see everything, even when you are not present."

"Good. Fear is what keeps them loyal. Gold fades, whores get old, but fear . . . fear stays."

As Stefan bows once more, my attention shifts to the sound of footsteps echoing in the hall. Commander Larn approaches, flanked by two knights dragging a trembling man between them.

Larn bows deeply. "Your Imperial Majesty, we bring Sir Barric. He disobeyed your orders regarding Noël during the guild's mission. He allowed Arnold to take her."

Barric stumbles forward. His knees hit the marble floor with a thud, and his voice cracks as he says, "Your Imperial Majesty, please! I was threatened—Arnold gave me no choice! I swear my loyalty to you, always!"

I raise a single finger, and his pleas cease. The hall falls silent, servants nearby quicken their pace, eyes cast downward as they pretend not to hear the pathetic display of a betrayer.

I stand slowly before descending the steps of the throne. "You swore your loyalty the day you took up that armor. That oath meant nothing to you, it seems."

"Your Imperial Majesty, I beg you! I never meant for this to happen! Mercy—please—mercy!" Barric grovels, his trembling hands clasped in front of him.

"Mercy?" I'm close enough that my shadow swallows him. "Mercy is for the strong, for the loyal. Tell me, Barric, what strength have you shown? What loyalty?"

His sobs grow louder.

"Take him to the dungeons. I will deal with him myself."

Larn bows again. "Shall I prepare for his execution?"

"Not yet." I glance at Barric, who is being dragged away. "Keep him alive. His suffering is far from over."

As the heavy doors to the dungeons close with a loud echo, I turn and make my way toward my private study. The corridors, lined with relics of my family's unbroken legacy, reverberate with my footsteps. My robe drags behind me as servants bow low with their faces turned away.

The fire in my study smolders, and its faint warmth does little to dispel the chill of the stone walls. Shadows dance across the shelves of ancient tomes and scrolls, over a map of Vathéria spread across the wall.

But no map, no power, eases the void inside me. Only one presence ever did.

If only she were still alive.

I move to the far corner of the study and push the map aside. Brushing against the cold stone, I descend the narrow spiral staircase. It is always cold and dark in my private part of the dungeons, and now, the scent of decay threatens to overtake the space.

At the base of the stairs, two stoic guards bow at the waist. I step inside, and the heavy door groans as it closes behind me.

The chamber is freezing, so cold it seeps into my bones. But it is what must be done to keep her whole. There, lying on the stone table, is Eyleen.

My beloved.

Her body, preserved in frost and time, is as beautiful as the day she defied me. Her skin, tinged blue, gleams under the torchlight like a sacred relic. I step closer, my breath visible in the chilled air, my heart both heavy and aflame.

I run my fingers along her frozen cheek, marveling at the icy smoothness of her skin. How beautiful can one be? A true blue rose before my eyes.

The touch sends a thrill through me, the same sense of possession I've felt since I first brought her here. My hand tightens in her hair, the strands stiff with frost, and I yank her head back, leaning down until my lips hover near her ear.

"Your daughter thinks she can escape me, as you have. She will learn, as you did, that there is no escape from my reach. She will walk the path *I* choose for her."

The rage boiling inside me softens as I look upon her lifeless eyes. The satisfaction of having Eyleen here soothes the storm that has consumed me for years. She was always the one thing I could never truly control—until now.

I release her hair, and my fingers move down to trace the curve of her jaw. My breathing deepens, the tension in my body growing taut. The sight of her, frozen, belonging to no one but me, fills me with a sense of victory.

The frigid air bites at my skin, but it only heightens the fire within me as my hands drop to my trousers. "You are mine," I murmur. "Always mine."

A knock at the door slices through the silence.

Oh, for god's rose.

"Come in," I call. Only one man would dare disturb me now.

The door opens, and Bard walks quietly across the chamber. His hood conceals his face, but I know him. My shadow, my ever-loyal instrument of order. As he approaches, he bows deeply. "Your Imperial Majesty," he begins. "I bring news."

I wave a hand for him to continue, undoing my trousers

with the other. My attention is split, half on Bard, half on my beloved.

I hope you will forgive me. I shall spoil you after so many years.

"Gregor has been positioned in the forest surrounding Ávera, as you instructed," Bard says. "He is ready."

I smirk as I take my cock into my hand. Gregor. A worm of a man, but useful. His desperation, his love for his sister, binds him like iron chains. He will serve, whether he wishes to or not.

"And Noël?" I ask, my breath quickening as my grip tightens.

"No sign of her yet, Your Imperial Majesty," Bard replies, his head bowed. "But our scouts believe she's hiding within the vólkins' land, in Ávera."

My hand is stilled momentarily by the anger pooling in my chest. Noël. That insolent brat, the daughter of the woman who dared defy me. My Eyleen. My perfect Eyleen, stolen from me by her foolish rebellion. My grip tightens again, rage and desire merging as one.

"Your daughter is fucking a wolf," I spit. "Just as you did." My hand moves faster now, the friction stokes the fire in my veins. "Were you not satisfied with me, Eyleen?!" My voice echoes off the stone walls. "No," I snarl, leaning closer to her frozen body. "You wanted more. But look where you are now. Still mine."

I force her cold, lifeless hand to wrap around my length. The chill of her skin on me is thrilling. I stroke myself with her hand, using her as she should have been used when she still lived. My breath hitches.

"Your Imperial Majesty." Bard's voice cuts through my frenzy. "The knyzya await your presence in the council chamber."

I laugh. "Let them wait."

My hand moves faster and harder. "Weak men," I mutter through clenched teeth. "Parasites. Feeding on my scraps. But I will remind them who the tsar is. Who the god of this land truly is."

My release comes with a growl, spilling onto the stone floor at Bard's feet. I shudder, though the satisfaction is fleeting, replaced by the endless void inside me. I release her hand to drop limply against the table.

"Oy!" I bark.

The guards stationed outside burst into the chamber.

"Clean this," I order, gesturing to the mess. "My wife prefers her chambers pristine."

The guards bow and move to obey. Bard waits for my command.

"Tell the knyzya I will join them shortly," I say as I refasten my trousers and straighten my robes.

"Yes, Your Imperial Majesty," Bard says with one more bow, then disappears into the shadows.

I turn back to Eyleen, brushing a hand over her cold cheek. My voice drops to a whisper. "And you, my love . . . You will see me tonight."

The heavy double doors groan as they open on the council chamber bathed in golden light from the small glass windows. The knyzya stand as I enter and bow as I approach. The scent of polished wood fills my nose, alongside the smoke of burning incense to mask the dampness of the ancient stone walls. As I make my way to the head of the table, the sound of my boots striking the floor reverberates in the wide room.

Caelan, his face framed by a trimmed beard, inclines his head as I pass. "Your Imperial Majesty, you've summoned us with haste. I assume the matter is urgent."

Letting my eyes sweep the room, I take my seat. "Sit."

The knyzya obey as they exchange glances with one another, then gazes lock on mine. These men understand my authority, though some are better at hiding their discontent than others. Like my two brothers, sitting across from each other.

"The vólkins are free," I begin. "The barrier has fallen, and their leader, Noël Ársa, gathers strength."

Gávril leans forward, his jaw tight. "A leader? A woman? And what do we know of her?"

"She is dangerous," I say. "And resourceful. A daughter of Eyleen Ársa."

A murmur spreads through the room, gasps barely stifled. Elias, the soft-spoken knyaz of Róstan, frowns. "Eyleen Ársa? The blue rose who—"

"My wife," I interject. "And her daughter seems intent on continuing the rebellion. She has allied with the vólkins, and they are more organized than ever before. She has their loyalty and power. A human sergeant, backed by an army of wolves."

When my men questioned Gregor, he revealed the truth. A vólkin stands by Noël's side. Her mate. They are unbonded—for now—but that is only a matter of time. Once their bond is complete, she will not settle for a quiet life in Ávera. That is not who Noël is. Noël Ársa is a force of rage and power, a woman made in defiance and driven by fury, just like her mother. She is not meant to live in obscurity. She is meant to fight. To lead. To silence the weak and to serve under my command, as she should have from the start.

Hākān clears his throat. "If what you say is true, Your Imperial Majesty, this poses a grave threat. What is our course of action?"

I lean forward, steepling my fingers. "The vólkins cannot be allowed to thrive. They are a crack in the foundation of our rule. If left unchecked, they will inspire rebellion across Vathéria."

The previous generation of vólkins was completely uninterested in the world beyond their eyes. Content with their mates, they turned their backs on the chaos happening outside their lands. But Noël is no ordinary woman. She is a blue rose, the Lidéřen. She will not rest in complacency, she will lead them into chaos, a storm waiting to be unleashed. I feel it in the marrow of my bones, an inevitability that cannot be ignored.

Across the table, Caelan smirks. The glint in his eye gets on my nerves. "And what would you have us do? March our armies into the forest? Hunt wolves like common peasants?"

I fix him with a glare. "Careful, brother. Your tongue dances close to treason."

Caelan Velstrād, my younger brother, the second born who was never destined for the crown. I allow him to govern Velháven to ensure my hold over the capital remains absolute. My ancestors secured Vathéria for the Velstrād family, and I will not fail in maintaining that legacy. All of it belongs to us— from Velháven's grandeur to the smallest, most insignificant village. All except Ávera. Ávera remains the one stain beyond my reach. For now.

Caelan's smirk disappears. "I merely mean to say, Your Imperial Majesty, that brute force alone will not suffice. Centuries ago, one of them killed a hundred armed men. A whole army of them leaves us with little hope."

Gāvril crosses his arms. "Then we extinguish the fire before it spreads. We crush them completely, leave nothing to rebuild."

Gāvril Velstrād, the third born, always excelled in combat and strategy. Entrusting him with Tárnov, the second-largest village in Vathéria and its most formidable military base, was a calculated decision on my part. Unlike our father, I recognize Gāvril's worth. While our father dismissed him, let him be overshadowed by me and Caelan, I see beyond tradition. Gāvril had to fight the hardest to prove himself, and that makes him invaluable. Where others see rank and birthright, I see potential and power. And he has that power.

Elias shifts uncomfortably in his seat. "A coordinated strike risks too much, especially if they've already fortified their numbers. We cannot afford to stretch our forces thin."

Elias Vorst, Knyaz of Róstan. It's no surprise that Gregor and his family hail from there—a land where poverty and hardship are a way of life. His parents succumbed to hunger and overwork, leaving Gregor and his sister, Linnéa, as orphans. *Gregor, what a selfish creature you are. You abandoned Linnéa to a lonely, wretched existence, tossing her a few silver coins each month as if that could make up for leaving her behind.* A pitiful man clinging to survival, blind to anything beyond himself.

I turn to Caspian, who has remained silent, his gaze distant and unfocused. "And you, Knyaz Tarn? What does Vódany advise?"

Caspian's voice is as deep and haunting as the waters he rules. "The vólkins are creatures of the land, tied to the spirits. They will not fall easily. The waters speak of a reckoning, Your Imperial Majesty. The goddesses are restless."

A hush falls over the room. Superstition always leaves discomfort among pragmatists like Gāvril and Caelan. I dismiss it with a wave of my hand. "Spare me your omens, Caspian. I need solutions, not riddles."

Hākān, my dear friend and Knyaz of Gráyárk, leans forward. "What of alliances? If this threat is as dire as you say, Your Imperial Majesty, perhaps it is time to reach out to others."

A heavy silence descends.

Orcs.

Before my ancestors created the barrier, they sought a power capable of ending vólkin lives. Using slaves and dark magic, they fashioned abominations—half man, half beast. At first, these creatures were failures: sickly and mindless, dying off one by one. But the tsar at the time, Aldrik I, refused to abandon his vision. He poured thousands of lives into his experiments, sacrificing slaves to perfect the formula. By balancing elements drawn from nature, he produced monsters that grew larger, stronger, closer to his ideal.

But it wasn't enough. Aldrik craved more. He wanted them to think, to reason, to speak and serve.

What a fool he was.

He introduced the essence of the blue rose into the mix, believing it would grant them intelligence. And it did. At a cost. The orcs were born, towering, intelligent beasts as large as the average vólkin. At seven to eight feet tall, with frames as wide as the walls of Velháven, they were formidable and terrifying. And they were as green as nature. But Aldrik underestimated his creation. The orcs, smarter than the average man of Róstan, refused servitude. They brought chaos, unleashed destruction on Velháven and the southern villages, laid waste to Yáarím and Róstan.

In time, they fled to the nearby continent now known as Thrā'kkor, named after their leader—the one who ended Aldrik's life with his own monstrous hands.

What a true fool he was.

Caelan is the first to break it. "You mean the orcs, don't you? Those savages?"

"Savages," I echo. "Savages who have the numbers and strength to obliterate the vólkins. They fight for blood and plunder, and we can provide both."

Edrin Haymoor, usually detached from political discussions, finally speaks up. "Offering them anything will bring chaos to the villages. The Orcs do not know restraint."

"That is why we will control them," I reply, my gaze sweeping the table. "We will make them an offer they cannot resist: goods, land, and women. In return, they will annihilate the vólkins."

The orcs are not creatures of nature. They have no females, no means to reproduce on their own. They will accept the offer, of that, I have no doubt. But I am not Aldrik. I am Varyán, Tsar Varyán II. With the promise of bodies to fulfill their desires, they will obey. No rational being would decline such a favor.

Caspian's frown deepens, and his fingers drum against the table. "The waters will not favor this decision."

"They are orcs, not vólkins," Gāvril snaps. "They don't pray to goddesses. They bleed and die like any other."

I allow a slow smirk to spread across my face. "Then it's settled. We will send a messenger to the orcs. They will have as many women as they want and more—slaves, land, and goods. We will offer them things they never dreamed possible."

The knyzya exchange glances, but none dare voice their objections outright. I rise from my seat, towering over them all. "The vólkins and their leader will fall. And when they do, Vathéria will stand unchallenged."

As I walk toward the double doors, I turn over my shoulder for one last glance at the knyzya.

"Let the Tafl begin."

44

THE VOLKINS, THE NÝMPHÁ, AND THE LIES OF A PUPPET

"This pup will either save the world or scorch it to ash. And if he chooses wrong, no goddess, not even your love, will bring him back. Pray he never loses what tethers him."
—Elder Aïna, to Vládan and Ánya when Theron was born

Theron

"Here!" Kaël leaps into the air, and his tail wags as his paw splashes into the water to grasp a glowing stone.

This is too easy. The nýmphí, who seemed ready to kill us mere hours ago, suddenly feel like less of a threat. So far, we've encountered seven teams, each boasting at least one item. It's as if the trial's true challenge has yet to reveal itself.

"That stone is ours," a low voice growls from the shadows. Across the pond, a dark-furred vólkin, Orïon, emerges from the trees with his team. His eyes are fixed on Kaël's find.

Kaël shakes off, the water from his soaked fur spraying in all directions as he climbs onto dry land. His paw remains tightly wrapped around the glowing stone, and his tail wags side to side. "The stone belongs to whoever holds it."

Orïon steps forward, and I do the same. We meet at the edge of the water. Does he truly believe we'll hand over the stone without a fight? Foolish. He bares his fangs, and his muscles ripple as he postures for dominance—a display that might cow a weaker creature, but not me. I wasn't chosen to lead the vólkins by chance. I earned my place through strength, strategy, and sheer will. I am the best, and that will not change.

"Move, Orïon," I growl, flexing my claws.

The trial means nothing to him. Revenge is all he cares about.

He drags a paw through the dirt as his eyes lock on mine. Then, with a burst of speed, he charges, closing the distance between us. I meet him head-on where we collide with a deafening crash, the force of which splashes water into the air. The pond ripples violently around us as we grapple, muscles straining, claws tearing.

Zephyr moves to approach us, but I fix him with a warning growl that freezes him in place. This is between me and Orïon. This is the moment to remind him—and every vólkin watching —who their leader is.

"Shall we sort this out?" Orïon's grin is wide. The glow of his burgundy crystals reflects his bloodlust.

"Very well."

My claws swipe upward, tearing into his face. The force of the blow sends him flying out of the pond. His body crashes into the earth with a thud that echoes through the forest. Water splashes around me as I stride forward, my focus locked on him. This isn't over until he knows his place.

The scent of his blood fills my snout. It mingles with the dampness of forest air. Orïon is already on his paws, snarling through the blood pouring from the gashes across his face. Rage burns in his eyes as he charges.

He slams into me, and his weight crushes me into the ground. The cold mud clings to my fur. His claws dig into my shoulders as he roars so loudly he shakes the trees near us. With a savage snarl, he grips the back of my head and slams it into the jagged stone beneath me. Pain explodes through my skull, the edges of my vision darken.

Not like this.

I twist, throw my weight to the side, and roll him over. His claws scrape against my skin, but I'm stronger and faster. My paw clamps over his snout, and I press down hard enough to feel the bones strain beneath the pressure. His blood stains my fur. Its acrid scent replaces the sweetness of my mate's that usually lingers there. The thought enrages me even more.

With my free paw, I strike. Aiming for his eye, my claws carve into his face. The soft pop of flesh and the wet sound of tearing are what I hear. Orïon's howl of pain tears through the forest as his left eye spills from its socket and is left hanging by a thread of sinew.

"Yield!" I bark, my chest heaving, my voice raw with rage. I tighten my grip on his snout and force his head back.

But he doesn't yield.

Orïon twists violently until he breaks free with a loud growl. Blood streams through his claws, where they clutch at his ruined eye, and soaks into the grass below.

I rise, tower over him as he stumbles to his paws, and then lunge, driving my shoulder into his chest and slamming him into the nearest tree. The bark splinters under his weight, shards of wood flying as his body crashes against it.

Before he can recover his balance, I lift him off the ground by his throat. His legs kick wildly, his claws scrape at my arm, and I press him harder into the broken bark. The scent of his blood saturates the air.

"This ends now." My claws tighten around his mane, his gasps grow weaker. The forest is silent save for the ragged sound of his breath, until I tighten my grip even more and breathing becomes impossible.

He finally stops struggling, and his body goes limp in my grasp. When I drop him to the ground, he collapses in a heap. He lies still, his chest rising and falling weakly. Then, slowly, with his head bowed low, he raises his paw in submission.

I snarl, stepping back and turning away. Let the others see this. Let them remember. I am their leader, and no one will challenge me without consequence.

No one moves. All eyes remain fixed on Orïon. Aeson and Zephyr release his team members, their earlier intent to separate us now abandoned. There's no need. They've seen enough.

"He lost his eye for his stupidity. Let this be a lesson to all." Without sparing Orïon another glance, I stride into the pond. The water is cool against my fur as I scrub his blood from my claws and arms.

Kaël moves to Orïon, reaching out to help him stand.

"Do not touch me!" Orïon's voice is raw with rage and humiliation. He stumbles to his paws, weak and beaten, his remaining eye open wide.

I understand his anger. If I ever lost a fight, if someone ever forced me to yield, I wouldn't be able to face my mate.

"Leave him be, Kaël," I say, stepping out of the water. The droplets scatter into the air as I shake them off.

If I don't stop this sort of foolish behavior, others might get the wrong ideas. My ears twitch at the quiet rustling to my right, and I turn my snout toward the sound.

"Mighty leader." A nýmphá steps gracefully from behind a tree, her glowing form illuminating the forest like a shard of moonlight. Her bare feet leave no trace on the mossy ground. "Her Majesty summons you," she says. "A man named Gregor is approaching."

Gregor. Isn't that the one my mate let be?

"How far?" I demand, closing the distance between us in a single stride. My shadow swallows her slender figure.

"Not far," she answers, her face calm as she tilts her head to meet my eyes. "He is with other vólkins, being brought to her."

My claws flex, itching to tear through him, to end the threat he represents once and for all. Loose ends are not good, and Gregor is a thread I've wanted severed since the moment I learned of him.

But Noël. If she knows he's coming . . . I can't act yet. Not until I understand why. I turn back to my team. "Continue without me. Finish this trial. I will deal with Gregor."

They lift their paws to their hearts, and I waste no time. As my legs carry me through the forest, the trees blur around me, and the cool air slices against my fur.

How has Gregor found himself here again?

He is a weak, fragile male, a pitiful creature who aided in the attempt to destroy my mate. He isn't worthy of her attention, let alone her mercy. Why did she hesitate? This human betrayed her, endangered her. Why let him draw another breath? Why take the risk?

As I approach the edge of the clearing, my eyes sweep over the familiar forms of my warriors. Their massive bodies stand tall. Their glowing crystals cast faint light across the darkened forest. The moment they see me, they snap to attention, paws lifted to their hearts in salute. Their discipline steadies my rage, if only slightly.

I scent piss and blood, and then I see him. Gregor.

He stumbles behind them, his body so broken and frail he can barely manage to stay standing. He looks even weaker than before, a husk. He should have died with the other male. I should have crushed him under my claws.

Striding into the clearing, I nod once to the vólkins, but my focus is locked entirely on Gregor. The tension in the air thickens as my shadow falls over him, and I speak with a calm, low voice. "How did you end up here again?"

Gregor's lips tremble, his words stumbling over each other like broken shards of bark. The vólkins exchange glances. They didn't know Gregor and I have met before.

Gregor collapses to his knees. "I was caught. Tortured," he stammers, his voice weak and whiny. "I-I managed to escape. I didn't know where to go. I was just wandering through the forest, and then . . . then they found me."

His words are pathetic, hardly coherent. He looks like a male who has been through the worst. But something about this doesn't sit right. The timing. The location. This feels too convenient. "Did they harm you?" I ask, turning my gaze to the vólkins. My tone is calm, but my claws flex.

Ívar, the leader of the team, steps forward with a low growl. "We wanted to . . . but didn't. This human said he knows Her Majesty."

I flick my eyes back to Gregor, who remains kneeling in the dirt.

"How is it," I say slowly, "that you happened to end up here?"

Gregor's eyes widen, the fear spreading across his face. He's shaking uncontrollably, his mouth opening and closing as he searches for words. But none come.

He's hiding something.

I remain silent, and my warriors watch quietly as well.

Let's see what your next move is, Gregor. It might be your last.

"I-I didn't mean to end up here . . . I was just trying to survive."

I step close enough to tower over his miserable body.

His eyes dart between me and the vólkins, desperately searching for a lifeline. He'll find none.

"And yet, you did end up here, didn't you?" My voice is low.

"Convenient, don't you think? Wandering through the forest until what?"

"I didn't have anywhere else to go," Gregor whispers, his voice cracking. "No one to trust."

"You should have died, Gregor," I snarl. "You should have died with the other human. Arnold."

Gregor's lips quiver, but he stays silent. It's like he knows that no matter what he says, I won't believe him. But why does Noël believe him? What does she see in him?

I glance at the warriors standing around us. They know as well as I do that this human should be dead. And yet, here he kneels, alive, trembling like prey at my paws. Ívar catches my eye, a flicker of agreement passing between us.

"Why are you here, Gregor?" I lean down until my eyes are level with his. My breath is hot, my claws flexing at my sides. "What are you hiding?"

"I'm not hiding anything!" Gregor blurts out, his voice frantic, desperate. "I don't know why I'm still alive, I swear. Noë— Her Majesty spared me . . . and I-I—"

"Get him up," I growl. I need to get control over myself, need to calm the storm raging inside me. "We'll take him to my mate."

Ívar nods, and two vólkins grab Gregor roughly by the arms to pull him to his feet. I turn away from the scene and toward the path that leads back to Ávera.

45

UNDER THE VEIL OF JUDGMENT

"There will come a day, my rose, when you must choose with hands that tremble and a heart that roars. Choose anyway, for even mercy carves wounds. Every judgment leaves seeds behind."
—Eyleen Ársa to Noël, on her sixteenth birthday

Noël

M y heart pounds louder in my chest as I sit at the table. My breathing feels shallow and uneven. It's nearly impossible to focus on the teams' progress. The whispers of the nýmphí, the chatter of Elder Aïna, Naïa, and Essin—they all blur in the background of my mind.

Gregor is on his way.

The nýmphí that usually walk about with carefree grace move more cautiously now. I noticed that my own feelings reflect on them. Like they're mirroring me. Mina took the younglings for a nap, sensing the tension in the air. *My* tension. I press my palms flat against the table and try to quiet the noises in my mind.

Why am I so on edge? Gregor isn't a threat. At least he shouldn't be.

Then what is it? Is it the knowledge that Theron will be furious? That his rage will ripple through the vólkins the moment Gregor steps foot in this place?

Maybe it's something simpler. Maybe it's because I don't even know how I feel about him myself.

I don't hate Gregor, but I don't like him either. He's done nothing truly wrong, and I'm not a monster. I don't kill without reason. The way he looked at me when Arnold . . .

I didn't let Theron kill him before. That much is true. But why? Was it because I cared for Gregor in some small, unspoken way? Or was it because after Arnold's death, I couldn't bear to hear another man's dying gasp echo in my ears?

Did I make the right decision?

I've turned the question over in my mind a thousand times in the past few hours. And still, I don't have an answer.

A nýmphá with beautiful golden hair rushes to my side. "They're here. The warriors have returned with the human, Gregor."

I rise from the table and glance at Elder Aïna. She meets my eyes with a nod. Together, we head toward the edge of Ávera, the place where I first arrived weeks ago. The others follow us both.

As we walk, their gazes burn into my back, watching, waiting for my next move. The breeze stirs the leaves around us, and from the tree line, the vólkins appear.

My heart pounds when I see Theron, leading the group of at least a dozen warriors. I haven't seen him all morning, and for some strange reason, I feel my body needing to be closer. Theron is a handsome wolf. So big and strong, with unnatural muscles. But then I see *Gregor*.

He hangs over one of the vólkin's massive shoulders, his

body slack like a rag doll. He looks worse than when I last saw him. His ribs are visible beneath his torn tunic, blood crusted around his mouth and eyes, his skin pale and splotched with bruises. He looks like a man who's been to the edge of death and clawed his way back. My stomach churns at the sight. What happened to him?

Seeing him like this, so small and fragile among the giant vólkins, makes me . . . need to protect him. He's human. He's *my* kind.

Theron's eyes soften as his gaze meets mine. There's something magnetic about him, a pull that I can't seem to resist. Half a day apart feels like too long.

Will this connection ever weaken?

When Mother would leave for days, I'd throw myself into preparing for her return—cleaning the house, tending to her roses, cooking her a warm meal. That ache of missing her, the joy of her return, it felt overwhelming back then. But this . . . of course this is different.

Am I falling for him?

The question is so out of place. Right now, it's the last thing I should be thinking about.

When Theron's gaze shifts to Gregor, all tenderness vanishes. His face hardens with distrust. It's in the way his jaw tightens, in the way his broad shoulders stiffen. He despises Gregor, sees him as someone who shouldn't be here. Not in Ávera. Not near me. His face says it all.

Theron made it clear before that sparing Gregor was a mistake. And yet, Gregor is here, barely clinging to life, surrounded by beings we were told to hate.

I understand that fear. I remember it from the first time I saw Theron, and then Ávera. The feeling of being so small, so out of place, fragile among powerful wolves. Walking into Ávera for the first time, surrounded by deadly beasts.

It overwhelmed me then, and I see that same fear in Gregor

now. His eyes, wide with terror, flick back and forth between the vólkins as if he's trying to determine which one might kill him.

Ívar, the warrior who holds him, unceremoniously drops Gregor to the ground at my feet. The sound of his body hitting the dirt makes me jolt, and a flash of anger burns within me at the roughness of it all. He's already suffered enough.

Beside me, Theron crosses his arms. He doesn't trust Gregor. Not one bit.

Gregor groans in pain when he hits the earth but doesn't stay down long. Shivering, he crawls toward my feet, his bloody hands leave streaks in the dirt as he drags himself forward. The sight of it makes my heart clench.

"P-please . . ." His voice is so weak. "Please, you have to listen to me."

Oh, poor thing.

I crouch and offer him a gentle smile. "It's alright, Gregor. You're safe here."

But as I speak, the tension rises around me. Some vólkins grunt, their eyes dark and judgmental. Theron's irritation radiates off him, his gaze never leaving Gregor.

I take a slow breath and focus back on Gregor. "What happened to you?" My voice is calm, but I can't ignore the knot forming in my stomach. I need to understand.

Gregor hesitates, his eyes on mine as his pupils dilate. His lips quiver as he speaks. "I-I was captured."

I frown. "Captured? By whom?"

His eyes lower to the ground, and I can see him trembling. "They tortured me."

What?

I was expecting something harsh, considering his state . . . but not this.

"Tortured?" I repeat. I instinctively reach out to touch his shoulder. "Gregor, who did this to you?"

He shakes his head. "I don't know . . . I don't know who they were. I only heard them call themselves the Shadow Guild."

I frown again. The Shadow Guild? I've never heard of them. "Who are they?"

"I don't know." His voice is frantic. "They—they didn't show their faces. Just shadows . . . moving in the darkness, asking questions I couldn't answer."

I glance at Elder Aïna, but even she looks troubled by his news. The vólkins stir behind me, muttering among themselves, clearly as unsettled as I am.

"Why would they capture you?" I ask. "What did they want from you?"

Gregor's face pales even further. "They—they kept asking about you. About Ávera."

This isn't good. Someone knows of me. Ávera is a known legend, vólkins a popular topic to discuss and condemn. But the fact that someone knows of me *specifically* raises alarms. I can't help but glance at Theron, who's watching Gregor with a look of barely contained fury.

"They wanted to know how to find you," Gregor continues, struggling to hold it together. "But I didn't know anything. I swear, I didn't tell them anything! I didn't even know how to get back here until I—until I stumbled into the forest."

My hand drops from his shoulder as I straighten up. There is no question we might be talking about the tsar's men. Unless there's a force I've never heard of. The Shadow Guild.

I keep my voice steady as I say, "I believe you, Gregor. We'll keep you safe."

The vólkins grunt again, unimpressed with his story. They have been in this place their whole lives, and the only human they know is me. As much as Elder Aïna taught them about humans, it is not enough to know the politics of my kind. Our system works differently from theirs, and while they want to disagree with me, I know better.

Their growls reverberate through the air, and Gregor flinches. He looks up at me, his eyes pleading, darting nervously toward the surrounding vólkins.

The silence that follows is loud. Theron is staring at Gregor with cold, unforgiving eyes.

Elder Aïna says, "Leadership isn't about making easy decisions, Ethereal Lidéřen. It's about standing by the ones you make."

She's right. I spared Gregor's life once. I need to stand by that choice, even if it's difficult. Even if it brings tension. *Especially if it brings tension.* "Gregor will stay in Ávera. We'll see to it that he heals properly."

"No."

I blink, taken aback by the sharpness of Theron's tone.

"He will not roam Ávera freely. He'll be locked up until we decide what to do with him. He's a danger, Noël. We don't know what he's capable of or who might come looking for him."

His words sting. The vólkins shift, their eyes moving uncomfortably between Theron and me. They've never seen us in disagreement like this before.

Neither have I.

I just stare at Theron as the tension pulls tight between us. He's not just protecting me. He's protecting Ávera, and I know he's right. Gregor could be a threat, even if he doesn't seem like one. I clench my jaw. I don't want to undermine Theron either, but I can't let him completely take control. He will kill Gregor.

After a brief pause, I nod. "Very well. Gregor will be kept under guard until we decide his fate."

Theron doesn't respond. The warmth I felt when I first saw him coming through the trees, that connection . . . it's now replaced by distance. I hate it.

I turn my attention back to Gregor who's still trembling at my feet. His fate is uncertain, but for now, he's alive. I spared him for a reason.

But did I really make the right choice?

46

CHAINS OF DISTRUST

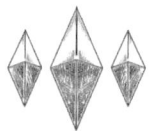

"To lead is not to be loved, and to protect is not to be forgiven. A leader chooses knowing that loyalty may break and blood may stain the soil where they stand."
—Láda Veléša, Goddess of Leadership and War

Theron

I stand, arms crossed, as Noël speaks to Gregor with such a soft voice that I feel the urge to end him right here and now. My jaw clenches, and my claws itch to extend. Every instinct in my body is screaming to stop this. He's a threat. The human doesn't belong in Ávera, and every moment he spends among us puts us in more danger. But instead of ordering his removal, Noël is . . . comforting him.

Sweet-talking him, smiling at him. Touching him.

The sound of her gentle words grates on my nerves. My claws twitch, wanting to dig into something. Into his skull. *She's being too sweet.*

I can't understand it. After everything we just heard, how can she continue to show him this kindness? Every time I look at Gregor, all I see is filth. His hunched body, quivering at her feet. And yet, Noël spares him again. The way she looks at him, the concern in her eyes—it twists the beast inside me. I want to protect her. I want to protect Ávera. I want her to look at *me*.

Noël finishes giving her orders. The way he looks at her, even now, broken and quaking, it disgusts me. There's something in his eyes. *Does he see her the way I do?*

He's looking at her neck, her hair, her eyes. He's looking at what's mine. But I hold my tongue. If I push too hard, I'll only make things worse. Noël's decisions carry weight, but so do mine. We need to work together if we're going to survive our next steps.

As Noël turns away, I step forward, my eyes locking onto the vólkins nearby. They stand tall, waiting for direction. Their paws flex, claws half-extended, mirroring my own unease.

"Chain him," I command. The vólkins snap to attention. "I want him guarded at all times. He's not to move without supervision. No one shows him mercy. Understood?"

They nod, baring their fangs as they exchange glances. *Good. They understand.*

"If he tries anything—anything at all—you report it to me. We're not taking chances."

One of the younger vólkins, his fur bristling, speaks. "Shall we begin the chains now, Theron?" I glance back at Gregor, who's still kneeling on the ground. His hands shake where they dig into the dirt. He doesn't look like a threat. Not in this state. But I know better. Weakness is a disguise predators wear when they want you to drop your guard.

"Do it," I say. "Don't let him out of your sight."

The vólkins move quickly. One grabs him by the arm and drags him to his feet. Gregor stumbles, nearly falling again, but my warrior jerks him up, his claws digging into Gregor's arm, just enough to remind him of his place. The other vólkin crouches down and secures his ankles with ropes of energy.

Gregor doesn't struggle. His head hangs low, his body limp as they lead him away.

They will bring him to the cages. We've never used them before, but right now, it's the best option for him.

We have at least a hundred empty houses, grown for future mates to bond in Ávera. Some of them will need a fresh start, as some vólkins prefer to live in the forest.

I watch them go. If Noël wants him to stay, fine, but it'll be on my terms. He'll be watched. And if he so much as looks at us wrong, I'll deal with him myself.

There is one more conversation I need to have, one that won't be easy. My mate stands a few steps away, her back to me, staring into the forest. Her shoulders are tense.

"We need to talk," I say, my voice softer than I feel. But she is my mate, and even if I'm angry with her, I shouldn't let myself unleash it. She turns slowly, and when her eyes meet mine, I see the unease there.

"You're angry," she says.

"Of course I'm angry," I snap, unable to hold back the growl in my throat. "You're letting him stay here, and you let him live. Again. You're still showing him mercy."

Noël's brow furrows, but she doesn't break eye contact. "I know what I'm doing, Theron."

"Do you? Because from where I'm standing, it looks like you're putting everyone in danger. He shouldn't be here, Noël. He might look weak, but these people who tortured him— they'll come looking for him. For us. You're risking everything, and for what? We've never faced threats from outside the forest. Ávera is all we know."

What if they're already here? Watching us? We know nothing about them. It's a threat I can't fight yet, and I hate that. Gregor's presence here is opening us up to danger.

"My instincts are telling me . . . something," she says. "I don't know how to explain it, but I feel like I need to keep him alive. He's human, like me. And he's never done anything wrong."

"Your instincts?" My claws flex in frustration. "We're talking about the safety of Ávera. What if you're wrong?"

Noël's eyes flash with a spark of anger. "And what if I'm right? What if Gregor has information that could help us? He mentioned the Shadow Guild. We've never heard of them before, and we need to find out more."

I exhale slowly. I hate this, feeling powerless against an unknown threat. As much as I want to dismiss it, I can't ignore the possibility that Gregor might have valuable information.

In his state, he surely didn't share everything he knew.

"I get it, Noël. I do. But you have to understand . . . you're not only risking yourself. You're risking all *our* people. Our land." The words come out harsher than I intend, but I can't take them back. If Gregor's presence led the Shadow Guild's eyes to us, we'd be fighting a war on unknown ground. Ávera's centuries of peace might shatter in a single night.

Noël's shoulders sag. "I'm not trying to push you away, but I have to follow my instincts. I can't ignore what I feel."

"And I can't ignore my duty to protect you. To protect Ávera." My voice softens. "We have to find a balance, Noël. I can't keep standing by while you make decisions that could risk everything we've built."

She's trying to do what's right, just as I am. But we're pulling in different directions, and that's a problem. Two leaders clashing over thoughts and beliefs. This is dangerous.

"We'll keep Gregor locked up," she says after a moment. "But we'll also question him. Find out what he knows."

It's a compromise, but it doesn't sit right with me. "Fine. But if he so much as breathes wrong, I'll deal with him."

Noël nods. There's no clear victory here, only the sense that something is shifting, something neither of us can fully control. And that's what scares me the most.

She made her choice. And I made mine. But I can't shake the feeling that one of us will regret it.

My mate has been gone for some time now, and I can't leave things as they are. I close my eyes and filter out all the scents around me to focus on hers.

My paws lead the way, and my soul warms as I approach the cliff I showed her yesterday. Is she in the cave?

I keep walking, and finally, I find her again. She stands on the top of the cliff, shoulders tight, fury simmering beneath her skin. In her hands, she grips a wooden branch three times the width of her arm and far heavier than any human should be able to manage with ease. Then I see her move.

Noël whirls with the branch like it's an extension of her arm, in perfect control. Each strike cuts through the air. Her motions are precise, but also elegant. I wonder how many times she's done this before.

She brings the branch down on a massive rock with a crack that echoes through the forest. The ground shakes with each blow. She strikes again, and again, faster, harder, until dust clouds rise around her and the rock begins to chip.

She is fascinating.

With a final groan, she lifts the branch high and slams it down with such force that it snaps in two. The broken end splinters in her hand, but she doesn't pause, she drives what's left of it into the rock, shoving until stone gives way with a grating crunch. A hole—no, a crater—carved into its middle. "Not enough," she breathes.

"Why not?" I ask.

My mate turns her head to me and throws the broken wood. "Noël."

She walks to the edge of the cliff, facing Ávera. "We had our first fight. I feel uneasy about it, but . . . what else can I do?" A deep sigh escapes her.

I come to stand beside her, watching Ávera too.

"Gregor's a man caught between power and horror. I feel like I understand him. He's endured so much, been thrown into a harsh reality he never asked for . . . just like me. I've seen what power can do, how it twists and corrupts. I know it all too well. All I want is to bring this place into a new era, where children can grow up free, surrounded by nature. Where women can live their lives on their own terms."

"It is as though you read my soul, my dove. I, too, wish for all of it, except for Gregor. He may be your kind, and you may feel those feelings, but you've left your old life to start a new one. In this life, everything changes." I rest my paw on her head and caress her gently.

She leans into my touch, and my soul sings. We turn to face each other fully.

"We will go with your decision, and we'll interrogate Gregor. We'll find out what's going on, and we'll restore balance. And after we fulfill our purpose, we'll finally rest and spend the rest of our days in a new world. A world where children run freely between the trees, where women are safe and those who dare to go against us bleed to nothingness under our wrath. My Noël, my sweet dove," I say, crouching to be as close to eye level with her as I can. "I wish for us to fulfill that dream."

Noël cups my face with both hands and looks into my eyes. "If we die in war—"

"Then they will bury our bones together," I complete her sentence.

She smiles and leans toward my snout. "I just wish we were one."

47

THE OUTSIDER'S EYES

"The best chains are not forged from iron or steel. The best chains are built from pity. Make them pity you, Gregor, and you will never need to beg for power again."
—Bard, during Gregor's final lesson

Gregor

I sit on the cold ground, my back pressed against a wall that feels alive, like the wood itself is breathing. I'm trying to process everything I've just seen. Ávera.

Bard spoke of this place, a hidden village in the depths of the forest where the vólkins live. He described towering warriors, their homes nestled in ancient trees, and strange, ethereal beings that roamed the woods. I knew it existed—at least in theory—but knowing and seeing are two very different things.

This place feels unreal, like I've stumbled into another world entirely. The vólkins themselves . . . gods, they're enormous. Twice my size, with fur that looks too soft for creatures so dangerous. Their eyes are the worst, sharp and glowing, they cut through me like they can see every lie I've ever told.

And the spirits. Little leaflike creatures with faces, flitting around like children of nature. They're alive. They move and giggle and shimmer, something out of a tale told to scare children into behaving.

The homes here defy logic. They're built into the trunks of trees so enormous they make human buildings look like toys. The branches cradle each structure like arms. This is a world no human knows. Except for me.

And Noël.

That thought should bring me comfort. We share this secret, this connection.

But I don't belong here.

Bard said there were only male vólkins. That much was drilled into me during my lessons. But he was wrong. I've seen females, tall, graceful, and every bit as terrifying as the males. What else did Bard get wrong? How much of what I was told is a lie? Even the Shadow Guild, with all its resources, doesn't know as much as they think they do.

And I thought of them as gods.

Two vólkin guards stand outside my cell, their bodies so massive they don't let the sunlight in. They don't move, don't blink, they just stand there as if I'm not here. I wonder if they even acknowledge my existence—or if they're simply waiting for the order to end it.

No one back at the base would believe this. Not the lieutenant colonel. Not anyone. Gods, even I wouldn't have believed it if I weren't seeing it with my own eyes. I can't even imagine the conversation back in the barracks. All we ever knew was stone and dirt, with a glimpse of nature only when we left the village. Even on the road to Tárnov from Róstan, it was the same. Trees and rocks on one side, the endless ocean on the other.

How would I even begin to tell the rookies about this place? About giant wolves walking like humans, speaking like humans, with their shining, colorful crystals? About the laughing leaves and the living trees?

They'd think I've lost my mind. Maybe I have. Maybe after everything I've been through, these living leaves are figments of my damaged imagination. Maybe my mind seeks colors and happy memories at last.

Heavy footsteps break through my thoughts, growing louder as someone approaches the entrance to my living cage of twisted branches and roots. My heart pounds, and I look up, dread curling in my gut.

A figure stands at the entrance.

A female vólkin.

She steps in, rests a big basin full of water near the wall on my right, and turns toward me. Her presence fills the space instantly. She's tall. Not as massive as the males, but her sleek gray fur, a band of crystals on her wrist, eyes as green as the entire forest, and straight posture give her an air of authority. My gaze flicks to her forehead. It's bare.

No crystals.

What does that mean? Bard told me that vólkins couldn't survive without their crystals. That removing them is a death sentence. But here she is, standing right in front of me. Alive.

But then again, I have a pink crystal up my arse.

Her green eyes sweep over me, and I can't decipher her expression. I also can't look away. I don't want to stare, but I can't stop myself. Every detail—the way she moves, the sheen of her fur in the dim light—it's a puzzle I don't have the pieces to solve.

How much of what Bard told me is wrong?

She doesn't speak as she approaches, and my body tenses. I shrink back, pressing myself against the wall of living wood. Is she going to hurt me?

The thought sounds absurd, even to me, but nothing in this place makes sense. Every rule I've ever known has been rewritten, and I'm at the mercy of creatures I don't understand.

She kneels beside me, her powerful body close enough I can feel the heat radiating from her. Is she going to grab me?

Instead, she extends her hand—or paw. It's something in between, covered in fur but shaped like a human's. Tiny talking leaves emerge from her palm. Except they don't speak now. I guess I wasn't imagining them. They are leaves, dressed in more leaves.

I stare as they move toward my ankles. The glowing, light blue shackles cling tightly to my skin. Shackles made of weightless ropes that appeared out of thin air when the vólkins restrained me. Bard's words about energy transfer come rushing back, but none of it prepared me for this.

The leaves reach my ankles, their tiny, expressionless faces focused on their task. Their small hands move around my shackles. I feel something, a strange sensation, like a delicate breeze brushing against my skin.

Before I can process what's happening, the shackles vanish.

The female vólkin straightens to her full height, and her voice is low but firm when she says, "Her Majesty wants you to bathe and clean the grime off before we heal you."

Her Majesty. Noël.

My throat tightens, and I nod stiffly. Words fail me. My mouth is dry. She's speaking on Noël's behalf.

The vólkin holds my gaze for a moment longer. Then she strides away, the living leaves scurrying back up her arm before disappearing altogether.

I'm left sitting there, staring at the spot where she stood, trying to make sense of what just happened. My ankles are free, my mind anything but.

Bathe?

The water in the basin she left behind is clear, shining with the light of a crystal nestled at the bottom. Hesitant, I dip my hand into the water.

It's warm.

Tears prick at the corners of my eyes. A warm bath. How long has it been since I've had one? In the barracks there were no baths, just rows of cold metal showerheads. In summer, the water would scald. In winter, it was icy enough to numb your skin.

The only time I truly enjoyed a bath was at a friend's house. Back then, we were allowed to leave the barracks once every few months, but I rarely went home. Róstan was too far, and traveling there for only a weekend didn't make sense.

One time, my roommate invited me to his family's home in Tárnov. I agreed, eager to see what life outside the barracks was like.

Walking into his house was like stepping into another world. Strong stone walls, furniture that looked like it belonged in a merchant's gallery, and the scent of real home-cooked food hanging in the air. His parents greeted us warmly, and his brothers ran around the house, their laughter echoing off the walls of their big home.

A family.

How different his life was from mine. A father, a mother, a real home. At least five siblings, maybe more.

Unlike me and Linnéa. Orphaned before we had a chance to know what a real family could be.

I glance over at the two guards stationed outside. Their backs are turned.

It's fine, right? Just to take off my clothes?

They don't wear clothes anyway.

Slowly, I strip out of the dirty, tattered fabric clinging to my body. Each piece drops on the floor with a heavy thud—a thud of blood- and piss-soaked fabric. The basin of water looks small, but I step in and carefully lower myself. I actually fit, as long as I don't stretch my legs all the way.

I'm no tall man, a little taller than Noël. And she's . . . well, she's a shorty. Probably around five feet tall.

Letting the warmth of the water seep into my muscles, I lean my head back. The tension I've carried for weeks begins to melt away.

Oh, this is incredible.

For the first time in forever, I feel like a human again. I close my eyes and relax.

"Human!"

My body flinches before my brain even catches up. Water sloshes around me as a cold shiver runs across my skin. I snap my eyes open and see a dark vólkin standing at the entrance of my cell.

A gasp escapes me as I instinctively try to move backward, but the basin doesn't allow much room for retreat. Right. I'm in this thing.

The giant vólkin lets out a heavy sigh, rubbing his snout with a clawed hand. His fur is pitch black, his burgundy crystals glowing faintly above a single, piercing blue eye. The other socket is empty with a jagged scar across it.

Oh gods. He has one eye.

"Y-yes?" I stammer as I close my thighs.

After the way the other vólkins mocked my body, I'm not about to give this one a reason to laugh at me too. Compared to them, I'm practically a runt. Gods, just his balls are bigger than my entire length. How could anyone even compare themselves to these creatures?

He tosses a bit of fabric at me, and I manage to catch it

before it falls into the water. My tunic and trousers, clean and dry.

"Thank you," I murmur.

"Shut your mouth," he snaps. "You've slept the whole day. Her Majesty is inviting you to the feast. Get dressed. I'll wait here."

His words are harsh, and now I'm not sure who scares me more—this one or Noël's mate.

I nod and stand, stepping out of the bucket. My skin feels soggy, my fingers wrinkled from soaking for so long. I angle my body to the side, avoiding his gaze. "Could you . . . turn away?"

He growls low. Of course not.

With a sigh, I pull the tunic on and savor how good the clean fabric feels against my skin. Then my trousers, no longer covered in piss. As I lace up my boots, a single thought comes to mind: *When will I get the chance to get this crystal out of my arse?*

"I'm done," I say, but the vólkin is already walking out of the cell.

Hesitant, I follow. One of the guards growls low, and I cower, then pick up my pace to stay close to the dark vólkin leading me.

It's already evening. The sun has set, and the cool breeze sends a shiver over my damp skin. As we walk, I notice small vólkin children peeking out from the towering trees.

Ávera's trees are like nothing I've ever seen. They're massive, ancient, and alive. They look older than the world. Older than the statue of the first tsar that stands in Tárnov's square.

The little vólkins scamper after us, curious but keeping their distance. The dark vólkin ahead doesn't seem to care. He just walks like he owns the ground beneath him.

I was scared for my life before, so I didn't get the chance to take a close look at these creatures. Like this one in front of me.

His muscles ripple with every step, shifting under his black fur like living stone. How does someone get like that?

Even the most elite soldiers under the tsar's command, the ones trained to perfection, could never look like this. Human bodies aren't made for it. I swear I'm seeing muscles I didn't even know existed.

Out of the corner of my eye, I notice more vólkin females. They're sitting under a tree, weaving flowers into the children's fur. A calm and peaceful scene.

It hits me . . . The sheer amount of color here in Ávera.

I've been so overwhelmed by everything—the danger, the strangeness—that I didn't grasp how vibrant this place is. The bark of the trees is a deeper, richer brown than any I've seen. The greenery is lush, every leaf full of life. The crystals on the male vólkins' foreheads shine in different colors, each unique.

Glowing orbs, light blue, move lazily among the branches alongside birds.

It's nothing like the human villages. Not the bleak, crumbling corners of Róstan. Not even the grandeur of Tárnov with its polished stone and orderly streets. Ávera is something else entirely.

In the distance, a massive stone, thick vines wrapped around it like a cocoon, comes into view. It stands tall, and all around it, blue roses. Real blue roses. I've heard the stories. That the tsar keeps a garden of them. That the blue rose is the essence of life, of nature. Maybe it's true.

We walk for a long time. Ávera is massive.

There aren't streets or proper roads, but there are clear paths. Wooden platforms form bridges in some areas, both on the forest floor and high above to connect the tree houses nestled in the canopy.

Everywhere I look, there are small figures carved into the trees. Each one has a different face and a unique shape. They're oddly charming, almost . . . cute.

Lost in thought, I step wrong and stumble, hitting the ground hard on my hands and knees. Pain shoots through my bruises, and I grit my teeth against the sting.

The vólkin grunts. Before I can move, he grabs me by the arm and lifts me to my feet.

Wincing, I brush dirt from my palms. "You didn't have to—"

"You talk too much." Without another word, he continues walking, leaving me scrambling to catch up. We barely spoke . . . I don't talk too much. Maybe I feel more comfortable now. Maybe it's because I feel safe. These vólkins listen to Noël.

"So, you're Gregor," a female vólkin says as she steps out of what looks like a room—or is it a house?

This isn't the same female who brought the basin earlier. This one has piercing yellow eyes and an air of toughness that makes my stomach tighten. She doesn't look like someone to mess with.

"I am," I reply.

She looks me up and down, then smirks. "Just as Naïa said, you're a disaster."

"A disaster?" I stop in my tracks, my brow furrowing.

Her smirk grows wider, and she waves a paw dismissively. "Her Majesty said to heal you, so come on. Hey, Oríon! Want to join us? Maybe we can find you a new eye while we're at it!" She bursts out laughing and disappears inside.

My heart thuds in my chest. Did she just joke about his missing eye?

I glance at Oríon, expecting rage or violence, but he doesn't react the way I expect. He simply grunts and walks away without a word.

"Oríon will be your nanny!" the female laughs, dragging me into the room.

My nanny? Like a caretaker?

"This is his punishment for going against Theron. If it was up to him, he'd be dead by now."

A shiver runs over my skin. I look at the female who said these harsh words without even sparing me a glance. This is the female with those beautiful green eyes.

I stand awkwardly just inside the open entrance. It's spacious, with furs scattered in the corners, and the furniture . . . Actual wooden cabinets that wouldn't look out of place in Tárnov. How did they get here? Did humans make them?

Shelves line the walls, carved and filled with jars of herbs and powders. It's so out of place in a world I thought would be all raw and primal.

Bard told me that, centuries ago, human women fled to the vólkins for refuge. It seemed far-fetched at the time, but . . . he might have been right.

Not about the part where there are no female vólkins. That's clearly false. I've already seen two here and more earlier. But he was right about humans and vólkins living together.

Well, Noël and her mate seem to prove that. I doubt he hasn't bedded her already.

"Come sit here," the livelier female says, gesturing to a large, cushiony seat. I move to where she's pointing and settle down. Oh, it's softer than it looks.

"What's your name?" I ask.

"Essin," she replies, then gestures toward the other female. "And that's Naïa."

"Nice . . . nice to meet you," I mumble, shifting awkwardly in my seat.

Essin seems approachable. But Naïa—well, she won't even look at me, and the tension in her stance speaks loud. She clearly resents me. I doubt either of them knows why I'm here, so their guarded behavior makes sense.

Naïa grabs the front of my tunic and pulls me close. "We're doing this because Her Majesty ordered us to. Don't mistake it for kindness. No one here likes you. Not even Essin, she's just smiling for some reason."

I nod, swallowing hard as the lump in my throat grows heavier.

"Naïa, I'd never expect such harshness from you," a calm voice interjects.

We both turn to the entrance. A new vólkin steps inside, a tall female with beautiful green eyes, like emeralds polished to perfection. A necklace with crystals hangs around her neck, glowing as she moves.

She approaches, and Naïa immediately releases her grip on me, stepping back without a word.

"He is our guest. As you know, we treat guests with respect," she says, her calm voice directed at Naïa. Her green eyes move to me, but her gaze has no warmth, not a hint of kindness. "If he were a prisoner . . ." She walks to one of the shelves, and retrieves a jar filled with what looks like dried rosemary. "We could handle him however you wished."

The discomfort settles in my chest. I don't feel safe here, not even a little.

"I am Mina," she says, placing the jar on a cabinet beside me.

"Nice to meet you, Mina," I reply, though my voice is tight. My eyes dart to Naïa. She doesn't acknowledge me, her attention fixed elsewhere.

"Take off your clothes," Mina instructs.

Are vólkin females as interested in human men as their male counterparts are in human women? Will they mock my body the way the males did?

I inhale and peel off my tunic. They look, but there's no sign of disgust. That's . . . something. I unfasten my trousers and push them down, then kick my boots aside.

Mina's eyes scan the cuts and bruises on my torso. She gestures for me to turn around, and I do as she wants. My face burns hot. The last time anyone inspected me like this, it was during my army enlistment.

The healer—a predator cloaked in authority— would prod us, inspect us far beyond necessity, and even massage us under the guise of his duties. Everyone knew he was a deviant, but no one spoke out. He had powerful friends among the higher ranks, and challenging him would've cost us our futures. So, we stayed silent.

"I'll apply vólkin saliva and rosemary to your wounds. They'll heal in no time," Mina says as she spreads the mixture onto my skin. The cool texture makes me frown. It's . . . unpleasant, to say the least.

"Whose saliva is this?" I ask as I raise my arms to keep them out of Mina's way.

"Just be grateful Her Majesty wants you healed," Naïa snaps without looking at me, focused instead on adjusting a flower in Mina's fur.

"Sorry," I mutter, lowering my gaze.

"You're not some kind of spy, are you?" Essin teases.

Oh gods. "Of course not . . ." The words come out in a rush as panic grips my chest. Was that just an innocent joke? Or do they actually suspect something? Everything has gone according to plan so far. Hasn't it?

"He's already scared, Essin. Don't push him," Mina says, her eyes never leaving my injuries.

The bruises and cuts on my skin begin to fade, disappearing even as I watch. "It worked . . ." I whisper, mostly to myself.

"Of course it did," Mina says matter-of-factly. "Vólkin saliva is precious, and the rosemary helps heal the damaged nerves."

I need to get some rosemary for myself if I want to send signals to Bard without the vólkin knowing I'm doing so. What a convenient ritual. I wish I had known of it when I was young. Being able to hide anything from unwanted eyes and ears. What a dream that must be.

"I have a very weak body," I begin. I must be careful now. Every syllable has to count.

Mina closes the jar and turns to me, tilting her head.

"I've been beaten so many times . . . and . . ." I need the tears to come now. Think of Linnéa. Think of Noël. Parents dead. No food. You're a failure, Gregor. You're the disgrace of the Fenrówe family. Frail and pitiful. Unforgivable.

My throat tightens, and my vision blurs. They come easily —because it's all true.

Mina watches me silently as I meet her gaze through my tears. It's not just an act. It hurts. It hurts because every word is real.

"Oh, goddesses," Mina whispers, her voice soft as she takes my hand. "You're stronger than you think. Look at what you've endured."

I close my eyes, letting the tears spill freely down my cheeks. Her kindness feels like a dagger to my chest. She doesn't have to care, yet she does.

"I'm sorry to ask this, but . . ." My voice trembles. "Would it be alright if I kept some rosemary in my cage? To hold . . . close to where it still hurts?"

What a pathetic excuse of a man I am. Pathetic.

"Of course!" Essin exclaims, her own eyes glistening as she hands me an entire bunch of rosemary. "It's all yours!"

I clutch the bundle to my chest, nodding as if it is my burden to bear. I'm so sorry, Mina. And Essin. You don't deserve my lies.

48

THE ROSE AT HAND AND
THE BLOOM OF DOUBT

"Beyond the cradle of the holy land, the threads of their fates are already woven. They must step into the unknown, for not all wars are fought with claws—some are won by finding the hearts still hidden in shadow."
—Elder Aïna, praying to the sacred stone

Noël

The roses bloom as they always have.

"Did your crystal stop pulsing because you've completed your mission, Father?" I whisper, gazing at the vibrant petals surrounding the grave. "I wanted to thank you for saving me in that carriage. I was so scared. Back then, I had no idea what horrors life could hold. And now, here I am, standing at the edge of war."

I trace over the cold stone, over my mother's carvings. "I will start this war, Father. I hope Mother is sitting beside you, listening. I hope you're together, watching over me." My fingers brush the edge of a nearby rose. "Can you watch over Theron too?"

The sound of flapping wings draws my attention upward. I follow the movement as a white dove lands on the gravestone. My stomach drops when I see my mother's handkerchief wrapped around its leg. There's something else tied to it.

"Where did you get that handkerchief, little one?"

The dove tilts its head to the side and makes a soft cooing sound.

"This handkerchief is very important to me. Please, give it back."

The dove steps sideways along the gravestone, inching closer, then lifts its leg to reveal that the handkerchief is secured with a piece of folded paper. Is that a sign for me to take it?

"You're trained, aren't you?" I ask as I gently untie the knot. "Who tied this handkerchief to you?" I unfold the paper. My breath catches in my throat.

No. No, this can't be.

Blinking hard, I shake my head. I must be imagining things. My vision blurs as my hands begin to tremble. Tears spill onto the paper, turning the inked dots a darker shade. It's a page from my mother's book, the one about the ritual called *Chains of Blood*.

I lift my gaze to the dove. It has moved to stand quietly beside the grave. Then it taps against the stone. My eyes follow its beak until I see the name. *Eyleen.*

"No," I breathe, the word breaking in my throat. My whole body trembles. "Mother?"

I scan through the words on the page. "In the time of veiled suns and forgotten stars, when the blood of the ancients stirs once more, one shall be given, not taken, willingly offered upon the sacred tether.

"Only by the hand of her own heart shall the first be sealed.

"Only then may the second, born of her line and bearing the soul-mark, cross the threshold. And when both steps are fulfilled, the Chains of Blood shall shatter, and the path between realms shall be undone."

A sacrifice . . . an ancient bloodline crossing paths . . .

I am the ancient bloodline. I am the blue rose. I am the daughter of the sacrifice. She gave herself so I could cross the threshold—the barrier.

"Mother!" I cry out, and the dove hops onto my thigh, cooing as if to soothe me.

"You followed me through every step of this path," I whisper, my voice breaking as I lean closer to the dove. "You gave Theron a sign . . . you left me so I could fulfill my destiny!"

A sob shudders through me. My fingers curl around the edge of the gravestone as if I could anchor myself in her presence. "I read your diary, Mother," I cry. "I know now. I *know* what you gave up."

My chest heaves, the grief clawing its way up like fire through my ribs. "You didn't deserve this," I wail, and it echoes in the still air. "You were never meant to carry the weight of a prophecy. You were meant to be happy. You were meant to live!"

The dove watches me with quiet eyes, and I swear I see something in its gaze. Something familiar, something achingly familiar.

"I'm so sorry. I'm so sorry you had to die so I could live."

The dove hops closer, then nestles into the fabric of my gown. I clutch the handkerchief to my heart, now broken wide open.

I sit in this position, crumpled over my knees, for a very long time. My tears have dried and the little dove is long asleep. "Thank you for looking after me." I take the dove in my palms, close my eyes, and lift it up, letting it fly free. I don't want to see it. It hurts too much to say goodbye.

"Please go."

Its wings brush against the air as it flies away.

I'm not sure if I feel relief or guilt, but I finally know what happened to her. If anyone killed her, I wouldn't have been able to cross the barrier. So she did it herself. She marked the page before I came, and took her own life so I could thrive. It hurts, but this was her decision. I should respect that.

"Your Majesty." Zephyr's voice pulls me from my one-sided conversation. I open my eyes and turn to see him and Kaël standing nearby. Kaël looks like he's on the verge of tears.

A small smile creeps onto my face. "You remind me of Essin, Kaël."

They step closer, but as they reach the edge of the roses, they pause.

"You can approach," I say, rising from the grave. "Come sit with me."

Kaël rushes forward and collapses to the ground in front of me. "I am so sorry!"

"For what?" Did they hear me crying?

"Yesterday when we were here," he stammers, his eyes welling up. Is *he* really about to cry? "You thought I was against you!" His words spill out in a wail, and then he bursts into tears.

His sobs catch me off guard. Oh, goddesses. What . . . what am I supposed to do?

"Kaël, you fool! Don't upset her like this!" Zephyr growls, grabbing Kaël by the mane and giving him a firm shake.

"There's no need to apologize," I say, forcing another smile. Do I smile? Do I pat him? Offer a blue rose? Scratch behind his ear like a pup?

"I swear I didn't mean to doubt you, Your Majesty! It was just . . . the way you looked at me. I thought you were going to claw my ears off!"

"I'm not going to claw your ears off, Kaël. But if you keep crying like that, I might drown in your tears before the war even begins."

Puppy eyes are a real thing, and I'm staring at them right now. With a deep sigh, I raise my hands toward the sky. "Leaf spirits, my dears, please bring us water and leaves for Kaël's tears."

The sound of light, tinkling laughter fills the air as the leaf spirits emerge from the trees, carrying a large leaf between them. Moments later, a few nýmphí appear with bowls of water in their hands.

"Thank you," I say, accepting a water bowl from one of the pretty nýmphí. She bows before sitting beside me, the others following suit. The leaf spirits flutter over to lay the large leaf near Kaël's snout. The rest of us flinch as he blows his nose into it.

"Thank you," Kaël murmurs, wiping at his tears and nose with the edge of the leaf.

I nod in response, and Zephyr lifts his paw to his heart. "We will fight in this war for you, Your Majesty."

"Yes!" Kaël echoes.

I take a sip of water to ease my thirst before handing the empty bowl back to the nýmphá. "You won't," I say firmly.

Both of them tilt their heads, their confusion written all over their snouts.

"I have a different mission for the two of you. And Aeson," I add. "Where is he, by the way?"

Kaël leans on his arm. "We were patrolling this side of the land. Aeson is stationed in the west area with his patrol partner."

The trials have been canceled for now. We have only one day left until the bonding ritual, and that day is critical. With Gregor here, anything could happen. Theron has already assigned a larger-scale patrol to prepare for whatever may come. Before we question Gregor, we need to be ready for everything.

With the feast approaching, it's the perfect chance for the vólkins to see Gregor in a different light. Not as a threat, but as . . . Maybe a friend. At least, that's the goal. For now, the vólkins are busy hunting—some for the feast, others to feed the warriors on patrol. Tonight, most of the patrolling warriors will eat in shifts, while the females, children, and a few warriors gather for the celebration.

"What's the mission?" Zephyr asks.

I straighten my spine. "As the strongest warriors, you will scout the land. Since you could sense that I am the leader from the prophecy, you'll also have the ability to identify the others. While we conquer lands and villages, your task will be to search for the other five women."

"By ourselves?" Kaël blurts out, his ears pinching back.

"Don't be a pup," Zephyr cuts in before I can respond.

"Yes, by yourself," I confirm. "Aeson will be sent north, given his white fur and origins in that region. The two of you will be assigned to other areas. Don't worry, we'll discuss the specifics after the feast."

This plan is our best option. Both Theron and Elder Aïna agreed. Finding the other five is essential, and their discovery will mark the true beginning of what needs to be done. Once my awakening is complete, I'll be ready to take the necessary actions. And to make this world a better place.

"It's time to get ready, Ethereal Leader," the nýmphá beside me says, rising before offering her hand to help me up.

Turning to Kaël and Zephyr, who still seem to be processing my words, I say, "Save your questions for after the feast. Go get ready, and we'll meet there."

The two of them rise to their paws before bowing.

More nýmphí gather at my parents' home as I prepare to get ready there. It feels comforting, like a small connection to my past. If I can't return to my mother's home, having this option is a blessing.

"When you're not with me, where do you go?" I ask the nýmphá brushing my hair.

"Some of us are always watching from afar, Ethereal Leader."

"Others tend to nature," another nýmphá says, resting her chin on my thigh. "We help animals in need, play with the leaves, and make sure Mother Nature doesn't suffer."

"If you're busy doing all that, who takes over your duties?" I ask, tucking a lock of her brown hair behind her ear.

"There are many of us, Ethereal Leader," she replies, her voice light as a song.

"How many?"

"Too many to count. Maybe hundreds?"

"Hundreds?" I repeat, turning to the nýmphá in surprise.

They giggle at my reaction, their laughter harmonious, like a symphony of voices layered atop one another. I could listen to it forever. Despite their thin bodies, they never eat, yet still radiate life and energy. As ethereal beings, they're sustained by their crystals and serve me as the Lidéřen of the prophecy they believe in.

"You summoned blue roses with your tears, Ethereal Leader," a nýmphá perched on the edge of the cabinets says, swinging her legs lazily. "Have you tried doing it with your will instead?"

"Can I do that?" I ask as the nýmphá behind me starts braiding my hair, humming a soft tune.

The nýmphá on my thigh lifts her head and gently takes my hand with a smile. "Focus your energy here."

With her hands holding mine, I close my eyes. If Theron could do it, maybe I can too.

"Trust that you already have one in your palm," she says. "When we truly believe we already possess what we desire, it comes to us."

I imagine a blue rose in my hand, but nothing happens. "I can't,"

"You can." She giggles. "You have the idea, but it's not clear.

Focus on the petals—their texture, their scent, their color. Picture the beauty of this rare flower. Think of the ones you've seen before, perhaps with your mother or Éva, the Mother of All."

A blue rose. Deep, beautiful blue. Its petals are velvety and delicate, their fragrance sweet and calming. Like the ones my mother and I used to water together. Or the roses glowing by the grave. Or even those I summoned near the ancient stone.

Beautiful, blue, and luminous, responding to my wish. *Come to me, pretty flower, appear in my hand.*

It does.

A light, airy sensation forms in my palm. When I open my eyes, I see a soft, glowing ball of pale blue. It begins to grow, forming the shape of a blue rose.

"Oh," I breathe.

The nýmphá leans in, inhaling its fragrance. With a warm smile, she reaches out and caresses the petals.

We run back to Ávera together. Since my awakening began, combined with Theron's nightly healing sessions, my body feels stronger every day. Not just stronger, but more keen. My vision is clearer, my sense of smell more acute. Not like a vólkin's, but certainly no longer like a human's either. I can only imagine what my abilities will be like when I fully awaken.

It's incredible to think that thousands of years ago, women didn't need bonding rituals to achieve this. Back then, they were so connected to their spirituality that they bonded souls with their mates naturally. What men have done to disrupt that balance is unforgivable, but soon, that will change. Soon, I will destroy every creation of men, and Ávera will stretch until it reaches the oceans surrounding the land. Spirits and humans will live in nature, free of chains, as it was always intended.

Mother Nature never meant for us to stress or suffer. We were always meant to live as free spirits. And this is my plan to restore balance.

When we reach Ávera, the scent of cooked meat fills the air. Tonight, they've prepared meals for two humans—Gregor and me. Gregor's arrival has unsettled everyone, and I can only hope this feast will ease the tension that hangs heavy over the village.

Theron promised we'd question Gregor together. The fact that he isn't here yet, and that Gregor seems more at ease than before, is a good sign.

"Her Majesty has arrived!" Mina announces, her voice carrying across the gathering.

Every vólkin turns to face us, bowing low. My gaze shifts to Gregor, and he bows as well. This is good. It makes him seem more relatable.

"You will sit with me," Oríon snarls at Gregor.

Gregor flinches, nodding quickly. Even from this distance, I hear their exchange clearly. It is amazing how my senses have sharpened.

"Oríon," I call.

He stiffens and snaps to attention. "Yes?"

I approach them, noting Gregor's forced smile as he greets me. "I would ask you to be nicer to our guest," I say, holding Oríon's gaze.

He grunts in response, and the sound grates on my nerves.

My tone is cold when I say, "I *didn't* hear your answer."

His jaw tightens as he forces the word out, each syllable dripping with reluctance. "Yes, Your Majesty."

I've dealt with men like him before—soldiers who had a hard time taking orders from a woman. The difference is, Oríon's resistance isn't about my femininity. It's about waiting. Or more specifically, being stuck in Ávera when he clearly wants to be anywhere else. But Theron already taught him that lesson, so I won't push.

Elder Aïna, Mina, Naïa, and Essin arrive as I take my seat, the same spot I sat during the welcoming feast the vólkins held for me when I arrived. I know Theron is with his patrol, but he promised he'd return when three stars appear in the sky. So far, only two have shown.

Tonight we'll question Gregor. I need to know everything, every detail he remembers about what happened. If Gregor feels welcomed and safe, he's far more likely to share valuable information, more than what he's already told us.

"How's our little guest?" Elder Aïna asks, settling beside me.

"Scared of Orïon," I reply. "But he looks better than before. The girls took care of him."

Elder Aïna hums thoughtfully as I speak.

"He's in shock, but honestly, he seems to be handling everything better than I expected, better than I would in his position, considering how new all this is for him."

"Perhaps it isn't as new to him as you think."

Her words make me tighten my grip on the goblet in my hand. That possibility hadn't even crossed my mind. "Do you think ..."

"You know what I think, Your Majesty."

Of course. How had I not seen it? Gregor was terrified, anyone would be after nearly being killed. But now that I think about it, he's been adapting to all this far too easily. I should ask Mina how he behaved during his healing.

Interesting, Gregor. Very interesting.

As the third star appears in the sky, my heart pounds loudly in my chest. I do not see Theron, but for some reason, my body reacts. What is this? Why am I getting wet?

Goddesses, why now?

I take a deep breath to steady myself and rise to my feet.

The vólkins are already seated. Gregor sits near Orïon, while the children gather together at a separate table. As I stand, silence falls over the crowd, and all eyes turn to me.

Elder Aïna places a reassuring paw on my knee.

"Tonight," I begin, "we mark the first and last day of the

trials. Our warriors have done well. Most teams found all three artifacts, demonstrating teamwork, strategic thinking, and strength. The forest was unkind, challenging them every step of the way. Yet, they prevailed, proving they are who they claim to be."

I raise my goblet without thinking, a habit from my human life. Though vólkins don't drink from goblets, no one seems to mind the gesture.

"The trials will not continue. As we all know, these are alarming times. From today forward, Ávera will be heavily guarded. I ask each and every one of you to remain on guard. If anything unusual occurs, report it immediately." I pause, swiping my gaze over everyone. Gregor included. "Tonight, we feast in honor of our warriors. In two days, we will celebrate the bonding. For now, enjoy the feast and offer prayers for our strong males patrolling to keep us safe." I lift the goblet higher. "Let the feast begin."

"Very noble, Your Majesty." Theron's voice cuts through the air as he takes a seat beside me. I'd almost forgotten how deep his voice is.

"Thank you," I reply, setting the goblet on the table.

"I missed you." His tone is low as he places strawberries in my bowl.

Heat rushes to my cheeks at his words. I clear my throat and pick a strawberry. "We need to talk about Gregor," I whisper.

49

A HOUSE OF SECRETS

"Thank yu for the coins, dir brother. I saved them carefuly and even skiped a few meels, so I could buy us somethin nice one day when yu com hom. I mis yu every day."
—Linnéa's first letter to Gregor

Gregor

"I swear to tell the truth! I swear on my mother! If I lie, let her be dead!"

We're sitting in my new house, a house I shouldn't have. I overheard Noël and Theron arguing during the feast. Theron wanted me locked in that cage, while Noël insisted I deserved a place of my own. She won the argument.

Now I'm here, in an actual house in Ávera. It's far bigger than my room back in the barracks, where twenty men shared one cramped space, bunk beds stacked like a child's puzzle. Here, I have walls to myself, a roof that doesn't leak, and silence that feels as foreign as the vólkin.

Not that I've had time to explore. The moment we arrived, Noël and Theron ushered me into the living area to question me. Now I sit on a wooden chair, my posture stiff. Noël, her expression warm, sits across from me. Theron doesn't bother to sit. He stands nearby, his eyes locked on me like the predator that he is.

"It's alright, Gregor," Noël says, her voice as warm as her smile. "I believe every word you say. We're not here to work against you. We're here to listen and do what's right."

She's so nice to me, so much kinder than I ever imagined. I never thought Noël could be like this. On the training grounds or in the dining hall, she always looked carved from stone, her face unmoving, expressionless. Now, though, she's like a different person. Has been so kind to me since I arrived. "Thank you," I reply, forcing a small smile of my own.

"You said these people called themselves the Shadow Guild, right?" Noël continues. "Do you think they're connected to the tsar?"

"Yes," I start, but Theron cuts in before I can continue.

"Why?" His voice is low.

I swallow hard. "When I was in their basement—it was underground, I think, since there were no windows—I saw tapestries with the same blue rose emblems you see in every commander's office."

"So they serve the tsar," Noël murmurs. Her eyes sweeping over me make me sit straighter, and the chair creaks beneath me.

"What did they do to you while you were there?" she asks. "Aside from torturing you?"

"And why were you beaten?" Theron follows. "Because you didn't cooperate?"

"I mostly sat with my eyes covered. They moved me from one place to another, blindfolded. Sometimes they'd ask me questions, especially when they saw how weak I'd become." A shiver runs down my spine, and goose bumps rise on my arms. I hate thinking about it—about the humiliation, the pain—but

I force myself to continue. "They beat me to remind me that I was nothing. Every time I refused to answer, they'd shove a cloth in my mouth and keep hitting me." My fists clench at the memory, the phantom ache of every blow tightening in my chest. "I was so scared . . ." My voice falters, and my eyes start to sting. And that cursed crystal—still inside me—feels like it's mocking me.

"What questions did they ask you?" Theron asks.

"Theron! Can't you give him a minute?" Noël stands abruptly and glares up at him. Her eyes blaze with anger.

Theron grunts in response, looking away.

Noël exhales and turns back to me, sitting down with a gentleness that calms the air around her. "Please don't mind him," she says. "He's just . . . very concerned for all of us."

I nod slowly, my throat dry. "They asked me if Noël—" I catch myself, panic flashing through me. "I mean, Her Majesty," I correct quickly, before Theron can tear my head off.

His eyes narrow, but he says nothing.

"They wanted to know if you had crystals on your forehead."

I glance between them, gauging their reactions. Bard taught me what that meant—how a woman spiritually awakens when bonded with a vólkin. The crystals that form on her forehead are a reflection of their shared element, always matching the bond. In Noël and Theron's case, it's the blue rose. That's why Theron's crystals glow blue. The room grows quiet. Every pause feels like walking on a sword's edge.

"Since they're the tsar's men, it's no surprise they know about it," Noël finally says.

"This also means they know we'll perform the bonding ritual at the full moon," Theron adds, leaning against the table beside him.

"You don't understand!" The words burst out of me before I can stop them. Noël's eyes widen at my sudden outburst, but I continue, my voice rising in pitch. "They're everywhere! They have shadows in every village! I saw one of them returning in disguise, dressed as a blacksmith!" My words spill out in a frantic rush, my fingers gripping my knees so hard it hurts. "They had me discharged from the army!"

"What?" Noël breathes, leaning forward, her wide eyes growing even larger. "How?"

"They brought me to the healer in Tárnov." My voice shakes as I explain. "At our base. He declared me unfit to serve. It was all arranged so no one would question my disappearance." I inhale slowly, trying to steady myself. "They hold so much power . . . I was so scared . . ." Tears streak down my face as I murmur those last words. The fear was real. It clung to me every day, every sleepless night. And it wasn't only for me. It was for Linnéa too. Bard had told me how she was holding up.

For months, I hadn't been able to send her money. My own foolishness burned through it when I started sneaking out of the barracks to the shadowy underside of the market.

The whores had their charms, luring men for prices that seemed reasonable—at least until you realized the madam pocketed every coin. The gambling houses, connected to one brotherhood or another, were even worse. If you couldn't pay, their enforcer would come, and suddenly you'd find yourself enslaved to their debts.

Those places were dark, dangerous, and of course, I was always stupid enough to go back. Month by month, I lost everything. I had nothing left to send her.

Poor Linnéa.

Bard said she was fine with them, that she had her own room at one of their bases. She'd be safe, he promised, so long as I didn't make a mistake, but his reassurance did little to ease my guilt.

"What else have you told them?" Theron demands. "It seems like there's more to your story than you initially claimed.

'I haven't told them anything' doesn't quite mean *nothing*, does it, Gregor?"

Oh shit. My heart pounds so hard it feels like it might burst from my chest. Cold sweat beads on my forehead, and my breath comes shallow and quick. Did I already screw this up? It hasn't even been a full day.

"No . . . No . . ." I stammer. "Try to understand!"

"Understand what?" Theron leans in close, grasping my jaw in his clawed hand. His strength is terrifying. I can feel the power in his grip, controlled but on the verge of something far worse.

Oh gods. Oh gods.

"I . . . I . . ."

"You. What?" Theron growls, his teeth bared, his face inches from mine.

"That's enough, Theron!" Noël's voice snaps through the room, and she pulls him away from me.

Oh thank the gods. Mama, I'll never swear on you again. I promise.

"He is lying!" Theron's voice is thunderous. "Don't you see that?"

"He is NOT lying, Theron! You've never been scared in your life. You don't know what it's like to stand before creatures twice your size, to feel so small, so helpless, knowing your life could be snuffed out at any moment." She slams her hand on the table.

The sound cracks through the silence, and I flinch, my body taut with nerves. *Noël.* Standing up for me like this.

"Do you think his mind was stable when he arrived here? When the vólkins treated him like nothing more than a piece of horse shit?" Her voice is a cold command when she says, "Get out of here."

What? How? She just . . . ?

Theron snarls, the sound reverberating through the house before he storms out and slams the door behind him.

I swallow hard. Did that really just happen?

Noël sighs, shaking her head as if she's used to this kind of display. Without a word, she walks to the kitchen area. She pours water into a small cup, then another.

I hesitate before following her. "Is . . . is everything alright?"

"Don't worry about him," she says, handing me one of the cups. "Vólkin pride is something else entirely, but I won't let him treat you like that."

I drink, and the cool water soothes my dry throat. Up close, Noël seems so much smaller than I expected. I'd only ever seen her from a distance during my time in the army, always carrying herself with an air of authority. Seeing her like this, soft and approachable, stirs something in me. She is, after all, a woman.

She takes my hand suddenly, her fingers warm against mine. Her smile is gentle. "Trust me, Gregor, I'll stand up for you every time."

Her words catch me off guard, and I can't help but smile back. I brush my thumb over her knuckles. "Thank you."

Noël leads me to a bed-like pile of furs in the corner of the room. My chest tightens with nerves as she sits and gestures for me to join her. I didn't expect this—being on a bed with a woman as beautiful as her.

"Tell me what you wanted to say," she says, her voice caring and kind. It melts away some of my nerves. "Theron isn't here to interrupt us now."

"The Shadow Guild. The man who was in charge of me . . . It was like he was more than human."

Her brows knit together. "What do you mean?"

"His name was Bard," I say, pausing to find the right words. "And Bard was . . . strange. In ways I don't even know how to explain. He could hear me whispering from the other side of

the base. He could smell what I'd eaten before even seeing me."
I scratch the back of my head. "He reminded me of a vólkin."

Noël's eyes widen, and her whole posture changes.

"He had heightened senses," I continue, lowering my voice
as if someone might overhear. "Like a wolf. Sensing scents,
hearing sounds no one else could. I was too scared to ask him
about it, but there was something unnatural about him. Almost
like he had human skin, but . . . something else underneath."
The room is so quiet, I swear I can hear her heartbeat.

After everything I've learned about vólkins, magic, and a
world I never knew existed, I'm not surprised anymore. But
judging by Noël's expression, she is.

"There's one more thing," I say. "Bard said it would be
logical for you to perform the bonding ritual on a full moon.
He explained what it means. So, I know . . . I know that much."

I take a deep breath. Time to say it. I can do this. "He's planning an ambush. An army to strike when you leave Ávera.
That's why I told you he has eyes and ears everywhere. Bard
isn't just anyone, he's one of the tsar's most trusted shadows.
They know you won't stay hidden here forever. They know
you'll want to attack. They're preparing for it. All the warriors
are ready." This time, I'm the one to take her hand. "So, Noël," I
say, looking directly into her eyes, "you need to be prepared.
The tsar's army is strong. You know that better than I do."

Noël's expression relaxes, her features melting into something affectionate and gentle. "Thank you for telling me,
Gregor. You just saved a thousand lives." She lifts her hand, and
her touch is tender when her fingers brush against my cheek.

I'm doing the right thing, I tell myself, the words echoing in
my mind as I nod slowly, eyes closed, her hand still warm
against my face.

Noël bids me good night, and as she opens the door, I catch
sight of Orïon outside, his imposing figure silhouetted against
the night.

Well.

I have a home in Ávera.

Clasping my hands, I raise my arms over my head and feel the sting in my muscles as they protest the stretch. Exhaustion weighs on me. It's been the longest day of my life. But before I let sleep take me, there's one more thing I need to do.

I head to the kitchen where I scan the small cabinet attached to the wooden wall. Essin mentioned earlier that the house was stocked with everything I'd need to cook for myself. If that's true, there might be salt somewhere.

Salt is a rare and precious ingredient, but in the army, when we were celebrating the tsar's birthday, we would get some meals with salt. It was a luxury all the soldiers waited for every year. The meat from the feast earlier had salt, so I figure there must be some here too.

Opening the first cabinet, I find a crooked wooden bowl filled with a few vegetables, another holding apples. Simple, but enough. In the next cabinet, there are cups neatly stacked, and there, the spices.

I pull out a sealed jar and open it, inhaling its contents. Dried thyme. Another jar holds dried sage, and the next, dried bay leaves. My lips twitch into a small smile as memories of my mother's soups come flooding back. She always used bay leaves to add flavor.

I put the jar back, my hand brushing past the others until I spot what I'm looking for. Salt.

I bring the small container with me over to the lower cabinet near the wall. My rosemary is tucked safely inside, exactly where I left it.

With the salt and a stalk of rosemary from the bundle, I head to the dimly lit bathroom. After setting the ingredients carefully on the sink, I undo my trousers with a sigh and toss them onto the floor.

Finally. It's time to get this thing out of me.

Crouching, I brace myself, one hand gripping the edge of the sink for balance. My other hand trembles as it moves toward the crystal lodged inside me. Gods, this is humiliating.

Tears sting my eyes, blurring my vision, but I don't stop. I can't stop. With a sharp exhale, I remove the crystal.

It feels heavier than I expected, or maybe that's my exhaustion and shame reminding me who I am and what I'm doing. My chest heaves as I clean the crystal in the water, watching as the traces of blood swirl away to leave the surface clean once more.

The tears fall freely now, but I don't wipe them away. Instead, I grab the salt and rosemary.

Time for the ritual.

Bard needs to know I've succeeded.

I stare at the crystal, its surface catching the faint moonlight shining through the small bathroom window.

After everything I said today, I wonder what Noël and Theron think was a lie and what was not.

50

MAMINKA, SYSTRITSY, AND BRATYA

"Women are the earth's oldest prayer. Soft as moss, fierce as fire.
They carry seasons in their blood, stars in their bones, and
rivers in their breath. To be a woman is to be the first miracle
the world ever knew."
—Eyleen Ársa

Noël

I sit on Theron's belly as he sleeps beneath me. Usually, he
wakes before I do, but the past two days have worn him
out. The room is quiet, the hushed sounds of the forest
outside barely breaking the silence in our home. It's still dark,
though the sun will likely rise in an hour or two.

For the past two weeks, I've relied on the sun, moon, stars,
and weather to tell the time. At first, it felt strange not having a
clock in every building, something I hadn't realized I took for
granted. But I've grown used to it. I'm no longer running after
time, no longer chasing hours that slip through my fingers.
It's . . . refreshing.

So much has changed in me over the time I've been here.

I lost my mother. I discovered who my father is. Arnold is gone. Gregor returned. I became the leader of a prophecy and met my other half. Never in my life did I think I'd say that—I have someone I will spend the rest of my life with. It's strange, but not in a bad way. I'd even say . . . it's good. Different, but good.

Tonight is the bonding ritual, our version of a wedding. In just two weeks, I've experienced more than I ever thought possible. A lifetime of events condensed into weeks. And from now on, I know things will only get scarier and infinitely more serious. But in a way, I'm doing what I've always wanted, what I could never do before. I'm a leader. Lidéřen.

My body rises and falls with Theron's steady breaths. He looks so peaceful. A massive wolf who could tear lives apart, now resting soundly in the nest-bed. The thought tugs a smile to my lips. When did I become so unhinged that the idea of him doesn't terrify me anymore?

Theron has changed me. More than I ever could have imagined possible.

And I'm grateful for it. I thought I was strong before I came here, but tonight, I'll become stronger. I'll awaken, fully bonded, and finally be able to harness the power within me.

I lift my hand, focusing on the living wooden wall to the side of the nest. A beautiful blue rose takes shape in my mind, its petals vibrant and lush, just like Mother used to love.

Within moments, the wall responds, and small blue roses bloom into existence. Seven vibrant flowers unfurl, their color deep and rich. My smile widens as I watch them, their elegance takes my breath away. I love them. They're so beautiful to me.

Then, I close my palm into a fist, my gaze fixed on the little bush. The flowers shudder, and thick, dark thorns twist from their stems. Some curve at their edges, transforming the serene beauty into something dangerous. A flicker of satisfaction sparks within me. Dark thoughts stir. I shake my head. No. Not that.

Soon, Theron will wake, and we'll part ways to prepare for the ritual. For our "wedding." But what if . . . A grin spreads across my face. Theron's shaft is already pressing against my lower back. I could—

The grin grows even wider.

Reaching for his tail, I run my fingers through the silky fur. Last time, I couldn't help myself. It's just so irresistibly soft. I trace my nails along the length of his tail, brushing against the skin beneath the fur. Theron's eyes snap open. With a jerk, he sits up, and I laugh as I tumble backward from the sudden movement.

Before I can fall too far, his large arms catch me and pull me back to him. His eyes, still heavy with sleep, meet mine. "My mate," he murmurs, his voice raspy with drowsiness.

A shiver runs through me at the sound. Goddesses, am I really this desperate? The damp heat pooling between my thighs answers for me.

"You're wanting," he says as he tugs me closer. His arms wrap around me, and my body clings to his, drawn to him as if it's beyond my control.

"Why do I react like this?" I ask, placing my hands on his chest, feeling the rhythm of his heart beneath my palms.

"Why do you find your mate desirable?" he asks back, a teasing glint in his tired eyes.

Leaning in, he traces his tongue across my face. I hum, savoring the warm, wet glide against my skin. The sensation, once strange when he healed me after our first meeting, has become something I enjoy, something that leaves me "wanting."

My gaze roams over his face. His beautiful eyes, the glistening wetness of his nose, and the gleam of his fangs. *He's so majestic.*

I wanted to give him a gift, but I don't have much here yet. A thought occurs to me. "Theron," I whisper, leaning toward him.

He hums in question.

"I want to express my gratitude, a gift, for everything that you've done for me."

"You are my gift,"

"Something for our wedding. Or bonding ritual," I say, lifting my right arm. I open my palm, and grow the most beautiful blue rose I've seen. It has the most petals, and it glows more than the others. More than the roses in my mother's garden, more than the roses around Father's grave. Even more than those I grew myself inside and outside our home.

This rose is special.

Theron watches in fascination as the petals bloom. "I've never seen a rose quite like this."

I smile and put the rose behind his ear. It suits him so much.

"Thank you, my golubenya rozia." His lids grow heavy as his breath slows and his pupils grow to swallow his hazel gaze.

"What's *golubenya rozia?*" I ask.

"Blue rose."

My heart pounds so frantically in my chest, it might shatter my rib cage. On impulse, I catch his tongue with my lips, and a low growl escapes him.

Theron moves fast, his paws gripping my thighs and cheeks, lifting me with ease to settle over his hard shaft. The moment he brushes against my aching core, I wince.

"Goddesses . . ." My sensitivity is unbearable, and it only makes me want him more. Leaning back in his arms, I look up at him, my chest rising and falling with shallow breaths. "We shouldn't." The words slip out even as I hate myself for saying them. The sun will soon rise above Ávera, and Theron will have to go.

"We have time." His voice, deep and low, sends shivers racing across my skin as his claws trace light patterns over me.

"We don't," I murmur, though a smile I can't hold back softens my quiet protest. "Did you choose your bratya yet? It's Zephyr, Aeson, and Kaël, isn't it?"

Theron hums, his mouth quirking slightly at the question.

Yesterday, after we questioned Gregor, we met with the three of them. Theron had informed them of their upcoming missions, and now, today will be their last day in Ávera.

We're truly sending the vólkins to scatter across the land, to search for the other five and prepare for what's coming.

We're truly going to war.

Aeson will go with two warriors of his choosing, as will Kaël and Zephyr. I know they'd prefer to go together—close friends bound by loyalty—but something in my gut tells me they need to go separately.

Theron, Elder Aïna, and I discussed this in detail, considering everything we know about their origins and strengths. Aeson, with his fur as bright as freshly fallen snow, is best suited for the cold north. Kaël's brown fur, tinged with golden undertones, fits the southern territories' sun-drenched lands. And Zephyr, his fur dark and rich like the forest floor, belongs to the west, where the woods stretch endlessly. It's the best strategy, but knowing that doesn't make it easier.

"We already discussed that we'd all be each other's bratya," Theron says.

Elder Aïna told me that when mates perform a bonding ritual, the vólkin must choose a few of his closest brothers to stand by his side, even if they aren't related by blood. These bratya help the groom prepare for the ritual, providing guidance and support.

The bride, on the other hand, must choose a maminka, literally meaning "mother." Traditionally, the bride's own mother would take on this role, guiding her through the preparations and overseeing the systritsy, the bride's chosen sisters. These sisters could be blood related or not, depending on the bride's circumstances. But I have neither.

Elder Aïna, with her wisdom and warmth, will be my maminka. Naïa, Mina, and Essin will stand beside me as my systritsy.

"Do you think Gregor believed our act yesterday?" I ask. The information he gave us is crucial, if it's true. But doubt lingers in the back of my mind.

"Of course," Theron answers with a grin. "We executed everything as planned. I was the bad 'officer,' and you played the good one perfectly." He pauses, his grin shifting into something darker. "I had to remind myself it was all an act. Otherwise, I'd have killed him on the spot."

Before I can respond, Theron moves with the speed and grace of a predator, flipping me over in seconds. His body cages me as his weight presses me into the bed-nest.

"Having you choose another over me was painful, my little dove," he growls, his voice rough and his eyes boring into mine.

The door swings open.

Both of us freeze, then turn our attention to Elder Aïna as she steps into the room.

"Now, now," she says as she motions with her paw. "Come on in."

In a flurry, dozens of nýmphí rush inside, their glowing forms filling the space. Before I can process what's happening, they lift Theron off me. *How are they even doing that?* Theron probably weighs more than all of them combined—thrice over.

"I trust neither of you has eaten a thing this morning?" Elder Aïna asks with a grin that's far too knowing.

Theron and I shake our heads like guilty children caught red-handed and pawed. The fasting was explained to me the day before as well. From the morning of the bonding ritual until dawn the next day, both mates must abstain from food. Mina said it was a precaution after a few unfortunate brides had food poisoning during their ceremonies. It also served to cleanse the body—*two rabbits in one claw*, as she put it.

But now, with all these nýmphí bustling around us, a new and horrifying thought strikes me. *Everyone in this room has already seen me bare.*

Dear goddesses above.

"Oy! Theron!" Kaël's voice booms from outside.

Theron exhales a long sigh. He leans down to me, still pinned beneath everything that just happened, and murmurs, "We'll meet tonight, my beautiful mate."

His gaze is smoldering, his arousal more than obvious. Then, with a reluctance that almost makes me laugh, he straightens and leaves the house. And just like that, he's gone, with a frustrated expression and a hard cock.

"They took him to the farthest stream from this one, Your Majesty," Naïa says as she helps me out of my dress.

We've arrived at a stream on the opposite side of Ávera. I still don't quite understand why Theron and I have to be separated for the preparations, but tradition is tradition. As long as it doesn't harm anyone, I'll go along with it.

Naïa folds my dress and hands it to a nearby nýmphá.

"What happens in the winter?" I ask, holding my hair in a loose fist as I dip my toes into the water. The coolness is a surprise, but not unbearable. "Do the mates still have to cleanse outside?"

Elder Aïna, standing nearby, brushes her paw over the crystals adorning another nýmphá. "In colder weather," she explains, "there are two options. First, the woman cleanses at home in warm water. Second, she dips quickly in the stream outside."

"Why would anyone choose outside when there's another option?" I ask, turning to face her fully. "Wouldn't it be easier to do this at home? All year round?"

Elder Aïna takes my hand in her paw. She steps into the stream, the water lapping just below her knees. Vólkin-style knees. For me, it will likely rise to my thighs.

"Mother Nature has four elements," she begins. "As her child, you must embrace them. The water you cleanse yourself in now is hers, created naturally and pure. It cleanses not only your body but your spirit."

I nod, stepping into the stream after her. The water is cool but invigorating, flowing around me gently.

"The second element is fire," Elder Aïna continues. "We will light a fire under the full moon. It symbolizes passion and your awakening." She gathers my hair in her paw, guiding me.

I dip beneath the surface, letting the water cover every part of me. With my eyes open, I take in the underwater world—the green moss carpeting the stones, the smooth pebbles beneath the current. It's beautiful.

Elder Aïna tugs my hair lightly, signaling me to rise. I break through the surface, the brisk air meeting my wet skin, and take a breath.

Mina and Essin rush to wrap me in soft furs before the shivers set in. The warmth is comforting, and I pull the layers tighter around myself. Mina's crystal necklace catches the sunlight, sending tiny flecks of light dancing around us.

"The third element is earth," Elder Aïna continues. "Theron will demonstrate his skill in energy transfer by creating a blue rose crown for you."

"A blue rose crown?" I echo, tilting my head. "Theron grew blue roses for me when we first met."

Elder Aïna hums in amusement and then chuckles. "Well,

then he's made this task even harder for himself. Now, he'll have to outdo himself to impress you."

A smile tugs at my lips. "Do I make a crown for him too?"

The idea of crafting a crown for Theron makes me smile wider. I can grow blue roses, and the thought of him with beautiful flowers adorning his head is . . . nice. He'd look so *pretty*.

But the moment the words leave my mouth, the air shifts. Every female around me freezes and turns to face me, their expressions ranging from confusion to outright horror. Each one stares at me from a different angle, as if trying to confirm they heard correctly. Nýmphí included.

Pinching the bridge of her snout, Elder Aïna sighs. "I'm almost afraid to ask what kind of traditions humans have these days."

I blink, completely baffled. "What did I say?"

Mina steps forward, her gentle smile trying to soothe the awkwardness as she begins leading me toward my home. "The entire purpose of this ritual," she explains, "is for *you* to awaken and for your mate to prove he's worthy of you."

"The goddesses may align two souls," Essin chimes in, "but the male must demonstrate his dedication, hard work, and sacrifice. Who would want a useless male?"

"How would a gift make Theron useless?" Am I missing something important here?

Naïa shakes her head. "You are a *woman*," she says.

"You *are* the gift!" Essin finishes with a dramatic huff, as if it's the most obvious thing in the world.

I should tell Theron to never, ever speak of my gift to him to anyone. For our safety.

51

AWAITING NIGHTFALL

"A crystal you are born. Yet a day shall come when you find a rose, not crimson, as men's songs tell, but deep as the endless blue of the sea. And in her, your soul shall awaken. In her, your destiny shall bloom."
—Ánya, holding newborn Theron

Theron

"I've never seen such a rose before!" Kaël gasps.

"My mate gifted it to me." I show off the most precious treasure I've ever received. I didn't expect one at all. The female is the gift, her very existence. Perhaps it's human culture for a female to do such a thing. But I love it, it's from her. Even if she gifted me a leaf spirit, I'd say thank you and cherish it forever.

Tonight, my mate and I will become one. Just the thought of it, of finally claiming her, of everything falling into place, sends heat coursing through me, unsheathing my cock. I've waited for this day for so long. Over four hundred years of yearning, of searching, of wondering when I would find the other half of my soul.

I stand in the stream with my bratya. Aeson is the first to step out of the water, his bright white fur glinting in the sunlight. Then Zephyr, Kaël, and finally me. Together, we shake the last of the water from our fur, and the droplets catch the light like scattered crystals.

I lift my gaze to the sky. The sun shines bright. The blooming season paints Ávera in different colors of nature. But this year, blue shines the brightest.

"The first of us to bond," Zephyr says, a smile tugging at his mouth as he rests his paw on my shoulder.

I nod in acknowledgment.

"It is a great honor, Theron," Aeson adds as he crosses his arms.

It is indeed. My mate is not only the Lidéřen from the prophecy but also the one destined to break the curse that has plagued us for generations. Pride swells in my chest. *My mate.*

"And we won't even be here to watch you celebrate your lives together!" Kaël whines, his tail flicking in frustration.

With a forceful sigh, I close the distance between us. Zephyr's paw falls to his side as I turn my full attention to Kaël.

"There won't be time for celebration," I say, my voice bitter. I wish it were different. Being the first bonded vólkin in centuries is an honor, but it comes with an unbearable weight. My mate and I carry the responsibility of starting a war—a war to end the suffering of this world. Where my ancestors chose complacency, we will act. Where they turned their backs, we will lead.

"Will you leave tomorrow?" Kaël asks after a moment of silence.

"Yes."

"After us?"

"Yes."

Our time joining together will be brief, as will any chance to enjoy the bond we've waited so long to form.

"The tsar's army waits, their ambush approaches. We cannot afford to wait. We must be ready. We must strike first and take them by surprise."

For centuries, we have trained as one, guided by raw strength and instinct. But now, Noël brings us something new. She transforms our chaos into precision, our instinct into strategy. She makes us more than brutal beasts.

The time of useless strikes is over. Tomorrow, we fight as a force united. Each warrior will carry more than raw strength into battle, they will carry purpose. Noël's vision has forged this into being, and from it, we have shaped three main forces:

Claw Force, the backbone of our strength, the fangs of our might. When they charge, the ground will quake beneath them, and nothing will stand in their path. Their purpose is to break and destroy.

Shade Force, the eyes in the shadows, the ears in the silence. They will see what others cannot, move where others dare not tread, and strike before the enemy even knows they are there.

Crystal Force, the healers and protectors, the salvation in the chaos. They will tend to the wounded, shield the weak, and save those who might otherwise be lost. The women and children we free may be hurt, and it will be Crystal Force that keeps them—and us—standing.

When we attack, the warriors will divide into packs, and each pack will carry the strength of all three forces: the might of the Claw, the cunning of the Shade, and the resilience of the Crystal.

This is the structure we bring to the battle ahead. No longer lost wolves, we are an army. Noël has given us this vision, and together, we will show the tsar's forces what it means when the vólkins rise united.

"Do you remember how Kaël tried to dig under the barrier to find his mate?" Aeson says, amused.

Kaël groans, rolling his eyes. "Oh, come on—"

"Only to discover the barrier continued underground," Zephyr adds with a chuckle.

A grin tugs at my mouth as I recall those days. We were frustrated, desperate, and willing to do anything to break free. It feels good to laugh about it now, even if the memory is painful.

"Before you decorate me," I say, opening and closing my paws, "I want to check on our 'visitor.'"

My fur is already dry, and soon, I'll be ready for my bratya to adorn me for my mate. As Elder Aïna explained to us during our bonding ritual lesson, males must always look their best for their mates, as a sign of honor and respect.

This is especially true for tonight. Until women awaken, they don't feel the bond as strongly as we do. And during the ritual, when the vólkin gives his vows, it is her choice whether to accept them or not.

Tonight, she will choose me.

I walk up to Gregor's house.

Though calling it "his house" feels like the wrong way to describe it. This is a vólkin home, grown for a woman who doesn't have a mate to create one for her. A skill this human could never master, no matter how long he lived.

Orïon stands near the entrance, his posture stiff and his expression dark. This is his punishment for reckless behavior, a fitting one.

"How's our guest?" I ask, stopping just outside the door. Gregor is asleep, snoring so loudly I don't need vólkin senses to notice.

"Still breathing," Orïon grunts. He's angry.

Not surprising. I don't think I've ever had a normal conversation with Orïon. Every exchange has felt like a competition, one I've won every time.

"Anything unusual about him?"

Orïon lets out a sharp *tsk*, his ears flicking in annoyance. "No," he finally says.

Fine. Nothing unusual it is.

"He's very talkative," Orïon adds after a moment.

I tilt my head. "What does he talk to you about?"

"Stupid nonsense, Theron," he bursts out. "Instead of training with the others, instead of preparing for war tomorrow like *everyone else*, I'm stuck here with this human! Standing around, listening to the *crap* that comes out of his mouth!"

"You were assigned to stay in Ávera with your pack," I say. "You're fulfilling a mission that is just as important as the rest."

His empty eye socket has healed, the scars from my claws permanent marks now. Within the vólkins, asserting dominance isn't new. It's part of who we are. Most of the time, we respect each other's achievements, keeping the balance Elder Aïna always preaches: "We are one big family, and we must treat each other as such."

But even in families, there are prideful warriors who can't resist the urge to challenge authority.

Orïon is one of them. If he were in my place, leading our kind, most of us would be dead by now. That's not speculation, it's fact. And it's why I'd never let him join us in the battle ahead, let alone lead.

Before Gregor arrived, he was tasked with scouting the nearby villages. Instead of returning with his patrolling brothers, as commanded, he struck out on his own. It took three warriors to drag him back to Ávera. Orïon has always been a loner, has always believed he can do everything by himself.

I've had my eyes on him for a few days now, since the farewell. Some of my warriors have been keeping me updated.

Orïon wants to do good, there's no doubting his intent, but his recklessness and foolish pride could destroy everything we've built. And I can't let that happen.

"Tonight, tell Gregor he can join the ritual from afar. My mate invites him," I say as I walk back to my bratya.

It is time to make myself even more handsome for my mate tonight.

52

A CUP OF BITTER CHOICE

"One day, you will walk alone into the dark, and you will think you are lost. But you won't be. The stars will light a path only you can see, and when you follow it, you will find arms waiting to carry you home."
—Eyleen Ársa to Noël, brushing her hair before bed

Noël

"This is for protection," Elder Aïna says as she slips a small trinket into my pocket.

I offer a quiet thank you as she does and ask, "Protection from what?"

"Under a full moon, ethereal beings are very sensitive," she explains. "And tonight, as you fully awaken, you will enter a state between human and spirit." She takes my hands in hers as Mina tugs at my hair, braiding it tightly.

My scalp burns, but I say nothing.

"Although," Elder Aïna continues, "you have already been in that state for some time now."

I nod, then wince when Naïa steadies my head so I won't

move. "Yes," I reply. "I've felt more sensitive . . . to everything around me."

"You see brighter colors?" Essin asks, leaning in.

"Y-es." I flinch as Mina pulls even tighter. Does it really need to be this tight?

"I'm sorry, Your Majesty," Mina says. "But the braid must hold perfectly for tonight!"

"Tonight, you'll seal the deal!" Essin grins. "Theron's seed must take root within your belly. That's the final part of the union!"

I glance at Elder Aïna, seeking reassurance, and she nods.

My chest tightens. I rise from the cushion as soon as Mina finishes the braid. My heart aches. Physically *aches*.

"What's wrong?" Naïa's worried eyes search mine.

"Are you having doubts?" Essin adds, her tone softening.

I shake my head. No, I'm not having doubts. I . . . want to be a mother, to raise a daughter surrounded by love and freedom. I picture her running through open fields, as carefree as a petal carried on the wind. But I know that dream isn't possible. Not now.

A beautiful nýmphá with red-brown hair approaches, carrying a cup in her small hands.

"Mates who didn't want more children would drink this," Elder Aïna says. "It prevents the seed from taking root."

The room falls silent.

War is coming. Tomorrow, we'll be on the move.

I can't bear a child now. I can't bring a new life into such a cruel, uncertain world.

Tears well up in my eyes as I take the cup from the nýmphá's hands. My fingers tremble as I raise it to my lips. I'll have to drink this every moon until the war is over. And it hasn't even begun yet.

Mina, Naïa, and Essin lower their eyes, giving me the space I need.

The bitter liquid slides down my throat, and the first tear spills over, tracing a hot path down my cheek. I rest my palm on my belly, shut my eyes, and turn my face away. The ache in my chest is unbearable.

It hurts to know I can't have a baby now, or a pup if I bore a son. But I can't have either. Not a beautiful girl or a handsome pup. Not while the world burns around us.

The tears fall freely, and I don't try to stop them. My heart cries with me. Warmth surrounds me, and when I open my eyes, I'm startled to see Elder Aïna's arms wrapping me in a gentle embrace. She holds me close, her fur soft against my skin.

It's been so long since I've been held like this.

I collapse into her, burying my face in her chest as the tears come harder. Loud, painful sobs rack my body, and I let them.

"You have made the right choice, child," Elder Aïna murmurs into my hair.

She's never called me *child* before. Always *Ethereal Leader*, *Lidéřen*, or *Your Majesty*—titles that carried distance, making me feel like I stood on a pedestal far from everyone else.

But this single word holds a warmth and closeness I didn't realize I needed. And I do, truly.

"Thank you," I whisper into her fur, clinging to her like an actual child. Elder Aïna has been more than a mentor to me. In some ways, she's filled the void my mother left behind. "Thank you for everything." I let go of her and turn to the others.

Mina, Naïa, Essin, and the nýmphí stand quietly.

"Thank you, all of you." My voice is steady despite the tears still streaking my cheeks. I wipe them away with the fabric of my dress and ground myself in the strength of their presence. "Thank you for supporting me, understanding me, and standing by my side. I will fulfill my purpose and make this world a place worth bringing a child into. I will protect all of you with my life."

Essin bursts into tears, rushing forward to embrace me. The force of her hug almost knocks me back, but I hold her just as fiercely. Mina and Naïa exchange hesitant glances before I smile at them, inviting them silently to join. They step forward, their initial reserve melting away as we fall into a shared embrace. For a while, we hold each other, whispering soft words of comfort to one another. This is my family. My people. I will protect them. Ávera is mine, this whole land is mine. I will protect them all.

The girls didn't even ask if I'd want to go bare during the ritual. They already knew the answer. Apparently, every woman who has ever been here walked bare. I can't imagine doing such a thing. Maybe I'm just too modest for that. I did agree to go barefoot, though. That's . . . something.

The sun is setting, its golden light slipping behind Ávera's tree line and painting the forest in shades of amber and shadow. My nerves are on edge. Tonight, I will bond with Theron. Forever.

This isn't a human wedding where you can run from an abusive husband or "accidentally" poison him. Here, we intertwine our souls.

"The rest of the ritual I'll guide you through step by step," Elder Aïna says as she adjusts the fabric of my gown.

I nod, turning to look at myself in the water basin.

Even with my eyes still slightly red and puffy, I'm beautiful.

My hair is long and perfectly braided, the length adorned with a few blue roses I grew myself, their petals bright against my dark strands. My new gown fits perfectly. It's looser than what I usually wear, but it's elegant and comfortable.

For a moment, I see the faintest hint of my mother in my reflection. Nina always said we looked like two drops of water.

I wonder if she's doing well. I hope she's not worried.

I also hope that Mother will be here too. Seeing me like this, beautiful and almost bonded with a great vólkin. I look to my right, half expecting the dove to appear on the windowsill.

I wish you could see me now, Mother.

Four nýmphí approach, carrying a length of white, almost translucent fabric draped across their arms.

"What's that?" I ask.

"A veil," Mina says with a warm smile.

"It will protect you from ill wishes," Naïa adds.

The nýmphí form a square around me and move as if dancing. Together, they lift the veil into the air, holding it high above me. Slowly, it floats down, landing over my head and covering most of my body.

Everyone in the room steps forward, each holding a candle adorned with carvings. The warm glow dances, lighting the room against the falling night.

"With this fire," Elder Aïna begins, "we will light the fire of your awakening."

"You will walk in the middle," Essin explains, her tone brimming with excitement, "and the four of us will be by your sides."

"And we, Ethereal Leader, will follow behind you," one of the nýmphí says with a kind smile.

Elder Aïna steps closer. "The woman shall walk a moonlit path, for all the witness circle to see."

"A circle . . . as in the circle of life?" I ask.

"You learn fast," she says with a broad smile, and I notice the pride in her voice.

I'm left alone in my home. Maminka and systritsy went ahead to ensure everything is in place. It might not have been the best idea to leave me by myself. Alone with my thoughts. My thoughts . . . they scare me sometimes. They pull me into places so dark I barely recognize myself. Sometimes, it feels like something takes over, whispering things I can't ignore. I was never a sensitive person, not much of a positive one either. I've always been running, always trying to meet someone else's expectations. My mother expected me to be the best at everything. My commanders were always watching, waiting for me to make a mistake so they could justify kicking me out. And the soldiers? They saw me as competition more than anything else. I've always felt the need to prove myself. Here, it's no different.

But what I've been through so far? It's nothing compared to what's coming. Now, I'm a leader—a leader of the whole fucking world. *Vathéria.* Do I take the north too? Two continents. Two worlds. How many lives will be lost? How many wolves will suffer?

What if I fail? Will I survive? If I die, Theron dies too.

I've never been in a war. The last one was lifetimes ago. Did my mother know she was preparing me for this? Did she ever think I'd end up leading armies? That I'd want to kill the tsar?

I do want to kill him. Not just for what he's done to Vathéria, but for what he did to her. He raped her. Over and over again. I'll fulfill her wish. When I get to him, I'll cut off his cock and make him hold it as he watches himself burn, bleeding into the fire. Yes. That's exactly what I'll do.

Here they are again. My dark thoughts.

But tonight, I must be free of them. I must let my mind find peace, if only for a while. Not the best timing, considering tomorrow I might die. But . . . I might not. It's not all as bad as I fear.

Yes. I'll free women, children, elders. I'll break their chains of suffering. I'm healthy. Stronger than I've ever been. I'm surrounded by people—vólkins—who trust me, who stand with me. And I know more about my mother now than I ever did when she was alive.

And then there's Theron.

My big, sweet wolf. Reserved most of the time, but always kind. He takes care of me. He's strong and steadfast. He never puts me down or tells me I can't do something. He didn't laugh or call me insane for wanting a war. He encouraged it. A smile tugs at my lips.

Maybe he's just as insane as I am. I miss him. The past few days, we've barely had a moment to be together.

Heavy thudding reaches my ears. Footsteps. Elder Aïna and the others. I stand, smoothing my dress as I inhale. The blue roses in our home seem to glow brighter than ever tonight.

It's time.

53

THE NIGHT THE BLUE ROSE
CLAIMED HER THRONE

"She will not slip quietly into this world, Ándor. She will be carved out by blood and broken by destiny. One day, she will wear a crown not of gold, but of thorns. And when she binds herself to him, the world will bleed to make way."
—Eyleen Ársa to Ándor, resting her hand over her belly

Noël

The moon hangs high in the dark sky, bright and beautiful, almost at its peak.

We walk slowly toward the sacred glade. Elder Aïna and Mina walk to my right, while Naïa and Essin walk to my left. Each holds a candle in their paws, their flames flickering in the night air. Two nýmphí follow close behind, holding the edges of my veil, and the rest trail silently after us. My heart pounds, and I feel every step I take. Literally.

Every blade of grass beneath my bare feet, every small rock pressing into my soles—I feel them all, as if each demands my attention. I can count them as I walk.

This isn't normal.

And I am *so* hungry.

The weather is perfect, as if the goddesses planned this night just for me. I'm grateful. Even through the veil, I can make out every detail. Every leaf on every tree is crisp. I think I hear the trees humming, soft and melodic, as if singing a song only I can hear.

This has never happened before. What else will I see when I'm fully awakened?

I fix my gaze forward, and as we walk, the sacred glade comes into view. Hundreds of vólkins are gathered, just as Elder Aïna said they would be. They stand tall and proud, encircling the glade in silence. Even the pups are silent. Everyone's waiting for me. And in the center, Theron.

He stands near the giant stone. My breath catches as I look at him. His broad chest is adorned with red circles and lines, symbols painted onto his fur. Blue roses are woven into his thick mane where they glow against his dark fur. That must have been Zephyr's touch. It has his style. I recognize my gift to him, the lush blue rose, nestled behind his ear. A smile stretches my lips.

How handsome he looks. Like a god of nature, standing there as if the earth shaped him with careful hands. Then he turns to me, and I freeze mid-step. His eyes pierce through the distance, locking onto mine with an intensity that steals the air from my lungs. I swallow hard.

"Keep walking," Mina whispers.

I force my legs to move, each step slow. The fabric of my dress brushes against my skin, and I'm acutely aware of how little I'm wearing. There's nothing beneath it—no cloth to hold my breasts, no undergarments. My arousal dampens my curls, and I bite the inside of my cheek to keep from faltering. Oh goddesses, his gaze. It's focused entirely on me, as if nothing else exists.

We're still far from the glade—at least a twenty-minute walk away—but I see him. I *feel* him. I feel his breath, his heart, his hazel eyes. I feel his fur, so thick and soft on his skin. And I know he feels me too. There is no shame in being attracted to him. This is how nature made us. How the goddesses intended us to be. Everything has a reason. Every life and every death. I arch my back and lift my chin. Why should I feel anything but pride?

I am Noël Ársa. No. I am *more* than Noël Ársa.

I am the one who will restore the balance. I am strong. I am smart. I am *ready*. It's not the result that defines us, not the end of the path.

It's the journey.

The journey that *enlightens*.

The candle flames around me roar higher, growing wild and violent. My fingertips burn with heat, as if I'm holding fire itself. The moon above looks down on me, and I *feel* everything. The air, clear yet heavy, the ground beneath my feet, and the charge in the atmosphere. As we near the glade, the gathered vólkins part to let us pass.

Theron's gaze is still fixed on me. His bratya stand at his side. A light breeze picks up, swirling fallen leaves and petals into a violent, dancing storm. Leaf spirits flit through the chaos to clear my path.

My step falters, my body sways as searing pain shoots through my forehead. It feels like it's about to explode. Was the tea bad? Did I not drink enough water today? To my side, Mina isn't urging me forward. None of them are. They're all bowing.

Heat spreads through me. It's as if my feet, my knees, my entire being is aflame. Theron takes a step closer, his expression shifting, but I lift my hand to stop him, and he does.

What is happening to me?

I close my eyes, inhale slowly, desperate for calm and to steady the storm of flames. But the pain in my forehead grows more insistent. Then, behind my closed lids, I don't see darkness, but light. Vivid, blinding colors—pinks, greens, blues, and purples—paint everything in front of me. I sway, knees buckling. I almost fall, but I catch myself. My hand moves to my forehead. It isn't smooth. A gasp escapes me. I feel strange bumps beneath my fingers. *Crystals.*

My nails tap lightly against them, the sound clear and true. I hear it so loudly. My eyes fly open. The tall stands around the glade are ablaze with angry fire—fire that Elder Aïna hasn't yet lit. And I hear it.

Murmurs. Voices.

Not from the vólkins. The glade is silent. Everyone is silent. The voices come from the forest, from the shadows, from the wild. Animals? I don't know. But they're calling.

I turn to Theron, and what I see stops my steps. He looks *delighted.* A warm smile in his eyes. What?

My gaze shifts to everyone around us. Their heads are lowered, gazes fixed firmly on the ground. Theron walks over to me, but he doesn't say a word. We now stand a mere few steps from the glade. He lifts a paw and traces his pads gently over the crystals on my forehead through the thin veil. It doesn't hurt anymore. I follow his gaze as it turns back toward the glade.

The entire area *glows.*

The enormous stone at the center—taller even than Theron —is alive with light. Its ancient carvings pulse with energy, shining brighter and brighter. The grass around it shimmers, the blue roses at its base emit an ethereal radiance, and the air hums with power.

A loud, bone-chilling howl suddenly rises from the forest. The sound echoes around us, primal and raw, sending a shiver through my body. I whirl around, searching for its source, my heart pounding. The nýmphí kneel, their heads bowed. The vólkins are still bowed as well, lowered to the earth. Everyone is silent.

Six figures appear before the glade, their presence taking me completely by surprise. Six beautiful women—*goddesses*—just as Elder Aïna once described. The six goddesses who have never appeared in human history.

And now, they stand before me.

At the forefront is Goddess Láda Veléša, the goddess of leadership and war. She is tall, commanding, and she radiates power. She looks just as Elder Aïna told me she would. Her braided hair is threaded with golden ribbon. She wears a flowing black gown adorned with red and gold embroidery depicting roses and twisting vines. Her headscarf is tied under her chin, the crescent moon embroidered at its center catching the glow of the glade. A circular halo surrounds her head, a weave of swords and vines. In her many hands, she carries her symbols. A sickle gleams in one hand, a sword glints in another. A scale rests in the third hand, a symbol of balance and judgment.

And in her fourth, she holds a small shield emblazoned with the blue rose insignia, the mark of divine protection. Her gaze locks onto mine, piercing my soul. This is the goddess who spoke to me in the darkness. I feel it.

And now, she is here.

Theron bows to the goddesses, and I follow.

"The Lidéřen never lowers her head." Láda Veléša's voice echoes.

A shiver races down my spine, and I straighten, meeting her gaze.

"Good," she says. "You have awakened before the ritual. That is a good sign."

My hand moves to my forehead, brushing over the cool crystals. They are *real*. I have crystals now.

"Why has this happened?" I ask and take a step forward.

"You are a child of nature, and you have understood its core," Láda Veléša says. She lifts the hand holding her sword, and the blade glimmers. A wave of wind rushes around me, removing my veil.

The sword in her hand is silver as moonlight, sharp as the claw of the mightiest vólkin, with patterns of roses spiraling around the handle.

"Lift your chin, ethereal being," she commands. "You are the chosen one. The one to be knelt before. The one who will restore the balance this world has lost through time."

I stand taller, my eyes drawn to the braids framing her face. Thick and beautiful, her braids, adorned with blue and red roses, cascade over her shoulders and chest.

"A leader must bear the heaviest burdens," she continues, "and wield both strength and mercy. In your hands lies the power to unite or destroy. Choose wisely."

With grace and wind, she extends the sword toward me.

I raise both arms and take it from her. The blade feels impossibly heavy at first, but as my grip tightens around the hilt, the weight disappears. It's as if the sword was made for me —it feels like home.

"Thank you for the gift and your wise words," I say, shifting the blade into one hand.

I raise the sword high, and the flames surrounding the glade surge upward, wild and untamed. They roar to life, higher and higher, lighting the night with their fierce dance.

Then I lower the blade, and the flames respond, quieting their rage, as if submitting to my will.

The other goddesses don't say a word, their gazes fixed upon me. Every goddess is different. Each radiates her own essence—power, flame, storm, soil, water, night—yet together, they blur into something greater, a circle of power older than the world I know. They are contrasts made whole: fierce and nurturing, storm and serenity, guardians and destroyers, all woven into a single breathless silence.

I turn to Theron, his crystals grow so bright.

"With the goddesses as our witnesses," I say loudly for the wolves in the forest to hear, "I want to hear your vows."

Though I awakened before the ritual began, I want this moment. This is my choice: to accept or reject, to seal fate or shatter it.

Theron straightens, his posture firm. He lifts his paw to his heart. "Noël, you are my soul," he says, the words reverberating through the air. "The air I breathe tastes of you, and the blood in my veins burns for you. My life is yours to command, my strength yours to wield. I vow to stand between you and every shadow, every enemy, and every spirit who dares to so much as think ill of you. I will hunt before you hunger, and I will bleed for your wounds." His voice grows softer, as if the entire world has faded, leaving only the two of us. "You are my Lidéřen, my heart, my body, and my soul. My reason to exist."

He lowers his paw from his chest and takes a step closer. "I vow to be yours, wholly and eternally, until the earth crumbles beneath your feet."

That is a beautiful vow. So raw and so *him*. If I agree, we're sealed together. If I agree, we bond completely and set off to war tomorrow.

I will never be free of duties. Free to chase my own choices and dreams. I might never have a child of my own. I might die before completing my purpose. I might even die tomorrow.

I lift the sword and point it at his heart. Theron doesn't move. He stares quietly into my eyes as I press the tip of the blade through his fur until I feel the resistance of his skin. The slightest pressure, and it gives way. If his heart stops beating, he will die. He isn't immortal.

The blade draws a thin line of blood from his chest, and he grins. That familiar, confident grin.

And I grin back.

Theron brushes his thumb over the blood, then reaches out to let it hover over my chest. "Do you accept, my little dove?"

I lower the sword to my own heart, piercing the skin with a sharp sting. Blood paints the fabric of my dress, and I lift my thumb to collect it.

Reaching forward, I press my blood against his chest, right over his heart. "I do," I say, my grin stretching wider as his matches mine. Together, we mark each other's hearts, sealing the bond with blood.

Mother, Father, I am bonded to my mate.

"The rose," Láda Veléša says, "and the guardian."

Theron and I stand before the goddesses, waiting.

"From the garden of Éva, six flowers bloom," she continues, her many hands moving in one direction. "The blue rose will lead them."

Six flowers? Is this a clue? My heart pounds as I focus on her every word.

"The peony will guard," she says, and a lush, pink peony appears in one of her hands. "The chamomile will heal." A gentle breeze carries the familiar scent of chamomile. It reminds me of the tea my mother used to make when I was ill. "The yarrow will fight." One of her swords takes on a burgundy hue as she speaks. "The rowan berry will know." Another hand forms small, red berries, glistening like drops of blood. "And the lotus will see." From her eyes, a white flower blooms, pure and radiant.

This is it. Everything falls into place.

I am the blue rose—the leader. The peony is the sentinel. The chamomile, the healer. The yarrow, the warrior. The rowan berry, the scholar. And the lotus, the seer.

The six who will restore balance.

Láda Veléša's gaze sharpens. "You will find them, Blue Rose, and together, you will bring harmony to this fractured world."

54

THE SEALED BOND

"Only when soul and soul are bound does true power wake.
Half a soul can bleed, but a whole soul can command the earth,
the winds, and the stars themselves."
—Mother of All, whispered into the roots of the first blue rose

Noël

"I've waited centuries for this. Tell me you feel it too," Theron breathes.

Carefully, he sets me on the table in our home. We wanted to spend this night here— one last time—before we leave tomorrow.

"I feel it, Theron." My heart races, and the weight of his eyes on me makes it harder to breathe. The need is overwhelming, literally unbearable. Heat spreads through me. Rubbing my thighs together doesn't help, it only makes it worse. Is this how he felt the moment we first met?

It's impossible to focus. The only thought in my mind is him. How big he is, how strong he is, how charming. I have to touch him. I reach for him with shaking hands, bury them in the fur of his mane, and I pull him to me.

Breathing long, uneven breaths, he leans in.

"Theron," I whisper. I can't wait another second. My hands fumble to remove the gown, and I pull it off as quickly as I can, my breath coming in short, desperate pants.

It's all too much.

Paws trembling, Theron grips my shoulders, his claws pressing just enough to make my skin tingle. He leans down to my neck while my gown slides off the edge of the table, damp with my arousal. Goddesses.

His broad chest rises and falls, each breath frantic and heavy, before he slowly lowers himself to the floor.

"You're on your knees," I pant, barely able to keep my voice steady.

"I . . ." His chest heaves as thick, white precum drips from the tip of his pulsing cock. " . . . am." His snout brushes against my knee, his warm breaths ghosting over my skin. The heat makes me shiver.

His paws grip the edge of the table, and his claws dig into the wood. With a loud crack, the table splinters beneath his strength, shattering in a second.

Before I can gasp in surprise, his arms are around me, catching me. We freeze, staring into each other's eyes, both wide in shock.

Is he even stronger now that I've awakened?

"I think I am." His eyes drop to his fist as if testing the strength in his paw.

"Did I say that out loud?" I ask, leaning back slightly to look at him.

"No, you didn't."

Can you hear my thoughts?

"I feel the confusion," he replies.

What?

"I can't feel yours, though," I say. "Shouldn't things like that be mutual? Since . . . our souls . . ."

"I don't know . . . Elder Aïna never mentioned anything like this." Theron's voice is strained as he pulls me close. His pulse is wild, matching the frantic rhythm of mine.

My body moves on its own, instinct taking over. I climb onto him, my knees resting on his powerful thighs. Control is slipping through my fingers. I'm at my *limit*.

Theron's snout brushes over my breasts, his cold, wet nose teasing my skin. His arms tighten around my lower back to hold me against him as my arousal slicks down my inner thighs and pools on his.

A small gasp escapes my lips as his fangs trace along my ribs, sending a shiver down my entire body.

Then, he sinks them in, piercing my skin. The sting draws a cry from me. "Why—"

Before I can finish, his tongue glides over the fresh wound, lapping up the blood as it trickles down my side. "Your blood is so sweet," he murmurs against me.

I feel dizzy, whatever is happening to me pulls me under. With a grin and hooded eyes, I grab the styled fur on his head and pull him back. "Is it?"

He hums in agreement, and only now do I notice that the red marks on his chest don't paint my skin. I should be a mess right now. *Why does it even matter?* I wonder with a chuckle.

"Your soul is light," Theron says with a half smile before he returns to teasing my chest with his tongue.

Pleasure overtakes me, and I lean my head back, barely able to hold on to him.

His impossibly hard cock is trapped between his stomach and my muscles. I will finally know what it feels like to have him inside me.

I don't know why, but I'm bold tonight. Is it because of my

crystals? Is it because I feel so powerful I could break a table myself?

I meet his beautiful eyes, then slide my hands down to his chest and gently push him back. Without hesitation, Theron complies, leaning back on his elbows. His gaze is intense, hooded, and majestic.

He is just so unbelievably majestic.

My navel presses against his hard shaft when I lean forward. The heat between us is overwhelming. Nuzzling his jaw, I plant small kisses along his snout, each one longer and softer than the last. The need to consume him, to have every part of him, pulses through me. Theron nuzzles me back, and my head swims, as though I've downed an entire bottle of ale in one gulp.

We shift together, rolling to our sides on the wooden floor, tangled in each other. I lie between the roses I grew, the soft petals caressing my skin as his arms wrap around me. He nips at my neck and leaves a trail of tingling pleasure. Along with my own dripping arousal, I feel his warm drops falling between my thighs.

Our most intimate parts are so close it makes my breath hitch.

Theron moves even closer, until his powerful body presses against mine as he takes my thigh in his giant paw, lifts it higher, and opens me farther to him.

With my leg resting on his waist, his shaved claws tease my entrance. A whimper escapes me as he slides the tip of his finger inside, achingly slow. It's not the first time he's done this, but I still feel exposed, vulnerable in a way that makes my pulse race. Before my thoughts can spiral, Theron pushes deeper, and my back arches.

A gasp slips from my lips, my eyes squeezing shut.

"Eyes on me, my mate," Theron murmurs, his voice deep and raspy.

I force my eyes open to meet his.

Goddesses, he's so demanding.

"Your eyes should always be on *me*." His tone is firm as his tongue traces slowly over my neck, leaving a trail of heat behind.

Having him in me and on me is a pleasure I welcome. He keeps as much contact as possible, as though he can't stand a single part of me not being his. And it makes me happy—truly happy.

Goose bumps rise across my skin as his fingers curl inside me, and then he adds another, pushes deeper. My mind blanks from the sensation of being so full.

Theron growls low in his throat, his body radiating heat, and adds another finger. The stretch is too much, but the way he moves—pumping into me—sends waves of pleasure coursing through my body.

My toes curl, and I can't stop the cries escaping me as Theron pants, his breath heavy and hot against my face. His muscles flex with every movement of his arm, and I don't know where to look anymore.

"Noël," he breathes as he withdraws his paw from me.

I hum in response, and my body clenches around the emptiness he leaves behind.

I expect him to lick his slick fingers like he always does, but instead, he moves them to his groin. My eyes follow the motion, watching as he strokes himself down to his swollen knot and lets out a low hiss. His nearly red cock glistens, now coated with my arousal, and goddesses, it's so alluring. Heat rushes to my face as I tear my gaze away, only to meet his. His pupils are so blown, they nearly swallow his irises entirely.

"Can I . . ." he pants, his voice shaky.

I nod, breathless just as he is. This is so fascinating. So overwhelming.

I'm about to feel him. Inside.

He leans forward, his hips pressing closer to mine. "If you want me to stop, just say it."

"Alright," I whisper, quivering as I shift my hips toward him —just a little.

He growls low in his throat, his paw grips my thigh while the other wraps around my waist. The tip of his cock slides over my entrance, teasing and slick.

I can't help but clench, the anticipation unbearable.

"Relax your muscles," he breathes, and I can see the battle raging in his gaze as he fights for control.

My heart pounds in my chest, but I force myself to take a breath, willing my body to comply. Slowly, he pushes in.

Oh dear goddesses.

I clench again, this time around him, and his sharp hiss pierces the air. His fangs glint in the blue light of my crystals as he speaks through gritted teeth.

"Please," he begs, rough and desperate.

My hands instinctively weave into his fur, holding on as he moves his hips, each thrust pressing him deeper.

His grip on me tightens, his claws just shy of digging into my skin, and the tension in my body feels like it's about to snap. The stretch burns, but it's so impossibly good, I can't stop the moans spilling from my lips. He's not even fully inside yet, but it feels like he's about to split me in half.

"You're in," I manage to whisper between shaky breaths.

"I am," he responds, his voice just as unsteady.

"It's . . . ah," I gasp, unable to form anything more coherent.

"It is," he growls, before pushing farther into me. His pace quickens, and with every thrust, my moans grow more frantic.

My body has been completely taken over, trembling and weak, as the intense pleasure consumes me. My gaze blurs, my mind unable to focus on anything but the sensation of him filling me.

With another deep growl, he shifts us, thrusting into me as

he moves. His arm slides beneath my head to cradle it gently as he rests his weight partially on top of me. The contrast of his strength and his tenderness sends another wave of warmth through me.

Suddenly, Theron pulls out, his entire body tense as a guttural growl rumbles through him. His muscles flex, and he leans heavily against me, his breath ragged.

The sudden emptiness makes me . . . sad? Like a part of me has been taken out. What just happened?

Theron pants against my neck, his arms wrapped tightly around me as if grounding himself as he whispers, "I'm sorry. I'm so sorry."

Sorry? "Why?" I ask, turning my face toward him, searching his gaze.

"I . . ." He exhales sharply, his breath still uneven. "I found release too fast."

Before I can process his words, he stands, lifting me in his arms with my legs straddling him. It's only then that I feel it— the warmth pooling between my thighs, the slick mess dripping onto the floor from my arse. Theron nuzzles me as he walks, holding me close. With every step, his fur brushes against my clit and sends small sparks of pleasure through me. I'm dazed, needy, and completely lost in him. I don't mind that he found release too soon.

55

SLICK FLOORS AND VOLKIN ROARS

"Even the fiercest bond wilts when the winds of war blow, Rose
and Guardian. Hold fast to each other."
—Elder Aïna, during the bonding ritual

Theron

I can feel her thoughts. She's disappointed.

What kind of male am I to disappoint my mate? After
centuries of control, after seeking release countless times
over the past four hundred years, I can't even hold myself back?

But she's so tight. So beautiful, lying between the most
precious blue roses. It drives me mad. I nearly lost it the
moment I was inside her, just the tip, and I was already on the
edge. Goddesses, give me strength. I swear I'll leave more offerings. I spilled my release on the floor. I didn't want to do it
inside her. Not yet. I want her to take my knot, to feel me fully,
to tremble beneath me as I bring her to the peak of pleasure.
My mate. My sweet mate.

I'm so sorry.

She's nestled in my arms as I carry her to our nest. Having

our first time on the floor wasn't what I planned, but something in my—our—minds changed. Instinct overtook plans.

Even though I only found release moments ago, I'm already hard again, swollen with need. I lay her on the furs, and for a moment, I can only stare. She is beyond beauty. My Noël, my little dove, is a goddess of both strength and desire.

The urge to be inside her again is unbearable. My shaft throbs at the thought of it. Taking a slow breath, I rise to my knees. She looks so small beneath me. A furless little dove, with dark eyes and curls between her muscled thighs. Hooded eyes, flushed cheeks, legs spread, waiting for me to make her mine.

And I will. That is my intent.

"I'm going to devour you," I groan. Before she can finish her gasp, I slide my cock into her swollen little cunt.

She slaps a hand over her mouth, stifling the breathless moan that escapes her lips.

I push her hand away with my snout and growl in her ear, "I want to hear you." And then I start moving.

I thrust into her, dragging her tight, slick heat around me as she grips my fur. The sounds we make—the wet, desperate slap of skin, the broken gasps leaving her lips—will be the end of me. She will be the end of me.

One arm wrapped around her waist, my other braced against the furs above her head, I lift her, then thrust faster, harder. I pull her up in time with every drive of my hips, forcing her to take me deeper. Every time she meets my swollen knot, she holds her breath.

"Theron," she pants, eyes glazed, nearly closed.

"Mine, Noël." I snarl the words, a primal claim, and I lose myself in her. My breath is ragged, saliva slipping past my lips and onto my mate's breasts. The droplets slide down her skin to pool in the hollow of her throat before rolling to the furs beneath her. The faster I move, the faster they fall. "Always mine," I growl. "From the moment you were born, you were mine." Another deep, guttural growl tears from me, vibrating against her skin as I rut into her like the beast I am.

"Ye"—she struggles to form words—"sss." Her beautiful crystals shine bright, nearly blinding me.

Yes, yes, yes. Mine.

Her abs tense every time I thrust. Her cries are breaking apart, ruined and perfect. *Because of me.* I drag my tongue along the curve of her throat, tasting the salt of her sweat, then I grin against her ear. "And, now."

With a final, brutal thrust, I force my knot into her, and the world goes white.

A violent snarl rips from my chest as I lock us together, as her body clenches down, so tight. It burns. The pressure is excruciating. My vision tunnels, black and red and pure instinct. My knees nearly give out, my entire body shakes.

Goddesses above.

I grip her hips so hard I know she'll bruise, but I need her to feel this, to feel me, to know she is mine.

"The knot," she chokes out, her voice barely there, her body wrecked beneath me. Her lashes flutter, wet with tears.

"The knot," I echo, dragging my teeth along her shoulder, sucking and biting.

We breathe each other's breaths, her gasps feeding my hunger, my groans feeding her release. I spill deep inside her, my body shuddering as her own pleasure detonates. She jerks, spasms, and milks me for everything I have. Her body takes everything from me. Her soul sings to mine.

And I answer.

My forehead presses against hers as I hold her tight, my claws digging into her skin, keeping her exactly where she belongs. This is how it should be.

Her belly swells with my seed, rounding before my eyes. A low growl rumbles in my chest as I watch her body take everything I've given. Too good. Too much. It can't be real. And yet, it is.

"Look how good you're taking me," I breathe.

"I . . . I . . ." my Noël gasps, her gaze unfocused, hazed with pleasure.

I trace my tongue over her face, soothing her. Vólkin semen is thicker than human, as Elder Aïna once explained. It clings to the walls of the female's canal and locks the knot in place. And I want it to stay there forever. I'll take her again. And again.

"I thought I might meet my mother," she murmurs with a smile as she lies boneless beneath me.

"And I thought I'd meet mine," I grin, nuzzling her.

She traces her fingers over her swollen belly. "I look like I'm with child."

"One day," I whisper. Still buried deep inside her, I shift us, pulling her into my arms and lying beside her before exhaustion claims me. If I don't, I'll collapse on top of her. I reach for more furs and tuck them around her so she's warm and comfortable.

"I thought your tongue was good," my mate mumbles before she quickly buries her reddening face in my chest. "What am I saying!!"

I chuckle, tugging her closer. My knot is slowly relaxing, so I shift my hips just a little.

She shudders.

So eager and slick. I move my hips back and forth. *I could do this forever.*

My mate moves her hips with mine, and I lean closer, half atop her, half sinking into the furs, unwilling to let her go. Then, a noise.

Both our heads snap toward the entrance of our home. With a sigh, I force myself to relax. "Come in."

The door opens on five nýmphí who bow to both of us before stepping around the mess I made on the floor and moving straight toward our nest. My mate's horrified gaze meets mine. She is so amusing to me.

"The Lidéřen must heal before dawn," one of the nýmphí says, crouching beside us.

I huff, tightening my hold around my mate, wrapping my arms, legs, and tail around her, locking her to me. Still buried deep inside her. "I can heal her."

Two of the nýmphí sigh before kneeling beside Noël. "If you do that, noble guardian, you will continue mating until dawn," one says, opening a small jar that smells of crushed herbs.

"While that is a good thing," the other adds, reaching out and gripping my tail.

I jerk violently, a growl tearing from me. My tail is sensitive.

The nýmphá does not flinch. "Tomorrow, we leave for war. So, please."

My instincts war against reason. It is true, if I stay inside her, I might rot in my mate for the rest of our days. But that is not a bad thing.

I don't want to pull out so soon.

"Theron, they're right." My mate sighs as she pulls away from me.

"I can apply the medicine."

The two nýmphí shake their heads in unison. "We will."

And before I can protest, they begin unwrapping me from her completely.

56

FROM THE SOIL THEY RISE

Afterthat night, the bonded woke earlier than usual, their hearts heavy with what lay ahead. Even though Ávera's air was always crisp and fresh, it was thick with tension as they met the warriors preparing to depart on their missions. Kaël, Zephyr, and Aeson stood ready, their hunts complete, their offerings laid out for the newly bonded mates—fresh fruits, fat boars, charged crystals, and flowers. At the edge of Ávera's ancient woods, they exchanged their final farewells before departing with their teams.

Theron knew this moment was inevitable. He knew he might meet them again one day, or perhaps he never would. But he had chosen wisely, and he trusted his brothers, not bound to him by blood but by soul. Parting didn't come easily. They had lived lifetimes together, grown under the same stars, trained side by side from sundown to dawn, hunted to feed their people, mourned their families. They had shed tears as pups and as warriors, and now, for the first time, they had to separate.

Kaël wept. His shoulders shook as he said his goodbyes. Zephyr sighed heavily, as if this moment might crush him.

Aeson stood silent, but his clenched fists betrayed his pain. They locked eyes with one another, a silent vow passing between them. They would survive, find the other five, and one day, they would reunite.

Theron clung to that hope, even as the ache in his chest threatened to consume him. His little dove stood by his side, sharing his pain. She, too, had come to like these warriors. They were the family she never had.

That morning, as a tradition of the newly bonded demanded, Noël and Theron planted a tree near their home. With hands and paws pressed into the soil, they whispered a promise: One day, their heirs would feast on the fruit it bore and run free beneath the open sky. Perhaps one day, their little girl or their little pup would run through these lands. Perhaps they would see the beauty of the world their parents fought for and eat the fruits of a healed land.

It was a gesture of gratitude to Mother Nature and a symbol of the future they hoped to create.

But the air was restless, not yet at peace. The birds sang songs of war, their melodies distracting in the morning quiet of Ávera. The Vólkins stirred, restless for the days ahead. Who could rest when the world was on the brink of change? And who could sleep after witnessing the goddesses? Their presence inspired faith in some, fear in others, and awe in all.

The females clutched their young, while the elders spoke of good omens. At the forefront, the warriors stood tall and strong, ready to set off. The Claw, the Shade, and the Crystal were prepared, standing with their packs in rows of four.

Noël and Theron scanned the army of Vólkins, their hearts swelling with pride. The warriors were a sight to behold— broad, tall, and brimming with strength. Many were eager, longing to see the world beyond the barrier, yearning to find their destined mates. But beneath their pride and want lay a quiet fear.

How could they not be afraid? They had spent their lives behind the safety of the barrier, sheltered from the unknown dangers beyond. Yet, no warrior would let that fear take over. The call to find their mate—their other half—was too powerful to set aside.

With chests puffed in pride, muscles tense, and gazes sharp, they stood in silence and waited for the command to march.

Amid the cries of the young and the quiet weeping of loved ones, Elder Aïna stepped forward to offer her final words. Her voice echoing through the clear skies, she said, "We will wait for you all to return to our embrace. May the goddesses protect your souls and spirits, and may the earthly ones find their way back home."

She leaned her forehead against Noël's sword, the blade pulsing with life and glowing blue, mirroring the crystals that adorned its owner. The Rose—named the night before— hummed in response, alive in Noël's grip.

Noël raised the Rose high, shining light over the gathered warriors. Blue roses sprouted from the soil beneath their paws, a blessing of the Lidéřen. Without a word, the warriors turned as one and began their march.

The journey had begun, and the world would never be the same.

For days and nights, they ran. Noël clung to Theron's back, her sword raised high, its blade catching the light that broke through the ancient trees above. It wasn't only a weapon. It was a declaration to the world that the Vólkins were coming. Behind them, the army surged forward like a storm. The earth trembled under the weight of two hundred wolves.

Ahead lay their targets: the villages of Róvgrad, Borodýn, and Velkýna. Smaller than the mighty five, but no less danger- ous. These villages stood as shields against Ávera's strength. They were always prepared, always armed, their weapons honed and their men hardened by years of training. Tárnov, the military capital, ensured their readiness. Its forges burned day and night, producing steel strong enough to tear apart even the mightiest of foes. These villages thrived on the fear of an attack that had never come—until now.

At least that was what the Lidéřen thought.

57

AT THE GATES OF BORODYN

"The old world rots at its roots. Tear it free with blood and
bone, Lidéřen, or be buried beneath it."
—Láda Veléša, Goddess of Leadership and War

Noël

T he nearest village is close. I hear human voices, the
crackle of burning coal, smell the scent of food
drifting through the air, tainted by the stench of
sweat and unwashed men.

It has been a while since I last stepped into a human village.
This is also my first time in one that isn't Tárnov.

For all its cold, oppressive presence, Tárnov is clean. If
anything falls to the ground, it is picked up immediately, fear-
fully, lest a soldier sees and punishes someone. The streets are
polished, the stones gleaming. I, myself, sent misbehaving
soldiers to scrub them clean, a shameful lesson for their families to witness. But this village smells foul.

Tárnov is the second-largest village, a military stronghold. I assumed other villages might not be as favored by the tsar, but I did not expect the difference to be this vast.

We have been running for days and nights. Now that I am no longer human, I can see how little sleep I need and how my strength remains unchanged. Colors are more vivid. Sounds are crisper. The day we left, I could hear everything. Not just the birds near our home, but the ones far beyond. The laughter of nýmphi by the forest pond. The rustling of animals far away from us. I could sift through the noise, channeling what I wanted to hear and blocking out the rest. It was easy to learn.

That night, when Theron and I became one, I heard nothing but us. That is a weakness I cannot afford. Even if having him buried inside me was a pleasure I never thought existed. This is why I put a cloth inside myself to prevent leaking. Even now, my body craves him.

From the moment we set off, the wolves have followed us. Even now, they run behind us—not too close, but never too far. They don't look hungry.

And I swear I heard their cries during the bonding ritual. That piercing, bone-deep howl still lingers in my mind. They want something. If not food, then what?

For now, it doesn't matter.

We near the first village, positioned northeast of Ávera. A small coastal settlement, yet dangerously close to our lands. If there's one thing I know about villages near Ávera, it's that they are always armed. And today, I will test my new strength.

We ascend a hill that should give us a clear view of the village below. Our pace slows, our approach careful and silent. The last thing we need is to alert the villagers too soon. What concerns me most is the ambush. Gregor's warning about the tsar's plan was no surprise. I would be a fool to think everything would go smoothly. Of course he's furious. His precious barrier, gone. The old plan to keep women locked in the villages, to ensure the blue rose never crossed it, is soon to be gone as well.

If he knows the prophecy, which he does, he will stop at nothing to prevent me from fulfilling it. What he doesn't realize is that I already know this. He tried to use Gregor, but failed. And his empire will fall, village by village, mistake after mistake. His first mistake was *me*. Had he not allowed me to join the army, I would be just another nameless woman, married off with a dozen children by now. Yet, something feels off.

There is no sound of gathered soldiers. No distant orders being given. No shifting of armor or weapons.

Nothing.

Theron halts and glances at me over his shoulder. The others follow his lead, coming to a silent stop, waiting for my signal. I turn to face my army, an unshakable force of giant, battle-hungry vólkins. Their gazes burn, muscles taut, ready to strike at my command.

I pulse my crystals once, a silent command. *Do not move.*

I nod to Theron, and he climbs to the edge of the cliff. My eyes darken at what we find.

A half-destroyed sign hangs from a wooden tower, barely clinging to the rotting beams. *Welcome to Borodýn.* The tower itself connects to a crude wooden wall surrounding the village, though calling it a defense would be generous. I only heard of Borodýn once. My commander mentioned that some villages were too poor to afford a starosta, a head of their own, forced instead to serve one of the five ruling territories. I knew that. What I didn't know was that it was *this* poor. The stench alone should have warned me. But nothing prepares me for what I see next.

An old man, his face twisted with self-satisfaction, standing at the center of a wedding ceremony. A wedding . . . *with a child.* The guests at his wedding cheer as the women remain silent. My grip tightens around my Rose, my jaw locks in place. Then, a cry.

My head snaps toward the sound just in time to witness, through an open window, a man striking his wife. She sobs, begging for mercy, and her body curls in on itself as he beats her without pause. I can't believe my own eyes.

The final straw is when my gaze lands on a statue of a woman in the village square. Even a *statue* has not been spared their depravity. Her chest is polished smooth, lighter than the rest of the stone. Men have been groping a damn statue. A slow, seething heat creeps through my veins.

Every single man here is guilty.

My awakening wasn't just a transformation of my body and spirit. It was a revelation. A stripping away of the veil that once hid the world's horrors from me. Now, I see the world as it truly is. And I will not stand by.

I lift my hand to signal to the nýmphí. They emerge from between the trees, shimmering under the canopy.

It begins. We raid Borodýn.

The blade of my sword ignites with a blinding blue light, pulsing with my raw energy. A scream erupts from deep within me, louder, more powerful than I have ever heard before.

"ENSLAVE THE MEN! LEAVE NO ONE BEHIND! SEARCH EVERY CABINET, EVERY BED, EVERY HIDDEN SPACE. NO MAN SHALL ESCAPE HIS FATE."

My voice echoes like thunder. It crashes through the trees, shakes the air itself. With that command, we charge. A storm of bodies, a force of nature, descends upon Borodýn.

The nýmphí move like wraiths, slipping through the village to rescue the women and children. The vólkins and I? We will destroy everything else.

An earth-shattering growl rips through every warrior's throat, and the sound rolls through the land like the voice of vengeance. The ground quakes beneath our feet. Theron roars, a deafening, primal battle cry that sends birds shrieking from the treetops.

With the nýmphí at our flanks, we crash through the walls of the village.

The wood splinters. The gates shatter.

Borodýn will fall. And the world will remember.

This is the rage of centuries, of mothers slaughtered, of daughters caged, of a prophecy forced into silence.

I leap from Theron's back to land in a crouch before pushing off into a sprint. Around me, the vólkins flood the village, their massive bodies tear through the narrow streets, storm buildings, and break down doors. Screams erupt from all sides—panicked cries from men, desperate wails from women. The clang of bells smashing together rings through the village, their alarm system echoing above the chaos.

My heart pounds. My pulse roars in my ears. I run.

The child. That is all that matters.

Theron keeps pace beside me. A man rushes toward us, swinging a rusted sword. Mistake. Theron grabs him mid-stride and hurls him into the side of a building with a sickening crunch. Another lunges at me, but I don't slow. With a flick of my wrist, my blade slices clean through his thigh. He collapses to the dirt with a scream. I don't spare him a glance. The scent of blood already thickens the air, along with sweat, smoke, and fear.

People scatter, some to flee, others foolish enough to fight. It doesn't matter. I see it from afar. The village square. The altar. The child bride.

The old man grabs the girl and runs. Rage blinds me. My entire body burns with it. I push forward, faster than I ever have before. My fingers tighten around the hilt of my sword as I near him. He won't get away.

With a single motion, I drive my blade through his skull. His body goes limp, he collapses, and he drags the girl down with him. Blood spills over her small wedding dress, soaking her in his filth. My heart slams against my ribs. My breaths come fast and sharp. *My first kill.*

Staring at the corpse before her, the girl cringes. Then, as the shock wears off, she bursts into tears. Of course she's terrified. She just witnessed death.

I crouch, lowering my sword, and force softness into my voice. "What's your name, little one?"

Her wide, glossy eyes go wooden.

I reach out carefully to wipe a tear from her cheek. "I came here to save you," I whisper. "I am Noël, and the wolves here have come to free all the girls."

She blinks, her tiny shoulders trembling as she processes my words. "Maya," she murmurs. "I'm Maya."

"You're very brave, Maya." With a smile, I open my arms, offering her a choice. A way out.

She hesitates, then, slowly, she pushes her feet forward. She leans into me, letting me gather her in my arms. I turn to Theron. He stands tall, chains in his massive paws, a few dozen men already shackled at their ankles and wrists. Their terrified gazes remind me of Gregor, back when he first arrived. But this time, I have no mercy left to give.

It takes only a few hours to crush those who dared to fight and bind the ones who surrendered. The nýmphí move around the village gathering the women and children, their soft whispers of comfort barely audible over the wreckage. The warriors sweep through the village, checking every abandoned space, so no one can hide from their fate. A few soldiers arrived with weapons drawn. They were dead within seconds. I have lost count of how many lives I've taken today.

And I regret nothing.

The shaking women clutch their children, fear still raw in their eyes. But soon, they will leave this place. Soon, they will step beyond these walls and enter Ávera, where they will be free.

As for the men, the guilty, they stand in ten endless lines, shackled and silent, their expressions etched with fear or empty resignation. Each will face judgment before they meet their end. Because this is justice. And this is how it should be.

I stride into the heart of the chaos. On my right, women, elders, and children stand in clusters, their faces streaked with tears, their bodies trembling. Some still sob, clinging to each other, while others have begun to calm, soothed by the nýmphí assuring them that everything will be alright. On my left, the rows of chained men stand in silence. But not all of them have learned their place. Some steal glances at the bare nýmphí, their gazes dark with the same hunger that once ruled this village.

Disgust curls in my stomach.

My eyes catch Ívar's, who stands near the closest line of prisoners. Then, I turn my attention to the one whose leering gaze lingers the longest.

Ívar follows my stare. He nods once, then moves. With force, he grabs the man's head and slams it down. "Eyes on the ground," he growls.

The other men flinch. One by one, their gazes drop to their shackled feet. Where they belong.

The moment I spot Theron, returning with the last of the captured men, I raise my chin.

He throws them down near the farthest row, and they hit the dirt with muffled grunts. Two warriors step forward, their paws glowing as they form the energy shackles that bind the new prisoners in place. Then, Theron walks to me, and our gazes lock. His fierce, battle-hardened expression softens immediately. And just like that, my soul feels light, as if a feather floats through my chest. I tear my eyes away. We can't. Not now.

I turn back to the crowd. "Listen closely to what I'm about to say." Silence falls. The warriors, the women, the children, the prisoners, all turn to me. I fix my gaze on the shackled men. "Some of you are wondering what happens now." Theron moves behind me, like a silent wall of power. "From today onward, you are my prisoners. My slaves. From today, you begin counting your days. Those who are guilty will die."

I drive my sword into the ground, and the blade sinks into the earth before a pulse of energy ripples outward. From the soil, a row of blue roses bursts forth to bloom in a perfect circle around the terrified women. Gasps echo through the crowd. Some of the children laugh in delight, reaching out to touch the glowing petals and brush their small hands against the roses.

At least . . . I've done this much.

"As for the women and elders." My tone softens, and I pull my sword free. "You will be given a choice. These vólkins," I say, sweeping my hand toward the warriors standing at attention. "I'm sure you've heard of them, beasts lurking in the shadows, hunters of those who cross their path."

A low, rumbling growl passes through the ranks of my warriors, standing tall in front of the women, as they lift their paws to their hearts.

"These vólkins are your shield and your sword. Your muscle and your claw." I wait a moment to let my words settle. "The first option is to stay in your village, free of the fate that shackled you. We came to set your souls alight."

A hush settles over the women. Some exchange glances, their faces torn between doubt and a fragile, desperate hope. The children remain distracted, fully entranced by the roses.

At least they understand I'm here to help. "The second option is to come with me. To Ávera." Mother, Father, I hope you see me well from above. "In Ávera, you will be given a

home. A place of safety. A place that glows with life, not decay."
My voice grows stronger. "You will see land untouched by
cruelty, filled with vivid color, fruits you've never tasted, fresh
water as clear as the sky, warmth that is not given as a privilege
but as a right." *This is what they were never allowed to dream of.*

"And you will be free."

Some of them gasp, some press hands over their mouths as
if afraid to believe it.

"The third option," I continue, "is for those who want more.
Those who want to build something greater." I let my gaze
sweep across the crowd. "I want to educate you."

A ripple of murmurs passes through the women. Knowledge was never theirs to claim. Not before.

"In Ávera, you will have the chance to learn. I will teach
you, and I will have educators to guide you. You will read, you
will write, and you will grow." I take a deep breath. "And I will
need healers to mend the wounded. I will need artists to shape
the new world. I will need minds to lead, create, and teach.
Those who wish to fight—to take up the sword and defend the
ones who cannot—I will train you."

Some women clutch their children tighter, looking into
their eyes. A spark.

I clench my fist, raising my voice to the skies. "The old laws
have no place in the world I am building." I point toward the
burning remains of Borodýn. "This—this—is what the old
world gave you." I press a hand to my chest. "I offer you something new. First, a home. Then, a future. And lastly, a purpose."

58

ONE VILLAGE CLAIMED, A THOUSAND MORE TO SAVE

"When Éva breathed life into the world, she shaped it for the bond between spirit and strength—for the woman and the vólkin. In their union, the earth itself finds peace."
—Elder Aïna

Theron

So many females in one place, and yet not a single warrior has found his mate.

There are too few vólkins compared to the number of females. Too few mates to be found. And none of these females are one of the five we are searching for. But this is only the first village. We have an entire land to conquer, a world to reshape.

Things take time. And no one understands patience better than a vólkin. Every warrior sniffs the air, desperate to catch a scent, to find her. But their snouts do not betray them. When I first scented my mate, my body acted on pure instinct. Had I not overpowered my own desires, I fear what I might have done to her.

Going against nature is a dangerous game.

Locking a few hundred vólkins away, forcing them to exist without their other halves, without their fated mates, was the worst kind of cruelty. Now, I know what it means to be whole. My soul is warm, a constant burn that soothes and heals. As if she is the cure to every sickness I have ever carried. I cannot imagine parting from her. I wouldn't survive it. The agony, the longing—it would end me.

"We've been here our whole lives, child. How can we believe you speak the truth?" An elder female breaks the silence. Among the hundreds of females staring at us with wide eyes, she is the only one brave enough to speak.

It is hard for me to understand their fear. We came here. We took their abusers. We offered them freedom. And still, they hesitate. Why? My mate even thought of the nýmphí, ensuring the females would feel safe. Their homes are nothing but dead trees, their air stagnant with dust and filth. The soil beneath them is lifeless, not a single plant grows where it should. They do not know what it means to breathe freely. They only need to see Ávera, and they will understand what my mate offers them. But this conversation is a human matter. So I will not interfere.

"My name is Noël Ársa, and I come from Tárnov," my mate answers the elder. I barely register her words before my gaze lands on one of the pathetic males shackled in the dirt. Disgust burrows into my chest. How could any of these females have ever mated with them?

Even if I had the longest claws in Ávera, I wouldn't lay a single one on them. Let alone take them as a mate.

Gasps ripple through the females. Why?

"You are the girl who is wanted!" one of them exclaims.

Another nods quickly, eyes darting between the others. "Yes! Yes! I heard from the farmers. There were men who helped you escape. They were hanged in Tárnov's square!"

I freeze. She never told me someone helped her escape. She was—

"I was kidnapped," my mate says, her hand sliding into my paw.

The moment our skin touches, I feel her soul grow lighter, and her warmth floods into me. A slow, dangerous heat builds in my stomach. Not now.

"They planned to throw me to the vólkins, to my death." She squeezes my paw, her gaze sweeping over the silent crowd. "As you see, I am well and alive." Then, she looks up at me, her next words striking like a bolt of lightning. "And this is my husband."

My ears twitch. My head tilts on its own. Husband? Is that what humans call a mate? If so . . . then Noël is my husband as well. I like the sound of it. She also declared we're mates in front of other humans. That fills my chest with pride.

The elders chose to stay. They have known nothing beyond these borders, nothing but the life they were given. Change, even when it offers freedom, is a terrifying thing.

I don't blame them, but I must make sure they're comfortable.

Five warriors I've selected will remain behind. These vólkins will control and oversee everything, the human slaves will rebuild what we tore down. Borodýn will become a village without chains, but still under our rule.

The mothers with children chose to come with us to Ávera, clinging to the promise of a life free from suffering. The never-mated females made their choice as well. They do not wish to be left behind in the ruins of their old lives. They seek a future.

For now, as we take more land, the females will be given

time to gather their belongings, though there is little worth taking from these broken homes.

My gaze sweeps over my mate where she stands with furrowed brows and crossed arms. Her gown is soaked with blood that isn't hers. Maybe she wants to have her belongings as well. Although we cannot take over Tárnov yet. It is too risky for us, since it's one of the most armed villages. It isn't the right time. Yet.

I've assigned another five packs to carry the females' belongings back to Ávera. That should be enough for now, since we need warriors for the next villages. The warriors will move in rotations. Every village we conquer remains under our watch. No territory will be left unguarded, no land reclaimed left unprotected.

And those stationed here will have their chance to meet the females from other villages, to find the mates they have been denied for too long. I will do whatever it takes to make sure my people find their mates. Because no vólkin should live without their other half. And I will not stop until every one of them is bonded.

"Not a single one!"

Ívar stomps closer, waving his paws in the air. Nér has just taken over his post with the slaves.

My mate catches my gaze before turning away and walking toward the females. She wants to speak with them, to ease their fear.

I tear my eyes from her to focus back on Ívar. "Calm your senses," I say.

"Hundreds, Theron! Hundreds! And none! Not even one!" His chest heaves, his claws flexing at his sides. "When will I meet my own?"

Everywhere I look, the females move in and out of their homes, carrying burdens they should have never had to bear. Some help the elders, others haul cloth sacks filled with whatever they can salvage. Warriors carry the heavy items. I think I'm seeing a table. Perhaps the female truly likes that table. Each female is different.

Just like us.

Some are pale like my mate, others as rich in color as the earth itself. Their hair varies like the nýmphí—red, golden, brown, light as sand—but none as dark as hers. Just as no other warrior is as white-furred as Aeson. We are not meant to be the same.

"That is why we will continue." My voice is calm. "Village after village, land after land. Until every warrior finds his mate."

Ívar lets out a harsh breath, his golden eyes narrowing as he looks over at the shackled males. "They're even uglier than the one who pissed himself."

Nodding, I smirk. I once thought Gregor was unpleasant to look at.

I was wrong.

These males—these pathetic creatures—couldn't possibly call themselves males. Even those who drooled over the nýmphí, their weak cocks standing uselessly, were . . . small. How could that possibly satisfy a female? A mate is meant to be strong, meant to claim, protect, and worship. This is why no one should ever go against nature.

Mother Nature decreed it so—there is woman and there is vólkin. That is the balance. That is the law. But Ádám created these males with a snake. Ugly, greedy, and weak.

With a weary sigh, I glance up at the sky, clear and blue, untouched by the chaos below. Yet, beyond the village walls, the wolves still wait. Watching.

Aeson, Kaël, Zephyr . . . I wonder how they fare with their packs. I've sent signals, but no response. They're already too far to reach.

59

OLD SONGS OF ELDERS

"They taught us to endure. We will teach them to bleed. A woman's silence is not peace, it is the howl before the slaughter."
—Eyleen Ársa

Theron

"What a handsome boy you are!" An elder female studies my face, nodding in approval.

"Why didn't we have men like this when we were young?!" another exclaims and clicks her tongue.

Before I can react, a cooked piece of meat is shoved toward my face. I open my mouth, I have no choice.

"If I were sixty years younger . . ." a third elder mutters.

I pause mid-chew. What is happening? What would she have done if she were younger? Does she not realize I'm older than her?

I sit here, on a log, chewing cooked meat, surrounded by a few dozen elder females as they inspect and feed me like I'm a small pup.

From Borodýn to Róvgrad, it took us nearly four sun cycles to arrive. Róvgrad was no different. Another weak village, another place stripped of nature, lifeless and gray. It was even smaller than Borodýn. Hardly worth a battle.

I ordered three packs to escort the females and children to the first village, so they were under protection. As before, most of those who chose to stay behind were elders, but unlike Borodýn, those elders were . . . different. Now, we stand in Velkýna, the third village we have taken as ours. Since we left Ávera, eleven—maybe twelve—passing suns have come and gone. I have never been away from home this long before.

The elders here are livelier than the last. I take another bite of cooked meat.

The moment Velkýna's females realized we had come to save them, not destroy them, the elders cheered. I hadn't expected that.

Even my warriors changed, they softened. One scented his mate, and they are now at her home, claiming what fate has given them.

It gave the others hope.

We have been gone from Ávera for nearly half a moon cycle, and finally, we have one pair. That is good.

Unlike Borodýn and Róvgrad, this village has color. The females dress in rich reds and vibrant blues with beautiful embroidery. Even the elders wear bright fabric, their head coverings far more vivid than the dull rags of the last two villages.

"So you're telling me you bedded Noël?" the elder woman in front of me asks, eyes curious as she inspects my crystals.

Bedded. The word comes from *bed*, my mate once explained. I grin, arching my back and letting my chest muscles flex under the firelight. "Of course."

They burst into laughter, some playfully smacking my arms. This is good, right?

"So when will you have babies?" another elder asks, shoving another piece of meat into my mouth before I can answer.

Both my mate and I want that. But we can't. I feel my shoulders sag on their own. She would be a great mother. I would be a great father. But the goddesses chose us for war, and the choice was never ours to make. I chew, swallow, and speak. "Not yet. First, we must free all the females. And enslave the males."

"So that vólkin is now bedding Nessya!" An elder's voice rises from the other side of the fire, her tone teasing.

The entire village gathered to celebrate our arrival, the first true welcome we've received. Compared to the first two villages, Velkýna had more soldiers and defenses, but they were nothing against vólkin strength.

"She's my youngest granddaughter, Lyuba!" another elder laughs, her weathered hands clapping together.

I nod. "Yes, they're mates." I move to the side of the log to make space as an elder moves to sit beside me. "The goddesses choose two souls, and the vólkin feels it in his core."

It is law. It is nature.

"You are such a charmer!" The elder grins, nudging me.

"Thank you," I reply.

These elders are different. Bold and filled with something the others were missing.

Warmth.

My mate was taken away earlier, the elders eager to steal her for themselves, though for what purpose, I do not know. At least she finished overseeing the disposal of the corpses before they dragged her away. I fed them to the wolves. And still, the wolves wait. They stick around at the edge of the village, never venturing too close, yet never leaving. They are watching, waiting for something.

"Have you tried mead?" A younger female approaches the

fire, carrying pointed jars in her hands. The moment she lifts them, the stench hits me.

I wrinkle my snout. "What is this?"

Behind me, I hear sneezes from my warriors. The scent is foul, strong enough to make even a vólkin recoil.

"Don't you have alcohol in Ávera?" the elder woman who has spent the evening feeding me cooked meat asks.

I shake my head. "It looks like water, but yellowed. What is it?"

"Oh, son, it is from Mother Nature!" She chuckles and takes a cup from another young female. "It is honey and water."

Honey? Bee offerings to the goddesses?

"Try it!"

I take the cup from her, lifting it to my snout—

And immediately sneeze.

The scent is pungent and sour. My fur bristles. What an awful stench.

"It might make you dizzy." The elder near me grins.

"You blind fuck! Don't you see his size? It won't even affect him," another elder scoffs.

I am big, but I do not trust anything that dulls my senses. I scan the gathering. Some of my warriors stand by the shackled men. Others help cook the hunt, a few talk with the females. Dozens have gathered by the central fire, filling the village with voices and laughter. Different scents cross my snout—blood from the fresh game, sweat from the males in chains, the scent of mating from a home nearby, and meals the females have brought from their houses. And then, the one scent that eclipses them all. Sweet and mine. My mate. And she is still far from me.

"You're a strong, big boy. But tell me, do you know how to please a woman?" My attention snaps to another elder as she approaches, carrying a wooden tray.

"Of course. My mate is very satisfied."

The elder hums, setting the tray down. "Do you use your tongue?"

"I do."

"Where?"

Isn't it obvious? "In my mate's cunt, of course."

The elders burst into laughter, their amusement echoing through the firelit clearing. The younger females blush, their faces turning red, just like my mate does. She would probably blush too if she heard this conversation.

"Just there?" The elder's eyebrows rise. "Do you kiss?"

I tilt my head. "It seems difficult. I do not have lips like you do." If they ask, then perhaps it means something important.

"Use your tongue," another elder chimes in.

I frown. "Where?"

"In her mouth!"

I freeze even as a gasp escapes me. *Of course.* How have I never thought of that?

Ívar, seated beside me, nearly chokes on his meat. I see the realization strike his mind too. He's already memorizing the information. Kaël would love this conversation.

I lean forward. "Please, elder, tell me more."

The scent of blue roses fills my snout, and I immediately turn toward its source, my mate in her full glory. My tail sways on its own, left and right, unable to be contained. They have changed her attire. She is wrapped in pale, flowing fabric, so light it clings to her like mist at dawn. The long sleeves drape past her hands, making her look too delicate for war, too fragile for this world.

But I know better.

White, blue, and gold adorn her. On her head sits a pointed

crown-like headpiece, its colors matching her dress. Her dark hair is woven into two long braids, falling down her back as she moves toward me. I rise to my paws.

"My, my! Dear, you are a delight!" Elder Lyuba exclaims, rushing Noël toward us.

"Delight," I echo, because I have forgotten every other word in existence. I stride forward and sweep her into my arms.

She laughs, loud and carefree. My snout twitches. Mead.

Did she drink it?

The females behind her burst into laughter, lifting the hems of their dresses in their fists as they rush forward.

"Theron." Noël giggles, and for the first time, I do not recognize my mate. "I"—she laughs, leaning into me—"must eat to sober up a bit. It's no good to drink on an empty stomach."

I turn on my heel, and my mate lets out a 'woo' noise as I move.

Mead is very dangerous.

"Elder Lyuba, could you please help me feed her?" I ask, settling onto the log with Noël perched on my thigh.

"We were just discussing you two!" The elder chuckles.

"You are popular." My mate giggles.

I huff, glancing down at her. She is a powerful leader. A warrior. The one chosen by the goddesses.

And yet, at this moment, she is a drunken dove, giggling in my lap. What have they done to her?

I cup her face, and she looks at me with a wide, dazed smile. My sweet dove. I cradle her against me as Elder Lyuba brings more meat. As I begin to feed my mate, the other females form a circle around the fire—elders and youths alike—each grabbing the back of the other's dress as they begin to move. Tradition.

It's beautiful. It makes me feel at home. Noël opens her mouth, waiting for another piece of meat, and I give it to her. Then, the first voice rises, melodic, timeless.

Daughter, daughter, hear my song,
The night is deep, the road is long.
The fire burns, the bread will rise,
A mother's love never dies.

One voice becomes many.

The circle moves slowly, in sync. Noël chews, eyes fixed on them.

When the wind calls, whisper low,
The trees will teach you where to go.
Moonlight fades but stars remain,
The river sings your name.

My fur bristles. This is nature. Feminine power, feminine voices. The sound vibrates in my bones. More females step forward, some carrying drums like the ones in Ávera. Elder Aïna once told me, the drums our warriors play today came from the human females who once fled to our lands.

Carry my voice, carry my name,
Daughter, my love, do the same.
Strength in your hands, fire in your soul,
Walk as the females before you once told.

Mothers sing to their daughters. My mate straightens, her body swaying to the rhythm of their song. She claps, her hands moving in sync with the females around us. The warriors join. They stomp their paws. They pound the drums. The fire roars higher.

Mother, Mother, hear my vow,
I take your words, I know them now.
I'll weave my fate, I'll braid my hair,
I'll carry your song everywhere.

The younger females release their grips, raising their hands to the open sky.

More females arrive, arms full of fabrics, objects, things I can't name. One by one, they throw them into the fire.

A young female steps forward. "For the fucking bastard

who took me young!" she shouts, hurling a pair of boots into the fire, boots that look just like my mate's.

Another woman follows, her voice trembling. She's furious. "For you, Soyer—for murdering my mother!"

More objects fly into the flames. More names are spoken, shouted, spat like poison. Their voices rise. Their rage turns to laughter, to screams, to release.

The fire devours their pasts, and the night becomes theirs.

I glance down at my mate, her eyes glisten. She doesn't look like she is about to cry. She looks like she will burn the entire land to the ground. I gather the long sleeves of her dress, keeping them from dragging in the dirt, and set her straight on my lap. She is tense, her body vibrating with rage.

"This is why we're doing this," she whispers, her voice low, dangerous. I feel it.

Her soul burns like an unyielding flame.

"Yes." I smile, nuzzling her face.

Daughter, my daughter, strong as stone,
Sing when you fight, sing when you roam.
With fire and heart, with love and with blade,
You are the flower that never will fade.

Both of us turn toward the fire. The flames dim, burning lower, as the females form pairs. One by one, gripping each other's hands tight, they leap over the embers. A symbol.

My chest swells with pride. This is why we fight. This is why we will never stop.

60

FLOWERS BLOOM IN ASH

"The blood of the earth remembers. The bones of the old world
still ache for your rage. Take it back."
—Láda Veléša, Goddess of Leadership and War

Noël

I rise from Theron's comfortable thigh. Before me, the
women jump over the fire in pairs, their sarafans billow-
ing, their voices rising in song. It is the most beautiful
thing I've ever seen.

When the grandmothers captured me earlier and dragged
me to their homes, I thought they meant to scold me. Instead,
they dressed me in this traditional gown. I saw women in
Tárnov wear them for grand festivals, but never like this. The
fabric, the braids, the chapel headpiece, it all fits me as if it
were made for me. They ate sunflower seeds as they worked,
chatting and humming like a secret sisterhood.

I had a few seeds myself, but Grandmother Raya, the one
who braided my hair, had tapped my wrist. "You cannot eat too
much before a proper meal, child."

The words made me smile. Mother used to say the same thing. But now, I stand before a sea of free women. This is our liberation. Every single one of these women has chosen to come to Ávera. I raise my arms to the sky and close my hands into fists.

The fire erupts, its flames turning blue at my will. "Dance, free spirits! Dance and sing! This is who we are."

The vólkins howl, their voices echoing through the night. The women gasp, their eyes wide as blue roses rise from the soil and bloom in the wake of their liberation. My power is beautiful. One burst after another, more and more roses explode from the dark earth. I sweep my hands through the air and summon the wind. Leaf spirits whirl to my command, dancing through the flames. More women jump over the fire, over the ashes of their pasts, their suffering. More burn belts, uniforms, hats, knives, watches—

Everything that once held them captive, burned to nothing.

To my left, nýmphí weave different hairstyles into the hair of young girls. To my right, children chase the leaf spirits, laughing with the crackling fire while grandmothers dance alongside warriors. One day, this is how the entire world will look, free from the children of the Snake.

"Oh gods!"

I turn to see a woman, probably around my age, with golden locks and beautiful blue eyes. The nýmphí guide her toward me, and the leaf spirits playfully tug at her gown.

"There are no gods in this world," I say, a smile curving my lips as I meet her gaze. The nýmphí bow, then retreat with soft giggles to join the others.

"No gods?" she echoes, her posture straightening. She stands just slightly taller than me, but the curiosity in her eyes makes her seem younger, almost . . . childlike.

"Didn't your mother ever teach you?" My smile widens. "Only goddesses exist."

Her eyes grow round. "That makes sense," she murmurs, tucking a golden curl behind her ear.

"It does. Men created a god because they couldn't accept that a woman creates life."

She stares at me.

I lift my hand, and with a thought, a blue rose blooms in my palm. Its petals glow in the firelight as I extend the rose to her. "When you understand this, you awaken."

With trembling fingers, she takes the rose. Its stem rests in her palm like a sacred offering.

"And when you do," I continue, my voice lowering, "you become your true self."

The woman presses the rose to her heart. "My name is Vasilisa." The blue fire shines in her eyes, reflecting together with the petals of the blue rose. She is stunning, not only in form, but in spirit. "And I want to be a warrior. To stand by your side."

I see the fire in her.

I feel it. Vasilisa.

A beautiful name for a beautiful soul. I meet Theron's gaze before putting my sword into his paws. Then, I turn back to Vasilisa and take her hand in mine. Without a word, we run. The fire roars before us, blue and wild. I tighten my grip on her hand, feeling her pulse race with mine. With my other hand, I lift the skirt of my gown. Laughter, bold and fearless, spills from my lips as we jump together, soaring over the flames, over the ashes of the past.

"Theron!"

I laugh as Theron nips at my neck, his sharp teeth grazing my skin before trailing up to my cheek. The glow of our crystals pulses bright in the dark barn. Apparently, the grandmothers taught him something new tonight, something he couldn't wait to try.

"Did you know," he murmurs against my skin as he lifts the hem of my skirt, "that we can kiss with our tongues?"

My eyes widen. Kiss with tongues?

Dear goddesses above.

I lean back against a wooden platform, my bare feet sinking into the piles of hay. The celebration continues outside, but we slipped away for a moment of quiet, our own private escape.

Theron grins. "I knew there had to be more options."

Shaking my head, I laugh. "I can't even imagine . . . How?" As the words leave my lips, an idea takes shape. Maybe it's the mead. Maybe I'm just dirty-minded? Either way, I find myself staring at his mouth. "Stick out your tongue, Theron."

A spark ignites in his gaze, he's as eager as I am. He opens his mouth and extends his long, dark pink tongue. And goddesses, I know exactly how good it feels inside me.

A rush of heat floods my body, my heartbeat hammers against my ribs, and I part my lips as I lean in. His breath mingles with mine, his scent fills my mind. So close.

I take his tongue into my mouth, and the moment I do, Theron tightens his grip, wrapping his strong arms around my thighs and pulling me closer. A whimper escapes me at the feeling. My mind is so dirty.

He groans, curling his tongue with mine, and I cup his jaw with both hands. Spreading my thighs wide, he seats me on the platform. One arm braces behind me, holding his weight, while the other moves with torturous slowness between my legs. He finds the cloth I placed there. With a rumble in his chest, he pulls it away and tosses it aside. My breath hitches, but I keep my lips locked around his tongue, sucking it until he presses his thumb to my clit.

A muffled moan bursts from my throat, my fingers tighten

in his fur, and the first nudge of his cock at my entrance has my entire body shuddering. Theron's purring growl vibrates against me, his massive body cages me in, and slowly—so painfully slowly—he presses inside me.

Gasping as waves of pleasure consume my body, I lose grip of his tongue. Oh, goddesses . . . I'm losing my mind.

Theron snarls, pressing his hips forward in one thrust. His cock filling me, his tongue in my mouth, I'm full in both directions. He starts to move, his hips snapping, each thrust forcing me closer to madness.

His deep growls, the raw sounds of our bodies meeting, the wet, obscene noises of my mouth sucking at his tongue. It fills the barn. It fills me.

Both of our heads snap to the side, instincts taking over. Eyes wide. Bodies frozen. Footsteps. Heavy. Numerous. Unfamiliar.

Not from the village, but outside. Theron's body goes rigid, his muscles tense like a beast sensing its prey, or its *hunters*. He pulls out, leaving me aching and empty.

Our eyes lock, breath ragged, hearts pounding. Not from pleasure anymore, but from the shift. The ambush we've been waiting for.

61

THE TSAR'S FAILED CREATIONS

"I shattered the bond and stole the breath of the earth. Let their broken forms wander, nameless, until the soil forgets their blood."

—Tsar Aldrik I

Noël

"**W**ith blood and roses, I will keep you all safe!"

My scream rips through the night as I leap onto Theron mid-run, gripping his thick fur as we charge forward. The warriors thunder after us, their claws digging into the dirt, their snarls filling the air. The village is secured, safe in the hands of the nýmphí and five packs. Now, the tsar's men will finally taste their own blood. Theron hisses as he runs, his sac still aching from our interruption. I know.

Because I feel it too.

I'm soaked, dripping, my arousal slicks his fur as we move. Very cruel timing. But we have no time to think, only to fight. My fingers tighten around my sword, my gaze locked ahead as heavy footfalls pound the earth. Too heavy.

This isn't normal. No human's footsteps should sound like that.

We run for what feels like an hour, though in reality, it's no more than ten minutes. Our speed is immense, our focus blade-sharp, but the tension claws at my chest like a caged beast. This is it. The night everything changes.

Tonight, the tsar will learn who truly rules this land. I will kill his army, and when the time comes, I will kill him too. But no amount of preparation could have readied me for what I see before my eyes.

Giant, green-skinned heads rise above the horizon, emerging like unnatural monoliths in the moonlight. The road ahead is clear of trees. This is open land, the kind where carriages, traders, or farmers travel. Not the kind where nightmares take shape. What is this? Who are they? "Theron," I grit out, my pulse hammering. "This . . . what is going on?"

He shakes his head, just as confused. My crystals blaze brighter, the glow spilling over the land. And then I see them clearly.

They have the shape of men, but they are not men. Their massive bodies are lined with powerful muscle, green skin in a spectrum of shades. Some as deep as forest shadows, others like sunlit moss. They are tall—vólkin tall.

And they are heavy. That's why their footsteps shake the ground. Their hair varies—some have their heads shaved, others wear braids. And then, the details hit me. Not only the countless daggers and spears.

The gold.

Rings pierce their pointed ears. Thick bands coil around their arms, their necks, their abs. Heavy chains drape over their massive frames like trophies of conquest. And lower . . .

Oh.

Oh dear goddesses. Even there? Even their cocks are adorned in gold.

The green men come to a halt, raising their hands.

My gaze narrows. What does that mean? Surrender? A warning?

I pulse my crystals once, a silent command. Theron immediately slows, his heavy breathing controlled despite the pounding of his heart still pulsing through him. The army behind us follows suit and stops. Now, we stand before these creatures, a mere fifty steps apart. A tense silence settles between us. And then, the front row of the green men tilt their heads back and sniff the air. My stomach drops. Oh, dear goddesses. Please. Let them not be scenting Theron's damp back, covered in my arousal.

"We have interrupted the Blue Rose and her mate. My apologies," says the green-skinned warrior at the front.

I just stare. There is no way I'm witnessing this madness. And then, they all bow. I blink.

What in Láda Veléša is going on? Did I fall asleep on Theron after we both collapsed into bliss? Is this some dream? I clear my throat before forcing my voice out. "Who are you?" *And why are you green?* I want to ask, but somehow, that question feels more ridiculous than the entire situation itself.

The warrior lifts his head. "My name is Thrā'kkor. I am the chief of the orcs."

My head almost tilts on its own, but I fight the urge to react. Orcs. I have no idea what that is or what they are.

"Thrā'kkor of orcs," I echo, slipping off Theron's back and landing with a solid thud of my boots. Theron instantly straightens behind me, claws flexing. As I step forward, so do the orcs behind Thrā'kkor. My warriors growl, fur bristling with instinct. From the edges of the field, the wolves that have followed us for days stand still, watching us. Watching me.

I don't know why, but I feel their waiting eyes. Their bellies are full of the corpses of rebellious men, the nýmphí even tried to calm them and scratch behind their ears. But nothing changed. So be it then. I lift my chin.

"What is the purpose of your arrival? Have you been sent by the tsar?"

Thrā'kkor nods. "We have." The moment the words leave his mouth, the orcs near him step aside.

A violent growl rips from Theron's throat, his body moving forward without hesitation. Our warriors mirror him.

I raise a hand. *Hold.*

And then I see why. The tsar's men. One. Three. Seven. Shoved forward like cattle.

I go still.

I would never mistake that uniform with the blue rose insignia, the symbol that is *mine*. The symbol he has no right to claim. My gaze narrows, burning with fury. The prisoners tremble, their bodies betraying them as fear coils around their spines like a vise.

One of them—a younger soldier, barely a man—clutches his mouth, his chest heaving. His face is pale, slick with sweat, eyes darting wildly between me, Theron, and the orcs. He sways. He's about to throw up.

Another, older, battle worn, collapses to his knees, gripping the soil as if it's the only thing anchoring him to this world. His fingers dig into the dirt like he's trying to hide himself from the horrors he's seen—or is about to see.

One of them lets out a high-pitched whimper. His entire body shakes so violently his armor clatters with every breath.

Another stares at me, unblinking, as if looking at something beyond human comprehension. His lips move soundlessly, forming words that never come. A prayer? Or maybe he's simply lost all ability to speak.

The last of them, a man twice my size but crumbling under his fate, slowly tilts his head upward. His eyes—dull and broken—meet mine. There is no defiance in them. What have they done to these men?

"The tsar wanted us to assist him against you and the vólkins, Your Majesty," Thrā'kkor says, his voice calm, almost amused. He called me by my title.

I narrow my eyes. "And I'm supposed to believe that?"

My crystals ignite with a fierce blue light that pulses from my forehead. The trembling men's eyes widen, beyond fear.

I tighten my grip around my sword, and in response, the blade surges with the same blue light. Its glow reflects in their terrified eyes, their minds scrambling between fight and flight, though neither will save them.

Suddenly, the wolves stir and point their snouts in the opposite direction, ears flat against their skulls. I flick my gaze toward them for just a second, just enough to register the change in their behavior. Then—

A sound like cracking bone shatters the moment.

Thrā'kkor moves. The orc chieftain reaches out and grabs the nearest soldier by the head. The man screams, thrashing wildly, his feet kicking against the ground. Frantic prayers to his nonexistent gods spill from his lips. With a fast tear, his body rips free from his head. The lifeless corpse collapses to the dirt, the severed head still caught in Thrā'kkor's monstrous grip. Blood arcs through the air, splattering the horrified faces of the remaining men. For a moment, there is nothing. Then, screams.

"Silence!" I command, my voice slicing through the chaotic panic of the soldiers.

The orcs stand tall at once, their eyes fixed on me. Behind me, Theron and my warriors stiffen. I flick them a sharp glare. They freeze in place.

My boots sink into the soil as I move forward. My gaze sweeps over the orcs. My fingers tighten around my sword.

"We have come to join you, Your Majesty," Thrā'kkor

declares when I stop in front of him. His deep voice is stoic, as if nothing happened.

My eyes narrow yet again.

He motions to the remaining messengers, the ones still trembling, still hoping for a miracle. Two orcs grab them and crack their skulls. Their heads are torn clean from their bodies. Blood spills in syrupy, steaming pools at their feet. "And we declined," Thrā'kkor finishes.

I don't flinch. I've seen enough death to stomach it. "Why?"

Thrā'kkor holds my gaze. "We were once human."

A shiver prickles down my spine.

"Four hundred years ago, we were created through dark magic," another orc says.

My blood runs cold. Dark magic. The goddesses used it to create the vólkin females. Four hundred years . . . The old tsar —the monster who burned vólkins' and women's bodies to create the barrier—he was the one who created them.

"Why would you join me?" I demand, my voice strong as I lift my chin to meet Thrā'kkor's piercing gaze.

"We were experiments," Thrā'kkor states. "Created to be the ultimate weapon against the vólkins."

A cold shudder ripples through me.

"Most of us perished," he continues. "The tsar twisted nature, testing and failing, again and again. Until he forged the perfect warriors."

The wolves whine, their ears flat, tails tucked between their legs. They feel it too. The wrongness. The weight of what was done.

Thrā'kkor lifts his massive green hand to his heart. "Our skin came from Mother Nature. Our brutal bodies were carved from the earth itself." He exhales, lowering his eyes. "And our minds—our will—came from the blue rose."

My heart beats so hard I feel it in my throat. I stumble back and crash into something solid. Theron.

He was behind me before I even realized it. He grips my shoulders, holding me still. Holding me together. "You came to fight for your mother," Theron says.

Thrā'kkor nods. Then, he bows. And then, they all bow.

A sea of massive warriors lowering their heads before me. "Noël Ársa," Thrā'kkor declares. "The Lidéřen we have waited for has finally awakened."

My throat tightens.

"It is our honor to fight for the true creator. The moment the messengers arrived, we knew our time had come. We began our journey from our land to Ávera. But—" He pauses, lifting his head. "We scented the blue rose earlier than expected. So we ran here. To you."

The blue rose. The lush gardens of the tsar's stronghold. The experiments. My mind spirals, a storm of fragmented pieces snapping into place. I turn to Theron, my breath shallow, my pulse pounding like war drums. Our eyes lock.

"So there was no ambush," Theron says.

But my chest tightens. A sick feeling coils in my gut. *Ávera.*

The wolves—their snouts lifted, their bodies rigid—aren't watching the orcs anymore. They're looking toward Ávera. Something is wrong.

A single, breathless word escapes my lips. "No."

The wolves knew all along.

62

THE HARVEST OF BROKEN SOULS

"I wove Ávera from the breath of the earth and the tear of the first bloom. It is the cradle of the six, the garden where balance shall rise again, or fall forever."
—Éva, Mother of All

Noël

Á vera has fallen.

We have run for so long since that night with the orcs. Too long. And now, it might be too late. We were too far. We were too foolish. *I* was too foolish. How could I believe Gregor?

The night air stings my lungs as we tear through the forest. Vólkins, nýmphí, orcs, we all run. A single force racing toward the land I swore to protect. But I scent it before I see it. Blood. Thick and pungent, rotting and fresh, coating the air like a death shroud. And beneath it—fire. Ash and decay. Ávera is burning.

The trees blur around me as we push harder, faster. My knuckles turn white around the hilt of my sword as I clutch

Theron's fur. My body moves in sync with his strides. A sliver of hope claws at my chest, that maybe we aren't too late. But the stench of death grows heavier.

The orcs run beside us, their eyes dark. They called me their creator, their mother—the one who will lead them. And now, they follow me to war. To the biggest war humankind has ever seen.

We near Ávera's borders, and the air claws at my throat. It's rotten. The odor of death thickens. What could have caused such a horrible stench? Unless . . . Unless everyone has been dead since we left. A shudder racks my body. I should have been smarter. I should have been more careful.

I should *not* be the Lidéřen.

Why did I ever believe this was something I could handle? Why did I ever think I was enough? The goddesses chose wrong. I have had everything handed to me—a loving mother, a military career, a prophecy, a mate, an army of orcs willing to follow me without question. All of it, given to me so easily. And I don't deserve any of it. This is why I will give my life for my failures. But.

If I die, Theron dies too. A violent sob chokes me. How can I end myself when his life is bound to mine? He doesn't deserve this.

Tears well in my eyes. I grit my teeth. The crystals on my forehead, a crown I don't deserve to wear, burn against my skin. I sent warriors to their deaths. Like some god I am not. I clench my fists into Theron's fur until my knuckles go numb.

Zephyr. Kaël. Aeson.

I'm so sorry.

Mother. You were wrong. I'm not strong. Tears slip free, trailing cold down my burning face.

The moment we reach the tree line, my stomach twists into knots, a deep, instinctual dread settles in my bones before my mind can fully process what I'm seeing.

This is not Ávera.

Not the Ávera I left behind, where the towering trees cradled glowing lanterns like fireflies trapped in an eternal dance of light. Not the Ávera where the rivers ran clear and reflected the sky in shades of sapphire, nor the Ávera where the wind carried the scent of fresh blooms and damp earth, where life pulsed beneath every root and leaf.

No. What stands before me is a massacre, a nightmare made real. The streams, once crystalline and pure, now run black, thick with filth and gore. The air is filled with the acrid tang of smoke and the metallic scent of blood. It coats my tongue even as I try to swallow down my nausea. The low, guttural moans that drift through the burning village blend with the crackling hiss of fire.

My entire body locks in place, every muscle tensing as a new horror unveils itself before me.

They are not human.

They move in the distance, long-limbed, grotesque figures, their bodies twisted into something barely recognizable, as if humanity was stretched too thin and left to wither in unnatural agony. Their bodies twitch as they move, jerky and uncoordinated, yet disturbingly fast when they shift their attention. Their limbs are wrong, too elongated, bending at impossible angles, their fingers tipped with jagged nails that seem to scrape against the very air around them. Their skin hangs in unnatural folds, some parts stretched too tight over sharp bones, others sagging as if melting, as though they are held together by forces beyond nature.

And their faces. Goddesses above, their faces.

Their mouths are too wide, split at the corners, jagged teeth barely concealed behind cracked lips. Their eyes are hollow, empty voids where life should be, black pits of nothingness that swallow whatever light dares to reach them. They stare, but they do not see in the way living things do. There is no soul behind those eyes.

A low, rolling growl rumbles from Theron's chest, his claws sliding free, his fur standing on end as he plants himself at my side like a wall of muscle and steel. But even he—my strongest, fiercest mate—does not lunge forward.

The tsar has played with dark magic, and this is what he has created. A perversion of nature. A mockery of humankind.

Some of these creatures move aimlessly, wandering through the burning remains of Ávera like lost shadows, their heads twitching erratically as if listening to something only they can hear. Others move with their rotting fingers curled around burning torches, the flames licking at their clawed hands with no reaction, no recognition of their own destruction.

And Ávera . . . Ávera burns.

The great trees, the ones that cradled our homes within their mighty arms, are now consumed by fire. The sacred wood screams, a desperate, cracking wail as the flames crawl up their trunks. Their golden lanterns shatter in bursts of light to fall like dying stars into the abyss of ruin below. And worse than the sight—is the sound. Screams.

Not just the dying groans of the trees, but the anguished, soul-wrenching cries of my people.

Vólkins lie broken across the land, their massive bodies torn apart, some still breathing, still twitching as their blood stains the earth in thick pools of crimson. Others—goddesses above, others—are being dragged away. The creatures haul them into the shadows, pulling them through the ruins, vanishing with them before I can even take a step.

The females and pups are gone. I can only hope they're safe in the shelters.

A thunderous roar erupts from Theron, his fury shaking the earth beneath us, but even that raw sound cannot drown out the chaos.

A creature stands over a fallen vólkin warrior, its skeletal fingers wrapped around his jaw, prying it open, tilting its grotesque head as if examining a specimen rather than a living being. The warrior growls, but he is too far gone to fight back.

The creature leans closer. Its mouth opens—wider, wider— splitting at the corners until its jaw unhinges. A voice spills from its throat in a warbled, broken sound. "Not . . . this one."

And then, like a piece of discarded meat, it drops him, turns away, and moves on.

Not this one. They are choosing. They are not here to kill indiscriminately. They are taking some. And they are leaving the rest to rot. They came to harvest them.

For what?

A fire unlike anything I have ever felt ignites within me.

A rage that consumes every doubt, every shred of restraint left in my body.

"Kill them." My voice is barely a whisper, but Theron hears it. He growls so deeply it shakes the marrow in my bones. And then I scream. The sound rips from my throat, shaking the skies and echoing into the night like a war cry from the depths of my very soul.

"KILL THEM ALL!"

The army erupts into motion, a wave of fury that crashes into the monsters that have defiled our home. I sprint forward, sword raised, and run it through the first creature that dares stand in my way. Its skin is too soft, it peels away beneath my blade as if cutting through rotting fruit. It shrieks, but still moves. And then, they all turn toward the sound. Their hollow eyes lock onto me.

They do not feel pain.

They do not fear death.

They only understand orders.

And whatever command they have been given, it is not yet complete.

The first monster lunges at me, its movements erratic. I swing my sword, the blade slices through its torso, but—nothing.

No scream. No stagger.

No death.

The thing keeps moving, as if I hadn't just gutted it from hip to rib. Its hollow eyes snap to mine, its lipless mouth curling into something grotesquely close to a grin.

I don't hesitate. I won't. I shift my grip, spin on my heel, and slash through its neck in a single strike. Its head snaps back, but it doesn't fall.

The body keeps moving, its decapitated head hanging on by nothing but threads of sinew. Still, it reaches for me. Goddesses, what are these things?

A deafening snarl rips through the battlefield as Theron barrels past me, his claws rake down a monster's back, tearing straight through flesh, tendons, and bone. He twists, jaws nearly unhinging before he bites into its neck and rips its throat out in one motion.

It doesn't die.

It still moves.

Theron throws the writhing corpse to the ground, crushing its ribs beneath his massive paws. He stomps its chest into the dirt and snarls when it still twitches.

The orcs fight differently.

Thrā'kkor wields a jagged axe, swinging it with such force that it cleaves a monster's entire upper body clean in half. But even as its torso falls, the arms still crawl forward.

Another orc crushes a creature's skull to splinters with his bare hands. It should be dead. It should be *fucking dead*. But it keeps moving, headless and mindless, clawing at the orc's chest. Nothing kills them. Nothing works.

I grit my teeth and move, slashing, slicing, tearing through flesh and bone, but it doesn't matter. Another monster rushes me from behind. Too fast.

I barely turn before claws drag down my shoulder, tearing into muscle, cutting through my skin like it's paper. The warmth of my own blood spills down my arm.

But I don't feel the pain.

Anger surges through me, drowning everything else out, sharpening my focus. The monster tries to strike again, but then, it stops. It stares at its hands. At my blood staining its rotting skin. And then it screams.

A piercing, earsplitting wail of agony.

Its body convulses, its veins bubble as if something is boiling beneath its flesh. Its movements turn even more unnatural than before, its hollow eyes bulge. And then it melts. Skin sloughs off in blackened chunks, muscle disintegrating into steaming, frothing rot. It collapses into the dirt, then shrivels into nothing. I freeze. My heart pounds so hard it hurts. What the—

Another monster lunges, but before it can touch me, Theron slams into it, tearing into its chest and ripping it apart limb by limb. And it still doesn't die. Enough.

I snarl and slam the blade of my sword straight through its skull, twisting it with a wet crunch.

It stops moving. Huh?

Not because of my sword. Because of the blood. A single drop from my shoulder drips onto its face. It twitches once, then collapses, shriveling into the same melted, rotting nothingness. I can barely breathe.

My blood. My blood kills them.

I don't know how. I don't care. I meet Theron's wide, shocked gaze. His chest heaves, his face covered in the blood of our enemies. I lift my injured arm, letting more blood drip from my fingertips.

And then I grin. "Theron," I breathe. My shoulder burns, but I don't care.

He grabs two creatures by their skulls and smashes them together with a loud crack. Their hollow eyes still stare as their bodies twitch. He turns to me, fur matted with blood. His blood. Their blood. "Yes, my dove?" His voice is rough, but his eyes are locked on me.

I lift my blade and drag my wounded arm across the steel. Theron's entire body tenses. His ears flick back, his tail lashes, his stance shifts as if he's about to lunge and stop me. But he doesn't. Because he understands.

This is the only way. If my blood kills them, so be it.

I take my good arm and slice my palm, then the other. The sting is uncomfortable, fire races through my skin, but I don't stop.

I raise my hands, coated in my own blood. It drips from my fingers, splatters against the dirt. My heart pounds. "LISTEN ALL!" My voice shakes the battlefield. Every single warrior—orc, vólkin, nýmphá, wolf—and every single twisted, grotesque monster turns their head toward me. They feel it. They hear it.

They know.

"EACH OF YOU, TAKE MY BLOOD. IT KILLS THEM."

Theron's gaze locks onto mine, understanding written in every part of his face. He knows what I need. He doesn't hesitate. Neither do I.

We move.

He smears his paws with my blood, and we run in opposite directions. Theron surges through the chaos, his massive paws crushing bones beneath him, claws raking through the flesh of those in his path. With every step, he grabs a monster, smearing my blood across their skin. And I do the same.

And just like that, they wither.

They scream and melt.

I dodge a monster near me, twist my body, and shove my

bloody hand against its throat. The monster seizes, its body convulses, its veins bulge. Then, with a wet, gurgling shriek, it collapses. It rots before it even hits the ground.

Another lunges, swinging a rusted blade, but I duck, pivot, and slam my palm against its ribs. One single touch, and it crumbles.

Everywhere, the battlefield is shifting.

The nýmphí move like shadows, slipping between bodies, nails slicing tendons and throats, dipping their hands in the blood I left behind. They cut, stain, let them rot.

They are losing.

They scream and wail, clawing at their melting flesh, writhing as their own bodies betray them. But it takes time. So much time, and my blood is limited. I can only give so much before I collapse.

The ground is slick with blood and corpses, with monsters half-dead, twitching, melting into the dirt. I don't know how long we fight. I just keep moving. Slash. Strike. Smear. Kill.

The battlefield becomes a slaughterhouse. Pain claws at my shoulder, my muscles ache, my breath is ragged, but I do not stop. The creatures fall, one by one, until only silence remains.

The last monster before my eyes looks familiar. *Commander Barric.* The tsar is the true monster.

He murmurs, "Blood of creator—"

I slash his throat. A silence thick with the stench of rot. A silence that rings louder than screams. The battle is over. Barric was the last one.

We have won.

"Theron!" My voice rips through the silence, my heart hammering against my ribs. I turn. Where is he? The battlefield is a graveyard, heavy with blood and decay, but my eyes see only one thing. Him. Theron.

He runs toward me, stepping over the broken corpses. He's

drenched in blood, so much blood. His fur is soaked, matted, dark, but he is still running, still breathing.

We did it. We won.

I don't think. I just run.

Fisting my ruined gown, I sprint to meet him. My vision blurs with exhaustion, with relief, with everything. Just a few more steps.

Just a little closer.

"My mate," Theron breathes, his voice raw, his hazel eyes burning into mine. Just a little—

A shrill whistle cuts through the air. An arrow. My head jerks up, my instincts screaming. Too fast, too close—

A flash of light erupts from my crystals. My fingers snap up, but too late. For a moment, I don't move. The battlefield spins. The world goes still.

The arrow broke my crystals. No . . .

But, we won. I don't understand.

My breath shudders. My legs weaken. My head sways. Just out of reach, Theron stumbles. No—

He sways, then falls to his knees.

No.

No.

This can't be happening. I haven't restored the balance. I haven't spent enough time with Theron.

I haven't had a child.

Is this how it en—

63

ASHES, CHAINS, AND
A LIFELESS CROWN

"Remember this, daughters of the earth: The Blue Rose and her
Guardian were carved from spirit and flame to rule what the
world has forgotten. Where they walk, life will kneel and death
will flee."
—Elder Aïna, to vólkin females

Mina

"Mama, when can we go out?" Little Árne's small
voice echoes through the underground cave, his
tiny paws padding over the stone floor as he
runs in circles.

I watch him with tired eyes, my heart aches. How do you
explain war to a pup?

"Hush, little one," Ciele murmurs, pulling her son close.
Her claws smooth over his downy fur, but I can see the tension
in her shoulders, in the way her tail flicks side to side. "When
Elder Aïna says we can."

It is the only answer she can give. I can smell the blood.

Even here—deep underground, far from the battlefield—it reaches us. That thick, metallic scent that does not belong in Ávera. The pups don't notice it. But we do.

"Elder Aïna!" Essin huffs, crossing her arms. "I can't wait any longer either! We need to go."

I glance at Naïa, who is rocking a pup to sleep. I see the same worry clouding her gaze.

"I feel my heart weeping." I swallow. "Am I the only one?"

Naïa meets my eyes, her fingers twitch in the pup's fur. We have been here too long. The day the warriors heard the monsters approaching, we were ushered into these shelters. Her Majesty ordered they be hidden beneath the earth, protected by a seamless entrance and surrounded with rosemary and salt. She thought of everything.

And yet—

It does not feel safe anymore.

"I have a bad feeling," Elder Aïna murmurs as she rises to her full height. The dim light of her crystals catches the silver in her fur, making her look older than she ever has. "The glade is standing strong." Her voice is calm, but her brows furrow. "However . . . it is covered in blood."

My heart stutters.

So much blood she can sense it from here. Silence falls over us. Even the pups seem to feel it.

"I will go investigate!" Essin declares, already moving toward the entrance.

I reach out to stop her. "Essin—"

"You are too foolish if you think to go alone." Elder Aïna's voice is firm, it leaves no room for argument. "Mina and Naïa shall go with you."

I nod.

Naïa tries to pass the sleeping pup to Elder Aïna, but she shakes her head. "I will go too."

My ears perk up. Elder Aïna is wise, and she is the strongest among us, but she's old. But if she thinks this is necessary, then we cannot refuse her.

I meet Naïa's gaze once more. We are going to see what waits above. Essin and I press our shoulders against the heavy stone, pushing together. The weight resists us at first, and then the rock moves, the grinding sound too loud in the silence of the underground shelter. I wince at the noise and glance over my shoulder to where the pups and the elder females wait, watching with wide eyes. I wish we had crystals.

Not for power, not for battle, but for something as simple as speaking without sound. If we could send signals to each other through thought, we wouldn't have to risk exposing ourselves now. But that is not a gift we were given. The males, the warriors, they have it, and we do not. That is simply the way things have always been.

Elder Aïna steps forward. With a motion of her paw through the air, the stone slides the rest of the way.

Essin flicks an ear, muttering something under her breath about how she and I just struggled with that same boulder, but there is no time for complaints. The moment the entrance is open, a savage, wet stench fills my nose.

My stomach lurches.

I have never smelled so much of it at once before. Even Naïa takes a few steps back. We have to move. We have to see what happened.

Elder Aïna is already walking, her ears forward and alert. I swallow down the knot rising in my throat and step out of the shelter beside Naïa and Essin.

The forest is eerily still, as though even the leaves have forgotten how to move. There is no wind, no rustling of branches, only the overwhelming scent of blood and decay hanging in the air. We move through the trees as silent as shadows. I'm not sure I'm ready to see what lies ahead.

My legs give out beneath me as an unbearable weight

crashes into my chest, and though my eyes refuse to blink, refuse to look away, my mind rejects what it sees. As if denying its existence could somehow rewrite fate, could somehow undo the carnage that spills across Ávera like a wound that will never heal. No, this is not real. It cannot be real.

And yet, bodies. So many bodies. Some are twisted, their shapes unrecognizable, grotesque, monstrous, just as the warriors warned. And though I have never seen these creatures before, I know, deep within my bones, that they were never meant to exist, that they are abominations of dark magic, things that should have never been given breath, never been given life.

But others . . . Others are ours. Vólkins.

Who are the green-skinned warriors? Doesn't matter now. The monsters' blood has stained the sacred earth of Ávera.

And those who remain standing, they are gathered in a circle, their faces hollow, their bodies still, their hands placing flowers over the dead. Flowers.

Ávera's warriors, Her Majesty's warriors, kneeling by the bodies of the fallen, offering beauty where only devastation remains, offering the final kindness they can give to those who will never rise again. I cannot breathe.

I feel my own heartbeat, a thunderous drum in my chest that threatens to shatter me from the inside out, and my gaze flickers frantically, searching, searching, desperate for something, someone, anything to ground me, anything to tell me this is not real, that this is a trick of my mind, a nightmare from which I will wake.

Elder Aïna's steps do not falter, though even she cannot hide the way her ears are lowered, the way her shoulders tremble as she walks toward the gathered warriors, toward the unmoving bodies, toward the sight I cannot bear to see.

But I follow her. Because I have to. Because I need to. Because if I do not, then I will stand here forever, paralyzed, drowning in my own denial.

Then I see them. Noël and Theron.

The air is ripped from my lungs in a strangled cry as I stumble forward, my steps uneven, my paws unsteady beneath me, my vision blurring with a flood of tears that refuse to fall because falling tears would mean acceptance. Their bodies lie together, side by side, unmoving. Too still. Too still.

Her Majesty—our leader, the soul of this rebellion, the one who led us out of the dark and into the light—she lies motionless, her crystals now dull and broken, a gaping wound where an arrow has lodged itself in her forehead and pierced the very essence of her power. *Just like four hundred years ago.*

And Theron—her mate, her guardian, her heart—is beside her, still and silent, his paw resting over her stomach, as if even in death he refuses to let her go, refuses to leave her, refuses to let the world take her from him. As if his final act was to hold on to her one last time.

A raw, broken sound wrenches itself from my throat, something that is neither scream nor sob but a soul-deep agony that has no name, only pain.

Naïa and Essin collapse, their bodies folding over them both, as if by shielding them, they can somehow protect them, somehow bring them back.

I turn blindly, blindly, reaching for Elder Aïna, pressing my face into her fur, clutching her as if she is the only thing keeping me from falling apart completely.

"Why?" The word is small, weak, nothing more than a breath. "Why—why—why?"

Elder Aïna bows her head and says nothing, because there are no answers. Because this is real.

Because the woman who led us all, who stood against the tsar and defied the laws of this world, who promised us a future, a world free of suffering, a world where we could be more than prisoners—

She is gone.

Theron, who stood by her side, who fought for her, who lived and breathed only for her, who swore to protect her with every last ounce of his strength, who would have torn the world apart for her—

He is gone too.

My tears dampen the fur on my face, blurring my vision, washing away the image before me, but no amount of tears can erase this, no amount of grief can bring them back, no amount of denial can change the truth that is right in front of me. And so I wail.

The nýmphí arrive with crystals glowing with healing energy, the leaf spirits gather around Noël's and Theron's life-less bodies, but nothing is enough. Nothing can undo what has been done.

"We will remember them," a rumbling voice says, and I lift my gaze to find one of the green-skinned warriors standing tall, his expression grim, his golden jewelry catching the moonlight. "Even though we did not know them for long, we saw what a true leader is."

Another green human speaks, his hands clenched into fists. "Her Majesty welcomed us," he says. "And we will honor her. Honor them both."

The warriors, both vólkin and green humans, rise as one. But then—

A growl rips through the silence. Low and familiar.

I snap my head to the right, my heart leaping into my throat as I stare toward the edge of Ávera. Orïon.

The sound of weeping—of shrieking—rises from the trees, a sound so unnatural, so gut wrenching, it makes my fur bristle. It's unlike anything I have ever heard before.

A gasp escapes me as figures emerge from between the blackened trees. More of them.

More of those twisted, unnatural creatures, their bodies

moving in broken ways, their soulless eyes fixed on us all, their very presence a stain on this sacred land. They step into the clearing, dragging the scent of decay with them.

And then I see Orïon.

He's shackled, bound in thick, thorn-covered chains that dig into his fur, wrap around his limbs, his torso, his muzzle. He trembles beneath the weight of his restraints.

They have muzzled him. Muzzled him.

A vólkin—one of our strongest, one of our own—bound like a beast. And at the end of the chain, holding him like a captured animal, stands a man. A human.

My claws curl, my stomach turns with rage. There are three of them. Three human males, walking through the trees as if they own this land, as if they have the right to defile it with their presence.

And between them, walking as if he belongs there, as if this is where he was always meant to stand, Gregor. My body locks, my breath stolen from my chest, my pulse thundering so violently I feel it in my ears.

The green humans, the vólkins, all of them, turn toward the unfolding nightmare, growls rising from their throats, their snarls breaking through the air.

Essin steps forward, her raw voice cracks as she roars, "Orïon!"

But Orïon does not answer.

Because he cannot. Because they have silenced him.

And Gregor is standing with them. I stare at him, my breath short, my vision darkening at the edges. And I do not understand.

"The tsar sends his regards," the man holding Orïon's chains sneers, and shoves him forward with a twist of his wrist. The heavy clang of metal rings through the growls of the warriors. His grin is ugly, stretched too wide over his teeth. "I believe it's quite clear who holds the prize now." His every word is designed to dig deep, to hurt. His gaze moves to Gregor, and his smirk widens. "Right, Gregor? Look at your friends."

Gregor doesn't respond. He doesn't even lift his head. He just stares at his feet. The monsters beside the humans remain still, waiting. And then the human laughs.

"Noël and her mate are gone, aren't they?" His fingers flex around Orïon's chain as he yanks it tighter, forcing him to stumble. He barks out another laugh. "I'm very skilled with my arrow."

My stomach twists. I have always known humans to be cruel.

But never like this. They are the real monsters.

The warriors around me shift, ready to strike. A low, warning growl rumbles from deep within their chests, fangs bared, claws twitching for violence. They are seconds away from launching themselves. And then, Elder Aïna lifts her paw.

The warriors freeze.

She steps forward.

"I have done it before," she says, closing her eyes. Her voice is calm. "And I will do it once again."

I shake my head, my entire body tensing.

I want to stop her. But I don't move.

The monsters charge, and their loud cries rip through the night like the wails of the damned. Their warped bodies jerk and sway, some moving on all fours, others stumbling upright with sickening, broken motions.

My breath catches in my throat, my knees threaten to give out. Every muscle in my body screams to run, to fight, to do something. But Elder Aïna does not move. Her paws lift toward the sky.

Not a single warrior dares to disobey.

Even the green-skinned warriors stand still, as if instinct itself warns them not to interfere. And then, the wind shifts.

A sudden, violent gust tears through the land, howling like an enraged spirit. The leaf spirits scatter in every direction, flung into the air by the force.

The ancient trees groan under the weight of something unseen, their massive branches creaking and trembling, knocking loose a storm of leaves that swirl through the darkened sky. The ground beneath us shakes hard enough to rattle my very bones. I don't know where to look. Everything is moving.

It feels as though the goddesses have reached down to twist nature before my eyes. The earth rumbles again. And more creatures appear from the tree line.

Their grotesque bodies spill from the shadows, pouring into the clearing like a wave of nightmares. They do not stop. They run straight past the humans and Orïon, their soulless eyes locked on us. But the moment they breach the clearing— they scream.

One by one, they collapse.

Writhing.

Howling.

Dying.

Frozen, heart hammering, I watch as the battlefield descends into madness. And then, Elder Aïna turns to us. Her eyes are wide, as if even she did not expect this.

She didn't...?

The earth shudders furiously, deep cracks splintering through the ground, splitting the soil apart. I stagger and barely manage to catch myself before I fall. Did Elder Aïna do this?

I knew she was powerful. I knew she could bend the forces of nature to her will. But this?

Even Elder Aïna's expression twists in shock, her pale eyes flickering as she watches the destruction unfold around us.

The nýmphí look just as lost. They quiver, their hands raised to shield the lifeless bodies of our leaders, their glowing eyes darting in every direction as if searching for something, an answer, a reason for the madness around us.

Thick, blackened vines explode from the cracked earth and twist into the sky like writhing serpents with jagged thorns so dark they seem to drink the moonlight. They spread through the battlefield, spiraling in all directions.

Ávera pulses.

The land hums with energy, the sacred blue roses shine brighter than the stars above. Their light is blinding, pulsing like a heartbeat, like a force awakened from slumber.

My fur stands on end. My fingers twitch, the raw energy in the air making my skin crawl.

I don't know what's happening. And then, a scream.

A scream that rips through the land, full of enough rage to shake the foundations of reality. The nýmphí collapse with their hands pressed against their ears, their bodies folded onto the bloodstained earth. My breath catches.

My entire world stops.

Because Her Majesty moves. Her body, once lifeless, once cold in the embrace of death, lurches upright. Her hand rises.

And with one motion, she yanks the arrow from her forehead.

A choked gasp bursts from my throat. My claws dig into the dirt.

This isn't possible.

This isn't possible.

The arrow falls from her hand, falls to the ground, and as it does, her eyes open.

They are not the eyes of the leader I once knew. They burn with blue fire. Flames swirl around her, licking at her skin, but they do not burn. They do not devour the grass beneath her feet. They do not touch the roses that bloom in her wake. They obey her. She rises—no, she ascends.

The air thickens, making it impossible to breathe. My throat constricts. The ground beneath her quakes.

"When the Blue Rose falls, Ávera will mourn. When Ávera mourns, I shall rise again."

The vines pulse.

The blue roses bloom. The land itself answers her.

And beside her, Theron moves.

64

THE BLUE ROSE CROWNED
BY BLOOD AND FIRE

"The flower that blooms after death is the one that will never
wither. Rise, Blue Rose. Let the earth remember your wrath."
—Láda Velésa, Goddess of Leadership and War

Noël

Breathing feels foreign. As if the world has been
reshaped in my absence. The land mourned me. I felt
its roots wrap around my soul and pull me back, whispering that my task was unfinished. My crystals feel heavier.
They thrum with every life lost, every drop of blood spilled in
my name.

Death was quiet. A slow fade into the dark. But returning is
like being thrust into the sun, seared back into existence by the
cries of those who refused to let me go.

I was meant to die. I know that now. But the prophecy was
never about my death—it was about what would *rise* from the
ashes of defeat.

*She who was marked for death shall not fall, but rise the flame
reborn in ruin's wake, forged not to perish, but to reign.*

Ávera told me the last part of the prophecy.

I am the Blue Rose, uprooted, but still I bloom. I am the flame-born heir who shall weigh a soul beneath the pyre's glow.

I am Noël Ársa, blood of the blue rose. No longer its daughter, but the bloom itself, crowned and sovereign.

Theron's soul held on to mine, a thread of fire and fury, tethering me to the world of the living. Even in death, I was warm in his grasp.

If the tsar believes this war is over, he has yet to understand the storm building outside his stronghold. He tried to bury me, but he did not know I was a seed my mother planted. I have risen, and I am not the same. For every drop of our blood, I will make them bleed *tenfold*. I will destroy and I will take what belongs to *me*.

Ávera has chosen me. The goddesses watch over me. I will not fail.

I exhale and look to Theron as words slip from my lips. "Rise, my soul. Our journey has just begun."

His chest rises. Barely, but it moves. His massive paws dig into the earth beneath him. Then, I turn around.

The nýmphí. The vólkins and the orcs. They are still. Silent. Staring at me as if I am a goddess. And Elder Aïna, her breath unsteady, her wide eyes locked onto mine.

A whisper of the land hums in my ears. A memory, a truth I did not know before death took me. I turn fully to her. "Ávera told me you are vólkar." My voice echoes through the land. "And so is Theron now."

Elder Aïna does not move. Does not speak.

Theron rises.

The earth crunches beneath his paws, the sound shivers across my skin. He is alive. Then, he opens his eyes. Those beautiful hazel eyes—once warm and gold—have turned pale. But he is still my Theron, my soul. We are alive.

The marks from our bonding ritual return, staining his fur as if they never left. A part of him now. Red circles and lines, the sacred symbols binding us. And there, over his heart, the mark I left on him. Mine. *Forever*. I turn my head.

The monsters crawl from the soil. They do not understand. So I lift my hand, calling the vines from beneath the earth. They obey my will and writhe toward me in a slow dance. A single vine coils into my palm, its thorns piercing my skin and pressing deep. My blood blooms against its dark edges as it drinks from me. With a twist of my wrist, I direct my hand toward the creatures. A single drop of my blood, and they *burn*.

Blue fire erupts from their flesh and devours them whole. Their limbs flail, their bodies convulse, until they crumble into nothing. Silence falls.

Not a single monster remains.

Now, at last, I have the time to savor Gregor's death. He trembles, drowning in terror, his wide eyes fixed on me. He knows. There is no more mercy. No more pleading. I never make the same mistake twice. He will *die*.

The tsar's men allow their cowardice to win out and abandon Orïon's bound body to dart away into the darkness. I barely shift my gaze toward Theron before he's moving—*a blur* —lunging after them like death itself. Faster than before. *Stronger*. But just as he reaches them—

"If you kill me!" a voice rings out. "*You kill her!*"

My gaze snaps toward the sound. One of the men yanks someone from the shadows. A woman, her body limp, her face obscured by tangled brown hair, her knees shaking.

Theron skids to a halt mere steps away from them. His body is ready to strike, but he does not move.

They have a hostage. The Healer.

A broken cry erupts. Gregor. He collapses to his knees, his fingers clutching at his hair, his entire form racked with something beyond fear. "*STOP!*" he screams. "*JUST STOP! I CAN'T*

TAKE THIS ANYMORE! KILL HER! KILL ME! KILL EVERYONE!"

It is the desperate, unhinged wail of a man who has lost all grip on reason.

"Gregor!" The woman's voice shatters the night. She thrashes in her captor's grasp, struggling against his hold.

The gleam of my blue flames flickers over her light brown hair, similar to his. A relative, perhaps? A sister? It doesn't matter. She is the healer from the prophecy, and no more related to this dead man. I pulse through my crystal to Theron. In a *blink*, it is done. Three men. Gregor. Oríon. Kneeling before me.

Theron stands behind them, a shadow of judgment. The nýmphí understand without words, and they dart forward to cut the healer free. She screams Gregor's name. Her cries echo through Ávera's forests.

"Three ways to go against me, and all of them kneel at my feet." I raise my bleeding hand and close it into a fist. The chains around Oríon shatter, and he collapses to the ground, gasping, freed at last. Gregor shudders.

Tilting my head, I consider him. He looks so *small* now. My boots are silent against the bloodstained earth as I step forward to grab him by the throat and lift him to his feet. His pulse thrashes beneath my palm. "I will take your life for all the lives you stole." My voice is ice, my grip tight. I tilt my head to the other side, and whisper, "And for mine as well."

Gregor's hollow, defeated eyes stare into mine, veins bulge from his skin. He swallows. A broken, pitiful sound escapes him. "I . . . I never wanted any of thi—" *Crack.* His body goes limp. I let him fall. The earth swallows him whole.

Now, the others. I turn to the three men still kneeling. "Which one of you killed me?"

The man in the center draws my attention, his lips stretching into something like a smirk, arrogant and too wide.

"I did." He tilts his head, studying me like a child amused by a toy he's already broken. "And you're even more of a tyrant than your father."

"Ándor wasn't a tyrant, you fool."

At that, he laughs. A wild, fractured sound that echoes across the silent land. "Look at you!" he gasps between chuckles, his shoulders shaking. "A vólkin whore, exactly like your mother was!"

Theron's growl rumbles behind him. His claws flex, his breathing sharp.

The man doesn't stop. He doesn't care. He leans forward, spitting poison with every word. "You think Ándor was your father?" He snorts and his voice turns cruel. "Eyleen didn't tell you? What a poor, lost child. Eyleen could've had a lavish life, the tsar's cock buried inside her every night. Instead, she ran pregnant into the forest like some pathetic wretch!"

A snarl tears from Theron as he grips the man's head, but the man just grins, his teeth bared like a wolf scenting blood.

"How dare you speak with such hatred for females?" Theron growls, clenching his claws and drawing blood from the man's forehead.

"No. He doesn't hate. He's afraid," I answer my mate. "He's afraid of women. *All of them are.*" I study the man's face. "That's why you try to make us small, keep us in the kitchen or in bed. Make us whores or mothers. And when we express our feelings, you call us hysterical. When we are strong, you call us whores. And when we seek power, you say, 'No, that's not feminine.'" I lean in, and my voice drops. "But what truly scares you . . . is not that we won't be feminine. It's that you will not be masculine enough." My crystals pulse, and I see my own pale eyes reflected in his.

"Come on, little girl! Kill me!" His voice rises, mockery and madness laced in every word that comes out of his mouth. "A child playing god with vólkins at her feet. Did you really think you were different? You think you stand against the tsar?!"

His smile stretches even wider. Unnatural. His eyes gleam as he delivers his final words. "You're going mad." A pause. A breath. "You are just like him. Or even worse."

My heart pounds, fury roars through my veins. The earth stirs. Blood pools beneath his knees, a crimson bloom spreading through the dirt.

He chokes on his laughter.

Thorned blue roses sprout from his own blood, curling out of his body, tearing his flesh. They twist, wrapping tight, tighter, until they snap his spine like a brittle twig. Eyes bulging, mouth frozen in an unfinished laugh, his head tilts back—

Then, it detaches.

His body collapses. The other two men follow, their screams hardly leaving their lips before the roses claim them too. And then silence. I lift my gaze, staring into nothing.

The battlefield fades, the blood, the bodies, the silence, all of it slips into the background as the pieces fall into place. I see it now.

She was *pregnant*. That's why she ran. That's why she fled the stronghold. To protect *me*. *Two mates can't be unbonded for more than six moons.*

The truth settles in my bones, a revelation so simple—so *obvious*—and yet, it shatters everything. It all finally makes sense.

I was born from the blood I vowed to destroy.

The battlefield is quiet now. The blood has dried, the ashes settled. What remains is only what has been lost. And what has been won.

I stand before them, the warriors who fought, the spirits who watched, the land that *chose me*. Vólkins. Orcs. Nýmphí. The very essence of Ávera. This is the moment that will shape the future. *Our* future.

With an inhale, I calm the storm inside me, then lift my voice so all may hear. So that every unseen creature will know who will shape this world.

"We have lost. We have bled. We have suffered. But we *are still here*."

The wind carries my words, the spirits whisper their approval, their presence felt in the rustling of leaves, in the gentle pulse of the glowing blue roses that now bloom across the battlefield.

"The tsar sought to break us. To burn us. To erase us from this world. But look around you." Spreading my arms, I motion to the warriors standing, to the land reborn beneath us. "He has failed."

I lock eyes with each of them—the vólkins, the nýmphí, the orcs who knelt before me but now stand as brothers.

"For centuries, we have been hunted. We have been called *monsters*." My voice hardens, the fire burning deep in my chest. "And yet, it was *they* who were the true monsters. The ones who ravaged our lands. The ones who took our homes. The ones who sought to turn us into nothing but whispers of the past."

A growl rumbles through the gathered warriors. Fists clench. Claws flex. Fangs gleam in the moonlight. Good.

"But we are not whispers." My crystals *glow*, my power pulses through the air. "We are the storm that will carve a new world. No longer will we kneel. No longer will we hide. No longer will we let the tsar dictate our fate. From this day forward, we *stand as one*—orc, vólkin, nýmphá, and woman." I place my bloodied palm against my torn gown over my heart. "We will build and rule. We will thrive. Not as the forgotten, but as the rightful heirs of this world."

And then Theron steps closer as a few nýmphí move aside for him. His pale eyes burn, his body still covered in the remnants of battle. He holds something in his paws. A crown.

But not of gold.

A crown of *blue roses*. Long, dark thorns stand tall around the circle. Theron lowers his head, presses his forehead to mine, and my soul sings. Feeling his touch and his crystals, makes me want to rise to the skies. He lifts the crown.

And places it atop my head.

A hush falls. The warriors, the spirits, and the land hold their breath. Theron takes a step back, his voice reverent as he says, "*Lidéřen.*"

My birthright.

And then, *they kneel*. All of them. Vólkins. Orcs. Nýmphí.

The land *itself* bows to me. The ancient trees curve to me, the moon blesses my soul.

A wind rushes through Ávera, carrying the scent of roses and blood. Eyes closed, I feel the weight of the crown on my head, the weight of every life lost, every sacrifice made, and the world that awaits me to be claimed.

And I swear, this is only the beginning.

"Noël Ársa, my husband," Theron says, and the only thing I can do is smile.

EPILOGUE

Since the day the leaders rose from death, the land itself began to heal. Earthly souls and ethereal beings alike worked together, restoring the sacred groves, rebuilding the homes that had been reduced to ash. It would take time, perhaps months or even years, but no one ever said war was easy.

The soil, though it had been drenched in blood, began to flourish once more. Seeds of fruits and vegetables were planted for the women who had come back home to the sacred land, their hands no longer bound by men but free to shape the world anew. A new era had begun. And at the heart of it stood Noël Ársa.

They called her Noël the Bloodthorn.

It was a name said with pride, given not by tsars or councils, but by the women who had once suffered under the weight of men's greed. To them, she was more than the Lideřen. She was their shield, their sword, and their justice. And so, Noël the Bloodthorn opened the Blue Rose Court.

The chamber of the court was carved from the heart of a

living tree. The scent of sap and ash lingered in the air, like the blood that was shed and the rebirth that followed. Above, blue roses bloomed, lighting the faces of every man captured in battle—*slaves and traitors*—who were brought before her, and their fates were sealed beneath the glow of the blue roses.

Noël the Bloodthorn, in her crown of roses, sat upon a throne grown from thorned vines and obsidian stone. Her eyes, pale with the power of the ancients, rested on the kneeling vólkin at the base of the dais. His name was Orïon.

Once, he was one of their strongest. A vólkin of honor and strength. But in his pride, he had broken that trust.

"You returned with Gregor to the tsar's men," Noël said, voice echoing through the chamber like wind through a field of corpses. "Not as a spy or savior, but as a warrior who thought himself the claw that could end a war alone."

Orïon did not lift his gaze. His broad shoulders rose and fell with the weight of what he'd done.

"Your recklessness cost us dearly," she continued. "You thought yourself clever. You were not. You thought yourself righteous. You were not. You brought fire to our land and believed it was light."

A hush fell. The gathered vólkins, nýmphí, and orcs watched in stillness, their judgment already spoken in the lines of their faces.

Noël stood.

"There are too few of our kind left to bury one more out of vengeance," she said. "But exile is not mercy. It is the slow death of belonging."

She descended the steps, her bare feet silent on the moss-lined floor.

"You will never set paw in Ávera again," she declared, lifting her hand. "You are unbound. Stripped of all honor. Your name will be remembered. Not as a traitor, but as a caution."

Vines slithered across the floor, circling Orïon. They did not strike. They did not bind. They merely glowed, and with them, the bond between him and the land dissolved.

Orïon did not beg. His silence was louder than any plea.

When he rose, his eyes met Noël's only once. There was no hatred there. He understood.

And then, he turned.

The court watched as he walked out. Past the vines, past the roots, past the arms that would never open for him again.

Banished.

The Blue Rose Court was silent once more.

Since the day the leaders rose, the vólkins who survived healed. Their wounds faded, and their pups ran through the land once more, their laughter ringing through the sacred groves. The women who had once been trapped in distant villages found their way to Ávera, adapted to its laws, its freedom, and its peace. And in time, more mates were bonded. More bellies swelled.

The land began to thrive.

And yet, Noël Ársa still could not walk among them as freely as the others. The women of Ávera had embraced their femininity, their nature, their right to be unshackled by shame. Many of them moved bare and untamed, at peace in their own skin. But Noël, Noël the Bloodthorn, was not ready for that freedom. Perhaps one day.

From time to time, Theron found his mate leaning against a baby's crib, a blue rose carved into its wood. She tugged the fur blanket tighter, tucking in invisible limbs, as though protecting a dream. Sometimes she added a white feather to the soft pile, gifts gathered during their walks through the reborn groves.

They would curl into each other, knowing the time had not yet come. Finding the remaining four and destroying the tsar was the priority.

Still, with a pained heart, Noël the Bloodthorn began

teaching women the once-forbidden knowledge of combat. Naïa taught them to read, Essin to write, Mina spoke of nature, and Elder Aïna guided them in spirit.

And through it all, Noël the Bloodthorn had one thing in mind.

Women don't want equality. They want revenge.

Not all blue roses are what they seem...

ACKNOWLEDGMENTS

To my family, thank you for being my anchor while I couldn't stop yapping about every single page written. You never told me to shut up (even when you should've), and that means more than I can say.

To D, E, and K, who kept me sane, hyped, and emotionally fed through every breakdown and breakthrough. This book wouldn't exist without you.

To my betas, who read this story back when it was more chaos than novel. Thank you for believing in it (and in me) since draft one.

To my editor, thank you for not only understanding this wild, rage-filled world but for helping me bring it to life exactly the way it was meant to be.

To L, thank you for waiting till the final draft was ready before editing. You will always be my angel, my sunshine.

And to K, who chewed my hand while the other one typed. Thank you for reminding me to take breaks and never eat in peace again. This book is yours too.

You all held my hand while I wrote this.

And for that, I will forever be grateful.

ABOUT THE AUTHOR

Nicole A. Sterling writes dark and spicy fantasy full of feral women and obsessive monsters. She believes rage is sacred, love should be all-consuming, and happy endings should still leave bruises.

When she's not summoning demons, she runs a business and tells plot twists to her dog.

Ethereal Ties: The Rose and the Guardian is her debut novel, the first in a series where women don't want equality, they want revenge.

FOR MORE ABOUT
NICOLE A. STERLING

Want more dark fantasy, obsessive monsters, and unhinged women? Let's connect:

Instagram: @nicoleasterling
TikTok: @nicoleasterling1
Website: www.nicoleasterling.com
Goodreads: Nicole A. Sterling
Facebook Group: Nicole A. Sterling's Monster Lair
Patreon: Nicole A. Sterling
Amazon: Nicole A. Sterling

ALSO BY NICOLE A. STERLING

Ethereal Ties Series
The Rose and the Guardian
The Peony and the Guardian (forthcoming)
More titles in the series coming soon.

Earthly Ties Series
The Warden and the Warrior (forthcoming)
More titles in the series coming soon.

Standalones
A Prayer to No God